Christmas
Wishes and
Mistletoe
Kisses

D1386293

Christmas Wishes and Mistletoe Kisses

JENNY HALE

bookouture

Published by Bookouture

An imprint of StoryFire Ltd.
23 Sussex Road, Ickenham, UB10 8PN
United Kingdom

www.bookouture.com

ISBN: 978-1-910751-55-8

Acknowledgments

I'd like to thank my husband, Justin, for his encouragement and support as I continue this journey.

An enormous thank-you goes out to Oliver Rhodes who's always right there at the perfect time to make it all happen.

I am thankful for my editor, Emily Ruston, for her guidance.

And lastly, my heartfelt thanks goes out to Tia Field for tackling my one million questions about nursing.

Chapter One

Twenty-six—that was the number of windows across the front of this house. Four—it had *four* chimneys. Abbey had only just counted them all as the enormous, Georgian-revival-style mansion came into view at the end of the mile-long driveway. She'd had to be let in via an intercom at a pair of iron gates bigger than her apartment building. As she'd snaked along the property in her car, miles of perfectly manicured grass—green, despite the winter weather—stretching out on either side of the drive, and the James River angrily lapping on the edge of the property under the winter clouds, her hands had begun to sweat. Abbey had always been impulsive, even though she'd tried very hard not to be, but she'd done it again.

She'd dressed up. She wasn't used to dressing up. Normally, she had on scrubs at work, and on her off time she wore hoodies and jeans. But this was a business meeting, and she'd wanted to look prepared; however, nothing had prepared her for what was in front of her now. She shifted her portfolio case on the seat of her car to keep it from slipping onto the floorboards. It was a gift from her gramps and had sat empty until now.

You can do this, she said to herself as she tried to keep the seatbelt from wrinkling her clothes. *You're gonna have to do this. You made your bed. Now you have to lie in it.*

The owner of this home was in a league beyond comprehension. He was the grandson of a woman named Caroline Sinclair for whom Abbey cared. Caroline lived in a small cottage on the edge of the Sinclair property, and Abbey had always reached her cottage using a private side road. The estate was so large and wooded that the cottage seemed to be all by itself; the main house wasn't even visible. Caroline had explained that she wanted it that way.

"If Nick is making me live on the property, I want to at least feel that I can come and go as if it's my own residence. I don't want to live out back of the house, or something demeaning like that. I want my own place, not a guest quarters."

Abbey had gotten the job caring for Caroline while working at an upscale retirement home. Nicholas Sinclair had called to ask if they had a service for in-home nurses. When she'd said that they didn't, he'd offered to pay her more than what she was making there to care for Caroline at home, because he didn't want to put her in a facility. Caroline had mentioned that her grandson, Nick, had a "big house," but this kind of wealth was something out of a storybook.

As Abbey looked at the house, it shed new light on Caroline's quirks—the way she'd held the thick mug that Abbey had gotten her for her birthday as if it were a delicate piece of art, the straightness of her back when she sat on the edge of her chair, the manner in which she nodded and said "thank you," for the smallest of things. It was all clear now. What had seemed like generally polite behavior had actually been the behavior of a privileged upbringing. Abbey had never met Mr. Sinclair face to face. She'd always just provided Caroline's current health status and data from her tests via phone—usually leaving a message—and he'd mailed her paychecks. Now, she wondered if she'd notice those small indications of wealth when she met him.

Abbey parked her car in the great, circular drive and turned off the engine. Snowflakes dotted her windshield as she took a peek in her rearview mirror to be sure she was as presentable as possible. She dabbed on some lip-gloss quickly and dropped it into her handbag. With a deep breath, she got out of the car, her heels wobbling slightly with her nerves. Hoping the snow wouldn't begin to pile up when she was inside, she clicked along the brick patio-sized pathway to the front steps. With every step, she could feel the crescendo of the pounding in her heart.

She stopped between two urns, each one containing a spruce tree the size of her Christmas tree at home, and pressed the doorbell. The double doors in front of her were so ornate and grand that she almost feared what was behind them. What was she thinking, telling Caroline she'd do this? Was she out of her mind?

The door opened, and, standing in front of her, was a short man wearing a charcoal gray suit and a red tie, his hair balding on the top. Abbey had heard about Nick Sinclair from the other nurses at the retirement home. They'd described him as tall, quiet, handsome—gorgeous, one had said—with dark hair and perfect clothes. While there was nothing wrong with the man in front of her, he was a far cry from the description she'd received.

He smiled, his lips pressed together, and took a step back to allow her to come in, the large door closing behind her as she entered the home.

She refocused on the man. "Hello. I'm Abbey Fuller. You must be Mr. Sinclair?"

"No, ma'am. He'll be with you shortly."

Wow, she thought. *He doesn't even open his own doors.* Her eyes moved around the space, taking in everything that surrounded her.

The floor was a white- and slate-colored marble, with matching columns that looked as though they were holding up the entire second floor. The upstairs ran along an oval balcony that completely circled the room. The space in that one room was the size of the house where she'd grown up. It was so grand that it had to have three massive chandeliers to light it, but the windows spanning every surface were large enough that the natural light coming in was plenty.

"Follow me, please," the man said as he led her across the marble floor, between the two wide, curving staircases flanking each side of the room, and through an ornate doorway with more pillars on either side, the woodwork all painted cream to match the walls. Each piece was carved into swirling perfection that rolled to a peak at the top of the doorframe. The more she walked, the more nervous she became, her mouth drying out.

Her breath caught, and she swallowed to cover it up as she entered the next room. A wall of windows on the east side offered an almost blinding white light from the clouds outside. The grass had been dusted with snow in just the amount of time she'd been in the house. In front of the windows sat a black grand piano, the top propped up, the keys so shiny she could see the reflection of the panes of glass on their surfaces. On the south side of the home another wall of windows stretched to the top of the thirty or more foot ceiling and overlooked the grounds. The walls had intricate woodwork framing their surfaces, the color between the woodwork the matching blue of the rug.

The man had walked over to two facing cream-colored sofas that seemed so comfortable that she wanted to snuggle up on them with a blanket and read. Their billowy cushions were juxtaposed to the formality of the blue and cream patterned rug that extended the entire length of the ballroom-sized space, and the general emptiness and sterile surroundings. He gestured for her to take a seat.

Abbey's eyes could not stay still in this room because she'd never seen anything like it in real life. It was such a stiffly styled room, yet those sofas were sitting at one end, and she wondered if anyone had ever sat on them.

What kinds of things would someone do in a room like this? Did Nick Sinclair play piano? Had he ever played for anyone before, or was it just a prop, a piece of furniture?

She sat down and the man left her alone with her thoughts, having never even introduced himself. Abbey put her hands on her knees as she sat on the edge of that gorgeous sofa. How impressed must Caroline have been with her decorating skills to suggest that Abbey decorate this mansion for her grandson? She couldn't even allow her pride to slip in because the whole situation was so baffling to her. She was shaking—partly from nerves and from the fact that the house was just slightly colder than she found to be comfortable. She shivered. The snow had really started coming down now in the few minutes she was there, already covering the ground outside. The scene played out before her through the towering windows, like a movie. Her mouth was so dry at this point, she couldn't even lick her lips, and she worried that her lip-gloss wouldn't last.

If she had to sit there much longer, she would explode—she needed to talk, have some kind of interaction—so she stood up to try to burn off her nervous energy. Her heels tapped on the marble floor that ran along the edge of the rug, and made hollow clicks that echoed throughout the room. "Rug" was an amusing term for this piece. It was half the size of a football field, it seemed. Her back to the room, Abbey looked out through the windows and, when she realized what was out there, she had to consciously keep her mouth from hanging open.

Covered in snow were tennis courts, a brick gazebo as big as a four-car garage, and, off in the distance, closer to the river, was a swimming pool. As she looked out at the grounds, the cold of winter seeping in through the icy glass in front of her, she wondered what Nick could possibly be doing. Why hadn't he greeted her at the door? Did it take him that long to walk from wherever he was in the house? She'd left a message, as he'd directed, and told him she'd be there at two o'clock. She'd just expected him to answer the door.

"Hello, Ms. Fuller," she heard the words echo across the room.

Abbey turned around. As she fixed her eyes on him, she had to work to keep her breath from coming out in ragged, nervous jerks. He *was* gorgeous. He was probably the most handsome man she'd ever seen. He had on navy trousers and a buttercream sweater with a thick collar that made the icy blue of his eyes visible even at a distance. His hair was perfectly combed, not a strand out of place, and his face looked soft, as if he'd just shaved a few minutes before their meeting. Perhaps that was what he'd been doing… Abbey shook the thought from her mind.

"Hello," she returned. She wanted to walk toward him, but she didn't trust herself in heels, and she worried that she might fall. He crossed the room and stopped in front of her, giving the two of them a large amount of personal space. He held out his hand in greeting, the starched cuff of his button-up shirt peeking out from underneath his sweater. She shook his hand.

"It's nice to finally put a face with the voice," he said. "Shall we head into my office?" He moved aside so that she could step up next to him. "We can discuss the details of your employment more easily there." He smiled. It was a pleasant smile, but it didn't seem to sit comfortably on his face.

They walked along the corridor, a lofty area so wide and open that it couldn't possibly be called just a hallway. It, too, was quite empty—no pictures, no accent tables, nothing. Abbey was shocked at the lack of decorations. The house was so cold and unfriendly that it made her wonder about Mr. Sinclair. Was he as cold as this house? They finally stopped outside what looked like Nick's office.

"You can just call me Abbey," she said, gripping her portfolio case to keep her hands steady.

He smiled down at her.

"Did you just move in?" she asked out of curiosity. There was nothing in this home to suggest that it was regularly lived in. There were no photos, no memorabilia anywhere—nothing to tell her about who he was.

"No," he said, sitting down behind a shiny desk with a mahogany finish. His chair rolled on the slick marble floor beneath it. Then, he made eye contact. "My grandmother tells me that you are a very good decorator," he said, offering that manufactured smile again. This time, Abbey could almost tell that he'd practiced it. Was he used to having to smile when he really didn't want to? She wondered what he looked like when he laughed—really laughed. What would his mouth do then? Would he keep still or throw his head back? Would she be able to see amusement in his eyes?

She sat down in one of the leather chairs facing his desk and crossed her legs at the ankle. With a tiny breath to steady herself, she put her portfolio case on her lap and unzipped it. She'd taken a few photos of her best decorating and had them blown up to a larger size for her presentation. "I've never had a project this size," she warned.

What she really wanted to tell him was that the only decorating experience she'd had was when she'd decorated his grandmother's cottage because Caroline didn't have the ability to paint and decorate herself. Abbey had worked hard to make her presentation professional, and there was a lot riding on this. She had Max to think about.

Abbey's son, Max, was in first grade. He needed lunch money, school supplies; he was on neighborhood sports teams. There were things she *had* to pay for if she wanted Max to have a regular childhood. Her poor judgment with his father had been her fault, not Max's. And the fact that her grandfather needed medicine that she had to help her mother pay for—that wasn't Max's fault either. Her son deserved nothing but the best, and she was going to give that to him, even if it meant that she went without. And she had before. Abbey had gone nights with no dinner, skipped parties with her friends, and lived on meager funds so that Max would never know that he was any different than anyone else. Secretly, she worried about him. Would he wonder why he didn't get beach vacations with his family? Would he wish that he could have big birthday parties with all his friends? She fretted about it all the time. And this was her chance to do something great for his future.

"I'm not concerned about any lack of experience. You come highly recommended by my grandmother, and she's hard to please, so I trust you'll do just fine."

She pulled back the flap on her portfolio and retrieved the first photo from it, turning it around for him to view. "I have experience decorating in a small variety of styles…" she said nervously. She'd practiced her presentation last night a hundred times but it was quite different with Nick's eyes on her. "As you know, this is a picture from your grandmother's cottage. I thought I'd start with hers first, since you could envision the before and after…"

He cleared his throat. "You don't need to sell me," he said. "I'm already hiring you." He offered a pleasant expression, but it was clear from his face that her presentation was over.

She slid the photo back into the case and closed it.

"Are you planning to charge a flat rate per square foot, or would you prefer a salary with a decorating budget?" he asked.

"Uh-mmm…" Abbey chewed on the inside of her lip, trying to scramble for an answer. She didn't know. She didn't have a clue. She'd only ever been a nurse. The idea of how to charge him hadn't even crossed her mind. That thought alone was unsettling enough to cause her chest to burn with anxiety.

Abbey had gone online during a few of her breaks, ordering things that were more extravagant than she'd ever bought, but she knew just how to place them to give them life in Caroline's cottage. She'd done it as a favor to Caroline, but she hadn't made any money doing it, and it never occurred to her to ask for any. She realized that she hadn't thought this through at all.

"I, uh…" She scrambled for an answer, feeling ridiculous that all she could produce were unintelligible sounds. *Get a grip!* she scolded herself. *Answer him!* This was too big a leap for her. She wasn't a decorator. She'd always dreamed of being one. She had files of magazine clippings just in case she ever won the lottery and was able to buy what she really wanted for her and Max.

Her passion for art ran deeply through her—she painted, she could draw, she saw art in everything—but when it had come down to it, she'd had to choose the career that would be the least amount of risk.

She'd had to pick something that would provide for Max. Because of that, she'd gotten a nursing degree as quickly as she could because it would give her that steady income. She'd taken as many classes as the local community college allowed, and she'd done nothing but study so that she could get her degree. Abbey still believed there was art in everything; she just didn't always have time to notice it anymore.

As she sat across from Nick Sinclair, she felt very small, heat filling her cheeks. She blinked to keep the tears at bay. Never had she come to tears about anything before now—not even raising Max alone. She'd always been able to handle it. So why was she about to cry now? Abbey tried not to process the answer, but it was bubbling up: She knew her artistic talent was that one piece of her that she could always hold on to when she'd lost everything, hoping that one day she could tap into it. It was the only thing besides Max that she was proud of. Now, finding herself out of her league, she didn't want anyone telling her that it wasn't good enough because that would crush her.

And the last thing she wanted was for Nick to think less of her, but she didn't know a thing about how to charge him for this job or the etiquette in a business relationship like this.

Abbey was silent, still trying to formulate an answer while not giving away how she was feeling. She didn't know what to say, so she just sat there, inwardly screaming at herself to say *something*. "I'll do it for free if you'll let me take photos for my portfolio when I'm finished," she said finally.

Then, his light blue eyes changed as he looked at her. He looked curious, but there was a gentleness in his face that she hadn't seen until right then.

"My grandmother has wanted me to do this for a while. Before she was set on having you do it, she'd even called around and given me quotes. I've had quotes for upwards of a hundred fifty thousand dollars, so, with that said, I won't let you do the job for free. My grandmother might disown me if I did. Why don't we settle for seventy-five thousand dollars to decorate the whole house?" He searched her face for a reaction. "And that will be your salary. Then, I'll buy whatever you need in terms of furnishings."

Abbey blinked to keep her eyes from popping out of their sockets. Seventy-five *thousand* dollars? That was three years' salary for her, and she was about to make it in a matter of weeks. All of a sudden, she felt lightheaded, her excitement swelling up inside. This could change everything. With money like that, she could pay for extra childcare—private sitters when she needed them. That would take the burden off her mother who was caring for her grandfather and watching Max. She might even be able to get Gramps that medicine he needed so badly.

"Does that suit you?" he asked. "Are you okay with those terms?"

"Yes." She couldn't say anything more than yes. Her emotions were getting the better of her. She wanted to get up and hug him and tell him what a Christmas miracle that money would be for her and her family. She wanted to thank him for being so generous despite the fact that, clearly, she was inexperienced.

"Great." He stood up and walked around to her side of the desk. She followed his lead and stood, tucking her portfolio under her arm.

He was so close that she caught his scent, and it caused a tickle in her chest. Abbey had never smelled cologne that good before, and she wondered what it was that he was wearing. Had she ever even heard of it? It was probably very expensive.

"Let me show you the rooms that you'll be decorating," he said, distracted, as he pulled out his phone and put it to his ear. She was glad to be up and moving again, and hoping to finally get to have a normal conversation, but he was already barking into his phone. "I don't care how much it costs," he said. "It's a car. Just buy it… I'd like it detailed and cleaned before it leaves the lot this time." After a minute's more conversation, he ended the call and looked down at her. "I collect cars—mostly Ferraris," he said, with an air of pride.

"Cars?" she asked. Max collected cars, but she wondered if he might be talking about a slightly different kind.

"There's a Lamborghini that's up for auction—very limited number of them. I've got someone bidding for me and I'm trying to manage that while I show you around. My apologies."

She stared up at him long enough to realize that it was becoming awkward, so she looked down at her feet. Her grandfather couldn't even buy the medicine he needed and this guy was wasting money on luxury cars.

"You need more than one car?" she asked.

He looked at her, the skin between his eyes wrinkling as if he were trying to make sense of what she was saying. "I *collect* them. I don't necessarily drive them."

"Where do you keep them?"

"I have a garage on the property. They're displayed there."

She knew that her face was showing her distaste, and she couldn't straighten it out no matter how hard she tried. She had no right to offer any opinion about what he did with his money. "So who comes to see them?"

He eyed her again. "No one," he said, his voice sounding slightly exasperated. "I collect them for my own amusement. No one else's."

She was quiet after that; the idea of all that money sitting somewhere in a garage helping no one had silenced her.

"Basically, you'll be decorating all the rooms except for a couple. I know that's a big job…" He looked down at her as they walked, changing the subject. Had he been able to interpret her opinions? "And you'll have only a short time to do it." He stopped, so Abbey did too. "I have family coming and I'm having a Christmas party. I want you to make the house look *lived in*."

A punch of laughter rose in her gut, but she cleared her throat to remove it. She remembered the ballroom with nothing but a piano and a set of fluffy sofas, and thought to herself, *How can I make a room like that look livable?*

If she'd chosen to be a full-time decorator instead of becoming a nurse, Abbey would take something like a cozy corner nook, paint it a warm color, add a pop of white furniture, and fill it full of book-shelves. She'd arrange the books on the shelves between knickknacks from various locations around the world that her client had gotten on his travels. She'd even drape a snowy-white throw across the arm of the chair and add a floor lamp for ambience. *That* would look lived in. This house was like a museum. It was too big to make it even *seem* like someone would live in it. But then, her thoughts went to Nick. He lived here. And as far as Abbey could tell, he lived here all by himself.

Caroline had never mentioned a family when she spoke of her grandson. She'd only said that he needed help with his home because he was too busy working to do anything with it. How sad to have to walk these giant hallways alone.

They rounded the corner and headed up a curling staircase to the second floor. Everywhere she looked, she saw lofty ceilings and bal-conies. It made her feel the need to take a deep breath to release the growing tension she was feeling about this job she'd taken.

All the doors to each room were shut, which was odd to Abbey, but then again, perhaps it was hard to heat such a large house. He stopped at the first one and opened it. It was another colossal expanse of space with vaulted ceilings, ornamental woodwork, and more chandeliers.

"This is a bedroom," he said as she walked around the room, snapping photos of walls and architectural features. She looked up at the intricate crystal chandelier above her, with its strands of diamond-like jewels dripping down, and took a photo. "There are eight bedrooms in total. I'd like each room to feel distinct, yet consistent with the style of the home. What you do with them is up to you. I trust you."

Abbey dragged her hand along the ornate woodwork in the recessed doorway, noticing how the patterns in the wood emerged from under the thick coats of shiny white paint. She'd keep that, she decided. She imagined Georgian-style furniture to maintain the integrity of the home, but with a few present-day traditional accents to make the look current. In such a large space, she'd want to focus on breaking the room up into smaller pieces—perhaps put a sitting area at one end of the bedroom. The key was to make this cold space seem warm and more personal. The walls needed neutrals but in inviting colors like light buttery yellows and subtle mint greens, rather than just plain white. She jotted down notes in the notebook that she'd included in the front pocket of her portfolio.

They opened the next two doors, and he explained the purpose of each room. She wrote down where the light came in and areas on which she wanted to focus. When they came to the fourth door on the hallway, he skipped it and walked ahead. She looked at his face, his thoughts seemingly preoccupied all of a sudden. It was subtle, but she'd noticed. What was behind that door?

"Did you want me to see this one?" she said, stopping in the hallway and pointing back to the closed door.

"No," he said. "I won't need you to decorate that room. It's fine." He walked ahead and opened the next door. It was just like the others.

"I'm sorry," she stopped him right there in the hallway. She was going to have to really make sure he understood if she ever wanted to feel comfortable in his presence. "I must drive home the fact that I haven't ever had a decorating job of this magnitude. Ever. I've only done the cottage for your grandmother and I've decorated my mom's house. I've never even been in a home on River Road before."

Everyone in the vicinity of Richmond knew where River Road was. It was more than just a road; it was a landmark, a stretch of real estate showcasing Richmond's finest. "I mean, my mother's house is nice. She's on the corner of Maple and Ivy Streets," she kidded, trying to joke about the insignificance of where her mother's house was located. Clearly, he didn't get it. Maple and Ivy obviously didn't have the same impact as River Road. Her joke had fallen flat.

He stared at her, as if waiting for something more.

"What I'm trying to say…" She swallowed. "What I'm wondering is…" She didn't want to *not* take the job. But telling him the truth was the right thing to do. "I'm inexperienced. With all the money that you have, why don't you just hire an experienced decorator?"

He was silent a moment as if he were trying to get his answer just right. "I mean no disrespect," he said. "This was my grandmother's idea. She thinks I need to make this house presentable for my family and friends when they come for Christmas. I agree, to a certain extent. And I think the emptiness bothers her in general. The problem is, I only want to make her happy. I don't care enough about it to spend time searching for a decorator. I just want it done, and if she thinks you're the person to do it, then so be it."

So he didn't care that she wasn't a seasoned professional. He didn't care about any of it. Any feelings of achievement she'd had by securing this job came crashing down. He was telling her loud and clear that it wasn't about him trusting her abilities; it was just something to tick off his list. Nick turned and headed down the hallway again. Trying to look on the bright side, Abbey walked along beside him, thinking of all the possibilities.

Chapter Two

Abbey opened the modest door to her mother's house and nearly fell over. There, on the living room hardwoods, right in front of her, were countless shattered ornaments, tinsel strewn about, and a brightly lit spruce monster writhing on the floor. Abbey's mother lunged for the outlet and unplugged the twinkling lights, the spruce monster going dark. A black bolt of lightning shot out from it, disappearing around the corner, leaving a heap of Christmas ruin in its wake.

With a huff, Abbey's mother lowered herself down on the floor and put her hands on her cheeks in bewilderment.

"What was that?" Abbey asked in horror.

"Señor Freckles got the tree."

"Señor Freckles is still alive?"

Her mom nodded.

Señor Freckles was Abbey's grandfather's cat. Born feral, he'd never quite gotten the hang of domestic life. He lurked in corners and crannies, only coming out to eat, and no one—as far as Abbey knew—had ever been able to touch him. He had to be at least twenty by now.

"Did Gramps bring that thing with him when he came to live with you?" she asked the question but didn't hear the answer, because she was too busy wondering how they ever got that cat into the car, and why she hadn't noticed him when she'd dropped off Max. But then again, he'd probably been lurking in a dark place somewhere. When Abbey looked up, her mother was nodding, so she guessed that her mom was now the proud owner of Señor Freckles.

Abbey nudged her mother's fallen Christmas tree out of the way, the ornaments tinkling together as they got jostled, just as Max came into the room to see what was going on.

"Hi, baby," Abbey said, giving him a kiss on his head and tousling his hair. He looked up at her with his bright eyes. They used to remind her of his daddy, but now, they were just his.

"Hi, Mama," he said, putting his little arms around her waist. "What was that noise?"

"Gramps's cat knocked over Nana's tree."

"Gramps has a cat?" Max said.

"Yes. He hides most of the time," her mom explained. "He hasn't been around all day," she said to Abbey, shaking her head. "I knew I should've waited until after Thanksgiving to decorate. I should've given the cat time to settle down after his move."

"Will that cat get me?" Max's face was serious with concern. His brows were pulled together, his lips pursed, a hint of a dimple showing on his cheek.

"No," her mom laughed. "That cat won't get anywhere near you, don't worry. He hates people."

"Then why does Gramps have him?" he asked.

"When Gramps found him, he was starving outside—skin and bones—in the cold of winter, and he felt like he could give him a better life. He loves that cat." She shook her head again. "But I think the affection is one-sided."

The front door wasn't latched—the drama of the falling Christmas tree had clearly distracted her as she'd come in—so Abbey shut it, the cold air now overwhelming them in the small entryway. The snow had really started to come down, and she noticed how the bottom edges of her high heels were now discolored from the melting precipitation. She kicked them off. "Please sit, Mom," she said. "You need to rest that ankle. Right now, I'll get the tree back up for you."

Her mom sat down, her face grateful.

As Abbey lifted the tree, the scent of pine making her nose itch, she caught sight of Señor Freckles in the corner. He was licking his paw until he noticed her glance. He stopped and stared at her unrelentingly as if he were about to pounce. She cut her eyes at him. "Don't even think about it," she said in his direction. "It's awfully cold outside," she teased. Her mom and Max both looked over at Señor Freckles too. The cat had turned his head and was now looking directly at Max, his gaze like lasers.

"I won't let her put you outside," he whispered to the cat across the room. "But you can't scratch me or anything."

Señor Freckles broke eye contact and began licking his paw again. In that moment, Max seemed a lot like his grandfather in temperament.

"Tell me about Nick Sinclair!" Abbey's mother said with excitement in her eyes. "Is he as handsome as I've heard?"

Abbey eyed Max who was still looking at the cat. "He is," she said. What she'd experienced earlier with him now felt like a dream.

"Is he nice?"

Abbey shrugged. "For a rich guy, I guess."

"What does that mean?"

"He has a very different life than we do."

"Obviously. Wouldn't it be great to live like that?"

Abbey contemplated that answer. She thought about Nick's indifference regarding spending thousands of dollars on decorators and cars. Did he realize that there were others out there who were struggling to make ends meet? "I wouldn't want to live like that," she decided aloud.

"Speak for yourself!" her mother laughed.

"You never told me *how* you hurt your ankle, only that you'd hurt it," Abbey said, changing the subject as she tipped the tree into the stand and set it upright. The water in the tray at the bottom had spilled all over the hardwoods, and she knew she'd need a towel to sop it up.

"I slipped on the ice outside. I was trying to keep Dad steady, and I fell."

"Oh, I'm so sorry, Mom," she said. Abbey was glad to be there to help her mother. Her arthritis was giving her enough trouble; taking care of Gramps was just adding to it. For so many years, her mom had helped her; now it was Abbey's turn to pay that back. "Where is Gramps?" she asked, as Max began to walk toward the cat. It skirted away, darting around the corner. He followed it.

"He's taking a nap in his room, but he could be awake. You should check on him and see. He's getting worse."

"The medicine's not working?"

"It is. But at some point, I worry it just won't work at all. And his insurance isn't great, you know. You and I can't afford to give him the care he really needs. All we can do is give him the best we have."

"I'll go see him now. I need to find Max anyway. He's probably chased Señor Freckles outside, and it's freezing out there. I don't want him out without a hat."

The house where Abbey had grown up wasn't anything grand—a single-level three bedroom with a small front porch and a deck out back—but it had a fenced in backyard, and her wooden play-set was still there, so Max could swing.

"I'll get the towels and a broom for the floor," her mom said, standing up and swinging her large cast out in front of her. "You go and see Dad. It'll make him happy. But after that, I'm dying to hear about your new job."

Abbey went down the hallway toward Gramps's room. He would ask—she was sure—how life was treating her. He always did. And she knew that he was hoping for some kind of exciting answer.

The problem was, growing up, Gramps had always told her, "You can do anything you want if you just want it enough." She could still remember the times he'd told her that, and, back then it had all seemed so feasible. Of course she could do anything she wanted—the sky was the limit. But when she'd gotten pregnant at twenty-four, she had to refocus. As she looked at Max the day he was born, she realized that what she wanted didn't matter so much. What she wanted then was for Max to be happy. That was all.

"So you finally decided to come and see me," Gramps said with a sly grin as she walked through the open door. He was sitting on the edge of his bed, trying unsuccessfully to pull on his cardigan. His hands were shaking so badly, he was struggling to hold on to the hem of the sweater as he tried to pull it around his shoulders. Abbey attempted to help him, but he batted her hand away gently. "How's life treating you?"

There it was—the question. The answer to it was so far out of her grasp that she could never get her mind around a good response. "I'm doing well," she said, unable to articulate anything else.

He stared at her, his head wobbling slightly back and forth from the Parkinson's. His eyes were telling her he could see through that answer, but he didn't say anything more. He just stood up and walked toward her. "Max is growing up quickly," he said, clearly deciding to focus on the positive. "I haven't seen the little guy for a few months and, I swear, he grew a foot!"

Abbey stepped aside to allow Gramps to maneuver down the hallway. After seeing how he insisted on handling his own sweater, she knew better than to try to help him.

"You'll be here tomorrow for Thanksgiving, right?" he asked over his shoulder as he led her down the hallway. "I feel like you spend all your time working these days."

"Of course I'm coming to Thanksgiving," she said with a smile. "I wouldn't miss it."

Nick floated into her mind—the thought surprising her. She imagined him all alone in that big house tomorrow for Thanksgiving. Did he have any family coming over? Was he going somewhere else? Would he see Caroline? He'd been so direct and quiet during their meeting that she almost couldn't imagine him sitting around a table, talking to his family. She wondered if he even cared about Thanksgiving at all.

They entered the kitchen and Gramps sat down at the small, oval table nestled near the bay window overlooking the swing set. Max was drawing in the dirt under her childhood swing with a stick. Abbey grinned at the sight of him and turned back to Gramps. Her mom was pulling his many bottles of medicine from the cabinet and lining them up on the counter.

"Have you bought the turkey for tomorrow, Abbey? If not, you'll want to get it soon or all the good ones will be gone."

Her mom hobbled toward the table, swinging her boot in front of her with every step, her broken ankle a reminder of the burden Gramps was putting on her. She set down the pills in a little pile and placed a glass of water beside them.

"I already have the turkey," Abbey said with a smile, glad that she was able to put her mother's mind at ease. "And I bought some of those oven rolls. All I have to do is make the pumpkin pie. I was hoping I could bring Max over tomorrow morning and make it here. Maybe Gramps could help since he was always so good at it. Gramps, do you still have your recipe?"

"You'll have to ask your mom," he said. "She packed up my whole house. She's put it somewhere, I'm sure."

"It's in the recipe box," her mom said.

"Would you make the pie with us tomorrow morning?" she asked.

With a shaky hand, Gramps picked up the pills and dumped them all into his mouth at once. He chased them with a swig of water. "Yep."

"Perfect," she said. "I'll come by first thing."

Chapter Three

"Hello?" Abbey said, her phone resting on her shoulder as she cradled the pumpkin mixture in a ceramic bowl, stirring it with a wooden spoon. Gramps was pressing the piecrust to the rim of the tin, his fingers so unsteady that the edges were uneven and lumpy. He used to cut holly leaves out of the crust and place them around the edges. They'd get golden brown in the oven, and Abbey would pick them off and eat them before she ate her slice of pie.

Abbey could see his frustration, and she wanted to help, but Nick was on the other end of the phone, and she was too busy trying to control her nerves. *Nick probably has a chef bake his pies*, she thought.

"Get it into the oven as quickly as you can, Abbey. We've still got the turkey to bake," her mother said before Abbey could wave her quiet. Abbey turned around and shook her head, pointing to the phone with the spoon.

"I'm sorry to call on Thanksgiving, but I'm trying to tie up a few loose ends. I wanted to find out what your timeframe would be," Nick said. "I remember you needed to check your schedule to determine what times and days you'd be available, and I'd like the house finished by Christmas."

She'd only told him she'd check yesterday. Nick Sinclair did not wait very well, did he? And now he was calling her on a holiday. Even though he'd apologized, it indicated to her that he didn't seem to put a lot of importance on the special day. Abbey wondered if she would be able to slip away later to check on Caroline. She didn't want her spending the holiday all by herself.

"I have the dates for you," she said, setting down the bowl and spoon and grabbing her calendar from her handbag. With pumpkin on her fingers, she thumbed through the pages. "I can start tomorrow…" She told him the hours each day when she was available, glad that Max would be in school for most of them.

Before she could finish the call, there was a crash! It scared her so much she nearly dropped her phone, fumbling to keep it from hitting the floor. She turned around to find Gramps shaking more than usual, bits of ceramic and splattered pumpkin mixture all over the floor. Señor Freckles had suddenly appeared and was licking it off the ceramic pieces. Her mom came running in, Max following.

"I'm sorry," she said. "I'm making a pie at my mom's, and I now have pumpkin pie mixture all over my floor. Can I call you back?"

"I apologize," Nick said, clearly startled. "I've interrupted your holiday."

"It's fine. It's not your fault."

She motioned for her mom to take Max into the other room. Her mother would only worry about everyone, and Abbey could easily clean it all up. Gramps was irritated—she could tell by his face. He wiped his hands on the kitchen towel, his head bobbing worse with his anxiety.

"It's okay," she mouthed to him.

"You don't have to call me back. Again, I'm so sorry," Nick said. "I've got the dates now. It's fine. I'll see you tomorrow. You're at your... mother's?"

She could hear remorse in his voice, uneasiness as he cleared his throat before trying to end the call. She hadn't meant to make him uncomfortable. As she bent down to pick up the pieces of broken bowl, Señor Freckles darted away, leaving orange paw prints across the floor.

She ended the call as gracefully as possible. Gramps was grumbling when she finally put her phone away. "It's really fine, Gramps."

"No, it's not. Those pills don't do a damn thing. I can't even make a pie anymore. And now, on Thanksgiving—the only time we ever eat pumpkin pie—I've gone and ruined it."

"You know what?" She moved in front of him. "The pie *is* ruined, but it doesn't matter. We're all going to have a nice dinner. We'll sit down, talk about everything and anything, and we'll forget about this one, lost pie," she said, her arms full of shards of ceramic.

His face stayed taut, annoyed.

"It's just a pie, Gramps."

With a thud, the pieces of ceramic hit the bottom of the trashcan.

"I'm sorry I snapped at you," Gramps said after Abbey had slid the turkey out of the oven and put it on the burners to cool. Max was at the table, coloring, and her mom was going through her serving dishes, setting them out on the counter. "I just get irritated. It bothers me that I can't do the things I used to do."

Max watched him out of the corner of his eye for a minute and then looked back down at his coloring book.

"I know. It's okay, Gramps." Abbey carved slices off the turkey and began arranging the slices on a serving plate.

They were beginning to settle in to the final Thanksgiving preparations when the doorbell rang. Abbey and her mother looked at one another. Who would be coming by on Thanksgiving right at dinnertime?

"I'll get it," Abbey said, pulling a piece of foil from its roll and draping it over the turkey to keep it warm.

Still wiping her hands on the kitchen towel, she opened the door to find an unknown man holding a picnic basket. "Hello," she greeted him, unsure of his motives.

"I'm looking for Abbey Fuller," he said.

What in the world could this be about? she wondered. "I'm Abbey Fuller."

"I figured, since this is the only house on the corner of Maple and Ivy Streets." He smiled, but Abbey's confusion clearly caused him to refocus and speed up his explanation for interrupting a national family holiday. "I have a delivery for you," he said, holding out the picnic basket.

She took it from him.

"It's from…" He looked down at his clipboard. "Mr. Nicholas Sinclair."

"Thank you."

He turned around and started down the steps, the snow now a sheet of ice after a deep freeze had set in. She shut the door to keep the cold from freezing the whole house, the jingle bells on her mother's wreath clanging against the door. Abbey looked inside the picnic basket. When she realized what it was, Nick's gesture gave her heart a flutter of gratitude.

"Who is it?" her mom called.

Abbey took the basket into the kitchen. "It's from Nick Sinclair. He's sent us pumpkin pies." She didn't recognize the bakery, and from the look of the packaging, she had probably never spent that amount of money on a pumpkin pie before. There was a complimentary card included. She pulled the card from its tiny, white envelope. It read, *I'm sorry about your pumpkin pie. I hope this reaches you. Happy Thanksgiving. Nick*

"How did he get a pumpkin pie delivered on Thanksgiving?" her mother wondered aloud. "Everything's closed."

"I have no idea."

"If the price is right, I suppose," her mother said, her eyebrows jumping up and down suggestively. "He must like you."

Abbey shook her head. "I doubt that."

Immediately, she wanted to call him and thank him. Initially, she'd been intimidated by him, but now she wondered who was really behind that reserved demeanor. Was there more to this man than his empty house and excessive car collection? She hoped that he didn't think the dropped pie was a result of his phone call. The fact that he'd sent a replacement made her wonder. Nonetheless, he'd been thoughtful tonight, and she wouldn't forget that. The thrill of it made her want to see him again and thank him personally.

"Let's hurry and eat," Max said. "I want some pie!"

The minute they had all the dishes on the table, as Abbey scooted her chair into place, Gramps said, "So, tell us about this mysterious pie-delivering man."

"Abbey has an interior decorating job," her mom cut in. She was still holding her knife and fork and talking with her utensils. "I've been dying to say something."

"It's just a favor for a lady that I provide care for," Abbey said, trying to play it down. Abbey didn't want Gramps making a big fuss over it until she'd been successful. She hadn't proven herself yet. But every time she thought about it, she got a tingle up her spine. What if she could actually do this? There were wealthy people coming to his Christmas party—possible clients for her. What if she got the chance to actually live out her dream of being an interior designer? She tried not to think about it because it sent her hopes sky high.

"He's paying her," her mom pressed.

Gramps looked at her, his head cocked to the side. He was interested, and for the first time since she'd arrived, he looked happy, relatively still. "Tell us more," he said.

"I've agreed to decorate his house. Well, I wouldn't really call it a house."

"What is it then, Mama?" Max said. He'd made a volcano with his potatoes, and he'd filled the crater at the top with green beans. She let it go. Normally, she'd say something, but if he wanted to eat a volcano-shaped dinner, then so be it.

"It's a house. Just a very big house. Bigger than any house you've ever seen," she told Max. "It has eight bedrooms, and a ballroom that's the size of *this whole* house. It's this giant mansion of a home but it's almost totally empty. It's so cold and sparse, it gives me shivers just being in it." Abbey turned back to her mother and Gramps. "You know what struck me most? There isn't a single Christmas decoration either."

"Well, not everyone decorates as early as we do. Even the early birds decorate tomorrow. I just wanted to get it done before Gramps moved in."

"Maybe he doesn't celebrate Christmas," Gramps said.

"Well, he said I could decide what to put in the house, so he's getting Christmas decorations. He said himself that his family is coming for Christmas and he's having a Christmas party! What would a house full of family be like on Christmas without a tree full of presents, stockings hanging on the fireplace, and plates of cookies and cakes waiting to be had?"

She noticed Max watching Gramps again. Gramps's eyes were wide, entertained, happy.

"You need to thank him for the pies," her mom said.

"Should I call him on Thanksgiving?"

"Why not? He called *you*."

"I suppose you're right." She didn't want to call Nick Sinclair all of a sudden. The mere thought of it sent another wave of anxiety through her. She tried to place why she was having that reaction just now, and the only conclusion was too alarming to think about, but it kept rising to the surface: she found him interesting. He was gorgeous, rich, and now thoughtful. She caught herself wondering about him. Suddenly, she couldn't eat another bite.

"It's just us here, Abbey. Don't feel like you have to be polite. Why don't you call him? We'll finish eating, and I can get some pie for Max."

Abbey nodded and excused herself from the table. She tried not to look at Gramps's giddy face as she dug around in her handbag. As she held her phone, her mind wasn't on the people at the table anymore. She'd see Nick tomorrow, and she could thank him then, but now her family was full of anticipation, excited for her, and she felt like she should go ahead and call. She went into her old bedroom and shut the door.

The springs on the mattress squeaked out their age as she sat down on her childhood bed. She'd redecorated the room for her mother, turning it into a guest room a few years ago. She pulled up her call history and, after a moment of hesitation, she tapped his number. The phone started to ring. Abbey fixed her eyes on the wall, trying to calm her beating heart. Why was she getting so nervous? Her palms were getting sweaty, a tingling sensation moving around in her limbs.

"Nick Sinclair," he answered.

"Hello, Nick."

"Abbey?"

"Yes. It's Abbey. I was just calling to thank you for the pies."

"Ah, good. I'm glad you received them. All I had to go on was your description of your mother's house: the corner of Maple and Ivy."

"How did you remember?" She lay down on her back, her blonde curly hair fanning out along the hunter green and cream color-coordinated comforter.

His slight amusement came through the phone in a short, quiet breath. "I hardly ever forget a detail. I can recall almost everything."

"Really? I'd love to remember everything," she said, but before she'd even finished saying the words, she regretted them. She wouldn't want to remember the sting of hurt when Vince, Max's dad, had left them, or the intense worry she'd had at a young age when she'd found out she was pregnant, and she hadn't made a life suitable for raising a child yet. She didn't want to recall with perfect clarity the conversation she'd had with her mother about her alcoholic father who wasn't allowed near her. Those emotions were now diluted with all kinds of other emotions that had happened over the years.

"Am I interrupting your Thanksgiving?" she asked suddenly.

He laughed quietly again. "No."

"Are you doing anything with Caroline today?" She knew it was a bold question since they'd just met. It wasn't to pry; she only asked out of concern for the both of them.

"I'm working, so no. And she hates turkey," he said, and Abbey could almost feel the smile in his words. "She refuses to eat Thanksgiving dinner, so it hasn't been a big holiday for us in a long time."

He'd said, "a long time," which meant that there was a time when he did celebrate Thanksgiving. Had he sat around that enormous dining room table of his, the chairs full of family members, passing dishes from one to the other, telling stories and enjoying each other?

"So, you used to celebrate Thanksgiving?" she asked. "Why don't you celebrate it anymore?"

The line was silent for so long that she pulled the phone back to view the screen to check that she was still connected. Just as she opened her mouth to say something, Nick said, "I just don't."

"I never knew Caroline didn't like turkey. She's funny," Abbey said, trying to lighten the mood after his last comment. It was clear he wasn't planning to share the details of his life with her, and she couldn't blame him. "It's a tough job, taking care of an elderly family member," she ventured.

"Yes."

"My mother and I take care of my gramps."

"Perhaps that's why you're so good with my grandmother," he said. "Your grandfather is lucky to have you to care for him."

"Well, he's always been there for me. I haven't seen my dad since I was four, and Gramps filled in when he wasn't there."

"I'm sorry you haven't seen your dad."

"According to my mom, he wasn't in the best shape to care for me. He died before I could really talk to him and find out his side of things."

The line was silent.

"Are you still there?"

"Uh, yes. I apologize. I'm just thinking about what you said."

"I wish my memory was as good as yours. I have fuzzy memories of my dad, but I wasn't quite old enough to really remember him. What bothers me the most is that my memories of him were good ones, and they didn't paint the same picture my mom painted once I'd gotten old enough to hear her story."

"What do you remember?"

"I remember his kisses before bed, the smile I got when he walked in from work, the way it felt to snuggle up next to him when I didn't feel well… He was nothing like what my mother remembers."

"What did she say about him?"

"That he was an alcoholic. Things could get heated… She wouldn't allow him near me." Abbey had never shared any of that with anyone before. "But Gramps was there for me every day. He taught me how to ride a bike, change a tire on my car, keep a checkbook… He was great."

"I understand," he said. "My grandmother spent a lot of time with us when we were growing up as well… Perhaps I'll stop over and see her today."

"She'd like that, I'm sure."

"Well, I won't keep you. I'm sure you'd like to be with your family. I'm glad you received the pies. Have a wonderful holiday, and I'll see you tomorrow."

"Okay," she said, self-conscious about opening up so much. She didn't even know him, but he was a good listener.

"Goodbye," he said.

"Bye." She dropped the phone onto the bed beside her and stared at the ceiling. The room was drafty. Her toes were like ice in her socks and her arms had goose bumps. She grabbed a pillow—encased in a matching green and cream sham—and laid it across her chest to keep warm.

There was a knock at the door and Max peeked his head in. "Mama," he said. "I cut you a giant slice of pie." He was smiling, his eyebrows up in anticipation. "I'm waiting to eat mine until you come out."

"You are?" she said, smiling.

"Yes! I want to see how much whipped cream you want on yours. I've covered my whole top with it! Nana said I could."

With another grin, she got up and followed Max to the kitchen to be with her family.

Chapter Four

The short man that continued to answer Nick Sinclair's front door was named Richard Smith. He was the house manager, and every decision regarding day-to-day happenings went through him. He'd sat Abbey down in Nick's office with the promise that Nick would be with her shortly. Abbey welcomed the silence as she waited, facing his desk.

She'd left Max with her mother and felt a touch guilty because Gramps was in a mood, and she worried that Max would have to entertain himself. Her mom had insisted they'd be just fine. Truthfully, Abbey didn't have any other options.

She'd had days like this one before—it was part of being a working mother—but this day was harder to swallow because she was leaving Max and burdening her mother in order to do something she didn't really have to do. She could easily just be a nurse, tell Caroline she couldn't do the decorating job, and apologize to Nick, but she kept thinking about how that money could change her family's lives, so she had to make herself do it. Plus, there was that dangled carrot in front of her: the idea that maybe—just maybe—this interior design opportunity could lead to something bigger, something amazing: the start of a new career, a new life for her and Max.

She'd been frazzled before she'd even left her mom's house, and, while the silence around her now was helping to calm her, her initial anxiety was being replaced by the zinging simultaneous excitement and fear of seeing Nick again.

"Sorry to keep you waiting," he said from behind her, as the sound of his footsteps got closer. She turned around. His gaze slid down to her sneakers, up her jeans, and back to her face. It wasn't an appraising look; it was more inquisitive than anything else. There was no way she was going to move furniture and sit on the floor to sketch in different rooms wearing her fanciest clothes.

Nick had on jeans today, and a gray sweater, the collar rolled and held together with a button. She could tell the quality of his clothes by the way they fell on his body, and she wondered where a millionaire like Nick Sinclair shopped. Did he have to order them? Were there shops for the rich and famous hidden somewhere in the city?

When she finally surfaced from her thoughts, she caught him still looking at her.

"What are you thinking about?" he asked.

"O-oh," she stammered. "Nothing. My thoughts get away from me sometimes." She resisted the urge to run her fingers through her wildly curly hair, which seemed to have a mind of its own in this weather. Her friends had always said it worked for her and people would die for her hair, but she'd always wanted that gorgeous sleek look that she saw in magazines.

"I've brought my sketchpad," she said, trying to get down to business so she wouldn't have to think about how gorgeous he was when he looked at her with those interested eyes of his. "I thought I could sketch out a plan for each room today. Then, once you approve the sketches, I can go to work finding similar furniture to fill the space."

"That would be fine." His gaze shifted above her head as a shiny, midnight-blue Lamborghini inched its way along the drive outside the window. It was clear that whoever was driving was meticulously careful maneuvering it in the snow outside. Nick's concern was evident on his face.

"I was also wondering," she said, trying to pull his attention back inside. She tipped her head up in front of his view. His eyes flickered back down to her. "I don't know if you require a certain dress code for your staff, but I think better when I can be comfortable." She looked down at her sneakers, wishing she could be in one of the bedrooms, behind a closed door so she could kick them off and go in her sock feet. "Are you okay if I wear jeans and sneakers to work?"

He laughed a little, his chest rising and falling with his laughter as he refocused on her face. There it was—that expression she'd been interested to see. She'd made him genuinely smile.

"You can wear whatever you like. I don't mind at all." He took a step toward her. "You're free to roam the house—food, drink, anything you want. If you can't find it, ask Richard. He's usually in the small office behind the kitchen or you can text him. I'll give you his number."

"I'm going to start in the ballroom with the piano downstairs. It reminds me of Cinderella," she said with a smile. "I loved that movie as a child." But he just looked at her so she continued, "Do you have any requests for the use of the room or anything you'd like me to include?"

He shook his head, his disinterest clear.

"Are you planning to decorate for Christmas?"

"I wasn't planning to. It seems like a waste of effort."

"Why?"

"It's just me here, and the family will be here only a short time…" His face shifted as if he were only just now realizing something. "You know, you should probably put up a tree somewhere. Robin's son will be coming. He still believes in Santa Claus. He may need a tree for presents."

"He may *need* a tree," she repeated, her confusion running rampant. "It certainly helps to have one when Santa leaves his gifts. Have you thought about Christmas morning at all? You're going to have guests."

"They are my family, remember? They know that I'm not much in the way of festivities. Knowing Robin, she'll have her own tree delivered."

"You're having a Christmas party, correct?"

"Yes."

"Would you not need decorations for a *Christmas* party?"

"I suppose. I was thinking you could just add a few in the ballroom. But you're the expert. Provide whatever atmosphere you'd like. That's why I'm paying you to do it instead of doing it myself."

"I'm not an expert," she said. "I just believe in the magic of the season. Wouldn't you enjoy fresh greenery and twinkling lights?"

"It is a formality of which I have no opinion one way or the other."

"Well, I think it would be fun to decorate. Do you own Christmas decorations, or do I need to buy them?"

"Buy them." He pulled his money clip from a back pocket and handed her a credit card. "And you don't have to show me the sketches. Just do it. Buy whatever you need. Richard is available for you and can arrange a staff when you need someone to install or move things." He headed toward the door. "I'll be in my office most of the day."

Nick headed out of the room, and she followed, turning in the opposite direction once in the hallway. Abbey pulled her eyes from him as he walked away from her, let herself into the ballroom, and plopped down on one of the two facing sofas. She let her gaze wander the space, wondering what she could do with such a room. She really liked the high ceilings and windows that stretched to the second floor, but they made it very hard to create a cozy space. In the very center of the room, on one wall, was a working wood-burning fireplace with a mantle as thick as the bow of a ship. It was painted white and empty of any decorations whatsoever. The snow outside had turned to a dreary rain, and, as she looked at this fireplace, Abbey thought that she definitely needed Christmas decorations to brighten things up. Then, it occurred to her just where to get them.

She pulled her phone from her handbag, stood up, and walked over to the fireplace. On her phone, she searched for the local Christmas tree farm where she and her mother always got their Christmas trees. As she scrolled through her search results, Richard peeked his head in.

"All okay?" he called.

"Yep! Thank you, Richard. Except… do you have any matches? I'd like to light this fire."

"I'd be happy to find you some, Ms. Fuller," he said with a smile. "Does it have enough kindling?"

"It looks like it."

"I'll see what I can find."

Once Richard had left, she called the Christmas tree farm and, after a bit of haggling, she ordered seven of the biggest Colorado Blue spruce trees they had and a few miles of fresh garland, and she got them for a very good price. With a smile, she also ordered a few bundles of mistletoe, thinking of all the places she could hang it around the house. What would Nick do if he were caught under it with her? The idea of him out of his comfort zone was enough to create a little giggle that rose in her throat. The Christmas tree farm worker promised to have it all delivered by noon, and it would come by truck, he'd said. Then, she grabbed her handbag and headed out to check on Caroline and find Christmas decorations.

"How was your Thanksgiving?" Caroline asked with a smile as she held the door open for Abbey to enter. Her shoulders were rounded forward from age, even though she was clearly attempting to stand quite straight. She had on a pair of slacks with a blouse that had fabric-covered buttons. Her white hair was curled and tucked behind her ears, showing off her pearl earrings. With a delicate touch, she pulled the door closed after Abbey entered.

"It was good." Abbey watched Caroline's face, wondering if the holiday had made her feel lonely, but she didn't look unhappy in any way. She never did. "Nick sent me two pumpkin pies." Caroline's eyebrows shot up in surprise. "Want to hear the story?"

As Abbey told her the story of Gramps and how he'd dropped the pies, and how Nick had been so thoughtful as to send her some, Caroline was almost smiling.

"I *knew* you'd make a good impression on him," she said, her lips pressed together as if to keep her smile from surfacing.

"Well, I haven't started decorating yet. He may have a different opinion when I'm done," she teased. "What if he doesn't like my choices? Decorating is so subjective. How do you know I'm the right person for the job?"

Caroline sat there, smiling now, thoughts behind her eyes. "Nick took a very long time to find me a nurse. He worried so much that he wouldn't find someone who could work to his—and my—standards. He was fully expecting to go through a few nurses before finding a good fit. But then you came in and I just loved you. You are so kind and thoughtful and careful. Even if you don't decorate like *he* would, I think he'll love it. You will surprise him at every turn, and I can't wait to hear all about it."

"I don't know…" Abbey worried aloud.

"I have never known Nick to send pie…" She put her fingertips to her lips to squelch the bubbling laughter for a moment before she continued, "I've never seen him send anything to anyone." She giggled again. "I think he'll enjoy having you around."

"Okay," Abbey said, standing up. She hoped Caroline didn't have some sort of ridiculous matchmaking plan going on or anything. She seemed awfully giddy. That was the very last thing Abbey needed. She'd promised herself that she'd never do that to Max again. She'd had a few boyfriends since his father, and they'd all ended badly.

Max's father, Vince, had been nice enough when Abbey had met him. He was always on the go—party to party, never settling down. Abbey had enjoyed the chase when it came to him. He was that bad boy she'd wanted to tame. And, for a while, she thought she had. Their relationship had progressed and, before she knew it, he was moving into her apartment. As a bartender, he kept crazy hours, but she delighted in the fact that he spent his free time with her, he took her to his parties, and he seemed to be in love with her. Until she got pregnant.

After Max was born, Vince had tried to be there for her, but when it came down to it, he wouldn't change his lifestyle to be with her and Max. She became more and more fed up with his party-going and lack of attention to her and their baby. He came in at all hours, stayed out, drank too much. Ultimately, she realized that he wouldn't change because that wasn't who he was. She confronted him during an argument and he admitted that he had never wanted to be a father. She didn't need to hear any more. He moved out the next day, and she hadn't heard from him since.

Dating people caused too many questions to answer for Max, and she could tell he felt the loss of those people in his life. She wouldn't put him through that again. "Let's check your meds and see what you need to have at the moment." She looked at her watch. "I need to take your blood pressure."

In just slightly over two hours, Abbey had returned from shopping, her little Toyota full to the brim with Christmas lights, ornaments, boxes, wrapping paper, ribbon, candles, and wreaths. Richard met her at the door and immediately called the groundsmen to help her, although she'd planned to bring it all in by herself. They deposited everything in the ballroom, the fire roaring in the fireplace. She sat down in front of it to wrap presents, dumping her coat and scarf on the floor.

The orange light of the fire reflecting on the surfaces of the great windows was helping with the ambience of the room already. Snow had started to fall again outside, and Abbey wished it would finally change over for good. It was as if the sky wanted to snow, and was trying to snow, but it just couldn't. She felt a little like that with this giant room. She wanted to make it beautiful, she was trying, but she just didn't quite know how to do it—it was so large. So she started with what she did know how to do, and that was decorate for Christmas. Abbey pulled out empty boxes that she'd purchased at the store and began folding them into shape. A log on the fire popped, sending an orange and yellow fizz up the chimney. After tearing the scissors free from their packaging and rummaging around in her shopping bags for the tape, she unrolled a section of bright silver paper. The blade of the open scissors slid along the sheet until it fell loose from the roll, and she began to wrap the empty boxes.

After kicking her sneakers off and warming her feet by the fire, Abbey was just starting to get feeling back in her limbs by the time she had finished an enormous pile of silver boxes. The cardboard spool rolled away from her as she unrolled the yards of wide, shimmery silver ribbon. Snipping and securing, tucking and folding, she tied each ribbon around a box until they looked like a perfect pile of presents on Christmas morning, their bows cascading down the side of each box. She pushed them off to the side and pulled out the Christmas ornaments she'd purchased.

Just as she'd gotten everything set out in one corner of the room, the Christmas tree farm called from the driveway. Abbey slipped on her shoes, found Richard, and asked him to round up the men to help once more. Seven trees were delivered: four twenty-five-foot trees in the ballroom, flanking the giant windows, two more in the entrance, and one smaller tree in the living room. She had the men leave the fresh garland on the floor of the entrance so that snow wouldn't collect on it. They also left twenty-six wreaths, each with an oversized red velvet bow at the bottom—one for each front exterior window.

As she held the large bundles of mistletoe in her arms, Nick came out of his office to see what all the commotion was in the entryway.

His brows were pulled downward, his mouth set in a slight scowl as if that were the resting position of his lips. "What is all this?"

"You said I could buy Christmas decorations." She shifted to get a better hold of the mistletoe. It was wrapped in paper, but the sheer number of sprigs was causing it to slip from her arms.

"I'd rather hoped you'd buy some furniture."

"I will."

"I just don't see the need in doing *all* of this. It's a waste of time."

"You said that you trusted me, so *trust* me when I say that I will have the house decorated by Christmas—furniture and all."

He shook his head, his chest filling with breath, and what she thought could be a slight smile on his lips emerged. Or was it a disbelieving smirk? He turned and headed back to his office.

By four o'clock, Abbey hadn't even stopped once, but she had both towering trees done in the ballroom. Each one had two thousand white twinkle lights and shiny silver and winter-blue ornaments to bring out the blue in the rug. She'd added silver tree skirts and then covered them completely with the silver faux presents she'd wrapped. Dangling from shimmery silver ribbons that the groundsmen had helped her pin to the massive ceiling near each of the windows were the sprigs of mistletoe, one hanging just over the grand piano, the tails of the bow cascading like tiny, velvet waterfalls, their reflection just beautiful on the surface of the piano's bench.

The fireplace was draped in spruce greenery and more white lights, a blue and silver bow with long tails holding it up at either corner. She'd placed silver stocking hangers perfectly centered along the front of the fireplace and from them, dangled cream-colored stockings with silver beading.

Abbey sat down on the floor cross-legged and pulled out her sketchpad. She turned around to view the trees she'd just decorated. With the warmth from the fire on her back, she peered up at the gorgeous trees, like bookends on either side of the windows. They'd already filled the room with so much character, their white lights glimmering against the window panes as the snow came down outside. Suddenly, inspiration was hitting her from every direction, and Abbey began to sketch out the room, her pencil moving as fast as it could go, her ideas bumping into one another on their way out.

She was going to make several seating areas in this room, each one angled so that everyone could feel the warmth from that gorgeous fireplace. Each group of chairs would have a small table in the center, allowing people to set down their drinks, talk, play cards, whatever they wanted. She imagined silver vases of Christmas greenery—tall shoots of holly branches with red berries. Above the mantle, she envisioned a colossal antique mirror with a thick silver frame. Her hands were sketching as fast as they could go, the side of her hand black from the lead of her drawing pencil.

"How's it going?" she heard from across the room and jumped, her concentration interrupted. Nick was standing in the doorway, his eyes moving up one of the Christmas trees. Then, he looked at Abbey, and she caught him stealing a glance at her sock feet before making eye contact. She tucked her feet under her self-consciously. He should be happy she wasn't wearing her shoes on the nice rug. He walked over to her and peered down at her sketchpad. "You've been busy," he said, his voice contemplating and careful.

"When I get ideas, I just run with them."

"Clearly," he said. His face showed no indication of his thoughts and it was driving her crazy. "You're keeping the piano, yes?"

"Yes. Is that okay?"

"It's fine." His gaze fluttered up to the mistletoe and then back to her. "Do you play piano at all?" he asked.

"A little."

With that answer, he cocked his head to the side slightly with interest. "Show me."

A swell of unease tickled her skin at his request. She was only facilitating conversation. She didn't really play. She'd learned a few songs at her friend's house when she was in high school. Now he'd put her on the spot.

Nick walked over and stood next to the piano. He was waiting for her to play something. Her empty stomach filled with nerves. Then, she got herself together. What did it matter if he thought she wasn't good at the piano? She was there to decorate his house, not entertain him. She padded over on her sock feet and sat down on the bench, crisscrossing her legs.

"You don't need the pedals?" he asked.

"Not for this song," she said with a nervous grin. Then, she banged out "Chopsticks" on the keys. She was the best at this song because she'd practiced it enough to be fast, and it generally sounded like the actual song, which was more than she could say for her other options.

Abbey turned to look at him, and he wasn't looking at her. He was looking at the floor, but clearly he was thinking about something, and the smile on his face told her that she'd done something right. His expression surprised her. She'd thought that he would be annoyed with her ridiculous piano playing after she'd said she could play, but instead, he seemed amused. His affectionate grin sent a wave of excitement through her.

He shook his head, that grin still playing at his lips, and then looked up at her. "Richard says you never ate lunch. I was just checking that you were okay."

"Oh," she said, only just realizing that she hadn't stopped, and it was nearly dinnertime. Perhaps it was adrenaline from having such a large project in front of her over such a short span of time and the need to impress him, or maybe it was her creative juices flowing, but she hadn't noticed the time.

"I'm having something prepared for you. I have a chef who cooks for me every evening. I've taken the liberty of having him make you an early dinner. You can have it here at the house, or he can box it up for you. Whatever you prefer."

Abbey figured she'd better eat there since it would be terribly rude of her to bring her own dinner to her mother's without having something for them. "Thank you," she said, surprised again by his thoughtfulness. "I'll have it here, if that's okay."

"Certainly. Why don't I have him serve you in the dining room?"

"Will you be eating?" She couldn't imagine the thought of sitting at the end of his long, empty dining room table all alone.

He stared at her a moment, as if he were trying to decipher her motives. The idea of eating with Nick Sinclair was a little stressful—she hoped her manners were up to par—but eating alone was just as terrifying. She never ate by herself; even when she was at her apartment with Max, she always made sure they ate together. The thought occurred to her that Nick probably ate alone every night.

Nick still hadn't said anything, so she filled the silence with an explanation. "I don't like to eat by myself," she said.

His eyes were unstill, that curiosity seeping out through his features. He smiled a little. She thought about the fact that she could be imposing on him. He'd only offered her food because she hadn't eaten. He wasn't necessarily offering his companionship for dinner. But she'd already asked him, so the damage was done. He was a big boy; he could get out of it if he wanted to.

"I'll have the chef serve us both in the dining room." He walked through the door and turned around. "It'll be ready in about twenty minutes. I'll see you then."

Chapter Five

What in the world was she about to eat? Was it pasta? Vegetables? It smelled delicious. Abbey draped her napkin in her lap and eyed Nick for strategies on how to eat the dish in front of her. Her natural inclination was to spin it around her fork, but she was worried that she'd break some kind of dining etiquette that she wasn't even aware of. Nick dipped his fork into the dish and began to turn it around in circles. Thank goodness!

"I forgot to ask," he said suddenly, abandoning his fork and setting his hand on the white tablecloth that hadn't been there before the meal. "Are you allergic to anything?" He nodded toward the pasta-like dish. "It's shrimp and zucchini noodles."

"No, I'm not allergic to anything."

He looked visibly relieved. "I'm not used to thinking about someone else. I just told the chef to make two, not even considering your preferences. I apologize. Do you even like shrimp and zucchini?"

"Yes," she said, although she'd never had a dish quite like this one before. "You just looked a little unsure."

She smiled despite herself. "I didn't know how I was supposed to eat it," she said honestly.

His brows pulled together in that handsome way of his, his lips turned down in confusion. "What do you mean?"

"I didn't know if I was supposed to just twirl it around my fork or not, but then, when you did it, I realized I'd guessed right."

"How else would you eat it?" he laughed, and she had to make herself breathe. His laughter went all the way to his eyes, and the corners of his mouth turned down just slightly when he smiled. His whole face changed. She was so happy to see a real laugh from him, and, by the way he collected himself right after, she wondered if he wasn't used to it.

"I didn't *know* how to eat it. That's why I looked at you!" she laughed too.

"Well, you can eat it any way you want," he said, chuckling again.

"Do you always eat in here?"

"Yes."

Abbey was sitting at the head of the table with Nick at her right, and the two of them barely covered one corner of that colossal table. It had five chairs down each side and one on the ends.

"Do you always sit in the same spot, or do you choose a new chair every night?"

"Ha!"

She couldn't help the flutter in her chest as she realized that she was making him laugh again, and she was so glad to see him smile. His face was quite different tonight than it was when she'd first met him. As she watched the fine lines forming around his eyes, the light creases in his forehead as his face became animated, the way his lips turned down at the corners in that way that was unique to him, she was happy to see his real smile.

"What would *you* do?" he asked.

"Sorry?"

"Would you sit in the same seat or would you choose a different one each night?"

"I'd sit in a different seat every night so I could see what the room looked like from the angles of every one of my guests. ...If I sat in here at all."

Nick looked around the room as if explanations of her last comment were hanging somewhere in the air above him. "Why wouldn't you eat in a dining room?" he finally asked.

"It's so big, the table swallows us right up. I'd eat somewhere comfier."

"Comfier?" His face crumpled, telling her that he had no idea why somewhere other than the dining room would be any better than where they were sitting now. "Where would you suggest then?"

His laughter had made her feel a sense of friendliness that gave her the courage to do what she was thinking of doing. "I'll show you," she said, standing up. "Grab your plate."

This time, *he* was watching *her* as she set her fork on her plate and grabbed her glass, her cloth napkin dangling between her fingers. With a slight reluctance, Nick followed her lead, that look of interest returning on his face. She caught him looking at her sock feet again as she led the way to the ballroom that she'd just decorated. The fire had dwindled to a low, orange glow, but the heat was still present. Carefully, she sat on one of the sofas that she'd arranged facing each other in front of the fireplace and folded her legs underneath her. With the plate and napkin balancing on her lap and the glass by the leg of the sofa on the floor, she began to eat.

"And why is this better than having a perfectly functional table at our disposal?" he asked, awkwardly holding his plate and trying to get the zucchini onto his fork.

"It's relaxing."

He didn't respond, and her thoughts were already somewhere else. Being next to him on the sofa with their dinners in their laps almost made her forget that they were so very different, the same way it had made her forget how big the room had seemed when she got there. "So, you said you remember nearly every detail? Will you remember everything I say tonight?" she asked.

"Yes, probably."

"You'll remember everything about the room and sitting here and what we ate?"

"Most likely."

"That's amazing."

He smiled, but it was his polite smile, not the kind she'd seen at the dinner table.

They ate for a while in the quiet of that enormous room, the fire popping every so often, the daylight fading on the newly fallen snow through the windows. He didn't talk anymore, and she wondered if he wasn't used to talking since he was accustomed to eating alone, but it was a comfortable silence. When she'd almost finished her dinner, she said, "May I test your memory?" She set her near empty plate down on the floor beside the sofa.

Nick set his dinner plate next to hers and twisted slightly to face her. "Okay."

"What kind of cake did you have for your ninth birthday?"

His eyes squinted as he attempted to recall the answer. "It was chocolate with vanilla icing, I believe."

"What did you wear on your first day of high school?"

"Our school uniform: a navy blazer with a white shirt and tan trousers."

"What was the weather like the Tuesday before last?"

He pursed his lips, as he sifted through the memories from that week. "Rainy. Icy, actually."

"It's easy to guess the weather this winter. It's either rainy or snowy lately. Are you lying?" she challenged him.

"No."

Abbey's thoughts were always muddled—she had hundreds of them all at the same time. She'd read once that creative people tended to think that way, and as a result, she'd had to work very hard to keep herself and her life organized so she didn't forget anything, misplace something, or let dates and events slip her mind. She was always running a hundred miles an hour, barely even processing things she did. Sometimes, she had to focus just to remember if she'd packed lunches or not. So the kind of memory that Nick had was fascinating—she couldn't even imagine it.

Speaking of remembering, she jolted upright. "What time is it?" she asked, looking down at her watch.

"Five."

Max was still at her mother's, and she'd stayed far longer than she'd planned. "Thank you so much for dinner. It was delicious," she said, standing up and grabbing her plate. He took it from her and set it back down. She hurried toward her bag, picked it up, and shoved her feet into her shoes. When she righted herself, Nick was standing by her. "I need to go. I'm late. My mom's watching my son, Max, and they're probably both wondering where I am."

"Absolutely. My grandmother had mentioned that you're a single mother."

"Yes." She shuffled toward the great entrance to the room that led to the front door. "I'll be over tomorrow at around noon. I'll be with your grandmother in the morning," she said as she paced to the front door.

"Perfect," he said, opening the door for her. "I look forward to it."

He would? He'd look forward to it? That comment was enough to stop her for just a second. She was glad he'd said it because she looked forward to it too.

He stayed in the doorway as she jogged through the snow toward her car, and he didn't shut the door until she was headed down the long drive to the main road.

"Let him sleep," her mom said as Abbey peered into her dark high school bedroom. Max was under the covers, his eyes closed. Abbey gasped and pointed, just realizing what she was seeing in the shadows. Two green eyes glared at her. "Is that Señor Freckles curled up at the foot of the bed?" she whispered. "I can't believe he's in there with Max." Then, before she could say anything else, she heard the thud of his paws on the floor and he darted between them and out the bedroom door.

"Isn't that funny," her mom said. "I haven't seen that cat all day." She stepped back and pulled the door closed, leaving a crack open for light. "Why not just let him sleep? You can drop his things off on your way to work tomorrow."

"You sure you don't mind?"

"Not at all."

"How was the decorating?" Gramps called from the kitchen. Abbey hurried down the hallway toward him to keep him from calling out again and waking Max. When she found him, he was dishing out a rather large helping of vanilla ice cream. He raised his eyebrows and pointed to it in offering. She shook her head with a smile and sat down at the table. Her mom joined her.

"It was amazing. I bought a bunch of Christmas trees today. Big, giant ones. They looked so beautiful."

"Did you see Nick Sinclair?" her mom asked, leaning on her hands, her elbows propped on the table.

"I did. I actually ate dinner with him."

Her mom's eyes bulged with interest. "Really? What was it like to be in the presence of a millionaire?"

"Surprisingly not much different than being with anyone else."

Gramps joined them with his bowl, the ceramic bottom of it rattling slightly against the table as he attempted to set it down with an unsteady hand.

"He's nice."

"Is he, now?" her mom said with a grin on her face. "He's sending you pies for Thanksgiving, having dinner with you…"

"It's not like that," Abbey said. She didn't want anyone mistaking his kindness for anything other than what it was. Nick had only been concerned about her in both instances, and he was just trying to make sure she had what she needed.

"You never know," Gramps said. "Your grandmother was quite wealthy. Her family owned a restaurant chain. She went to fancy schools and she was quite the southern belle." Gramps smiled, his forehead creasing in three large folds with his smile, pushing his white hair back just slightly on his head. "I had no business asking her out. I was from a working-class family, and I didn't feel that I had anything to offer her, but she looked so pretty sitting there at that soda fountain that day that I just had to take a chance and ask her out."

"And she said yes," Abbey said, trying to recall her grandmother's laugh. She always loved her laugh.

"Nope. She said no."

Mid-memory, Abbey turned and looked at Gramps. "What?"

"She said no. Then she got up and walked out."

"What did you do?"

"I chased after her. It took me a week. I think Fran finally said yes just to shut me up," he said with a laugh. "But once she said yes, we were inseparable from that moment on."

"I can't remember her laugh," Abbey fretted. She kept wracking her brain over and over, memory after memory. Fear swept through her as she realized she was losing her memory of Gran.

"It was like bells," Gramps said, his hands beginning to wobble more than they had. His spoon tapped the inside of the bowl relentlessly. "High-pitched, tinkling giggles. Her eyes would squint and she'd press her lips together as if she wanted to hold it in but always her giggles would escape. I remember it perfectly. God, I miss her laughter."

Abbey wished she could love someone like that. It occurred to her then that it had been quite a while since Gramps had laughed.

"I'm just saying, don't rule anything out," he said. "But you're not there to get a date anyway. You're there to work. And it sounds like you've gotten a good start."

"Yes," she said quietly. She couldn't agree more, but the pressure to please Gramps was mounting. He'd always pushed her to use her artistic gift, but the truth of the matter was that she had to support her son. That was what made this project so important to her. If she got it right, she could add it to her portfolio, maybe Nick would even mention her name at that Christmas party. She could potentially get clients and make a lot of money, and maybe even be an interior decorator full time. "I have to work in the morning, and then I'll be back there for a few hours to start on one of the bedrooms."

"I'll bet you'll do an amazing job," he said smiling, his hands becoming less shaky as he looked at her.

"I hope so."

"I've been having trouble getting a deep breath, and I keep having a fluttering in my chest," Caroline said as Abbey tried to listen to her heartbeat. She was usually quiet when Abbey checked her vitals, but today, she was quite chatty. Abbey closed her eyes to focus on the heartbeat. She jotted down the number in her log and pulled her stethoscope from her ears.

"Still? Let me see." She fished out the printout from the EKG that she'd received from the doctor at Caroline's last visit. It had come back abnormal, and they were awaiting more tests. Years of practice had taught her not to show any alarm, but as she looked at the paperwork, she did feel that it was possible Caroline could have an arrhythmia. This would not be good, given the fact that she had also complained of hip pain. Caroline's hip problems were coming on the heels of a diagnosis of arthritis of the spine.

"What is it?" Caroline asked. Her face didn't show any worry either, but she never would. She wasn't the type. Instead, she almost looked annoyed. "What do I have wrong now?"

"I'm not a doctor. I wouldn't want to try to diagnose you. We need a specialist to take a look." What she didn't want to say was that, if they needed to operate for any reason, an arrhythmia might complicate surgery, if not eliminate the possibility of it. It would just be too risky. Abbey mentioned none of this as she packed away her instruments.

"Have you been to Nick's today?" Caroline asked.

"I'm heading over there after I finish checking you over."

Caroline pursed her lips. "Nick's little decorating job is dipping into my conversation time. I'm getting jealous," she teased.

"It's your fault," Abbey teased back. "You were the one who set it up."

Caroline smiled. "Ah, well. It's far worse for him to be alone than it is for me. It'll be good for him to have some company." She shifted uncomfortably in her chair. "It's an awfully large home to have all to himself."

"I thought that too."

"When he bought it, he was married."

"Oh?"

That annoyed look consumed Caroline's features again. It was clear to Abbey that she had strong feelings relating to her comment, but her manners were preventing her from saying anything. "He's divorced now."

"I'm sorry to hear that." Abbey knew all too well what it was like to have a failing relationship. She knew that a divorce was only the tip of the iceberg and all the heartache and loss and disappointment were lurking under the water where no one else could see. Telling people she'd broken up with Max's dad was a tidy way to discuss it, but all of that emotion had been there.

"I'm not. Sarah wasn't right for him. She put too much pressure on him. She was never happy." Caroline shifted in her seat again, her leg clearly giving her some trouble. "Sarah's remarried now. She has kids."

Abbey knew how unsuccessful relationships had taken a toll on her. She was absolutely over Max's father, Vince, but there was always that lingering feeling of wanting to be with someone who loved her. She didn't often allow the thought to process, but sometimes, she wished she didn't have to go through life alone and raise Max all by herself. It would be so nice to have someone to experience life beside her, someone she could share it all with. But, as soon as the thought entered her mind, she reminded herself of how lucky she was. Max was a good boy, he had a great temperament, he was healthy, and she had enough money to put food on the table. Wishing for the luxuries of life only made her feel guilty.

"Things happen for a reason. I believe that," Caroline said.

"I hope you're right."

"I am!" She winked at Abbey. "I'm right about this as much as I'm right about you being the person to decorate Nick's house. Go talk some sense into him. Tell him he needs area rugs."

"Haha." Abbey looked at her watch. It was time to go. "I'll call the doctor and make you an appointment."

"Sounds good. And when you talk to Nick, tell him I'd love another visit."

Abbey nodded and packed her things. Then, she headed out to Nick's.

Chapter Six

When Richard let Abbey in, he allowed her to find her own way, assuming she knew where to go by now. As she stared at the sparkly Christmas trees she'd erected, the most gorgeous music came toward her. It was like nothing she'd ever heard before—sad, and light at the same time, the notes circling her like a musical cyclone. Every sound echoed through the large space, the deep notes filling her ears and settling in the pit of her stomach. It was so beautiful. She followed it to see where it was coming from, but she had a pretty good idea.

As she walked into the room with the piano, the sound crashed around her like a cool wave on a summer's day, and she found herself mesmerized. She stood in the large doorway, and allowed her head to rest on the frame as she watched Nick from behind sitting at the piano, under the mistletoe. His hands moved along the keys so smoothly, it made his arms look as though they were dancing. His head was tipped down, turned to the side, in total concentration, as his foot tapped the pedals. The top of the piano was propped open, allowing the glorious music to penetrate every space in the room and beyond.

She was transfixed, watching his fingers on the keys. They were gentle and careful as he played each note. She'd seen him hold his pen, flip papers on his desk, turn zucchini with his fork, but she'd not seen his fingers move like that. She wondered what else he was capable of. What would it feel like to have those fingers touch her skin? She snapped her head upright. What in the world was she thinking? Abbey mentally corrected herself for having those kinds of thoughts about the man who was employing her.

As she watched Nick playing alone at his piano, she could feel her heart aching for him, and she knew she shouldn't, but she couldn't stop the emotions she was feeling. They assaulted her against her will.

"Hello," he said, his head turned in her direction. She realized then that the music had stopped. "You're earlier than I expected." He stood up and walked over to her.

"That was beautiful."

"Thank you."

"What was that you were playing?"

"Chopin."

Nick's Chopin was a far cry from her "Chopsticks" the other day. She'd never experienced anyone playing piano like that, and yet he played like it was nothing to him, when it was the most beautiful sound she'd ever heard in real life. How many hours had he practiced as a child? How many lessons had he had? While she was playing softball, her hair in a ponytail and her cleats kicking dirt on the field, he had been learning classical piano.

Their worlds couldn't be any more dissimilar yet there was an art to his playing that she felt on another level. She knew that it took just the right person to know when to leave one note and begin another; he had it down perfectly. It was the same way she'd always felt with her art when she was in school, knowing when to taper that brush stroke just enough to make the painting create a feeling. In different mediums, they were both aware of how to create emotion, and that fact made him so interesting to her that she could hardly take her eyes off him.

"What's the matter?" he asked, and she realized that her thoughts were apparent on her face. She was terrible at hiding them. "You look worried about something."

"I'm fine," she smiled, straightening her face into a more pleasant expression.

"You sure?"

"Yes." She took in a deep breath and let it out. "I'm going to start on the bedrooms today."

"Perfect. As I said before, you have free rein of the house. Use whatever you'd like. You have my credit card. Please feel free to use it however you need."

"Thank you."

"You're welcome. I'll be out most of the day, but I should be home to see your plans and what you've done with the rooms before you leave."

"You'll be out?"

"I'm flying to Kentucky, to Turfway Park. I'm betting on a horse out there." He said it with an air of satisfaction as if he thought it would impress her or something.

"Horse racing?"

"Yes. The odds are good, otherwise I wouldn't bother." When she didn't respond, partly because she knew nothing about horse racing and partly because she'd always thought that there were better things to do with money than gamble it away, he added, "I'm also doing business. I'm meeting someone from New York about his corporation."

"So, instead of meeting at his office, you're betting on horses?"

"Yes."

Max needed new jeans. She'd bought some but she was saving them so that she could wrap them up and put them under the tree for Christmas because it would give him more to unwrap and she didn't have enough money for both his clothes and Christmas presents. His current jeans barely grazed the tops of his ankles, and she was glad for the snow outside so he could wear his boots to school to cover him up. And here was Nick betting away his hard-earned money. "And if you lose?"

"No big deal. It's only a thousand."

"Dollars? A *thousand* dollars? For one bet?"

He studied her for a moment while she tried unsuccessfully to hide what she was feeling and then—she could see it—realization sheeted over him. "It's the price of business," he said. "That's just how things are done."

"And you don't mind doing business that way?"

"It doesn't make a difference to me how I get it done as long as I get the signature on the dotted line."

"Don't you think there are better uses for that thousand dollars?"

"I consider it an investment toward a bigger bet. I'm trying to get someone to sell me his entire corporation. It will make me millions, and the thousand dollars is a blip on that scale." He started toward the door but turned around. "Is there anything else you'll require before I head out?"

"Caroline said she'd love a visit."

He nodded and then walked past her through the door and into the hallway, leaving her standing there. In the silence that remained, she was still pondering the fact that he was going to bet all that money. In an attempt to refocus herself, she tried to recall the sound of the piano, and at that moment, she wished she could have Nick's memory to remember it perfectly. But the betting on horses was still weighing on her.

"Wait!" she called after him.

He turned around.

"What if you win? Then what?"

He stood silent for a moment, pondering her question. "What would *you* like me to do with the winnings? You choose."

"If you win on the horse, I'd love you to donate your winnings to charity."

He smiled. "Okay. I promise. I'll let you pick the charity." With another smile and a wave, he headed down the hallway.

Feeling pleased with her arrangement with Nick, she slipped her shoes off and set them on the bottom step before walking up the curving staircase to the second floor as she tried to get herself together. When she got to the top, she opened the door to the first bedroom, walked inside, and, still trying to recall the sound of the music, she opened her sketchpad and began drawing.

She looked up, taking in the shadows of the room, the color of the walls, the way the fixtures reflected in the winter light. Then, with her hand moving as fast as Nick's had on the piano keys, she sketched, long, gray lines, shading in at the edges. She drew a four-poster bed, stark linens, and romantic lighting. More sketching—tall dressers with rounded corners, and warm rugs to cover the cold hardwoods. Her pencil moved along the paper effortlessly as the ideas came to her. When she was finished, she looked at her creation, and was happy with what she'd drawn. Despite her initial frustration over the way Nick spent his money, his music had stayed with her and actually inspired her. She set her pad of paper down and walked the space, getting a good look at it from every angle.

The next two bedrooms went just as smoothly. Abbey had a wonderfully colorful list of furniture to look for, and she couldn't believe she was going to buy so much. Before she left each room, she checked the closets just in case there was anything in there that she could use. They'd been empty, and she almost didn't check the one in the third room, thinking it, too, was probably bare. But something made her check, and was she glad she did.

Abbey let out a gasp as she squatted down in front of the most gorgeous framed picture of a landscape. At first, she wondered why it wasn't hanging up somewhere, but then she realized that Nick's ex-wife had taken all the furniture, so why would he have this one picture up anyway? She pulled it out to get a better look. The picture itself had an overall green tone to it, the landscape full of trees and underbrush with the most incredible white waterfall slamming down onto jagged rocks below. It was some sort of print, she figured, but it was absolutely amazing—the scene looking more like streaks of color than an actual waterfall, even though it was clear that it was real.

As she looked at her plan for the room, she realized that she'd gotten this room wrong. This picture needed to be the focal point. It was perfect in every way, and she couldn't believe it had been abandoned in a closet. Since it was already there, it also boosted her confidence. This picture was certainly elegant enough; it had a dark wood frame and creamy-white matting. Abbey imagined gauzy fabrics in white with green accents, perhaps a lamp with the tiniest floral pattern on it. She saw bookshelves and dark wood furniture, a bright white oval rug to cover the dark hardwoods. She flipped her page over and began sketching, the picture inspiring her.

When she was finished, she slid it back into the closet. This would be her surprise. Finally, she'd found something of Nick's to include in her decorating. Even if it meant nothing to him, he'd said she could have free rein of the house, and it moved her. It was the perfect piece to include—almost like putting her stamp on the room. Abbey would pull his personality into this house any way she could. She felt such a need to make it his.

With a smile, she closed her sketchpad and left to buy furniture, paint, and décor.

When Abbey returned, Richard informed her that her dinner had been prepared yet again, and Mr. Sinclair was waiting for her in the dining room. She didn't want to be excited, but the truth of the matter was that she was happy about seeing him again. If it continued, however, she would have to mention that she should have some say in the matter. What if she'd already eaten?

Abbey walked into the dining room and found Nick sitting in the same spot as last time, to the right of her plate. He stood up, greeting her with a smile. She sat down, and he followed suit.

"Thank you for having dinner with me," he said.

"You're welcome." She was trying hard to act like this was a totally regular occurrence.

"I took the liberty of having dinner prepared, hoping that you hadn't eaten while you were out."

"I haven't," she said. "But I do promise I'll start packing food so that you don't have to keep feeding me."

He smiled again, his face amused. "You don't have to pack lunches and dinners for yourself. Richard can easily have meals arranged."

"Are you sure?"

"Yes." He took a sip of his iced tea. She took in the flecks of silver in his blue eyes, the slight auburn strands in his dark hair, the masculinity of his hands up close.

"Did your horse win?"

He smiled. "No. I'm sorry."

She smiled back, trying not to think about the fact that he'd lost that money. She couldn't even imagine what it would be like to have the loss of a thousand dollars have no impact on her life.

"The reason I've asked you to dinner tonight is because I wanted to discuss what you think is going on with my grandmother. I went to see her today, and she said she's having trouble breathing. She also said that you looked quite worried about it."

Abbey had made sure not to show any emotion when she'd checked Caroline. How did she know that Abbey was worried? "I won't be concerned until I have a formal diagnosis. I'm not able to pinpoint her exact condition, so I can't offer options for her. I told her I'd make an appointment with the doctor."

"Will you keep me informed of her condition, please?"

Abbey nodded.

"I also wanted to have a chance to discuss the Christmas party with you. I hope you don't mind having a working dinner."

"You're always working," she said with a smile. She'd meant it to be a lighthearted comment but there was no shred of amusement on his face. She looked down at her plate. It looked like chicken. At least she knew how to eat that.

"I'm pleased with what you've done in the ballroom," he said, draping a linen napkin in his lap. "I was wondering if you could buy a freestanding bar for one end so that I can hire someone to bartend.

It will need to be substantial—holding a small refrigerator and wine cooler. There are outlets hidden in the flooring—you'll have to figure out where they are to install the bar." He cut a piece of chicken and left it sitting on the fork in his hand.

"Are you getting into the festive spirit?" she asked, glad to hear he'd given the party some thought.

"I'm making sure loose ends are tied up," he said, but she did notice a slight acceptance in his eyes. "I'm planning around a hundred people, plus my family. My sister, her husband, and her son will be heading down from New York. My mother will be coming as well. They're scheduled to arrive Christmas Eve. I'm hoping we can have it all finished by then. I'd like you to help plan the party as well. Just the ordering mostly. I'll get you the information that you need."

"Sure."

"Can you think of anything else for the ballroom that would facilitate a gathering of that size?"

"Hmm. Let me think about it." She reached down into her handbag and pulled out her sketchpad, jotting down a note to herself.

"Tell me about your progress. How are the bedrooms coming?"

"I've sketched out a basic plan for the first three, and everything has been ordered. The furniture should be arriving early next week. The bedding and decorations will trickle in within the next few days, and I'll be working on paint and lighting soon. Would you like to see my sketches?" She turned the pages back and began to show him, but he dismissed it, holding up his hand to stop her.

"Forgive me. You have the artistic eye. I trust your vision. Please. Eat. I'd hate to be a host who serves cold food."

"Does everyone always do what you say?" It was a bold question, but his eyes had given her the courage to ask.

"Everyone who works for me, yes."

"But I want your approval on my ideas. I want to know that I've met your expectations."

"Believe me," he said, a slight smile playing at his lips. "You've exceeded my expectations."

She wanted to do a good job, finish the deal. This money would give her enough to have a real Christmas for Max, one where she could get him everything on his list and make it the best Christmas ever.

Max had asked her once why some kids in his class got such big things from Santa, but he didn't. He'd worried that he'd been bad somehow, and he didn't know it. Her heart ached when he'd said that. Under the pressure of that moment, she'd said that Santa did his best to get everyone what they wanted, but he didn't have enough room in his sleigh to do that for everyone. She promised Max his year would come, but as he was getting older, and the items on his list were more specific and more expensive, she feared it wouldn't happen. She was running out of years. Pretty soon, he wouldn't believe in Santa anymore, and she wouldn't have the chance to prove her statement true.

Abbey cut a piece of chicken. They ate quietly for a while before Nick finally spoke. "Something is troubling you. I can tell by your face."

She shook her head a little too quickly, heat burning her cheeks, and she knew he saw through it. He was quietly watching her with those beautiful blue eyes, waiting for her to come clean. She chewed on her lip as she tried to find something to say. She didn't want to tell him that she needed the money. She was too proud for that.

"You're paying me to decorate your home, yet you don't want any input in it. It just worries me a little," she said, offering him half the truth.

His gaze was unstill as he searched for an explanation or an answer—something in response—but she spoke again before he could say anything.

"Would it be okay if I ask you some things to try to get a feeling for who you are? It sounds silly to you, I'm sure, but it would be so helpful as I'm putting things together. Nothing too personal or anything," she smiled shyly. "Just to get to know you."

"Of course."

Abbey took a moment to collect herself. She was sitting opposite a millionaire in his home, and she was able to ask him anything she wanted. Who got this kind of opportunity? Questions were coming to her in rapid fire, and she didn't want to waste the chance by asking the wrong questions.

"What were you like as a kid?" she asked, immediately worrying that she'd just asked him too personal a question after she'd said she wouldn't. But these were the kinds of things she needed to know if she wanted to do a good job for him.

"Quiet." He smiled at her, and it twisted her stomach so much that she looked down at her plate and cut a piece of chicken.

"You just have one sister?" She looked back up at him.

"Yes."

"Who's the oldest?"

"Robin. She is four years older than I."

This idea warmed her. Second children had very independent personalities, she once learned in her psychology class at the community college. But they did their own thing, they were often the quiet leaders, they could manage people well because of their empathy for others and their easy-going nature. She thought about the pies he'd sent over.

"I think four years apart is good. Perfectly spaced. I think about these kinds of things and I only have one child." She smiled.

"You'd get along with my mother," he chuckled.

"Where is she?"

"Colorado. She moved away after my father died."

Had that been why he'd gotten quiet on the phone before when she'd talked about her father and how he'd passed away? They had that in common, and now she wanted to know his story. "I'm sorry."

"It's okay."

She waited to see if she should delve into that any further, but his expression seemed to be anticipating her next question, so she pressed ahead. "Are you more like your mother or your father?"

His face was thoughtful, but it was clear the answer was already on his lips. "My father."

"Why?"

"How is this helping you decorate my house?" His expression made her feel as though she could be playful a little with him. She liked that.

"I'm getting to know you. It helps me pick things out that I think you might like. How are you and your father alike?"

"We both have relatively even temperaments. We believe in fairness." He stopped and cleared his throat. "If you stay with traditional décor and don't do anything too over the top, I'll be happy with what you choose," he added, obviously trying to put an end to this questioning.

"What was your dad like?" she asked anyway.

He took in a deep breath and let it out. She was pushing him. The complete exhilaration she got talking to him and learning about him made it all worth it. She smiled at his slight frustration with having to answer yet another question. He caught it, his features softening slightly.

"Busy." He looked down at the table, blinking his eyes a little more than usual. He was clearly uncomfortable sharing this bit of information. Then he looked up at her. "He worked most of my childhood. I barely saw him. Most of the time it was just my sister and my mother around."

"I can understand what that's like," she said. "Remember, I grew up most of my life without my father."

He nodded.

Their similarities seemed to hit home with him, and Nick fell quiet. They ate for a moment before he said, "My dad died before I could really know him as well. That's why I'm determined to make his business successful."

"How does making his business successful help you to know him?"

"It doesn't." He took a sip of his tea and set the glass down slowly. "But, I know he loved us, and I feel as though his work was so important to him that it kept him from us—the people he loved—so to honor his memory, I feel like I need to do this for him, to show him how much I loved him. Even when he worked all the time."

"But what if working all the time wasn't necessarily the best choice on his part, and now you're following in his footsteps?"

"The difference was that he had a family and I don't. I did, but I don't now so it all worked out."

"It all worked out?"

"I'm not meant to have a family. It's not who I am. It took a misstep before I realized it."

"Your marriage was a *misstep*?"

"My ex-wife, Sarah, was the 'right' girl for me on paper. She was raised in a similar family. I dated her long enough that when she began hinting around for marriage, I proposed. It was a logical step. I figured the least I could do for her was give her the big ring and decadent wedding. But once we were under the same roof, her insecurities were overwhelming. She was always trying to keep up with everyone else. She wanted more and more from me—a family that I wasn't ready for, this house in Richmond..."

Abbey's own experience with Vince paralleled Nick's in a way. Vince hadn't wanted a family either; he hadn't been ready, and it had happened anyway. She couldn't help but find a comparison to Nick. The difference was that Sarah hadn't gotten pregnant. "So you left her?" she asked.

"I had to work quite a bit to bring in enough money to keep her happy. I didn't mind that because I wanted the business to be successful for my father, and it kept me away. I knew that if I spent too much time with her, she'd want a baby and it wasn't what I wanted. My life wasn't in a place where a baby would be a good idea. I'd grown up missing my father, and I didn't want that for my child. So, one night I came home to find her on the sofa. She'd been crying. She told me that she wanted me to stop working so much and to build a family with her, and if I didn't, she'd leave me. I struggled with it, but in the end, I couldn't give it to her. She left the Thursday of that week."

"I didn't plan on having my son, Max, and I wasn't necessarily ready myself for a family, but now, I can't imagine life without him."

"We're all different, aren't we?" he said with a melancholy smile.

What Abbey had learned from Vince was that she couldn't convince someone who didn't want children to want them, so she decided that she'd better leave this conversation now. If she couldn't persuade the father of her child that family was a blessing, she certainly wouldn't sway Nick tonight over dinner. So she decided to lighten the mood.

"What do you do for fun?" she asked, resuming her questioning to change the subject.

"I collect cars," he said.

"I need to understand your motivation for this," she said. "You have a ton of cars that you don't drive. You just look at them?"

"Yes. But it isn't a *ton*. I have about ten."

"Oh, only ten," she teased.

"I have a Ferrari I'm donating to charity. You would probably like that, right?" He said it as if that would make everything else make sense.

He threw that word around—charity. "Do you have a passion for whatever cause it is?" she asked. Or did he just give things away to justify the rest of his spending habits?

"I have a friend whose son has multiple sclerosis. So, I donate to that charity."

She liked his answer. "I'm sorry to hear about your friend's son. Do you know him well?"

"Yes. His name is Michael."

"And you're donating a car to his foundation?"

"Yes." He was smiling, proud.

"Have you ever been to see Michael?"

"Not recently. Since he was diagnosed the family has been pretty preoccupied, but we used to get together quite a bit before."

"I'm sure the family is very thankful for your donation," she said carefully, "but do you think that he might like a visit from you instead?"

She could see the defensiveness swell up in his face, covering it like the gray clouds covered the sky outside. It was clear that he didn't like it when someone questioned what he did.

"I didn't mean to pry. It was just a thought. I'm sorry," she said, and she meant it. "Let's change the subject. What else do you like to do?"

"I attend other charity events or play polo…"

She'd never known anyone who actually played polo before. Did they even have a team in Richmond? She'd never heard of one. The idea of it seemed so ludicrous that she couldn't fathom it. It reminded her again how different their worlds really were. Her discomfort came out as a laugh, and she quickly tried to squelch it, worried she'd offended him.

"What in the world could be funny about that?" His brows were pulled downward, his face set in a curious frown.

"I'm sorry," she said again. "It just surprised me, that's all."

"In what way?"

"The closest I've come to a charity event is bagging up old clothes to donate to the second-hand shop in town. And, when it comes to sports, I generally stick with something like softball," she answered honestly.

He nodded, thoughtful.

"I played softball because that's what girls did, but I prefer to play baseball with the guys. I always felt like I could hit an overhand pitch more easily. It's probably all in my head. Have you ever played baseball before?"

His eyes found hers and stayed there as he shook his head.

"Never?"

"No. I've never even been to a baseball game."

Abbey thought about the old white jeep she'd had as a teenager, the battered sides that unzipped, allowing the wind to blow her hair around as she pulled up to the baseball fields to watch the game, the smell of roasting peanuts, popcorn, and burgers assaulting her when she parked the car, the red dust from the fields rising into the air under the heat of the sun. She remembered sitting in the folding metal seats, slipping out of her flip-flops, and propping her feet on the bottom of the seat in front of her as she tried unsuccessfully to keep the ketchup and mustard from sliding off her hotdog and onto her hand. The cheer of the crowd, the blinding white lights as the sun went down, and the quiet calm that happened between plays was a fond memory for her, and she couldn't imagine not having that experience to keep her warm during months like these.

"You'll have to go to a game sometime," she said, wondering if he would enjoy himself somewhere like that.

He smiled, but it was that pleasant smile that she was learning he offered when he was just trying to be polite. He probably wouldn't like it at all, she thought. She swung her feet back and forth a little under the table to try to keep them warm, wishing she could be in front of the fire in the ballroom like they had been the other night. Clearly, he was more comfortable in the dining room. When she focused on him, he was studying her, his eyes following her hands, her face, her lips, and he was still watching her now.

"Why are you looking at me like that?" she asked.

Her question caught him off guard and he quickly looked down at his food, and stabbed a piece of chicken with his fork.

"I don't mind," she said, leaning into his view. "I just wondered, that's all."

"You are…" he paused. "Different than anyone I've ever met."

"I'll take that as a compliment," she said with a smile.

Chapter Seven

"I'm cold, Mama," Max said, shivering under his blanket, beads of sweat on his forehead.

He'd been like this all day yesterday and the day before. Abbey had been able to stay with him the first day since it had been Sunday. She'd called Nick to tell him she wouldn't be there like she'd originally planned, and the burden of missing a day to decorate had bothered her. Then she'd missed Monday. She hadn't seen Caroline or done any decorating. When she'd called, Nick had understood, but she knew she didn't have much time.

Today was December second, and she had only twenty-two days left to get it all done. Now it was Tuesday, and Max wasn't any better. She knew he couldn't go to school with a lingering fever and she dared not leave him at her mother's house to get everyone else sick—especially Gramps. She wanted to be there for Max, take care of her little guy, and make him feel better. He needed her, and she didn't need anything else getting in the way of caring for him.

"Can you eat anything?" She pushed a small Spider-Man plate toward him on his dresser. The crackers had been there all morning and he hadn't eaten yesterday.

He shook his head.

"I'll be right back. Call me if you need me," she said, getting up.

She was going to have to let Nick know that yet again she wouldn't be there. She rubbed her forehead as she looked down at the timings sheets she'd made to ensure that every detail was complete before Christmas. Her to-do list was mounting. She picked up her phone. When she dialed Nick's number, her hands were shaking as the phone began to ring.

"Nick Sinclair."

She sat up straight, repositioning the phone on her ear. "Hi. It's Abbey."

"Ah, Abbey. I'm glad you called. A ton of boxes arrived yesterday. I had Richard put them in the upstairs hallway for now. Some of the furniture is in place, but you may need to tell him if it isn't in the correct room. He tried to match what you'd ordered. I've also had a call that one of the bedroom suites you've ordered is being delivered today. Apparently, they weren't sure if they could do the delivery that quickly, but they had an overstock at the warehouse…"

She bit her lip. This job not only meant a lot of money for her family, but she felt good doing it. Just hearing the lift in his voice as Nick told her about the items that had been delivered made her want to do this right. He said he didn't care much about it, but she wondered if the changes were growing on him.

"Max is still sick," she said into the silence. She struggled with even saying it. She knew that Nick would probably understand, but she didn't want to miss another day. "Would there be a way I could bring him?" she heard herself ask. Guilt swelled in her stomach as she thought about dragging poor Max across town to this job. She knew she shouldn't, but she didn't have any other ideas.

"I'm sorry that he's still ill," Nick said.

The buzz of silence that followed was absolute torture. It was un-professional to bring a sick kid to work, but she had no other options if she wanted to be finished in time for Christmas. She needed to see Nick's expression, to read those blue eyes of his. What was he think-ing? She waited, blindly, for his answer.

"Do you feel you'd be able to work and tend to him at the same time? Would that be too much on you?"

"I'll be fine."

"You're sure?"

"I'm sure."

"Then bring him."

"Thank you," she said, her voice giving away her relief.

"You're welcome."

Feeling the stress of the situation lift off her shoulders, she ended the call and headed back to Max's room. He was sitting up in bed, nibbling a cracker. She smiled. "Hi, sweet pea. Your tummy doing okay?"

He nodded.

She climbed into the bed with him and pulled the covers around his waist as he sat beside her. "Want to know something?"

He nodded again, a few cracker crumbs falling into his lap.

"You are going to get to see a real mansion today. And, the floors are so shiny that you can ice skate in your socks if you want to. Do you think you're up for going?"

His face showed about as much excitement as a sick child could muster. "That sounds like fun!"

"Well, let's get all packed up, then! I'll grab your sleeping bag in case you get tired." She rummaged around in his closet and pulled out the bedding, neatly rolled and secured with a handle. "Do you want to bring a few toys?" She handed him a bag. "You choose what you want to bring and I'll get some clothes for you."

"Whoa, how many people live here?" Max said, perking up more than he had in the last few days. They rounded the great drive that took them past the James River and up to the house.

Abbey looked over at her son. "One," she said, glad to see how excited he was. Perhaps getting out would be good for him.

"One person lives here? Why?" He looked back at the house.

With her free hand, she reached over to smooth Max's hair, which had popped back up despite her many attempts to comb it down this morning. "The man who lives here doesn't have a whole lot of family close by and he lives by himself. His name is Mr. Sinclair, but I call him Nick." She realized only then that she didn't know if she should call him Nick, and she couldn't remember if she'd ever addressed him as such, but in her mind, that's what she'd called him.

"What should I call him?"

"Maybe Mr. Sinclair." She stopped the car and turned off the engine. "Ready?"

When Richard answered the door, Max did a deep, dramatic bow and said, "Hello, Mr. Sinclair." Richard clearly attempted to keep a straight face, and Abbey shook her head infinitesimally while tugging on the shoulder of Max's shirt to make him stand up.

"That's not him," she whispered. "And you can just greet Mr. Sinclair like you greet everyone. This is Richard."

"But that's what they do in movies."

Richard bowed. "Hello, Mr. Fuller," he said. He took a step back to let them enter. Abbey smiled at his gesture. "I hope I've put all the furniture in the right rooms," he said to Abbey. "I think I've got it, based on the size of it all. Just call me if you need to move anything. Don't try to do it yourself. The boxes of decorations are all in the hallway still."

"Thank you, Richard."

Max took his shoes off and lined them up at the front door. He peered up at Abbey with an unsure look. The color was coming back into his face a little. He'd held down the crackers she'd given him earlier, and he'd even had some juice before they'd gotten there. She smiled and left her shoes beside his. "Before we go upstairs, do you want to see a giant piano?"

"Yes!"

Abbey took him into the ballroom. She figured she'd check for those hidden outlets while she was in there. "Isn't it beautiful?" she said, clicking on the lights for each of the Christmas trees.

Max was standing in front of the piano, his gaze moving from one side of it to the other.

"It's so shiny."

"I know."

Max moved over to the bench and sat down in front of the gleaming keys.

"Don't touch them," she whispered gently. "You might get your germs on them. We don't know if you're still contagious or not."

"It's all right," Nick said from the doorway, and Abbey turned around. "Hello," he said, walking toward them. "You must be Max," he said, producing that generic smile. He stood at just enough distance to make Abbey worry that he thought Max might get him sick. She wished that she hadn't had to bring him.

"This is Mr. Sinclair," Abbey introduced him. "He's *very* good at playing the piano."

Nick smiled.

"Would you like to try to play?" Nick asked Max.

Max nodded.

"Go ahead then."

Max scooted the bench closer, creating a hollow screech throughout the room, and Abbey cringed at the thought of what it might have done to the floors. She hoped he hadn't scratched them. She looked over at Nick, but he didn't seem fazed. He seemed to be thinking about something else. Max tinkled out a few notes, the sounds getting deeper as he made his way down the keys, and Nick focused on him again.

"Lovely," Nick said, but his thoughts still seemed a little preoccupied. "Well, it was nice to meet you, Max." He turned to Abbey. "Is there anything that you'll need from me to help you get started?"

"I think Richard has everything under control."

"Okay." Without another word, he left the room.

Abbey stood there a moment as Max continued to play on the piano. Nick had always been somewhat reserved, and he wasn't forthcoming with his daily goings-on, but today, he'd been less focused, his mind clearly somewhere else. Something about his features just now made her feel like he was worried about something—maybe it was the crease between his eyes that hadn't been there before, the smile that wasn't his real smile… Something wasn't right. If she hadn't had Max with her, she might have tried to find out what was wrong, but she didn't want to get into anything that might not be appropriate for little ears. Plus, to judge by the way he left, it was clear that Nick was quite busy. She found the outlets and jotted their locations on her sketchpad.

"Want to see the upstairs?" Abbey asked Max.

He slid off the bench and ran across the room to her. When he tried to come to a stop, his feet were not on the large rug, but on the slick floors surrounding it, and he slid across them until he bumped into his mother.

"See?" she giggled. "I told you that you could slide on the floors in your socks."

As they walked through the entryway, Max continued to get a running start so that he could slide toward her, his laughter rising into the air all the way up to the second floor. It was good to see him feeling better. When he got close to her again, she felt his forehead. It was still a little warm, but it wasn't nearly as hot as it had been.

When they got to the bedrooms, she checked that everything was there. It looked like most of the furniture had been delivered, but Richard had put one of the bedroom suites in the wrong room. She pulled out her cell and texted him using the number Nick had given her when she'd first arrived. It didn't take Richard long to appear at the door to the bedroom.

"Everything looks great, Richard. Thank you so much for arranging to have it all assembled and put into the rooms."

Max tugged on the hem of her shirt, and she put up her finger to ask him to wait his turn.

"Did I get it all right?" Richard asked.

"Nearly," she smiled. "I'm going to need to switch this room with the one beside it. I'm so sorry, but is there any way I could get someone to help move it?"

"Mama, can I go downstairs and slide in the hallway again? I'll come right back up."

Abbey nodded, trying to keep her focus on Richard. It would be good for Max, give him something to do while she explained what needed to go where.

"No problem at all. With the snow coming down again, they'll be able to help you right now. They've already shoveled the walk, and there isn't a whole lot to do outside in these conditions."

It didn't take long before the men showed up, and they moved the furniture that she'd asked them to switch. As they'd disassembled the enormous beds and taken them piece by piece to the other rooms, Max had called up to her from downstairs, showing her how quickly he could slide. Whenever he wobbled, he'd bend his legs and slide on his knees. He was having so much fun, and it was working out because she could pull out the bags of things she'd bought for the rooms and begin to piece things together. The first bedroom was already the color she'd wanted, and she was keeping the crystal chandelier, so it was the easiest of the bedrooms. She spent all of her time arranging the furniture and putting the final touches on the room.

When everything was in place in the first room, she clicked on the lamp on the bedside table, giving the room a warm and cozy glow. The bottoms of both tables flanking the enormous bed were bookshelves that she'd filled with all her favorite books. She had candles lit on the dresser, the scent of vanilla filling the space, and a cozy throw across the bench at the foot of the bed. While she'd decorated for Nick, clearly this was a room suitable for a woman, and she wondered if his sister would like it. When Abbey had gotten the bedroom nearly decorated, she peeked over the railing to find Max.

"Max?" she called down quietly. He wasn't down there. "Max?" she called again, padding down the steps, the enormous space completely silent. Had he gone looking for a bathroom or something? She walked into the ballroom, glancing from one end to the other. "Max?" No answer.

As she went in and out of rooms, she started to fear for him. Had he gotten himself lost in this big house? What if he'd gone outside and couldn't get back in? Was he somewhere crying because she couldn't hear him? How long had he been gone? Her heart pounded with every step she took. She checked the dining room—nothing. She went to the kitchen. No one there. Her hearing sharpened as she listened, willing herself to hear his voice. Then, she tipped her head to the side to try to make out the sound she heard. Was that Nick's voice? She followed the faint sounds, listening, as her eyes darted in every room for Max. The talking got clearer until, to her mortification, she could hear Max's voice. Was he in Nick's office?

She bit her lip as the conversation became clear. Abbey stopped just outside the office, out of sight, and listened for a moment, trying to figure out the best way to apologize. She could hear the clicking of computer keys as Max talked.

"Is this where you do all your work?" Max asked.

"Mmm hmm." More clicking of keys.

"What is your job?"

"I buy and sell companies."

"What's a company?"

More clicking. "It's... a business."

"Like those big buildings downtown?"

"Yep. Like those."

"Did you know your floors are really good for sliding?"

Abbey heard a burst of laughter escape, and her heart did a leap. "Are they?" he said. The clicking continued, and she knew that she had to go in and relieve Nick. It was terribly unprofessional, and she had no idea how long Max had been there. Nick was probably getting nothing done. But she'd never heard Max talk to another man like he was talking to Nick. He seemed so interested, so chatty. He hadn't been like that with any of the other men in her life, other than Gramps.

"You should try it sometime."

"Perhaps I may."

"Want to try it now?"

Oh no. She had to go in!

"I really have to work. I'm sorry. Maybe another time?"

Abbey was about to walk into the doorway when she stopped. Max said, his voice disappointed, "Okay." It was a quiet "okay," and she could tell, for whatever reason, he really wanted Nick to try it. She wondered if he'd be satisfied if she did it with him. Maybe during her lunch break, he could show her how to slide. But, the reason that Abbey had stopped was because when Max said "okay," like he had, the clicking stopped.

There was quite a long moment of hesitation as she waited to hear what would happen next, and then she heard the squeak of a chair. It sounded like Nick had stood up. She should've just gone in right then, but something held her back. It was almost like she could feel Nick's deliberation all the way through the wall. Or maybe she was just hoping that he was deliberating. He was probably trying to figure out how to get Max out of the room. At any time in the conversation, however, he could've said, "Let's go find your mother," but he hadn't. Nick had answered Max's questions, even if they were short answers.

"I suppose I can take a quick break," she heard Nick say, and she covered her mouth in astonishment. Was Nick Sinclair actually considering sliding around his house in his sock feet?

Abbey walked into the room. "Hi. I'm so sorry," she said. "I didn't know Max had wandered down here. Please, sit back down. I'll take him back with me."

"Mama! Mr. Sinclair is going to slide in his socks with me. He said he would."

Abbey felt awful to have put both Nick and Max in this situation. She knew Nick had work to do, and she also had an inkling that, because he was thoughtful, he'd follow through with Max's ridiculous request. She could feel the heat under her skin and the worry creeping into her stomach.

"You can call me Nick," he said again, now standing beside Max. Nick's eyes were curious, looking at her son—curious like they'd been when he'd looked at Abbey. The only difference, though, was that he wasn't smiling. He was more cautious, almost too careful, like he was a little uncomfortable.

"You really don't have to do this," she said quietly to him as they followed Max out of the office.

"It's fine."

They walked in silence to the entrance of the house. All Abbey could think about was how preoccupied Nick had seemed this morning. He'd barely smiled. And how they were disrupting whatever it was he had been doing.

When they arrived at the entrance, Max stopped and bent down. He began untying Nick's shoes. "Oh, honey." Abbey tried to pull him up. Those shoes looked like they cost more than her monthly salary. "Nick can do that himself."

"I'm just helping," he said, tugging the laces from the wrong spot and causing them to knot.

"It's okay," Nick said, bending down and helping Max. He slipped his shoes off and set them aside.

There was something about seeing Nick assisting Max with the laces and now in his sock feet that made Abbey smile. Had he ever been allowed to do this kind of thing as a boy?

"Okay," Max said with authority. "What you have to do is get a running start. Like this!" He took off from one side of the room. "Then, just stop real quick and you'll start to slide." He slid across the floor. "If you feel like you're gonna fall, go down on your knees. Here, I'll show you." Max demonstrated the knee slide. "Think you can do it?"

The corners of Nick's mouth were twitching just slightly, and Abbey wondered if he wanted to smile. Then, to her complete surprise, Nick took off across the room. Abbey watched him as he ran, his body moving effortlessly with every stride. He stopped and slid toward Max, coming to a stop in front of him.

Max let out a loud laugh, putting his hands on his knees and giggling uncontrollably. "Isn't that fun?" Max said.

Nick laughed too. "Yes. Thank you for teaching me," he said with happiness in his eyes. He walked over toward his shoes.

"Wait!" Max stood up.

Nick turned around.

"Let's do it again but race this time."

"Max, Nick has work he has to do."

"Please?"

Abbey thought about how entertaining this was for Max, and a pang of guilt swelled in her gut. He was either at school where he had to sit at a desk most of the day, in their little apartment with no room to run around, or with her mother and Gramps, where he had no one to play with. He was craving interaction, attention from someone. While she didn't want to bother Nick, she wished he would do this for Max's sake.

"Would you like a head start?" Nick said, and Abbey almost fell backward with excitement. There was absolutely no reason in the world for Nick to race her son, but he was doing it!

"Give me just to that Christmas tree."

"Okay. Where do you want to begin the race?"

"Right here."

Nick followed Max to the starting point and lined up next to him. While his curiosity was still evident, the uncertainty that she'd seen on Nick's face was easing slightly.

"On your mark," Max said, his eyes darting over to Nick. "Get set. Go!"

Nick let Max have the head start until he got to the Christmas tree. It was clear that Nick, who could easily beat the thin, tiny legs of her son, was running slower to allow Max to win. Max yelled to slide, and they both hit the brakes, sliding side-by-side until Nick slowed himself down, allowing Max to reach the stairway at the other side of the room.

"I won!" Max said, giggling. "Wasn't that so fun, Nick?"

Nick was smiling, the edges of his mouth turned down in that way of his. A chuckle escaped his chest. "Yes. That was fun, Max. Thank you for teaching me. Now I'll be able to do it any time I want."

"Yes!" Max said. "You could do it on the way to bed every night! I would. Where *is* your bedroom? Is it upstairs?"

"Max," Abbey said quickly, realizing that Nick hadn't ever shown her his bedroom. Max didn't need to keep Nick from work any longer, nor did he need a tour of Nick's private bedroom. "Let Nick get back to work. I'm sure he's busy." She turned to Nick. "Thank you for taking time to play with Max. I'll make sure to keep him with me from now on."

"It's fine." He smiled, but there were thoughts behind his eyes that she couldn't read. "And you're right. I really do have to get back to work."

"Max," Abbey said. "Let's go upstairs and finish decorating." She felt his head again. "You feel much better. Perhaps I can take you to Nana's."

"It's fine if he stays here," Nick said.

"Can I watch you do your work?" Max asked, and Abbey put her hand on his shoulder to try to stop his forward behavior. "It's more fun than watching Mama decorate." He made a face and Nick chuckled again.

She didn't want to put Nick in a situation where he was babysitting. He needed a decorator, not a single mom with nowhere to leave her kid. "Come with me," she said, putting her hand on his back in an attempt to lead him toward the stairway.

Max seemed to interpret his mother's tone because he complied without any further discussion. But, as they started up the steps, he called back down to the entryway, "Bye, Nick!" Nick turned and waved, but his face was serious as he watched little Max heading up the stairs.

"Can I come again tomorrow?" Max asked.

"I think you're well enough to go back to school," Abbey said, with a little laugh.

"Aw. But I like talking to Nick."

"What do you like about it?"

"He looks like the daddies that come to my school sometimes. They eat lunch with the kids in my class at the special parent table. It always looks like they have lots of fun over there. I liked talking to Nick like they talk to their daddies," he said as he smiled up at his mother.

She smiled back at him, but inside, Abbey felt very, very empty. She felt responsible for making the choices she had, but at the same time, she knew that if she hadn't made those choices, she wouldn't have Max in her life, so she didn't really know how to feel. It wasn't guilt as much as it was a longing for things to be different. As he grew up, who would answer his questions in a way that only men can answer? Who would show him that men can read bedtime stories and cook dinner? With Gramps's illness, he wouldn't be able to do those things for Max like he had for her. All Max had was his mother, and she was doing the best she could, but she wanted more for him.

"I'm glad you had fun with Nick," she said as they got to the top of the stairs.

Abbey looked at her watch. She had just enough time to get the bedroom with the picture in order to show Nick tomorrow. She hoped it would be a wonderful surprise. She whispered what she'd planned to Max as they made their way toward the room. In his excitement, Max ran ahead and opened the wrong door. It was the fourth door, the one Nick had said didn't need any decorating. Max swung the door open, peered inside and then stepped back into the hallway. "This isn't the room," he said, but Abbey had stopped cold.

"No," she said, barely able to get the words out. "It's a baby's room."

Chapter Eight

The light was coming in at a slant through the stark white, gauzy fabric of the nursery curtains that stretched from the top of the room to the bottom. They were tied back with long sashes of white satin, their tails dragging the floor. The wood floor was dark against the shaggy area rug that looked like a bright white cloud, floating in darkness. In the center of the room sat an enormous circular crib. Abbey almost didn't notice the little green and white embroidered roses on the bedding, or the perfectly tied bows of the bumper pad because her eyes had moved to the vaulted ceiling and the glass mobile floating above the crib like stars in the night's sky. The whole room looked like something from Heaven, all white and dreamlike. The only color was a small olive green and pearl white teddy bear that sat all alone in the center of the crib.

There was hardly a thing in the entire mansion, but this room was completely decorated, the white looking almost ghostly-stark all of a sudden as Abbey worried about the child for whom this room was meant. What was this room?

Quickly, she ushered Max out of it and shut the door. "Follow me," she said, refocusing and making her way to the third bedroom where she had the most decorating done. She needed to stay on track if she wanted to finish.

This was her surprise bedroom for Nick, and she hoped he liked it. The groundsmen had left her a hammer and, with a few taps, she secured the picture hanger on the wall for the large waterfall photograph. She hung it between the posts of the bed, and stepped back to take a look at it. The thick, dark wood of the frame was the perfect accent to the smooth hour-glass shape of the bed posts. The posts looked as though they were reaching upward to showcase that gorgeous picture, the sheer canopy she'd pleated like curtains softening the space. She'd chosen to decorate the room in white before she'd seen the nursery, and now, looking at the room, it looked oddly similar. She hoped that wasn't a bad thing. An antique chair sat in the corner, the green seat embroidered with flowers, the dark wood back and arms matching the bed. She fluffed a deliciously puffy throw pillow and cornered it in the bend of the chair. The colors of the chair looked so rich in the light of a floor lamp nearby. Abbey didn't know why—maybe it was that photo that made her feel romantic, but she hung an extra sprig of mistletoe by a dark green ribbon from the canopy above the bed. For such a large room, it looked livable and warm—the kind of room she'd want to stay in. She cornered a few books on the table and took a look around.

Max played with his toys on the floor while Abbey did the final dust and room check. He'd asked several times to go down and see Nick, and she'd made him stay upstairs with her. So, when it was finally time to show Nick this room, she told Max to go find him.

"Okay, Mama!" he said, more lively than she'd seen him in a while.

Abbey hurried to put Max's toys away as Max went to get Nick. He'd been pleased with the ballroom, but this was the first room she'd decorated that felt like it could fit who he was. It had soft lighting, billowy comforters and pillows, glass vases with sprigs of holly right now and, she imagined, daisies in the warm months. It felt like somewhere she'd want to live, and with that gorgeous photo above the bed, she was nearly sure it would be somewhere Nick would want to live as well. Could she convince him that he needed a *home* rather than just a house? Her confidence was soaring as she looked around.

"Keep your eyes closed," she heard Max say, and her fingertips were tingling in anticipation. She couldn't wait to show him.

Max led Nick into the room and Nick awkwardly bumped the doorframe. "Oh, Max," she laughed nervously, "You didn't have to really make Nick close his eyes."

Nick was standing in the doorway, holding Max's hand, his eyes closed, and his face set in that cautious expression. He looked vulnerable right then, which was such a contrast to his usual commanding presence. There was a softness to his face, a gentle look about him, and she imagined what it would be like to see him sleep. How peaceful he must look.

"Ready?" Max said. "Open your eyes!"

Abbey waited for his reaction; at the very least, she thought she'd get the look of polite approval that he'd shown in the ballroom downstairs, but she was hoping for a bigger response. In her mind, she'd nailed this room. Would he think so? She waited for him to say something about this gorgeous surprise she'd found in the closet. What did he think of her interpretation of its mood? The greens and whites of the photo were like a blast of color, and she knew it had to evoke something in him.

What she hadn't planned for was the kind of emotion she saw on Nick's face.

His jaw was clenched, his lips set in a straight line, his eyes like daggers on that photo. "Where did you get that?" he asked, his voice controlled and careful. His eyes were filled with a myriad of feelings—she could see them: anger, hurt, irritation, sadness. How could this photo cause all that? What had she done?

"I found it in the closet," she answered, her voice small. "I was only trying to surprise you."

"What's the matter, Nick? Are you mad at my mommy?"

Without a word, Nick turned around and left them standing there.

Abbey's mothering instincts kicked in immediately as she simultaneously tried to recover from his reaction. Max had asked Nick a question and he'd flat ignored it. She felt like she needed to do damage control. She didn't want Max thinking that a response like that was okay or that he'd said anything wrong. Nick should have acknowledged his question. Max was a kid, for goodness' sake! Max had taken to Nick today, and now she didn't want him to get hurt.

"Something about that picture has upset Nick so much that he can't even speak," she explained to Max. "Normally, he would've answered your question, I'm sure, but for some reason the photo made him sad. Can you remember a time when you felt really sad about anything?"

"I've never been that sad," he said.

"Well, we all get sad from time to time, and sometimes, things can make us very sad. I'm glad you haven't had anything make you feel that way." Abbey picked up her bag. "We should probably go. I've got to be up early tomorrow, and, from the looks of you, so do you! You're much better, so back to school tomorrow."

Abbey sat on the sofa in her apartment, still thinking about Nick's reaction to the photo she'd put up. Scenarios ran wild in her mind.

She worried because she hadn't talked to him about it and she wanted to make sure he was okay. The thing about Abbey was that she was a talker, and when something was bothering her, she wanted to talk even more. She couldn't just sit quietly. It was eight thirty at night, a little late to call Nick.

She texted him: *Sorry to bother you. Are you awake? I want to talk.*

A response came through to her phone: *Yes. I'm awake. Shall I give you a call?*

Abbey didn't want to talk on the phone. She wanted to read his expressions, see his gestures, his mannerisms.

She texted back: *I'd like to come over. Would that be possible?* Her mother had heard the whole story earlier and Abbey was nearly sure she'd pop over to sit at the house while Max slept so she could see Nick.

Silence…

She texted again: *I know it's late.*

He finally responded: *I'll wait at the door. Be careful driving.*

Abbey texted her mother next to see if she would stay with Max, and she came over immediately, bless her. Once her mother was comfortable on the sofa in her apartment with her boot propped up on a cushion to keep her ankle from swelling, and after a ton of hugs and thank-yous, Abbey got in her car and headed to Nick's. As she shivered in the cold of late evening, her little Toyota engine working overtime to run in this icy weather, she mentally braced herself for his reprimand, but every time she thought it through, she knew that she hadn't done anything wrong. He'd told her to use whatever she wanted, that the house was hers. How was she supposed to know that the picture was some awful memory of his? His reaction had deflated her, made her feel like she'd done something wrong when she hadn't.

She needed to see him. She didn't want to wait for the next day. She'd never sleep, feeling the way she was feeling.

She glanced at the clock in her car. It was nearly nine o'clock now. Whose decorator would come to his house at such a ridiculous hour, and ask questions about his personal life? She turned between the large gates and headed down the drive. *It's only a quick visit*, she tried to convince herself. The truth was, she wanted to know, and if she didn't see him, she'd have to wait until a better time. Would there be a better time?

She parked the car and Nick already had the door open. His hair was gorgeously messy, his feet bare, which surprised her. Had she caught him just before bed? "Hi," she said as she walked up the steps.

He watched her carefully, almost as if he were worried she'd slip on the ice. When they were face to face, he allowed the tiniest of smiles to emerge. "Are those your pajamas?" he asked.

She looked down at her red and white flannel pajama bottoms, her Chuck Taylors seeming out of place against them, and nodded. She'd been so worried about his reaction to that room that she hadn't bothered to look at herself in the mirror. She walked in and he shut the door. Only then did she finally feel warmth. She took off her shoes and set them by the door. Then she wadded her coat and set it on top of them.

"Is that Mickey Mouse on your T-shirt?" he asked with a larger smile.

"It's vintage," she said, offering a grin in return.

"I see." He led her to the ballroom where a fire was already going. He offered for her to take a seat on the sofa.

"Is everything all right?" he asked.

"No." He'd knocked her confidence today. He'd made her feel like she'd ruined everything. She'd been so sure of herself, and the first bedroom she'd shown him had been all wrong. She took a deep breath and said, "I wanted to apologize for the picture in that room upstairs. I just found it in a closet." She bit her lip, thinking. She didn't know what to say. "I just wanted…" She struggled for the right words. "I just wanted to be sure that I hadn't overstepped any bounds. I was under the impression that I could use anything I found in the house."

"You've done nothing wrong. It just took me by surprise. I never go in that room anyway, so you can leave it up if you'd like. It doesn't matter."

Again, a wave of disappointment washed over her as she saw his indifference to all the hard work she'd put into that room.

He was quiet, not offering anything more.

She got up and walked to the window, nervous energy zinging through her.

To her surprise, he followed, pacing up beside her. "I have questions," she said, turning toward him. As she did, she realized they were standing under the mistletoe together. It felt ridiculous at that moment. "Tell me," she said. "Why do you have a baby's room all decorated and you didn't bother to tell me? Why were you so upset about that picture? I have to know these things to get it right. I want to do a good job for you."

His seriousness was different this time. There was a slight uncertainty to his face, and pain—she could see it. But lurking underneath it, it looked like he wanted to tell her. Out of nowhere, he started talking, and she couldn't take her eyes off him. "The baby's room was Sarah's idea of encouragement. She thought I'd fall in love with it and want a baby like she did. But I don't. And you're right: this house is meant for a family. So I left it, not knowing how long I'd stay here."

He wasn't planning on staying in this house? His words hit her like bricks, but the magic of where they were standing, the mistletoe hanging above her—for some reason it all gave her a little hope that everything would be okay. She'd do a wonderful job, so good he'd love it and want to live here forever.

"But you are still here," she said.

"For now."

As she digested this, she realized that *she'd* created this magical atmosphere—the trees, the stockings, the greenery. It had all come from her mind, and none of it was real. After Christmas, it would all be gone. What about him? Was he planning to be gone as well?

"What about the picture? It's a gorgeous picture. It's a shame it was hidden in the closet."

Abbey thought about the pies Nick had sent over, how he'd followed her lead and had dinner on the sofa even though it was clear how uncomfortable it was for him, how he'd looked when he was running with Max. He hadn't had to do any of those things, but he'd reached out, and for that, she was grateful. Now she wanted to reach out to him. He stood silently, looking at her, so she continued. "It looked like that picture really upset you. You've been very kind to me and Max, and I just want to make sure you're all right."

"I'm fine."

"You didn't seem fine. Look, I know it's none of my business, but your reaction to my choices in decorating is. I put something in your house that made you upset, and I feel terrible about that. If you don't want to tell me, then don't. You seem like a very kind person, and I just worried about you. That's all."

After she said that, his face changed. There was an interest in his eyes—she'd seen it before, but this time, the intensity behind it was startling. Was she the first person to say she worried about him? "I was at the waterfall depicted in the photograph the day my dad died."

"Oh." She covered her mouth. "I'm so sorry." Abbey thought about how Nick didn't easily forget things, and she wondered if the feelings for the loss of his father were as fresh as his memory of it. "Why did you preserve that memory with an enormous photo, if you don't mind me asking?"

"It was just after my wedding. Sarah had insisted that we go on our honeymoon. Dad had barely made it through the wedding—he was really sick, but he'd come anyway. His cancer had spread; he was so thin…"

How hard it must have been to celebrate the beginning of his life with his new wife while being terribly worried about his father. Abbey led Nick back to the sofas, her eyes on him, still listening. They both sat down, and he continued.

"We had a two-week stay in the Turks and Caicos. I wanted to postpone it, but Sarah had talked me into going. She said it would be good for me to get my mind off my father's battle. We spent Tuesday of the second week at that waterfall, just the two of us enjoying ourselves completely. Meanwhile, here in Richmond, my father was dying. I never got to say goodbye. I will always regret it. It makes my day at that waterfall feel completely selfish. I should've been with him."

"There was no way to know, Nick."

"What upsets me most still is that I allowed Sarah to sway me. I knew in my gut that I wanted to stay with him, and I permitted her to change my mind."

"I'll take it down as soon as I get here tomorrow. Or I can take it down right now…"

"It was nothing but a memento that we picked up while we were there. At the time, it reminded us of somewhere wonderful. You can leave it up. Like I said, I won't see it anyway."

"But don't you want your home to be a sanctuary where you can relax and unwind? Knowing that photo was on the wall in my home, I'd want to take it down."

"I relax and unwind when I'm sleeping. And I don't sleep in that room. Having you decorate is merely an exercise to appease my grandmother and keep my family quiet. The last thing I need is everyone giving me flak for having an empty house. For them, it would mean that I wasn't settled or happy, neither of which should they be worried about."

"They probably just care about you, that's all."

"My home is the very least of my worries. Now, I've kept you long enough," he said gently. "I apologize for upsetting you. I'll let you get home to Max and to bed."

He stood up. She didn't want to but she didn't want to keep him up all night either. She followed him out. Her pile of things was still at the door with Richard most likely off for the night. She picked up her coat and put it on. As she slipped on her shoes, she thought about how Nick had opened up to her tonight. He'd told her a very personal story about his father. She looked up at him, and in that moment of quiet, that big house all around them, it felt intimate.

"I'll see you tomorrow," he said as he opened the door. A gust of frigid air blew in.

She smiled at him.

"I enjoyed our talk."

Even though she'd driven all the way out there for only that short amount of time, she was glad she had. "Me too," she said, wishing she could stay but knowing that she shouldn't. "I'll see you tomorrow."

"Yes." He smiled then, a big, affectionate smile. "I'll see you tomorrow."

She headed to her car, the excitement of tomorrow already zinging through her.

Chapter Nine

"How's life treating you?" Gramps said as Abbey took a seat next to him at the kitchen table.

"Okay," she answered, not sure what he wanted to hear.

"Glad you could stop by."

"I had a free hour before I have to take Caroline Sinclair to the doctor to run some tests."

"How is she doing?"

"I'm not sure. She's complaining about shortness of breath. It could be a lot of things. I'm hoping it isn't an arrhythmia."

Gramps nodded, his head wobbling involuntarily. Señor Freckles darted across the room, rubbed up against his leg, and, as he put his hand down to pet the cat, he ran away before he could touch him. Gramps's movements were slower these days.

"Crazy cat," she noted.

"He's all right."

"Why do you keep him around? He's the worst pet ever."

Gramps looked over at the cat. He had climbed to the ledge of the window overlooking the backyard. His black fur was so shiny, and if she didn't know better, she'd think he was just any other domesticated cat. "He needs me. Remember when I found him? He was skin and bones. When I started putting food out for him, he'd never let me get close, but I could hear his purr. It made me happy."

Abbey could understand that. She'd felt the same way with Vince, wanting to give him a better life. She was a lot like Gramps. And now, given his health, caring for that cat was something he could still enjoy, and he was successful at it.

"He did just rub your leg," she said, seeing the cat in a slightly different way now. "That's the most affection I've ever seen from him."

"How's the decorating going?" Gramps asked, and Abbey could see the anticipation in his question. He'd clearly been waiting to ask. She dared not tell him that she'd dragged Max to work with her when he was sick, or that he'd made Nick do sock races, and to make things even more interesting, she'd decided to remind Nick of one of the saddest times of his life.

"Totally fine," she said with an encouraging expression.

"Good, good," he said, his face cheerful.

"Gramps, why do you get so happy whenever I mention this job?"

He grinned at her. "When I was younger, I was an airline pilot. I loved it. It was the thing that got me up in the mornings. There was nothing more exciting than feeling the lift of the plane at my hands. My flying time was that one time each day when I was in complete control of everything, and it made me the happiest. Later in life, I found that same joy in woodworking. It was my form of art, and I expressed myself through it. When I see you head off to Caroline Sinclair's in your scrubs, your hair pulled back in that little curly ponytail of yours, and I watch you wave goodbye, you don't have the fire in

teased, reaching for the doorknob. As she did, Señor Freckles darted away, rounding the corner to the hallway. Abbey shook her head and let herself out.

"Oh," Abbey said, startled, as Nick answered the door of his house. "Is Richard sick?"

"No." He opened the door wider to let her enter.

Snow was falling again. It was very early in the year to have snow, but there was a southern slow-moving system that just wouldn't leave, hovering over Richmond. None of the snow had managed to stick, though, leaving a sloshy mess on the roads.

"I just wanted to catch you before you started work to see if you had any information about my grandmother."

"I took her to the doctor this morning," Abbey said. "They ran some tests. We should get a call in the next day or so, but my intuition tells me there may be some kind of arrhythmia." She saw concern on his face, and, since she wasn't a doctor, she couldn't tell him for sure what was wrong. "That's only my guess, though. And sometimes arrhythmias don't cause a problem at all."

"But."

"But sometimes they can be life threatening, which is why I made ee a doctor. We just want to keep ahead of anything that may be 'ing as she ages."

ıodded.

ƚlad to see your concern for her," she said. "She says she would visit more."

er as much as I can with my workload." He took in a ƚ it out. "But I'll try to stop by more. The rest of the furniture arrived for the other rooms. I hope you'll find it where it all belongs," he said.

"Would you like to see it?" she asked, hoping he'd feel obligated.

"I can't. I have work to do. I really should get back to it. I was just checking on my grandmother."

"You can't spare five minutes to walk upstairs and see what your seventy-five-thousand-dollar investment is getting you?" she said with her best persuasive smile.

He looked at her, with deliberation on his face, and took in another visible breath and let it out. She was pushing him; she knew that. But at the same time, there was a part of her who wanted him to be happy, to love where he lived. She wanted to ensure that happiness.

"I know what it's getting me—peace of mind. When Sarah left, she took everything with her, and I allowed her to do that because it didn't matter to me. But, what I found out was that living in an empty house makes other people uneasy. So, that seventy-five thousand dollars is giving me the peace of mind to know that my family will not flock in and pity me. I'm perfectly fine, and the last thing I need is people thinking that I'm not."

"I'm glad you're fine. But I want you to be *happy*."

"Why do you care if I'm happy?" he asked, that curiosity lurking in his face.

Maybe it was his generosity or the fact that he'd been so good with Max. She couldn't stop the feeling. "I just like making people happy," she said, heat burning her cheeks. "Pretty please, will you see what I've done?" If it came to it, she'd start batting her eyelashes. She was being silly, and she didn't know if he was in that kind of mood at the moment. He was always so serious. He needed to lighten up.

Nick looked down at the floor as if the answer were there, his eyes not focused, his head shaking so subtly that she'd almost missed it. Then he looked at her, a smile lurking beneath his serious expression. "Five minutes," he said. "Then I *have* to get back to work."

Without prompting him for acceptance, she grabbed his arm and pulled him forward to walk with her. He clamped his eyes on her hand, but she noticed the tiny hint of a smile still there, so she didn't let go.

Chapter Ten

"How can you not love this four-poster bed, custom made in…" Abbey looked at the paperwork attached to one of the posts. "Tennessee…?"

"Ha!" Nick laughed at the insignificance of her statement, the mood considerably lightened from before.

"You know you like this vase," she said, playfully caressing a silver goblet-style vase monogrammed with an engraved *S*. Monograms were the theme of this particular room. She hopped onto the bed, picked up a deep red, shiny velvet pillow and traced her finger along the curly *S* sewn in cream that matched the beaded lampshade on the bedside table. She'd arranged a bouquet of roses under the lamp, and she caught Nick looking at them before his gaze settled on her. She'd been teasing him, and the more she did, the more she saw affection in his eyes. And she loved to see him laugh. The sight of it filled her stomach with flutters.

"How can you look at it all and not love it?"

Nick's face sobered, but his grin remained. "It really doesn't matter to me at all what is in this room. That's why all the rooms were empty." He said the words, but this time, there was less force behind them, and she wondered if he still believed what he was saying.

"Is your bedroom decorated? I only ask because you didn't show it to me. I'll decorate it as part of the original salary you quoted me, if you'd like."

"My bedroom is fine." His statement was matter of fact, but his gaze was swallowing her up. What was he trying to tell her? Was she getting through to him, showing him what living in a real home was like as opposed to just rooms with four blank walls?

She cut her eyes at him playfully. "I'll bet there's nothing in it."

He shot her a challenging look—she was learning that he showed all his emotion through his eyes—but he didn't say anything.

"I'm right, aren't I?"

"No one will be staying in my bedroom."

"Don't you want a little Christmas cheer in there? I could put a small tree or some winter floral arrangements."

"The only time I'm in there is when I'm sleeping, so I won't see it anyway. There's no need."

Nick was debating the idea with her, and he'd said he'd stay for five minutes but they'd been talking about decorating for at least twenty. He'd patiently walked through all the rooms she'd decorated and listened as she explained her reasoning for her choices. He'd nodded at all the right times, his hands clasped behind his back as he paced around the rooms. He'd laughed with her. He seemed relaxed and content. And now, when she'd asked him about his own private bedroom, he didn't flinch.

"What if one of your family members is looking for you and they stumble into your room?"

"In the middle of the night?"

"You never know," she teased.

She was really pushing now, but he was allowing it, so she continued. "I actually just want to end my curiosity. Where does Nick Sinclair lay his head at night?"

"You're *curious* about my bedroom?" he asked, raising an eyebrow.

"I'm willing to bet that there's nothing but a mattress in your bedroom," Abbey said, ignoring his statement purposely.

"And what are you willing to bet?"

He was playing along and it sent a shot of excitement through her chest. She hadn't thought about what she was willing to bet—again, she'd been impulsive.

"If you win the bet, I'll cook your dinner. If you lose, you have to cook mine." She waited for his answer, hoping he'd take her up on it. Either outcome would get him to have dinner with her, and she'd love to have more time to talk to him.

"So, if my room is decorated, you have to cook me dinner?"

"Yes."

"Follow me."

As they walked down the hallway, Abbey noticed the authority in his walk, the gentle swing of his arms, the masculinity of his stride. He had broad shoulders and a thin waist. His hairline was perfectly trimmed, his neck smooth, and she wondered if he had someone come in to touch up his neckline every morning.

When they got to the end of the hallway, they stood, facing a closed door. Before he opened it, she stopped him.

"Why do you keep all the doors in your house closed?" she asked.

He looked down at her, the skin between his eyes wrinkling in an adorable way. "I'm not sure. I suppose that it's a way of finishing off the job. When the staff has tidied the room, and it's clean, they shut the door then move on to the next room."

"Like closing the cereal box before you put it in the cabinet?"

The confusion returned on his face. "Something like that."

She wondered if he'd ever put a cereal box back in a cupboard in his life. Did he even eat cereal? Probably not.

He reached for the doorknob.

The minute the door opened, she was completely surprised. His room was perfectly organized, a large bed in the center, its headboard—patterned, dark leather—nearly spreading across the entire wall. The linens were tan with navy accents, a mass of throw pillows covering the top. Two sleek dark wood bedside tables flanked each side, their lines perfectly straight and angular, but coupled with the lamps and the softness of the bed, they looked quite comfortable. The walls were painted a dark tan, but the thick, white crown molding, paired with the vaulted ceiling, made the room look light and airy. Across from the bed was a flat-screen television bigger than her kitchen table. She wondered if he ever sat in bed and watched it.

"I prefer vegetables to fruit," he said. "Otherwise, I'm not difficult to please."

It took her a minute to realize that he was making a joke. She had to cook him dinner!

"There are a lot of pillows on that bed," she said, ignoring his joke, but not hiding her grin. He followed her gaze.

"Yes."

"Do you sleep with all those pillows?"

"No."

"Then why do you have them?" Until now he'd always said he didn't care about décor. So why did he have all those throw pillows for decoration if he didn't care about what the room looked like?

He grinned at her. "I have them because they came with the bedding. And it is customary to have blankets when one sleeps."

"Who decorated this room?" she asked in a playfully interrogating way.

Nick was chewing on a grin, and she could feel the affection for him rising even though she tried to push it back down.

"I did."

Her mouth hung open in an exaggerated gasp. "You're holding out on me!"

Nick laughed, the corners of his mouth turning down the way only his did. It made Abbey smile and, no matter how hard she tried to look serious, her smile pushed through her expression.

"It was the only room where Sarah let me choose what I wanted. I told her the house was too frilly. I hate frilly."

"I'm not a frilly decorator."

"I know. Well, apart from the flowers in every room. But the decorating itself is not frilly at all. It's very classic."

"So, you're saying you might *like* my decorating?"

He smiled again, and she had to remind herself to breathe.

"You can admit it. I won't tell anyone that you're happy."

He shook his head, still grinning. "How long will you be staying tonight? Do I need to have dinner prepared or will you be cooking?"

"Oh!" Her memory jolted her back to reality. "I planned to leave at four o'clock today. I'm taking Max to see Santa."

"Okay." He walked her out of the bedroom. "Now, if you will excuse me. I have a lot of work to do. You are the only person who can somehow pull me away from my work."

He'd stayed far longer she'd ever expected. He left her with her bag, her sketchpad, and a fizzle of excitement.

Abbey pushed her hands through her hair in frustration and tried the ignition again. It rolled over and didn't catch. The snow was starting to come down once more, and this time, it was actually sticking to the ground. Helplessly, she looked through her windshield at the mansion—the windows all twinkly and Christmassy as they reflected the decorations inside. She did not want to have to go in and find Richard and tell him that her car wouldn't start, but she had to leave in the next few minutes to get Max. She tried again.

There was a knock at her window, and she jumped with a start. Nick was standing outside her car, wearing a ski coat and gloves, his breath coming out in billowy puffs. She rolled down the window.

"Is there a problem with your car?"

"It doesn't want to start." Mortification crawled over her skin like spiders.

"Try it again," he said.

The car spit and sputtered but didn't start. Abbey got out of the car and shut the door, frustrated.

Nick paced back and forth for a moment, eyeing her car. Then, he pulled his cell phone from his back pocket and punched a few numbers. "I texted Richard. I know just what to do." There was an odd smile on his face.

She and Nick were both shivering as a bright red Ferrari came around the side of the house from the drive leading to the garage. It cut through the snow and slush like a knife and Abbey was trying not to wince at the muddy water splashing along the perfectly clean sides of it as it came to a stop in front of them. Richard got out, tossed the keys to Nick, and then went back inside.

Nick held out the keys, that weird smile still on his lips.

"What is this?" she asked.

"For you."

"You want me to drive that?" She couldn't even get the words out without laughing. She wouldn't even know how to drive a car like that, and there was no way she was taking something that expensive on the main roads. She'd be a nervous wreck.

"No. I want you to have it."

"What?" Abbey was at a loss for words. Surely he was joking. It was so ludicrous that she started laughing again.

Confusion crawled across his face. "It's yours. I'm giving it to you."

"You're giving me a car?" There was no way he could be serious.

"I was going to donate it anyway."

"I can't accept this," she said, looking at the keys as they dangled from his finger.

"Why not? I said I was donating it. To charity. What's the difference?"

Her heart plunged into her stomach. She let her gaze settle on the hood of her old Toyota. Did he think she was a charity case? "Well, I really can't accept it." She could hardly say the words without them catching in her throat.

"Look, your car broke down. I offered you a way home. I like you enough to give you the car. And if you don't have the money to buy it, that's one thing, but I do. And I'm choosing to put that money to good use."

"I have a few friends who are mechanics. For the cost of a burger and a few beers, I can get my car fixed. You're *giving* away an extraordinary amount of money and I just don't feel right taking it."

He was quietly watching her, studying her words as she released them into the air between them. He was listening, and the sight of it made her shoulders relax a little.

"Okay," he said. Nick was quiet again, the red Ferrari beside them taunting her, reminding her how no matter what things they'd shared, they were both very different people. Nick pulled his phone out again. "Richard is sending out Kenneth who is one of our groundsmen but he also knows quite a bit about cars. His father is a mechanic, and he taught him the trade. Maybe he can figure out what's wrong with it."

"I need it to start right now. I have to get Max and I'm late," she said, still trying to get her emotions in check.

Nick texted something else while Abbey got back into her car and tried again, unsuccessfully, to start the engine. She looked at her fuel levels and engine temperature. Totally fine. Then, her focus shifted to the most gorgeous black Mercedes she'd ever seen in her life, rounding the drive at the side of the house. Another car?

Nick opened the back door to her Toyota and pulled the booster seat from the backseat. The car came to a stop and Richard got out. He held the key out to Nick and Nick traded him, giving Richard the Ferrari key, his head shaking back and forth subtly to let Richard know he'd best take it back to the garage.

"Thank you, Richard. Would you have Kenneth take a look at Ms. Fuller's car? If he can't fix it, please have it serviced and then delivered to her home." He handed Abbey his cell phone through the open window. "Text your address to Richard, and he'll get your car fixed for you." He opened the door of the Mercedes and set Max's ratty booster in the backseat. "In the meantime, I'll drive you to get Max." He motioned for her to leave her car and get in.

As she slid into the car, she expected the leather interior to be cold from the winter weather but the seats were soft and warm. She tried to keep her feet in one place so as not to dirty the floorboards as she looked around the car. It was a convertible. What would it be like in the summer when he put the top down? She could only imagine the heat of the beating sun on her face, the wind in her hair. Her gaze slid to the console. There were so many buttons that she didn't know if she was in a car or an airplane. Nick got into the other side and the car came to life, a screen lighting up in the center. She'd never been in anything like this before.

"You were going to take Max to see Santa…"

"Yes," she said, trying to focus on his face and not the millions of shiny buttons all around him. "I'll just have to explain to him what happened."

"He'll be disappointed?"

"Probably. He was really looking forward to giving Santa Claus his Christmas list. But as soon as my car's working again I can take him."

"I'll drive you and Max to see Santa."

"Oh, you don't have to."

"I know I don't have to, but I will. I'd already planned on it after you wouldn't take the Ferrari. That's why I put Max's booster seat in the back." He threw his thumb up in the direction of the backseat and Abbey turned to look at it. Max's shabby plastic seat, its center fabric spotted from spills and dirt, sat on the plush leather, and she had to fight the urge to brush the crumbs off the top of it.

Nick put the car in drive, the engine purring.

"I'm sure you have better things to do," she said, knowing that she'd already kept him from his work earlier by insisting he see the decorated rooms.

He glanced over at her, a grin on his face. Perhaps he'd enjoyed their time together today.

"So you *want* to take us?"

"If I didn't want to, I wouldn't have put the seat in the back. I was serious when I said it the first time."

"Okay," she said, still not convinced.

As they drove, and she started to get used to the comfort of the Mercedes, it dawned on her that, if they were getting Max, Nick was going to have to go into her apartment. He would meet her mother who was watching Max. She knew her mom would probably want to freshen up, and tidy the apartment, but she didn't know how to warn them.

"Which way?" Nick asked as they came to a four-way stop.

"Straight. …I'm just going to text my mother and let her know she needs to have Max ready. Maybe she can even send him out, so we won't have to get out of the warm car. Let me just make sure Max has his Christmas outfit on…" She pulled out her phone and quickly texted: *Nick Sinclair is on his way over to my apartment! I'm with him! You have five minutes. Put Max in his red sweater and make everything look awesome! I owe you!*

Her phone lit up in her hand moments later. *WHAT?! HE'S COMING HERE! I CAN'T…* Abbey quickly swiped the message away so that Nick couldn't see it and dropped it into her handbag.

As Abbey directed Nick to her apartment, she was thinking about the impression she'd be making. She thought about her tiny Christmas tree, the red felt stockings she'd made with Max, their names in wobbly glitter across the tops. She wondered if her bed was made. Had the dishes been done? Had she left that little pile of dirty clothes in the corner of her bathroom?

They pulled up to her apartment and parked. "I'll just text Mom and see if she can send Max out." She pulled her phone from her handbag.

She typed very quickly: *Mom, send Max out.*

Only a moment later her phone immediately lit up: *I can't find his red sweater. I texted that to you but didn't hear back.*

She wracked her brain for any idea as to where that red sweater was. She texted back: *Is it on the dryer?*

Her mom: *No.*

Abbey: *How about in his third dresser drawer?*

Nick looked over at her. "What's the problem?"

"My mom can't find Max's sweater."

"So why don't we go in and help her?"

Abbey bit her lip as she scrambled for a response.

Nick turned off the engine, got out, and walked around the back of the car. He opened her door and motioned for her to get out. With a feeling of dread, she exited the car and headed toward the staircase leading to her apartment. Her phone was still lighting up but she ignored it. When they got to apartment C8, Abbey slid the key in the lock and opened the door.

"Mama!" Max came running toward her, holding on to his Spider-Man action figure. He wrapped his arms around her and buried his head in her torso. Then, he pulled back and looked up. "Hi, Nick!" he said with a big grin.

"Hello," Nick said to Max with a smile before looking up and greeting Abbey's mom. She had clearly put on lipstick, the color clashing with the red of her shirt. Abbey knew how she felt. She wanted to spruce *everything* up. "Nick Sinclair," he said with authority as he shook her mom's hand.

"Leanne Fuller." Her mom smiled nervously and took a step back. "Would you like to have a seat?" In a rush, she collected the storybooks, one of Max's pillows, and a few toys from the sofa cushions.

Nick thanked her and sat down.

"Would you like something to drink?"

"No, thank you. I'm just fine."

An awkward silence slithered between everyone after that. Max had run off to his room, and her mom was still smiling, wringing her hands, and glancing back and forth between Abbey and Nick.

"We've had a slight change of plans," Abbey said, breaking the silence. "I've had a little car trouble so Nick is taking us to see Santa."

"Oh!" her mom said a little too enthusiastically. "How wonderful."

"Did you find his red sweater?"

"No," her mom said.

"Would you help me look for it?" Abbey asked, trying to tell her more with her eyes as she asked the question.

Max came running out with his magic question ball. "Look what I have, Nick!" he said, climbing onto the sofa and leaning on Nick's lap. Abbey worried he'd wrinkle Nick's perfectly pressed trousers. "It answers your questions. Watch." Max turned the ball over. "Will Santa think I'm a good boy this year?" He shook the ball and read the answer. "It is probable." He looked at Nick. "What does probable mean?"

"It means that it's likely. It's possible."

Abbey grabbed her mom by the arm and yanked her down the hallway.

"Would you like to explain to me what's going on?" her mom whispered, her voice breathy and almost desperate for answers. "Quickly."

"My car didn't start at his house!" Abbey said as quietly as she could. "He just showed up and offered to take us to see Santa. I didn't ask him. You know I never would."

Her mom clasped her hands over her mouth to stifle an excited giggle.

"Shhh." Abbey batted her laughter away. "Help me find Max's sweater before Nick gets a chance to take in any more of my house! I wish I'd have known. I would've cleaned better."

The two women rummaged around in Max's room, tossing things left and right. They were quiet but the nervous energy was palpable. It wasn't often that Abbey had a millionaire sitting on her sofa, his Mercedes parked out front, waiting for her to get herself and her son together.

"Found it!" she said, grabbing it off the top of a pile in the closet. She held it up, and her mom looked visibly relieved.

Abbey walked out into the living room. Nick was still on the sofa, but he was sitting on the edge of it, Max on his lap, and they were asking the magic question ball questions. Max was bouncing on Nick's knee and the two of them looked so natural and relaxed, like they'd known each other all their lives. Max looked up.

"Let's change your sweater," she said. She worried about Max taking a liking to Nick. Their time was limited, and Max might be disappointed when he didn't get to see him again. "And then we get to take a ride in Nick's fancy car!" she said, trying to shake the worry.

"We do?" Max hopped up and ran over to his mother while simultaneously pulling his arms inside his T-shirt. Abbey pulled it over his head and draped it on the chair. Her mom came in behind her and scooped it up, headed for the laundry. Then, Abbey put the sweater over Max's head, and he assisted her by finding the sleeves himself and pushing his arms through.

Her mom came back in with a comb. "Just check his face and hair," she said, handing Abbey the comb while she bent down to adjust the cuffs on his jeans.

"Get your coat," her mom said, clearly displacing her nervous energy on Max. "It's cold. You'll need to bundle up. How's his hair?" She turned him around. "You look fantastic."

"Let me get my list!" Max said, pulling free and running down to his room. He returned with a small sheet of paper wadded in his fist. As Nick opened the door for Abbey, Max smoothed his list out. "Nick, do you know what I'm asking Santa for this Christmas?"

Abbey mouthed, "Thank you," to her mom and her mom smiled, waving in return as she closed the apartment door.

Max was reading his list to Nick as they walked side by side down the walk to the car. The snow was really coming down. Her sneakers were covered in snow, the canvas feeling wet against her feet. Max was rattling off the end of his list to Nick as he looked up between items, trying to catch snowflakes in his mouth.

"That's a great list you have there," Nick said.

"It's all my favorite things. I hope Santa will get them for me, but Mama says sometimes he just can't fit it all in the sleigh. I tried to make my list full of small things so he could fit them."

Nick nodded but made eye contact with Abbey, thoughts clear on his face. Was he reading between the lines? Did he realize that she didn't have enough money to pay for Max's presents? Well, this year, she would. He opened the car door for Max.

"Whoa!" Max said, climbing in. "It's like a space ship in here!"

Nick smiled as he allowed Abbey to get in. She slid inside, and he shut the door for her.

"Mama, this car is cool!" Max said. Nick smiled again as he got in on his side. He seemed to enjoy making Max happy.

"It is cool," Abbey said.

Nick started the car, the windshield wipers pushing the snow to the sides of the glass. He put the car in gear, and as they pulled away, he looked back at Max once more. "Off to see Santa Claus."

Chapter Eleven

"I thought we were going to the mall?" Abbey said as she realized that Nick wasn't driving in the correct direction. She said it quietly, trying not to let Max hear it. She didn't want to alarm him.

"Santa isn't at the mall," he answered, his eyes not leaving the road.

"Yes he is," Max said from the backseat.

"Santa is at the Children's Museum."

"What's the Children's Museum?" Max asked, and a swell of shame pelted Abbey's cheeks.

The Children's Museum in Richmond had replicas of caves for children to explore, real working trains on which to take rides, whole rooms for painting and stages with all the dress-up costumes one could imagine. It was a child's dream. Abbey always tried to give Max the best of everything, but funds were limited, and she'd only been with Max to the Children's Museum a handful of times. It's not that she didn't want to take him to a kid's wonderland full of the latest educational activities and toys, but she just didn't have enough money. Clearly, it had been so long that he didn't even remember.

"Do you remember the place where you sailed the boats in that big water table?" she asked him, recalling how he'd stayed there for hours when he was only about three years old.

"No. Will I get to sail boats today?"

"If you want to," Nick said. "We can play after we see Santa."

Abbey didn't want to have to admit that she didn't have enough cash to pay for all their entrance tickets to the museum, and she was nearly certain that the photo packages for Santa were going to be more money than she had. She'd planned to snap a few photos on her phone, and she didn't know if she'd be allowed to do that at the Children's Museum. It was a good thing she was getting paid for decorating. She'd have to put it on her credit card.

As a child, she'd heard of the Santa at the Children's Museum. He used to be at the old department store, Miller and Rhoads. Her friends at school would talk about having tea with him or the big Christmas breakfast that was offered for those who had the money for the most expensive tickets. Her mom, who was a secretary before she retired, had the same money dilemma that Abbey now faced, and Abbey had never been able to go to Miller and Rhoads.

She'd always gone to the mall. As a kid, she'd heard that the Miller and Rhoads Santa was the *real* Santa and all the others were just his helpers. She remembered looking very closely at Santa's beard to see if she could tell if it was real. Luckily, her mom had always found a pretty good Santa, and so, when Max was born, they made sure of the same.

Nick pulled the car to a stop in the parking lot. The lot didn't look very busy, which was surprising since she'd heard that the line usually snaked around the whole place and poured out the doors at times. Since it was just after Thanksgiving and a weekday, they'd gotten lucky.

The heat of the Children's Museum lobby warmed her, giving her a shiver, as she ushered Max through the glass doors. Nick was holding it open for her, and she had to duck under his arm to get in. Burgundy velvet ropes stretched throughout the lobby like an enormous Christmas maze, and at the front were a few families waiting to get in. Max ran ahead of them through the ropes.

"Slow down, Max," Abbey called. "You don't want to ruin your clothes by falling."

Once Max was out of earshot, she turned to Nick. His face was calm and content as he looked down at her. "We could've just gone to the mall," she said. "I know you have work to do—I've kept you from it all afternoon."

"You get to do this every year," he said, his face honest. "But I don't. It's been a long time since I've seen Santa Claus."

Happiness swelled in her chest, making her smile at his comment. He certainly could be charming when he wanted to. "It *is* fun," she said, looking over at Max.

They caught up with Max and moved through the double doors to the carpeted, plush room where Santa sat. The line was busier in there, the snaking velvet ropes continuing on through that room as well. The throne was large and golden, the seat and back a deep spruce green.

A gorgeous red Santa hat with a dangling white snowball at the end was draped on the back corner of the throne, but Santa wasn't there. Abbey noticed the concern on Max's face as the line shuffled forward. A girl dressed like an elf sat smiling at the register. The throne was sitting on a slight stage, and behind it was a real-looking fireplace. On that stage, at the very corner, sat a young woman in a white dress—the dress was so beautiful it could've been a wedding dress. She was wearing a diamond tiara, long, white gloves, and what looked to be a very small microphone. It was hardly noticeable.

"Santa will return shortly," she said, her voice like wind chimes. She was so young and strikingly beautiful that Abbey almost believed she could be someone magical. "He's just feeding his reindeer. If you'd like, children, you can sit quietly in your places in line until he returns."

Max sat down, a giant smile on his face. He didn't sit long though before he popped up. He gasped and pointed at the fireplace. Abbey followed his line of sight. To her astonishment, there, floating in the empty space inside the fireplace were two thick, black boots. *How did they manage that?* she thought. Abbey was just as captivated as her son.

With a thud, they hit the ground, and she could see the dark red fur of Santa's costume. Slowly, carefully, he bent down, his white beard showing just as the sound of jingle bells came from somewhere on the roof. He ducked out of the fireplace and stood with a loud, "Ho ho ho!" It all was so realistic that Abbey got goose bumps and she had to rub her arms to relieve them.

Santa's hair was long and white, perfectly combed and parted down the middle. His cheeks were rosy like they were in the storybooks Abbey had read as a child. His coat was thick and furry, deep red like his trousers, with white fluffy cuffs that met his white gloves. His beard, clearly real, curled just slightly against the front of his coat. Santa pulled off his gloves and set them on the side table next to his throne.

"Thank you for waiting, children," he said in a deep dreamy voice that projected across the entire room. "My reindeer get hungry and if I don't take a break and feed them, they start stomping on the roof! It's very annoying. Now, let me just get comfortable," he said, sitting down on his throne. "Our snow queen, Catherine, will keep you company while you wait your turn."

Abbey watched as the first child walked up to the woman in the big, white dress. She looked every bit the part of a snow queen. "Hello," she said quietly as Santa wriggled himself comfortable in his chair. "What is your name?"

"Timothy," the little boy said shyly.

"Timothy," she said slightly louder, and Abbey caught on to their theatrics. "Timothy," she said again, "have you come to sit on Santa's lap?" Santa scratched his ear as the boy nodded. "Well… *Timothy*, you may go right ahead."

Across the stage, Santa, who seemed too far away to hear Timothy's conversation with the snow queen, turned and said, "Well, Timothy! It's great to see you! How have you been this year?" The boy climbed up on Santa's lap, and Max turned around with an astonished look on his face. Watching it all play out, seeing Santa Claus greet every child by name as they climbed up on stage—it was like a real fairytale.

Before she knew it, it was Max's turn and he was talking to Catherine. After she spoke to him, she was nodding, smiling, and he looked nervous standing on that stage under the bright lights, but as Santa called out, "Max!" his face lit up and he nearly ran to Santa and climbed on his lap.

A bright bolt of light flashed, causing Max to blink several times. When he seemed to clear his vision, Max unrolled the balled paper in his hand and began to read his list. "I'd like an iPad, a skateboard, a scooter, a Willie Mays baseball card…" That baseball card was because of Gramps. It was his favorite player. The bare minimum value for a Willie Mays card was probably a hundred dollars. They went up to the thousands. Abbey swallowed to alleviate the lump that was forming. This Christmas, she'd have the money for all those things.

With a wave to Santa, Max came barreling toward her, slamming into her and wrapping his arms around her waist. "That was the *real* Santa!" he said.

Max would know better next year, and he'd never believe the mall Santa was the real Santa. She'd have to bring him back here next year. Making sure to keep the magic of believing in Santa alive was important to her.

When Abbey was a girl, her mom had worked hard to keep the magic alive, and when she'd finally told Abbey the truth, she explained that Santa was really a way to explain faith. We have to have faith in things we can't see sometimes, and if we believe, we may discover goodness beyond our dreams. That had stuck with Abbey all her life, and she wanted to be able to have that same talk with her own son. But she wanted the timing to be just right. She didn't want that magic ruined by a Santa at the mall that didn't live up to this moment.

Nick stepped away just as Max pulled at her arm. "Mama! Can you believe we really met the real Santa? He was so different! We've been going all this time to the mall and that was only his helper! He knew my name! Maybe that's why I never got what was on my list! Now, I'm sure to be one of the kids this year!"

Abbey tried to squelch her worry. If they continued to visit the Children's Museum each Christmas to see Santa, would Max expect to get everything on his list every year?

Nick returned, carrying a small white bag. He handed it over to her. "I got five three-and-a-half-by-five-size photos, six five-by-sevens, and four eight-by-tens. Just to be on the safe side, I paid to have the digital image emailed to my personal account because that has copyright release. I'll forward it to you. I would've gotten your email, but I was already paying, and Max had your attention."

She opened the bag and slid an eight-by-ten out to view it. Max was adorable. He had a gorgeous smile on his face as he looked up at Santa Claus.

"Thank you," she said, feeling a little uncomfortable about taking the photos. Nick had easily just spent a hundred dollars or more and she wasn't used to receiving gifts of that size. She wouldn't be able to repay him with a gift of comparable sentiment.

"You're welcome."

"Can we play with the boats now?" Max asked.

"Yes, we can," she said, rummaging in her purse as they crossed the lobby to the ticket counter. She only had seven dollars. That wasn't enough for one admission ticket. She pulled out her credit card.

Abbey had one credit card for emergencies. She never used it because she was terrible at keeping track of what she'd spent, and she didn't make enough each month to pay it off. She believed that if she couldn't pay for things with cash, she didn't need to have them. Even knowing she was getting the money, it felt odd using it.

"Two, please," she said to the woman behind the counter.

"I invited you," Nick said. "It's my treat."

The woman behind the counter paused, holding the credit card, clearly unsure of how to proceed.

"You don't have to pay for us," she said.

"I'm sure I don't, but I want to. As a friendly gesture."

"Do you want me to run this credit card?" the woman said from behind the counter. Max was sitting on the floor, waiting, his knees pulled up, and his arms around them.

"Yes, thank you," Abbey said back to the woman. She turned to Nick, feeling awkward about having her employer spend his money on her. Even though he had it to spend, she wanted to do this on her own. "Thank you so much for your offer, but it's really fine."

The woman walked from behind the counter with a pen so that Abbey could sign the receipt. With one hand, Abbey pressed the receipt against the wall and wrote her name with the other.

Max ran ahead to a life-size apple tree. It spit red plastic balls out of chutes that kids could collect with baskets as if they were apples. "Max, the boats are over here," Abbey said, smiling at his excitement.

Max dropped his basket and followed her to a long, narrow water table that snaked through the museum. It had little waterfalls, canals for the boats, and different levers and hinges to change direction.

One of the attendants bent down next to Max. "I'm Carrie," she said with a warm smile. She grabbed an apron from a peg on the wall nearby and put it on Max, tying it in the back. He already had his hands in the water, grabbing different boats and moving them along their paths. Abbey smiled at the woman's easy way with children as she helped each one up to the water table.

"This really is an amazing place," Abbey said to the woman.

"I agree," Carrie said. "I transferred here last year from Wilmington. I love Richmond. It's a good place to raise kids. My husband, Adam, and I are expecting our first! Well, I have two stepchildren—twins. They're very excited."

"Congratulations," Abbey said.

"Thank you! We're all planned and ready!"

"Look, Nick!" Max said, pushing his boat under a waterfall that made it spin and go in a different direction. Nick smiled and leaned over his shoulder to see.

Abbey watched Carrie walk away, hoping she knew how lucky she was to be having children at a time when she felt completely ready.

How much easier it would've been for Abbey if she'd been able to plan and prepare. She'd had to build her confidence as a mother, but now, looking at her son, she wondered if things really did happen for a reason. They were just fine now.

"I love boats," Max said, making a motor noise and pulling a handle to change the path.

"Have you ever been on a boat before?" Nick asked.

"No. Have you ever been on a boat, Nick?" he asked.

"I have." Nick smiled down at Max, and Abbey could see a gleam in Nick's eyes. He was enjoying himself.

Max played for ages. When he had finally told Abbey that he was getting hungry, she asked if Nick would take them home. Nick politely drove them through the city headed to her apartment, but something in her clicked. Maybe it was the spruce wreaths on all the buildings, the Christmas trees on every street corner, or the white wicker animals the city put out every year that peppered the lawns of the high-rises, every inch of them covered in white lights. Abbey felt, suddenly, that she wanted to do something for Nick. Why did *he* have to show *her* a good time? She had an idea.

"May I take you somewhere?" she asked.

He turned and looked at her as he pulled up to a stoplight.

"Max," she said, twisting to see him in the backseat. "Want to take Nick to La Esquina Loca?"

"Yes!" Max said as he wriggled in his booster seat with excitement. "May I get the tortilla chips?"

"Absolutely." Abbey laughed quietly. She'd never told him that the tortilla chips were complimentary. She turned to Nick. "Feel like a little Mexican food tonight? It's delicious."

"What's it called again?" he asked, putting on his blinker and making a turn.

"La Esquina Loca, The Crazy Corner. Ever been there?" It was famous for its one-dollar-taco night and strong margaritas, and it belonged to her friend, Alma. It was time she showed Nick Sinclair how *she* had fun.

"I haven't been there," he said.

"Wanna go?"

"Of course I want to go. I have to see what The Crazy Corner is all about."

"Well then," she said with a big smile. "Turn right at the next light."

Abbey gave directions until they pulled up at a small, freestanding building that used to be an old mechanic's garage. It had been completely transformed, but the original garage doors remained and their masses of square windows were full of twinkle lights and light-up strings of red peppers. Nick reached around Abbey to open the restaurant door, jingling the bells that were tied to it.

"Abbey!" said a young woman with olive skin and jet-black hair, her gold hoop earrings giving her the air of a movie star. She gave Abbey a hug with one arm, the other filled with menus. Afterward, she tousled Max's hair. "Have you been taking care of your *mamá*?" she asked.

"Yes," he giggled.

Abbey turned to Nick. "This is Alma. She's my good friend and part owner here."

Nick held out his hand in greeting and Alma shook it as Abbey finished the introductions. "Alma, this is Nick."

"Nice to meet you," she said with a smile that could light up a room. "Come with me. I have a table ready right now. The mariachi band will be starting soon."

"Awesome," Abbey said with a devious smile.

As Nick led Max to their table, Alma caught Abbey's eye and offered a loaded wink in her direction. "Cute," she mouthed in encouragement.

Before they could even get comfortable, a waiter set down a basket of tortilla chips and poured a bowl of salsa, then disappeared. As Max dipped into the tortillas, Nick looked around. Abbey followed his gaze, seeing the restaurant through new eyes. The walls were stucco-style, with a warm yellow finish, Mexican paintings with bright reds, blues, and greens dotting their surface. Potted palm trees sat at the corners, their trunks covered in multicolored Christmas lights, the light from the traditional Mexican lanterns matching them almost perfectly. The table was decoupage, with postcards from Mexican beaches. The whole place was just lovely.

A few moments later Alma stopped by their table and slid across two enormous frozen margaritas, the rim salted heavily with large rock salt, and floating in the center was a paper umbrella and a plastic snowman figurine. "On the house," she said with another wink. "Merry Christmas."

"Aw, thank you!" Abbey said feeling affectionate toward her friend. It was a very nice gesture.

Another man came up behind her and set down a small kids' drink for Max. It, too, was frozen but pink in color, and it had a snowman wearing sunglasses hugging a rainbow-colored straw. "*Feliz Navidad*," he said with a smile that showed all his bright white teeth.

"Merry Christmas," Abbey returned to both of them with an appreciative nod.

"Have you ever had a margarita?" she asked Nick as he studied the menu.

"I've never had one like this one before," he said with a smile.

"It's really good, but if you drink it all, you may be calling Richard to come get us. Be careful. It's potent."

"I'm not sure what to get," Nick said honestly as he looked over the menu.

"The tacos are so good, Nick," Max said as he colored his kid menu with the little pot of crayons the restaurant had supplied next to the salt, pepper, and habanero hot sauce. "Alma makes deeeeelicious tacos."

Abbey giggled at her son. "Alma doesn't make them all. She has cooks who do it," she said.

"Well she makes them at our house and they're yummy!"

"I'll have to tell her that," Abbey said. She looked over her menu at Nick. "All the recipes here were passed down from Alma's mother and grandmother. She makes amazing pork tamales. But Max is right. She makes wonderful tacos too."

"It's settled then," Nick said as he closed his menu. "If Max says the tacos are the best, then I'll have to try them."

"Looks like we're all getting tacos," Abbey said.

"Try the salsa," Max said, scooting the small molcajete-style bowl in Nick's direction.

Nick pinched a tortilla from the basket and dipped it in, scooping a large pile of salsa onto his chip. He took a bite, having to hold his napkin over his mouth to keep the salsa from dripping into his lap.

"It's a little messy sometimes, but it's good!" Max said.

"It is good," Nick said.

A man that Abbey recognized as Alma's brother, Carlos, came to take their order. Abbey ordered for everyone. Just as they were left alone again, the mariachi band started in the far corner. It was a large group all holding instruments: eight violins, two trumpets, what Alma told her once was a guitarrón, and a guitar. The music was loud, fast, and Abbey could feel the excitement of the notes bouncing through her chest. She sipped her margarita, the alcohol warming her cheeks while her fingertips stayed cold from the ice. Nick turned toward the band. They all looked so sharp in their black suits with silver accents, red scarves, and sombreros. It was a departure from Nick's classical piano, but their skill was evident immediately.

Men in white shirts and sombreros entered the small dance floor where the mariachi was playing followed by women in brightly colored, big, flowing skirts, the hems made of lace. The women grabbed the men's hands and began to spin around, their skirts fanning out along the dance floor, revealing their black, heeled shoes.

Nick's eyes still on the dancers, he grabbed his drink off the table and took a sip, his eyebrows rising in surprise.

"Do you like it?" Abbey asked over the music.

"It's amazing," he said, still not making eye contact.

The women flipped the hems of their dresses to the music while leaning toward their male counterparts. Max was sipping his drink, tortilla crumbs on the table in front of him as he jiggled to the beat of the music. Then, Abbey saw Nick's eyes widen as the dancers began to pull people onto the dance floor. Since they were waiting for their food, she knew that it was a possibility they'd be chosen, but she also knew Alma well, and she would probably have interpreted Abbey's earlier "Awesome" comment, when she'd mentioned the band, and told the dancers to choose Abbey's table.

Sure enough, two of them were standing in front of Abbey and Nick, their hands outstretched, waiting for them to stand up. Nick looked over at Abbey for what to do next. With a grin, Abbey stood up and took the man's hand. Reluctantly, Nick took the woman's and they were on the dance floor. As the man spun Abbey around, she leaned over mid-spin and said to Nick, "I'll teach you how. Alma taught us this dance, didn't she, Max?" Max, who'd been scooped up by one of the women, was wriggling his way down her torso, trying to get to the dance floor himself.

"Yes!" he said, his little feet tapping to the music.

Alma walked by and grinned in Abbey's direction. The two dancers paired up, leaving Abbey and Nick together.

"Hold my hand," she said, clasping her fingers in his and pulling his arm above her head. She began to spin, and she noticed his eyes were on her with each turn. After a few spins, she let go and fanned out an invisible skirt just as the dancers did theirs, and she shuffled her feet back and forth. The trumpets sang out their blaring, feisty music alongside the violins as the two of them moved to the beat, Abbey showing Nick where to put his hands and feet. He followed her every movement, his eyes intense and happy in a way she'd not experienced before.

They danced for quite a while, completing the same three or four steps she'd taught him to keep things easy. Once he'd gotten the hang of it, Nick was strong as he held her, deliberate with his movements, and confident as a lead. He pulled her close, just as she noticed that it wasn't a rehearsed dance move. His arms were around her. He looked down at her, the music loud in her ears. He smiled and leaned toward her.

"Thank you for bringing me tonight," he said into her ear, his breath tickling her, giving her a shiver. As he pulled back, his lips grazed her cheek, and it would've been so easy to catch them with her own and touch her lips to his. She'd only realized then that they'd stopped dancing. He was looking down at her like he wanted to kiss her, and she was willing him with everything she had inside to give into the impulse. The music dwindled to a stop, and Max grabbed Abbey's hand and pulled her away from Nick against her will.

"The food's here," Max said.

They all sat down and Nick took a huge swig of his drink. Abbey did the same. It took her a minute to come down to earth from that moment on the dance floor.

Nick took another drink of his margarita as he watched Abbey pick up a taco. She noticed how his shoulders had slacked, the way he was leaning against the back of the seat, his arm draped along the chair beside him and a smile on his lips. She'd never seen him this relaxed.

"Try it," Max said, nodding toward the tacos on Nick's plate.

With his eyes still fluttering to Abbey and a smile, he picked one up and gingerly took a bite, his eyebrows raising as he chewed and swallowed. "It's very good," he said.

The band continued to play as they ate, the wait staff whooping and whistling to the music off and on. Nick's gaze hadn't been still all night, and Abbey wondered if he'd ever had a night like this.

When they'd finished and the bill was left on the table, Abbey snatched it up. "This is on me," she said with a smile, pulling out her wallet. Nick didn't protest, but he did shake his head just slightly with a grin.

As they said goodbye to Alma and walked into the cold of winter, Nick put his arm lightly around Abbey to draw himself closer, surprising her. "I had a great time at dinner," he said.

"I'm glad," she said.

Max fell asleep in the backseat, and besides his breathing and the hum of the Mercedes, there wasn't another sound between them.

"Thank you," she said as Nick opened her car door once they were parked outside her apartment.

"Thank you for what? You bought me dinner." He smiled, and it was clear that he was teasing.

He leaned toward the backseat to get Max. Was he going to try to carry him inside? Abbey watched as he reached in, positioned his hands under Max's arms, and lifted him with ease out of the car.

"I can get him," she said, trying to keep her emotions in check. Max, still asleep, wrapped his arms around Nick's neck. Abbey understood the gesture completely. Watching his careful and gentle way with her son made her want to wrap her own arms around his neck.

"I'll take him upstairs for you," he whispered.

"Thank you," she said.

As they walked up the steps to her apartment, Abbey watched the slow, caring way Nick walked with Max. Max's head was turned to the side, his cheek on Nick's shoulder, and with every step Nick stopped to look down at him as if he were worried he'd wake him, as though he wasn't aware of how perfectly he could manage the task.

Abbey slid the key in the lock just as Max opened his eyes. "Hi," she smiled at him. "We're home."

Nick set him down inside the front door.

"Is Nick coming in?" Max asked, his voice groggy.

She looked at Nick. "I'm sure he'd like to go home," she said, worried she'd already taken too much of his time.

The curiosity she'd seen in Nick's face was replaced by seriousness. What was he thinking about? It was the kind of look that made her want to put her hand on his face and reassure him like she did with Max. "I suppose I should go," he said, but the tone in his voice sounded as if he might have thought otherwise.

"Thank you for a wonderful night," she said.

And with a kiss on the cheek, he was gone.

Chapter Twelve

Abbey had been at Nick's all day. She'd ordered the bar for his ballroom, and she was dying to show him what she'd picked out, but he hadn't shown up. It was unusual since he normally found her to at least to say hello. She decided to walk down to his office and see if he was there.

When she got to the office, the door was shut which she hadn't seen before. She knocked. No answer. Was he not at home? She pulled out her phone and texted: *Hi, Nick. Where are you? Are you at the house?*

She'd waited just long enough to think that he wasn't going to respond when a text came through: *Was that you knocking? If so, open the door. I'm in my office.*

She opened the door and walked in to find Nick hunched over his desk. He looked up, and his eyes had dark circles under them, his face tired looking, his lips set in a straight line.

"Hi," she said.

"Hi," he said, looking exhausted. "I'm sorry I didn't answer the door. I didn't know it was you and I've told Richard not to disturb me."

"Oh. I'm sorry... How are you?" She couldn't help the question. He seemed so worn out. Was he wearing the same shirt from yesterday? Had he slept at all?

"Busy." His voice was soft but direct.

He looked nothing like the man she'd seen at the restaurant last night. Even his face seemed different, his features wracked with tension.

"Are you okay?"

"I'm struggling with something and I need to focus."

She walked over to his side of the desk and turned his chair on its swivel until he was facing her. "What's wrong?"

"What's wrong," he said quietly, "is that I have committed to doing this job for my father. It's important to me that I do it. You and Max have become a distraction—albeit, a very nice distraction—but my work is suffering. I am not in a position to take care of people, and I feel I've been selfish in spending time with you. I don't want to give you false hope that I have time to devote to anything other than my work."

"False hope?"

"Of being someone in your life who is more than what I can offer."

"You didn't give me false hope," she said. "But I thought perhaps having a distraction was good for you. Last night you seemed… happy."

"When Sarah and I split, I had to decide where my focus needed to be. I'm good at what I do, and all my concentration needs to be on that," he said and she could almost swear he had sadness in his eyes.

"I understand," she said, trying not to visualize his face as he'd carried Max up the stairs last night, but it was coming into her mind despite her efforts. "I'll let myself out. Text me if you need anything."

"Thank you," he said with a small smile and then looked back down at his computer.

Without another word, Abbey turned and left the office, the clink of the latch as she shut the door echoing in the empty hallway.

"I've fallen, Abbey," Caroline's voice poured through the receiver on her phone. Abbey was relieved that Caroline had listened to her when she'd said to be sure to have her phone on her at all times. Caroline had complained that she didn't know how to even work the "darn thing," she'd called it, but Nick had gotten it for her, and Abbey had insisted she learn how to use it. Now, when it mattered, she could get help.

"I'm on my way. Don't try to move if you can help it. I'll be right there." She was already putting her shoes on. Richard had left them by the front door for her as he always did about a half hour before she left for the day.

It wasn't her scheduled visit time, but Caroline was in trouble. Abbey could tell by her voice. Caroline was always sure of herself, always in control of every motion, every facial expression, every word. But on the phone just then, she'd sounded quite helpless.

Luckily, she was still at Nick's, so in mere minutes, Abbey pulled in to the drive at Caroline's and ran inside. Caroline was on the floor of the kitchen, a mop tilted haphazardly toward her, the very end of it held up by the kitchen chair.

"I was trying to mop a spill," Caroline said from the floor. Abbey could see the humiliation on her face. Caroline clearly didn't like losing control. However, she seemed to be following Abbey's direction to keep still. She wasn't moving a muscle.

"It's natural, as we age, to have more difficulty recovering our balance when we start to fall…" Abbey checked Caroline for any sign of injury. She pressed on her ankles, legs. "Does this hurt at all?"

"No. It feels fine. I have a little pain in my hip though."

Abbey did her very best to keep her face neutral, especially knowing how easily Caroline could read her. She didn't want Caroline to have any pain in her hips at all. That could mean fracture, and that would be a painful recovery at the least, particularly given her arthritis. She pressed gently but firmly against her hips.

"How does this feel?"

"Fine."

"How about this side?" She pressed again.

Caroline winced. "A little."

"How about if I do this?" Abbey put her palm on the top of her hip and pressed downward with her other hand.

"Just a bit."

Abbey let out a breath. She hadn't realized she was holding it in until just then. "Well, it seems like you may have just strained it. The pain isn't indicating anything more, but we'll still need to get you to a doctor to be sure." She pulled two kitchen chairs over, scooting one by Caroline's head and one by her feet. "Can you roll over to your side?" Abbey assisted her by tugging her skirt past her knees where it belonged as Caroline rolled over with a bit of a struggle.

"Thank you for helping me," Caroline said, now facing away from Abbey.

"It's perfectly fine. I don't mind at all. Can you get up to a kneeling position?"

Caroline lifted herself up onto her knees and Abbey scooted the chair toward her. "Hold on to this." Caroline put her hands on the chair.

"I know this isn't part of your hours, and you should be with your family," Caroline said. "I could've called Richard…" She put her hands on the chair and attempted to lift herself up, scowling again at the pain in her hip. "But I didn't trust that he would know what to do…" She stood and leaned on Abbey, locking eyes with her. Caroline's eyes were so wide, so youthful looking that she wondered right then what she'd been like as a girl.

Caroline's eyes were also glassy with emotion, Abbey noticed. "I don't just like you taking care of me," she said, and Abbey wondered if years of training in keeping her emotions in were paying off. "I like talking to you. I feel like you're part of the family." She was quiet, clearly trying to keep herself in check. "Life moves along and we have to move along with it." She smiled, "The older I get, the more difficult it is to move along with anything."

"Everything will be okay." Abbey found herself saying the words to console Caroline, but she didn't really know if they were true. Caroline would be better off having someone with her all the time in case things like this happened. What would she do in the middle of the night if she fell?

Caroline walked carefully into the living area and lowered herself down on a chair. "I'm sure it will," she said, but she didn't look convinced either.

"I should call Richard in a few minutes and tell him you need a ride to the hospital. We have to check that hip."

"Yes. Absolutely. And you need to get home to your family, but first, let's have coffee. I feel good enough for coffee."

Abbey smiled, knowing she was right about being home with her family but she felt bad leaving her all alone again. She was glad for the offer. "Will you be okay?" she asked.

"I'll be fine. My hip feels better already. When will my test results be available?" Caroline asked, clearly changing the subject. Abbey wondered if she was trying her best to not be a burden on anyone. She'd just fallen yet she was insistent on making coffee and talking about her tests. It was clear she wanted to brush over the fall.

"Monday." Abbey felt exhausted suddenly and was glad for the coffee. She had to wonder if it was the stress of what had happened in Nick's office earlier. She hadn't wanted to think about it, but it kept floating to the front of her mind. While she didn't want to admit it, their night out *had* given her false hope. She knew better than to hope for something to happen between them, but she caught herself wishing anyway.

Caroline seemed to notice because she said, "You're tired."

"I'm fine," she lied.

"How is Max? Is he feeling better?"

"Yes, thank you." Abbey got up and made them both a coffee from a pot that Caroline had warming in the kitchen. She added cream and handed one to Caroline who had followed her into the kitchen. "He's back at school now."

Caroline sat down at the table. Abbey noted how controlled her hands were as she held her mug in her delicate fingers. Caroline was so different than Gramps. But then again, her issues were on the inside, eating away at her, and Gramps had to deal with the exterior complications of aging. On an off day he couldn't even hold a mug. Caroline never complained, she never showed pain, she never let on that anything was bothering her.

The opposite was true for Abbey. When she was upset, she wanted to talk more than she usually did. The problem was that she really couldn't explain to Caroline how she felt about Nick. She didn't know where to begin, so instead she was quiet, and Caroline knew she was never quiet. Caroline was watching her, an inquisitive look on her face. It was as if she were waiting for everything to come pouring out.

"How's the decorating?" she said, as if reading Abbey's mind.

"Fine," she lied again.

There was a shift in Caroline's face—it was small, but she'd caught it. Caroline sensed something. How did she do that? "Has Nick been helpful? Is he getting you what you need?"

"Yes, thank you."

"He told me that you all went to see Santa Claus last night."

Abbey nearly choked on her sip of coffee. "He did?"

Caroline nodded. "Mmm hmm." She took a slow sip of her coffee, her eyes on Abbey. "He enjoyed himself. I called him just as he had gotten home."

"He made it very clear to me today that he doesn't plan to allow it anymore. He called me a *distraction*."

Caroline's eyes widened with that comment but then she ironed it out. "Well, that's to be expected. He's never had anyone pull him away from his work before. He has to learn how to handle it. It totally took him by surprise. I think he finds you very interesting, and he cares what happens to you."

Caroline was very perceptive. She'd said Nick enjoyed being with her, but this morning, he'd made his wishes pretty clear. Abbey wished she could talk to *him*: the man she danced with in the restaurant last night, not the man behind his computer.

She finished her coffee and said her goodbyes to Caroline. Then, she headed home.

"I wanted to tell you my thoughts about Caroline." Abbey had turned the car around and gone straight back to Nick's after seeing his grand-mother. Despite Caroline's insistence that she was fine, Abbey had worried on her way home and decided she needed to talk to Nick. While seeing him sent a wave of happiness through her, she kept it all business. "I think she needs to live with someone."

"I was thinking the same thing. She called me after you left and told me about her fall. I want to ensure that she's safe." He was standing in front of his desk, leaning back on it.

Abbey explained the nature of Caroline's fall and her concerns that something could happen when she wasn't there. "She really needs to be careful with that hip."

He pushed himself off his desk, looking thoughtful. "Would you be interested in moving into the cottage with her? I would, obviously, increase your salary…"

"What about her moving in with *you*?"

"Abbey, I'm in and out. The staff all have jobs in the house and can't be at her beck and call. She needs an experienced nurse. She needs you."

"I have Max. There isn't enough space for the both of us in her cottage. We'd need more room."

"You know where there's a lot more room…" He looked around dramatically.

"Are you saying you'd want me and Max to move in here?"

"We could start on a trial basis—see how it goes…"

"I don't know…" She sat down in one of the chairs. This wasn't a decision she could make lightly. There were all kinds of things to think about. How would a move of this scale affect Max? Would he want to move into such a large home? And would she want that for him? She liked doing his homework at the small table in their kitchenette, under the lamplight in the silence of their little apartment. She enjoyed lining up all his various bottles of bubble bath on the tub and playing mad scientist with the different colors with him. Would she be able to do that in one of Nick's bathrooms?

"I'll double your salary and we can discuss your health benefits and retirement plans. I can contribute to those as well. If you work full time for me, we can set all that up."

He was looking down at her with those blue eyes. She bit her lip, considering. "I really need to speak to Max about this. I don't want to just uproot him. It would be a big move…"

"Why don't we try it just through Christmas? It's only a few weeks. If it works, you and Max can move in permanently. How about that?"

"Max has school for a few more weeks. The bus doesn't come out here."

"I'll send Richard to pick him up. Max can come straight here after school."

"What about his homework? I'll be working…"

"You write your hours. You can be on call only, whenever you need to be with Max. We'll find a way to fit it all in. I really feel strongly about having you in particular for my grandmother. She trusts you."

"Max doesn't have any things here. I'll need to pack all his toys, his books…"

"Richard and the staff can help you pack them. You just tell them what you want to bring and they'll ensure they arrive."

"Where will we sleep?"

"I have enough bedrooms. Pick one."

Abbey chewed on the thought for a moment. She really wasn't sure at all. She knew she should be there for Caroline's sake but it was a tough decision when Max was involved. Nick was wonderful with Max. Having him there, even for just some of the time, would be a great thing for her son. But then she'd recently seen how Nick could get when he was working. Would Max disturb him? Did Nick realize what it was like to live with a child in the house?

Max would love the idea, she was sure, and she could get her decorating done. She'd finally be able to relieve her mother of childcare duties. "Okay. Just until Christmas. Then we'll reevaluate."

A smile spread across his face, and she had to remind herself not to get her hopes up. She was there to work.

"What are you looking at, Mama?" Max asked as he stood beside Abbey in the kitchen. They'd only gotten back from her mother's house about a half hour ago, and she was just now going through Max's school papers. After everything else she'd had to do, she'd also had to run over and help Gramps understand why he needed to take his medicine. He'd sworn that he was the same on or off it. Finally, much later than she'd planned, she was just now looking through Max's backpack. He was standing beside her, wearing his Christmas pajamas.

"It's a flyer from school," she said.

"What does it say?"

The one thing Abbey wrestled with every day was trying not to shield Max too much from the realities of life, but also not to overwhelm him with them. "It's a list of the festivities for the school leading up to Christmas."

"What are they?" he said, clearly becoming excited.

"Well, next Saturday is the Christmas festival. They're going to auction off gift baskets. The basket theme for your class is 'Stay Warm and Comfy.' We're supposed to donate things like hot chocolate, blankets, slippers—things like that." She was so glad she was getting paid for decorating Nick's house. The closer she got to finishing the job, the more comfortable she felt spending a little money. She still had his teacher to buy for as well.

"What else does it say? What's that?" He tapped the box for Wednesday.

"The Wednesday after that is…" she paused, unsure of how to handle the situation. Should she just tell him?

"What?" Max asked impatiently. He was clearly so excited about everything going on. She didn't want to put a damper on things.

"It's 'Bring Your Daddy to School Day'." She tried to keep her face as neutral as possible.

"Everybody will have their daddies there," Max said, his face looking anxious.

"Probably not everybody."

"Not me."

"How do you feel about that?"

"Sad. Like I'm different… Hey! I know! Could I bring Nick?"

"Nick?" She could hardly control her surprise. Gramps, yes. But Nick?

"Yeah. I like him."

"What do you like about him?" There were a ton of things Abbey liked about Nick—the way he knew how to play piano, the interest he showed on his face when he looked at her, the gentleness he'd had with Max, the fun they'd had together…

"I like that he lets me show him stuff. He's nice. And I like that he took us to see the real Santa. If I had a daddy, I'd want him to be like that."

"Max, you know that Nick probably won't be able to come. He's my boss. I work for him. He isn't your dad, so we can't just ask anyone to come."

Max looked disappointed. He would be fine; Abbey knew that. She was providing a stable home for him, good memories, and lots of love. Abbey had grown up with only Gramps in her life, and she was fine too. But Abbey had a natural inclination to want to give Max what would make him happy. She knew he wanted to be like the other kids in his class, and the only reason he wasn't like them was because of her poor judgment when it came to men. It would never happen again. Abbey was tired of trying to fix people. Now, for Christmas, she just wanted a happy family, however small.

Max sighed and focused on the flyer again. "What's the last thing on the paper? Number three—what does it say?"

"On the nineteenth, you have your school winter party with all your friends."

"Oh, that sounds like fun!"

"Yes! Now, Mister, it's bedtime. Let's go brush your teeth."

Chapter Thirteen

"Tomorrow," Abbey's friend, Adrienne, said on the other end of the phone as Abbey got into the car. "My party's *tomorrow*. I have no food."

"Did the caterer say why she had to cancel?" Abbey threw her handbag on the passenger seat and set her coffee in the cup holder of her car.

"She's sick. It's just her. It's a small business but great for the money. The only problem is there's no one to take over in times like these."

"Well, you don't want a sick person serving food to your guests. How many are coming?"

"About twenty."

"You and I could cook."

"We only have one day."

"I can probably leave Nick's around five or so. Mom can stay with Max if you need help shopping," she said, feeling guilty for leaving Max yet again. Adrienne had a child too, but her childcare options were even more difficult to manage. It had taken an endless string of phone calls to family members before she'd found an aunt who agreed to watch her little girl for this party.

"Could you?"

"Of course." Abbey put the car in reverse, the exhaust filling her back window in the cold air outside. "Let's make a list. What should we have?"

"Something Christmassy. You could make your Christmas casserole—the one with the sausage and stuffing. That's delicious."

"Okay," she said, mentally accounting for the ingredients in her cupboard. That would be easy; she only needed an onion and ground sausage. A quick trip to the grocery store on the way home would be all she had to do. "Want me to pick anything else up?"

"What else? We need some finger foods. Oh! You could make those pinwheels! I love those."

"Are *you* making anything?" Abbey teased.

"No. I'm going to make you do it all. It tastes so much better when you make it."

Abbey laughed.

"I'm just kidding. I'm going to do ham biscuits, veggies and dips, and all the sweets."

"I'll do the pinwheels and the casserole. I'll get it ready Friday night and then bake it all Saturday and bring it over before the party. How does that sound?"

"Perfect!"

Abbey had been working in silence all morning. Nick hadn't been up to see her at all, and she'd finished sliding all the new furniture to the center of the room and covering it with plastic so the painters she'd called could change the color of this room. Right now, it was a boring white but there was a fireplace in this bedroom with the most beautiful gray in the marbling surrounding it, and she'd found a matching gray paint and scheduled a painting company to come. They were coming tomorrow which meant she was right on time. She looked at her watch—five o'clock. *Perfect*, she thought. *Just enough time to get to the store for Adrienne and home to see Max.* As she headed downstairs, she ran into Nick.

"I spoke with my grandmother," he said. "She wanted to make sure you were being taken care of. I assured her that you were. In light of that fact, I took the liberty of ordering you dinner. I figured it was a little late for you to cook it. Maybe we can plan that over our meal." He smiled.

She'd forgotten about their little bet, but of course he hadn't. She was supposed to cook him dinner but they'd gone out the last time. Any other night she would've loved the gesture.

"I can't," she said. She didn't want to feel disappointed but she did.

She tried to shake the feeling she was having. She hadn't seen him all day. He'd warned her that he was going to focus on work. She needed to get used to it. The Nick she'd had seen those few times—the one who stopped everything just to be with her, the one she could easily persuade to spend time with her—he wasn't what she was going to get if she lived with him, so she might as well get her head around the idea that things would be different. He wouldn't be following her around the house, listening to her blab about her decoration choices. But now, he'd had dinner made. Had he planned to eat with her?

"My friend's having a party tomorrow night and her caterer canceled. I have to help her make food and I need to go shopping," she explained.

"Oh. That's no problem. Would you like me to arrange to have a caterer for her?"

"No… You don't need to intervene." Any caterer he hired had probably never set foot in a party like the kind Adrienne was throwing. Crème brûlée wouldn't complement the annual red and green Jell-O shooters.

"But don't you need a caterer?"

"If you want to help, you could help me do the cooking." She was only kidding but she could see he was considering it.

"Why would we cook when we clearly aren't as qualified as caterers?"

"To show that we care."

He looked at her as if her comment was the most ridiculous thing he'd heard.

"How would you show someone that you care if you didn't have your money to fall back on?" she asked.

He stared at her. He didn't have an answer. She didn't have time to help him understand. She needed to go, but the problem was now he'd had food cooked for her. She could smell it and it made her tummy rumble.

She struggled for a way to make everyone happy. She had to somehow not waste Nick's dinner he'd had made, shop for Adrienne, relieve her mother, and spend time with Max—all before cooking for the party.

"Come with me," she said in desperation. Her mouth dried out before the words had left her lips. *What are you saying?* she immediately thought. *You shouldn't be asking this.* "Box up our dinners. I'll share mine with Max." *Max will be delighted.* "We can eat at my apartment." *I haven't cleaned…*

That curiosity that she'd seen before was all over his face. "I'll get our coats."

She couldn't help the rush of excitement. Despite their conversation earlier, she could still distract him. She didn't have time to ponder the consequences.

It had only taken a few minutes, and she found herself being let in to her own car by Nick, their dinners in his hand. She slid inside and eyed the old stray receipts and a tube of lip-gloss on the passenger seat. Quickly, she scooped them up and stuffed them into her handbag. Nick got in, fastened his seatbelt, and set the large brown paper bag of dinner on his lap. The smell of it was so rich and strong that her stomach growled again.

They drove quietly, the two of them eyeing each other as they made their way to her apartment. Once, they'd glanced over at each other at the same time, and he'd smiled at her, sending her stomach flipping.

When they arrived at her apartment, Nick got out and followed her toward the stairs.

Before they could get up the steps to her door, she saw Max peeking through the blinds. Then, the door swung open and Max came running down the stairs toward them. "Hi, Mama!" he called just before breaking into a bigger grin. "Hi, Nick!"

"Max," Abbey giggled. "Go back inside. You're barefoot!"

"What do you have in that bag, Nick?" he asked as they met him on the stairs and Abbey ushered him toward the warmth of the apartment, his hand skipping over the red velvet Christmas bows on the railing as he held on for support in his bare feet. Max walked beside Nick.

"Dinner. Do you like spaghetti?"

Max nodded.

"It's like fancy spaghetti."

Noticing the uncertainty in Max's eyes, Abbey said with a grin, "I have chicken nuggets we can heat up if you don't like it." Max was a somewhat picky eater, and she wasn't at all that sure he would give Nick's dinner a try.

When they opened the door, Abbey's mom was busy wiping down counters, looking out of breath, and Abbey wondered if she, too, had peeked outside. It warmed Abbey that her mom would try so hard to make her apartment look presentable. Her mom smiled, tossing the rag behind her back.

"Hello again," she said, nodding in a way that made her look like she was in the presence of royalty. Abbey chewed on a grin.

"Hello, Leanne," he said with a charming smile, and Abbey could tell he was trying to put her at ease. Nick set the bag down on the counter separating the small living area from the kitchenette.

"Well, I have to be going," her mom said. "Your grandpa's alone at home with no one to keep him company."

"It was nice to see you again," Nick said as her mom grabbed her bag off the sofa and shuffled over to the door like she was imposing.

"Same here." She eyed Abbey, giving her the oh-my-goodness look. She was asking with her silence what in the world he was doing back at the apartment again. Abbey knew what her mom was probably thinking. She was thinking there was something going on between them.

Abbey told her "thank you" and her mom let herself out with a nervous wave.

Max went to the kitchen sink and washed his hands for dinner. "Nick, can you get the soap, for me please? I can't reach it," he said.

Why was he asking Nick? Abbey was closer and he always asked her. She normally was conditioned to just pull the soap forward for him, but with Nick being there, she'd been a little sidetracked. Dutifully, Nick walked over and handed him the bottle. He shrugged off his coat, draping it on the chair in the small breakfast nook and rolled up the sleeves of his impeccably pressed shirt. Looking down at her son with a smile, Nick put his hands under the stream of water and washed beside Max.

Abbey knew why Max liked Nick so much. He was attentive, polite, and interesting. Max hadn't ever had a man around the house before. He hadn't witnessed a masculine presence. Even as they washed together, his movements, his stance—it was different than having a female around. So many times, Max had probably watched those fathers at his school, the men at church, or the coaches on his team and wondered what it was like to have a man in the house. Abbey wondered if Max looked at Nick and thought, "Finally, someone like me." For whatever reason, Max looked up to him.

"Nick," she heard her son say. "Will you come to school with me?"

Oh my God, Abbey thought. She was going to have a heart attack right then and there. This would put Nick in an uncomfortable position. Abbey knew he had work demands, and Max's Daddy Day was during a workday.

Nick looked down at him again, ripping off a paper towel and handing it to him, then getting one for himself. Nick looked as though he had questions, but his expression was gentle for Max's benefit. She could hardly stand to see him look at Max that way. It made her like him too much.

"We have 'Bring Your Daddy Day' at school, and I don't have a daddy to take."

Nick's expression had changed. It was an understanding, caring expression. Was he sympathetic toward him? What in the world was he going to say?

Nick squatted down so that he could be eye level with Max, his wrinkle-free trousers creasing at the backs of the knees. "I'd love to go," he said, and before Abbey could process what was going on, Max had wrapped his arms around Nick and was hugging him in thanks.

After Christmas, Nick would be gone from their lives. And Max would miss him. She knew he would, because she herself had already thought about missing him.

She'd always thought that she could provide all the love Max needed, but did he long for someone else like Nick in his life? She'd played soccer with him outside, built racecar tracks out of cardboard, all kinds of things. Was it not the same?

Nick stood up, grabbing the dinner bag. "If it's okay with your mom, I'll get her to tell me when it is, and I promise I'll be there." When he looked at Abbey again, she smiled to hide her thoughts. He pulled the bag open. "Are you hungry? Let's eat."

Chapter Fourteen

Max had spent most of the dinner talking to Nick. Abbey had eaten in near silence, still worried about her son. Nick talked to Max about their move into his home, which only sent her further into her thoughts. As she watched his caring smiles, the way he listened as Max was talking, it made her feel as though all of this could be real somehow. She caught herself wishing that Nick could be there every night, talking to them, watching over them. She felt safe having him there, and happy to see how Max reacted to him. She knew, without a doubt, that after Christmas she would certainly miss Nick, so it was only natural that Max would too.

Abbey had not only seen Nick, but she'd watched Max, too, from across the table. He'd even tried the linguini with roasted vegetables that Nick had brought. He would never have tried that for her. Max had talked more than she'd ever seen him talk. Max asked Nick about his job, what it was like to ride a horse when he played polo, his "fancy" cars, and she realized that those were all subjects that she wouldn't have anticipated would interest Max, and also subjects that she couldn't discuss at length because she didn't have the answers he craved.

He was still talking to Nick after dinner, as they drove in her car to the grocery store to get the supplies for Adrienne's party.

"Are you okay?" Nick asked.

She looked at Max in the rearview mirror and then back at Nick. He seemed to be waiting for her answer.

"I'm fine," she said with a smile.

Nick nodded, but his eyes remained on her for a few seconds longer before Max pulled his attention away with more questions.

They parked the car in front of a pile of slush, left from the earlier snowfall. The big storm was still holding off, and Abbey was glad for that because she hadn't bought new tires in a while, and she didn't want to slip and slide on the roads. It was bad enough already. What had fallen previously had frozen, sheeting everything in an icy glaze. And now, they were predicting an upwards of ten inches of snow. The only problem with the storm holding off was that the grocery store was a madhouse. There were people everywhere, their carts full of food, anticipating the closed roads and slippery highways. Whenever there was a storm of this magnitude, it took days before the plows could clear the roads, so everyone had to stock up on essentials.

Abbey turned around as Nick was helping Max out of the car. She stepped up next to them and they walked past the rows of bundled Christmas trees lined up against the wall and into the store. She got a cart and led them to the produce section to get what she needed for her recipes.

They'd picked out an onion, a green pepper, and a lemon when Max said, "I have to go to the bathroom."

She spun around quickly to ensure that he didn't look at Nick for help. That would put Nick in a very awkward position, and she honestly didn't know if he'd suggest that she take him or not.

"I'll take you," she said, swinging her handbag into the top basket of the cart, her cell phone and lipstick flying out of it and hitting the floor. She bent down to retrieve the fallen items and dumped them on top of her handbag along with the shopping list. "Could you stay with the cart for a second, please?" she asked Nick. "The bathrooms are over there."

"Certainly." Nick walked around to the front of the cart and stood. Abbey ran off with Max, weaving through the crowd.

It took ages just to get to the bathrooms. When they did, Max shut himself in a stall and it was taking him forever.

She took a minute to look at herself in the mirror, and she played with her hair a little under the harsh fluorescent lights to try to keep the frizz from showing too much. Leaning forward, she had a good look at her face. With her fingers, she wiped a little runaway mascara from below her eyes. She turned away from her image just as Max opened the door.

"Done!" he said, and he came out. She helped him wash his hands.

When she and Max came back, Nick was standing at the cart, a smile playing at his lips. Abbey gave him a suspicious look and waited for an explanation.

"I got almost everything that was on your list," he said, still smiling. Why was he looking at her that way? He held up her phone. "Your friend, Adrienne, says you can bring a date tomorrow." He turned it around so she could see the messages that had floated onto her screen. To her horror, there were a few more that she couldn't read because he was holding the phone too far away. She swiped at it, and he playfully held it out of reach—only briefly though, and then he held it out to her.

When she read the messages on her screen, embarrassment hit her face like a bolt of lightning. She read them one after another:

Don't forget you can bring a date tomorrow.
Bring the hottie millionaire! I dare you!
I'll bet you wouldn't ask him anyway.

"So," he said, still smiling playfully at her. "Who's the 'hottie millionaire' you're hanging out with?"

He was baiting her, and he knew it. He knew that there weren't any other millionaires in her circles. She stood mute for a moment, already thinking of ways to torture Adrienne when she saw her tomorrow. He leaned in for an answer and she focused on his gorgeous eyes.

"You know," she said. "Just someone I met at the… furniture store…"

"Mmm," he said, nodding.

"Millionaires have to shop at furniture stores too, you know," she teased, her heart pounding a hundred miles an hour at the sight of the affection on his face.

"Not the ones I know. We hire beautiful ladies to do it for us. What kind of millionaire is this?"

She tried to hold in her laugh but it came out anyway. "Clearly a hot one," she said through her giggles. "…according to my friend, Adrienne."

"How would she know unless you told her?"

"I can't help it if I find millionaires who shop at furniture stores attractive."

"Then I'd better find one quickly," he said, looking around. "What do I still need? A new desk...?"

She laughed again.

"So, are you going to take him to the party?"

"He wouldn't want to go," she said.

"Says who?"

"Me. I know him too well," she said, trying not to give away her growing fondness for him. "He will probably be working. I wouldn't want to distract him," she said with a sly smile. "Now do we have everything we need?" She didn't want to admit to him that, even if he agreed to go with her, Adrienne had only been kidding, and if she actually showed up with Nick, her friend would probably die of nerves trying to entertain him. But the way he was looking at her was making her think that he wanted to go with her. Max was waving his hand under the lights of the vegetable shelves, trying to turn the little misting sprinklers on. "I think they're on a timer," Abbey told him, trying to divert Nick's attention.

"Are you worried I won't enjoy myself?"

She thought about what it might be like to be with a bunch of very rich people, eating food she didn't recognize, talking about things she'd never experienced in her life, and then imagined it the other way around.

"Yes," she answered honestly.

"Why?"

"I'm afraid you won't have anything in common with them." She began pushing the cart toward the bread aisle to get the few remaining items that weren't on her list. Max jumped on the back of the cart, taking a ride.

"You and I don't have a *whole* lot in common—apart from the fact that we both play piano, mind you—and I enjoy being with *you*." She remembered the day that she'd played "Chopsticks." It seemed like ages ago.

He'd been kidding just now, but one fact hung in the air between them. He'd admitted to enjoying being with her. He must. Why else would he be hanging out at the grocery store with her and her son? She reached the shelf with the dried stuffing and grabbed a bag. Didn't he realize what he was doing? He'd said he didn't want to get her hopes up but he was.

He'd flat told her that he didn't want the kind of future she wanted and she wasn't in any position to play games. He had to be careful about the relationships he was building because, if he didn't want a family, eventually, he'd let them down.

"I'm not trying to persuade you," he said. "I'm not going to invite myself. I'd never put you in that position. I'm only kidding with you."

She smiled.

She still hadn't given him an answer when they'd checked out, and it was clear that Nick knew there was a reason. She was falling for him, and it scared her to death. He pushed the cart full of bags while Abbey grabbed Max's hand. The ice had gotten really bad since the sun had gone down, the air so frigid that it made her skin hurt. She picked up the pace to get Max back into the heat of the car.

The car ride was quiet, Max clearly getting tired. Abbey had a lot on her mind. She had a millionaire in her old, dirty car, and he was coming to her apartment. He hadn't followed her in his car. How was he planning to get home? Would someone come and get him? He surely wouldn't plan on staying. She didn't have a guest room…

It took Abbey a minute to register what she was seeing once they pulled up at her apartment and parked. Nick had gotten out of the car and was standing outside, a ton of grocery bags in each hand. Max was standing beside her, looking up at the building with her. Before she could say anything, her neighbor, an elderly woman named Ms. Johnson, came out with a small suitcase.

"There's no power," Ms. Johnson said. "It went out a while ago—the ice got to the power lines—and it's freezing inside with no heat. With the big storm coming, I wonder how long it will take them to fix it. The newsman said it could be up to a week." She shook her head. "I'm going to my daughter's house for the time being."

Abbey was unsure of what to do next. She had all the food for Adrienne's party that would have to be refrigerated, and now, her refrigerator wasn't working; she had electric heat in the apartment, so that meant no heat; it was dark outside—no lights. She wondered if her mom had enough room in her fridge for all the food. She and Max could sleep in her old bedroom.

She turned to Nick who was typing like crazy on his phone. "Richard will be here in less than five minutes," he said, still looking at his phone. "He's in the area running errands anyway. Tonight's his late work night." Nick read what looked like an incoming message and then typed again. Finally, he looked up. "We can put all of this in my refrigerators at home. You and Max are welcome to stay at my house if you'd like until the power comes back on. You might as well pack a large suitcase for the both of you and we can move Caroline tomorrow. There's a large flashlight in the trunk of my car. We can use it to pack you up once Richard gets here."

A shiny black Lincoln town car pulled up, and Abbey spotted Richard in the driver's seat. He must have been closer than he thought. Ms. Johnson, who had been opening the door to her own car, stood gawking at the Lincoln, not bothering to realize that she'd stopped still, her mouth slightly open, her eyes roaming the gleaming surface of it. Abbey looked back at Nick. She thought about all those bedrooms, the fresh, clean linens, the space. At her mom's, they'd be tight. She probably didn't have room in her small refrigerator for all of the things that Abbey had bought. Staying at Nick's would be easier.

"Can we stay at Nick's, Mama? Please?" Max asked, his eyes pleading.

Abbey looked up at Nick. He had curiosity on his face again. "I suppose so," she said.

Richard put the window down as Nick approached the car. "Would you wait here a few minutes please, Richard? I'm going to go inside with Abbey and help her pack. Keep the car running," he said as he popped the trunk and grabbed the flashlight. He put the groceries in the trunk. "The food back here will go in one of the refrigerators in the kitchen when we get home. And have a few of the guys get coolers out of storage and pack up Abbey's refrigerator and freezer in her apartment for her. I'll have her leave you a key."

I can't believe this is happening, Abbey said to herself while they climbed the stairs. What in the world would she and Max do all night in that huge house with barely enough time to think through her packing? Would Nick feel like he had to entertain them? Would she feel guilty pulling him away from his work again? She felt uneasy at the thought as she fumbled to unlock her door in the dark.

Chapter Fifteen

By the time they'd packed, arrived at Nick's house, gotten in and settled, and she'd given Richard her key to the apartment, it was after eight o'clock, and Max was really tired. She'd tucked him in to bed upstairs in the bedroom that she'd decorated with the framed picture, and met Nick back downstairs.

"Is he asleep already?" Nick asked.

"Yes. He must have been exhausted."

They stood together in the open entryway, the silence of the night surrounding them. The staff had all gone home, and there was no one else there.

"You were quiet tonight. Would you like to tell me what's been bothering you?" he asked.

"Let's go into the ballroom and sit," she said. She started toward the ballroom and he followed.

He sat down beside her and turned toward her, concern on his face.

"You've been spending time with both of us—me and Max, and I really like having you around."

"Then what's the problem?"

"You're going to Daddy Day for Max," she said. "It just makes me worry. He likes you."

"It worries you when I reach out?" he said.

Abbey sighed, wondering if she was making too big of a deal out of things. "None of this is your fault. It's my problem. I'm just protective of Max."

He looked at her for a long while and she waited with anticipation for what he had to say. "What are you afraid of?"

Her nervous energy was getting the better of her. She didn't want to say it. She got up and walked over to the piano and tapped a few keys. He followed and sat down beside her. She looked up at the mistletoe above them but his eyes were on the keys and he hadn't noticed. Her fears were mounting and she didn't want to say what she was going to have to tell him.

"I'm afraid he'll fall head over heels for you, and he'll have to experience what it's like to not receive that affection in return." She was speaking about Max, but thinking, too, about herself. "I feel like things are moving quickly. He's just asked you to do something very personal—his Daddy Day at school—and you've accepted. I don't want to take things this far without any promise that they'll continue."

Nick's face dropped in contemplation, and he put his hands on her arms, rubbing back and forth to try to soothe her. "I'm sorry," he said in a quiet whisper. "I was just excited. You forget that for a while now I've been by myself too. I'm not used to having to think of others before I make decisions. I just said yes because he asked me and I didn't mind going. But he's your son. I should've put him off until I spoke with you. I promise to do that next time."

"Thank you," she said, relieved and interested at the same time. *Next time?*

"Can I get you anything? A glass of wine?"

"That sounds nice." She took in a deep breath to settle herself. "And I still have to make the casserole and pinwheels for Adrienne's party."

"I'll help. Let me show you where the ingredients are."

He led her down the hallway to the kitchen, which she'd seen but not spent much time in. She entered the room and was floored by the number of cabinets that ran along two of the walls. There were so many that they almost looked like walls of paneling. Nick opened one that stretched nearly to the ceiling, and to her surprise, hidden behind the cabinetry was a refrigerator.

"Your cold items are in here," he said, shutting the cabinet. There were so many that she hoped she could remember which one it was. He opened another cabinet. "Your other things are here." He closed the door. "Let me get you that glass of wine."

She tried to see if she could find any trace of obligation in his face but all she could see was kindness. "Thank you," she said.

"Is red okay?"

"Yes." She watched him retrieve a bottle from the wine cooler and uncork it. He pulled two glasses down from the cabinet, filled them over halfway full, and handed one to her.

"So," he said before taking a quick sip of his and setting it down on the gigantic marble countertop. "What are we making tonight?"

"Sausage casserole and pinwheels," she said smiling.

"I've never had either."

"And you'd like to help me cook?" She had no idea if he was just being polite, what plans he had for the night, or if he had work to do, but since he was standing in the kitchen with her, drinking a glass of wine, she figured it was probably okay.

"Definitely." He took another drink of wine and then unbuttoned the cuffs of his sleeves. He rolled them up just under his elbows and turned on the water at the sink. It was more than a sink. It was a huge basin made of some sort of ceramic or porcelain—she wasn't sure. It was bright and shiny, the faucet a gleaming silver. She set down her wine and joined him.

"You know, this room could do with some decorating too," she said, looking around as she washed her hands. "Maybe put some fresh flowers here on this ledge. Hang some greenery along that doorway for Christmas…"

"It's fine," he said with a smile.

Toweling off her hands, she opened the refrigerator and pulled out the vegetables. "I'll need a knife and a cutting board," she said. "You might actually do something other than work if you had your home the way you like it." She grinned at him to let him know that while she was serious, her comment was lighthearted. "If there was no work at all, what would you do? Read? Watch sports? What?"

As Nick retrieved her supplies, she rinsed the onion under the water and shook it off.

"I'd probably…" He fell silent.

She waited, hoping he'd come up with something. "You don't know?"

"It isn't a reality. I'll always have work, so it doesn't matter."

"We're going to need to dice this onion." She chopped the ends off and set them aside. Then, she began to cut large rounds of onion, her knife rocking back and forth over the rounds to dice them up. Her eyes were stinging, starting to tear up, and her nose was getting sniffly. "Sorry. I get like this when I have to chop them."

Nick handed her a tissue from a silver container. She wiped her eyes.

"Let me give you a break," he said, walking around the counter and standing beside her. "What's next?" He handed her wine to her.

"We need to brown the sausage," she said. "And we haven't finished discussing what you would do if you weren't working." Being with him like this felt natural for her.

"I'd... play piano, I suppose. I haven't thought about playing piano in a long time. Not until you came." He got out a stainless steel skillet and a spatula. "These okay?" He was smiling, his expression and her exhaustion making the wine go to her head faster than it should.

"Perfect."

He put the skillet on one of the eight burners he had on his stove—the giant trapezoid-shaped hood on top of it was probably the size of her car. She retrieved the sausage and handed it to him. With a sizzle, it began to cook in the pan the minute he put it in.

"The house is coming along nicely," he said, stirring the meat in the pan. The spicy smell of it saturated the air around them. Watching him cook, she'd never know that he had people who prepared meals for him. He looked like he'd handled a pan and spatula before. "What's left on your decorating list?" He wiped his hands on a kitchen towel and turned to face her.

"Well, I have painters for one of the bedrooms coming tomorrow. I have to finish the exterior. I'm planning to put some white lights outside. There's the informal living room, and then the bathrooms and hallways. I also have to make sure the bar in the ballroom gets finished and is all set up for your party... You know how to cook," she pointed out.

"Yes." He looked at her, perplexed.

"I didn't know you could, since you have someone cook all your meals."

"Oh. That's just because I'm busy. I don't have time to cook."

"But you are now."

"Like I said. You distract me." He grinned at her.

"Well, maybe that's because talking to me and cooking are more fun than working. Maybe I don't distract you, I just shift your focus."

"The work won't get done by itself," he pointed out.

"But it also doesn't need to be done right now, does it? It's late."

The ground sausage behind Nick popped and he turned around, picking up the spatula and stirring it. His back was to her, so she couldn't see his face, but she wanted to see it. He stirred in silence until, finally, he set the heat to low and put down the spatula. Then, he turned around, his face serious but gentle.

"Sarah didn't want me to work and she wanted children from the minute I met her," he said. His words were more careful than they usually were. It was clear he was choosing what he said very cautiously. "Do you want to have more children?" he asked, out of the blue.

"Um… Yes. I do. I want lots of kids. But only if I find the right person and we have them together. I don't want to raise them all by myself. Raising Max is hard enough sometimes."

Nick nodded, his face full of unsaid thoughts. "I know what you mean about finding the right person. Sarah wasn't the right person for me, and it's a lonely, guilty existence when you're with someone who wants different things. I'm never going to have kids and that's just the way it is. But she's moved on, and she has her family now, so she's happy."

Abbey had heard the rest of what he'd said, but one particular statement had nearly knocked her backwards even though she'd heard it before: *I'm never going to have kids and that's just the way it is.* Even though she knew that she couldn't change him, she wished that she could.

"Never?" she asked. "You seem very sure that you're never going to have kids."

"I am sure."

"How do you know? You don't like children?"

"It isn't that."

"I know it isn't. I've seen you with Max." She moved closer to him. "Last year, I got the flu. I was so sick I could hardly move. Max, only five years old, rubbed my back for a whole hour until he fell asleep. I dozed off too, and when I woke up, he'd taken his blanket and left to go to bed for the night, but before he'd left, he'd placed a box of tissues next to me. He was only five, but he'd learned that when people need us, we should take care of them. That's what we do for people we care about. Who will take care of you when you have the flu? Certainly not your work."

He didn't answer but his eyes were unstill as he looked down at the counter. Would he ever understand? They were drinking wine, cooking together, acting like two normal people do when they enjoy each other, but would it ever work between them? Sarah hadn't changed his mind. Who was Abbey to think she could?

"It's not as easy as you make it seem," he said, finally. "My father tried to do both and he failed. I don't do well with failure. I almost fell prey to that same life, but I managed to escape it. The protectiveness you feel for Max—I'd feel that for my own child, and I couldn't live with myself knowing that kind of guilt when I had to put in the hours that I do. The only way to make the kind of money I do and have this amount of success is to work at it. Corporations don't sell themselves. And if I'm not there, someone else is, and sales will get lost. In this market, people don't work nine to five. They work around the clock. I can't let my father's business fail."

"You are very loyal to your father."

He nodded.

"What's your favorite memory of him?"

Nick smiled and took a sip of his wine before answering. "I was probably four or five. We went sailing one evening on Martha's Vineyard. It was chilly, and we all had to wear jackets, but the sun was so bright. I remember my dad wearing sunglasses. I hadn't seen him wear them before. He rarely took vacations with us, so this was a treat. We sailed out and anchored in the water. We ate dinner on the Nantucket Sound that night—grilled lamb chops. As the sun went down on the water, its reflection turned the ripples bright orange, and the water looked like it was on fire. I remember, because it got colder after the sun went down, and I thought to myself how it should be warmer with all that orange so close to us. My father wrapped us all up in quilts that he'd bought for my mother in town, and I remember her, all bundled in one, scolding him gently about them getting dirty on the boat. He teased her about letting her children freeze for the sake of the quilts and she relented with a huff. He bought her new ones the next day and we kept the ones we'd used on the boat. We used them every time after that."

"That's a beautiful memory," she said.

"Yes."

"Aren't you worried that you'll look back on your life and have no more memories like that one? You make all this money and have all this success but you never get to enjoy it."

"I enjoy the thrill of the success."

"That's a rehearsed response."

"It may be. But it's my answer. For that one memory, I have a ton of others where my father wasn't there for me. I'm not putting anyone else in that position."

She couldn't argue with that. "Let's just cover this and put what we've done so far in the fridge. I can do the rest tomorrow morning," she said.

"Are you sure? You don't want to do anymore prep work tonight?"

"No," she said, feeling even more exhausted, given the way the conversation had turned. There was no sense in discussing it any further. Things weren't going to change, no matter how much she liked him. "I'm tired. I'd like to turn in."

Abbey opened her eyes. White light poured through the windows. She looked over at Max. He was still asleep. She'd climbed into bed with him after cleaning up her prep work in the kitchen last night with Nick. What Nick had said about children bothered her so much, even though she'd known it all along. It had made her toss and turn during the night, and now her eyes burned from lack of sleep.

She got up and walked across the room to the window. To her complete dismay, she took in the view. The storm had hit overnight. Snow was covering the grounds. She couldn't even see where the drive was—it was nothing but a blanket of white. Her car was gone. She had parked it in the loop outside the front door, but it wasn't there now. She was hoping to slip out with Max and take him to school, but now she was certain that school would be canceled due to the road conditions—it always was with snowstorms like this. Abbey grabbed her phone to see what time it was, and when she did, she saw Adrienne's text: *The streets are so bad that nobody can get down them. I tried to run to the store this morning, and I had to turn around and go back home. I'm going to cancel the party. I hope you haven't bought the food yet.*

Abbey squeezed her eyes shut, the sting returning. Max didn't eat pinwheels, so she'd be eating those for the next week, and Nick had made so much sausage last night that they'd have to eat her sausage casserole for dinner every night for the next week. Not to mention, if the streets were that bad, how was she going to get home to pack her things properly when she did find her car? Abbey slipped into the bathroom to get ready for the day.

A call lit up on her screen and she answered it quietly so as not to wake Max. She shut the bathroom door. The painters couldn't come due to the snow and their next availability was three weeks out. That wouldn't work. She accepted their apologies—it wasn't their fault— and tiptoed back into the bedroom to look at her decorating timeline. She shook her head. That room had to be painted. It looked awful in all white and if she didn't paint it, none of the bedding would work. It would look dreary next to that bright white. She thought about calling more painters, but she knew she'd have trouble finding someone in this weather.

When she was finished getting ready, Max was still sleeping. She'd tried a few more painters while she was in the bathroom, and just as she suspected, they either weren't able to fit her in or they couldn't get out to do the job because of the snow. Abbey decided that if she wanted it done, she was going to have to do it herself. It would put her behind, but she had no other options. She'd painted before, and she could do a good job, but her hand wasn't very steady, and she needed to line all the woodwork with tape to keep her paint lines straight. Abbey dug through her handbag for a scrap piece of paper and a pen. She wrote in her simplest words so Max could read them, *I'll be back. I'm going to find Nick.* She put the paper on the nightstand next to Max, and then headed out to find Nick.

On her way downstairs, she ran into Richard.

"Good morning," she said. "Do you know where I can find Nick?"

"He's working."

"Okay. In his office?"

"He's asked not to be disturbed."

"Well, I need my car. Do you know where it is?"

"Ah, yes. We still had your keys so Nick had us pull it into the garage in case the snowstorm hit. Good choice, since it did."

"How do I get to the garage?"

"Ms. Fuller, I'm so sorry, but there's no way just yet that we can get your car out. The snow is too high. We have the groundsmen working on it, though. They've got the plow up and running."

She nodded, feeling helpless.

"In the meantime, would you like any breakfast?"

She shook her head.

She knew there was nothing Nick could do about the situation, but she found herself wanting to talk to him anyway. He'd helped her when her car wouldn't start, and he'd made sure all her food didn't spoil when she'd lost power. He was good at taking care of her, and she was not only attracted to him, but to his caring nature. She didn't want to get hurt, but she knew that, inevitably, she would. She decided to leave him to his work.

"I'll go up and check on Max and we'll come down to the dining room. Does that sound okay?" she asked Richard.

"I'll have something ready in about twenty minutes."

"I need some painter's tape. Is there any in the house?"

"I'm nearly certain the groundsmen have some. I'll check for you. Does your son like eggs and bacon?"

"Yes. He likes scrambled eggs."

"Scrambled eggs it is then."

"Thank you," she said. Abbey headed back up the steps and rounded the corner to the room where Max was sleeping. When she peeked in, he was sitting up, looking around.

"Good morning," she said, walking in.

Max rubbed his eyes, his hair pressed upward in the back.

"Did you sleep well?"

"Mmm hmm." Max was clearly still swimming out of his sleep. He fell back down into the fluffy bedding. "This is the best bed ever," he said, his voice muffled by the pillow.

Abbey smiled and crawled back up under the covers with him.

"I love it here," Max said.

She knew why he loved it there. It was the most amazing place he'd ever been. It was the most amazing place *she'd* ever been.

"Are you hungry? They're making breakfast for us downstairs."

"Is Nick making breakfast?"

"No," she said. "He's working today. Nick has somebody who cooks for him." Abbey wondered about the elusive cook who'd made her all those wonderful meals. She'd never even met the person before. The staff had all stayed hidden for the most part, and she hadn't really seen anyone other than Richard since she'd arrived. Was that how Nick wanted them—out of sight?

"Will we get to see him?"

"I don't think so." She worried about what Max would do all day if they were stuck there and couldn't leave. How would she ever entertain him while painting an entire room? She'd have to at least spend some time with him this morning. Perhaps they could play in the snow and then he could help her paint. "How about if, after breakfast, you and I make a snowman—the biggest one we've ever made?"

"Yeah!" Max jumped out of bed and ran into the bathroom to get ready.

There had been no sign of Nick during their breakfast, and Abbey had felt odd having the staff wait on her when she didn't live there or pay their salaries. To her relief Richard had come in to tell her they had a ton of painter's tape. When he had, he very kindly brought her the most perfect carrot and two olives on a plate after she'd mentioned making the snowman. "It's all I could find," he'd said with a smile.

"We have to pack the snow really well before we start rolling the snowball," Abbey said, the snow sliding down into her shoes. She hadn't come prepared to play in the snow, but Max had worn his boots yesterday, so he had them today, and his feet were nice and toasty. That was all that mattered.

"Like this?" he said, holding a very small ball of snow in his hands.

"Yep. Just like that." Luckily, it was the perfect kind of snow for snowman making. Abbey had made a ball too, and she placed it on the ground and began to roll it, modeling for Max how to do it. They rolled and rolled, her fingers feeling the chill of the snow through her thin gloves. When they finally stopped, they each had quite a snowball. Together, they rolled one more.

"Now how are we gonna get yours on top of mine?" Max asked, laughing at their creations. His cheeks were pink from the cold, and Abbey couldn't help but think how adorable he looked.

She tried to pick up her snowball. She could hardly get her arms around it, it was so big. She lifted with all her might. It didn't move.

"It's too big," Max said.

Abbey moved around the other side of the ball to see if she could get more leverage. When she did, she saw one of the windows, its yellow light glowing against the white sky and falling snow. She could make out a shadow, and she knew who it was by the build of the man. Nick was sitting at his desk, his head angled downward; he was typing something. Did he know they were right outside his window?

She put her arms around the ball and tried again. It wouldn't budge.

"You can do it, Mama!" Max cried. He was clapping and jumping, his navy blue cap sliding down over his eyes. He pushed it back with a mittened hand, snowflakes sticking to the yarn of his hat.

"We should get Nick! He could lift it!"

"He's working. We probably shouldn't disturb him."

"But he hasn't gotten to play in the snow at all."

Abbey smiled. "I think he was probably up before us. If he'd wanted to, he most likely would've played in the snow already before we were even out here."

"No he wouldn't."

Abbey looked down at him. "Why do you think he wouldn't?"

"He'd be by himself. It's hard when you're by yourself," Max said. "When I'm at Nana's, I don't play in the snow very much because no one is out there to play with me. I'll bet Nick feels like that. We should tell him we want to play with him."

Abbey felt a stab of sadness for her son. It was tough being an only child. She wanted to be able to fix it, to give him friends nearby and siblings in the house, but she just couldn't. She felt sad because she knew that it was Max who wanted someone new to play with. That was why he'd suggested calling Nick.

"Can we text him?"

Despite her reservations, Abbey pulled her phone from her back pocket. What would one morning in the snow hurt? She typed: *Max and I are trying to build a snowman, and Max wants you to help build it. Would you like to take a break, by chance? If not, I completely understand. I know you have work to do. But if so, it's freezing. Dress warm.*

Her phone lit up and she couldn't stop the smile from spreading across her face. She read, *Give me two minutes.*

"The snowman's gonna need buttons," Max said.

"Maybe we could use rocks."

Max ran off, the enormous grounds nearly swallowing him right up, and searched for rocks. Abbey watched him bend down, dig under the snow until he found one, inspect it, and then throw it on the ground. He did this a few times until she saw him put one in his pocket. When he had three, he returned. But as he neared her, a giant smile broke out on his face and he walked past her. She turned around.

Nick was standing in the snow, wearing some kind of large hiking boots, jeans, a dark coat, and leather gloves. Dangling from his fingers in his gloved hand was a black top hat. She'd only ever seen one in the movies.

"Where did you get that?" she said with a grin.

Max ran up to him and eyed it as he held it up into view. "It was for a costume party," Nick said as his icy blue eyes met hers. "I thought Mr. Snowman might get cold without it." He set it on Max's head.

"We can't get the snowballs stacked," Max said, still wearing it over his stocking cap.

Nick looked at the enormous balls of snow. "That's quite a snow-ball," he said.

Max puffed his little chest out in pride.

Nick leaned down and hugged the snowball, bending his knees in anticipation of the weight of it. With relative ease, he lifted it, but it was big enough to block his line of sight so Abbey stepped in.

As he hovered over the other snowball, she said, "Move just a little to the left."

Nick swayed left.

"No. Too much!"

He moved right.

"Left again. There!"

Nick attempted to set the ball down on top of the other one, but with a small misstep, the snowball teetered precariously, ready to roll back onto the snow and possibly break apart.

"Oh no!" Abbey cried and all three of them put their arms around the ball to keep it from falling. When they finally got it steady, Abbey said, "No one let it go. I'm going to pack snow around the base of it to glue it to the snowball below it."

Nick and Max held the ball in place and Abbey grabbed a fistful of snow. She packed it against the base of the snowball until it was steady. As she did, she had to duck under Nick's arms to pack snow on his side. She stole a glance at him, and he was grinning down at her.

"One more to go," she said.

He lifted the smallest ball and set it on top. They put snow around that one, and Abbey pulled her scarf off and wrapped it around the neck of it. Max added rocks as buttons, still wearing the top hat.

"I can't reach to do his face," Max said.

Without even a moment to consider, Nick lifted him up and Abbey had to pull herself together. Max was sitting on Nick's arm, his little legs dangling down against Nick's body, as Nick helped him remove his top hat and place it on the snowman. Anyone looking would think the three of them were a perfect little family when things couldn't be farther from the truth. She caught herself wishing for more time with Nick, and she knew it wasn't right. What he did with his life was up to him, not her.

Abbey handed them the small plate of olives and a carrot, their surfaces now dusted with light snow. Max pressed them into the face of the snowman and then Nick set him back down.

"Look at our snowman!" Max said. They all took a step back to admire it. It was perfect. "I'm so glad you came out to play, Nick!" Max said running around the snowman. "Let's play something else!" He bent down and picked up some snow, rounding it in his mittened hands. "Now, you're in trouble," he said, his little voice teasing him. "I hope you can run fast." Max held up a snowball, aimed at Nick.

Nick's face was swimming with curiosity as he watched Max prepare to throw the snowball. Had Nick ever had a snowball fight? Had he been allowed to run around, chasing his friends outside? There was a *smack!* and Nick's dark coat had an explosion of snow on the arm of it. Max ran away, giggling and gathering more snow.

Abbey worried for Nick, not wanting to put him in an uncomfortable position, but when she looked up at him, he was smiling. He bent down and picked up a handful of snow. When he did, Max went screaming across the yard in anticipation.

"You can't get me!" Max yelled.

Nick, with the lightly packed ball of snow in hand, began jogging toward Max, making Max burst into a fit of giggles. Nick cocked his arm back and released the snow as Max dodged it, falling down and scrambling to get back up, laughing in loud bursts. Max had hidden a ball of snow when he'd fallen and he got Nick right in the chest, surprising them both.

Abbey watched them as they threw snow at each other, bobbing and weaving around trees, Nick laughing loudly, his face lit with the thrill of it, and she couldn't take her eyes off him. Then, suddenly, he stopped. "You know what?" he called out. Max walked from behind a tree to hear. "We're leaving your mother out. I'll bet she wants to play." Nick turned toward her, his fist full of snow.

"You wouldn't," she said, cutting her eyes at him playfully.

His lips were set in a devious grin as he pulled his arm back.

"Run, Mama!" Max said, but Abbey didn't run.

Instead, she picked up a pile of snow and began to pack it gently in her hands, her eyes on Nick. "You don't think I'm going down without a fight, do you?" she said, now armed with her own snowball. Nick grinned at her, sending her stomach into a whirl of exhilaration.

"Are we at a stalemate?"

She raised an eyebrow. "You may be. I'm in attack mode." She pulled back and released her snowball, sending it right into his gut. It exploded in a fan of snow on his coat. Before he could react, she'd already filled her hands with another snowball.

Max stepped up beside Nick, more snow in his hands.

"You can't have backup," she teased, winking at Max.

"Two against one!" Max said through his giggles, and he took off after her, Nick following behind.

Abbey tore off through the property, darting behind as many trees as she could while Nick gained on her, his lengthy stride much bigger than hers. She turned around and beamed a snowball at him, hitting him in the upper arm. He stopped, looked down at it for just a second and then took off after her again. She bent down to scoop up more snow and when she stood up, she gasped as Nick had his arms around her.

"He got you!" Max called, and Nick released her.

She turned around, not making a fuss about his embrace, her game face still on. "No he didn't," she said with a grin. "He still has yet to hit me with a snowball." She offered him a challenging glance. He was too close to her to throw anything at her without hurting, and he couldn't bend down to get more snow. She had him.

But then, with a quick look to Max, he took a step closer and, before she knew it, he had his gloved hands on her face, but they weren't warm. They were freezing because they were full of snow! He smeared it all over her face as she tried to wriggle free.

"I'm going to get more snow!" Max said as he ran off.

"That was dirty!" she laughed, using the back of her arm to wipe the remaining snow off her cheeks. It had given her goose bumps all the way down her arms.

Nick smiled at her as he tried to help her get the snow off her face. This time, he'd pulled his hand out of his glove and it was warm against her skin. Gently, he trailed his fingers down her face to remove the melting snow. She didn't feel cold anymore.

"Look at me!" Max said, breaking them from the moment.

Abbey turned toward the spot where Max was playing. He was on his back, making snow angels.

"I see you!" she called out. "That's a great snow angel!"

"Nick! You do one!" Max yelled over to them.

As if jolted by some invisible force, Nick checked his watch. "I can't, buddy. I'm sorry. I have to go back in."

While Abbey would've liked to have him stay longer, she knew she'd already taken more time from his day than he'd probably like, so she didn't intervene. "Thank you for coming out today," she said, genuinely glad that he had. "It was fun."

"Yes, it was," he said with a smile. Then, with a quick wave to Max, he headed in.

Chapter Sixteen

Richard had started the fire for Abbey and Max in the ballroom. It was odd for her to choose that large room, because originally, she'd felt that no one should have a room that big, but the memory of sitting in front of that fireplace had stuck with her, and the sofas kept drawing her in. Max had put his pajamas back on and was curled up at one end of the two facing sofas with a pile of his books while Abbey attempted to rearrange her decorating timeline. It was going to take her all day just to tape the ceiling of that enormous bedroom, and it had a ton of woodwork to tape around. She felt anxiety creeping in at the thought of one person trying to paint it but she just couldn't leave the room white. It would put her way behind.

All her life, Abbey had dreamed of being an interior designer. Even though she had never had a formal class, it just fit as a career for her. She could do it with ease. The problem she was finding as she looked at the timings was that she needed a team for a house this size. She might have to pull an all-nighter just to get this room painted, and stay relatively on track.

Abbey noticed Max eyeing the grand piano on the other side of the room, and she smiled to herself, remembering the sound of the notes as Nick had played. She remembered the curve of his back, the tilt of his head, the ease in which his hands moved over the keys. She wished he were playing now. She looked around the ballroom at the amazing Christmas trees she'd decorated, the pop and sizzle of the fire, the piano, the mistletoe on giant ribbons—this really was the stuff of fairytales.

She had to remind herself that this wasn't a fairytale. Niggling at the back of her mind was the fact that she kept letting Nick into her life *and* Max's life. It was too easy for him to be involved, and she could feel her resolve to keep things professional slipping.

Abbey had used nearly all the paper in her sketchpad, drawing with Max. They'd played in the snow again, read all his books; Richard had brought a deck of cards and they'd played "Go Fish" and "War". They'd had lunch in the kitchen, they'd walked over to Caroline's for her daily check, they'd played "Hide and Seek", and they'd even tinkered on Nick's piano. In between all those things, she'd been able to tape some of the bedroom off for painting. The ceiling was done, and the fireplace, but she had none of the doorways or crown moldings finished, and she hadn't done the floorboards. The sun was setting, and still, she'd only seen Nick that one time.

When Richard walked past the bedroom where she and Max were reading a book, she grabbed his attention and walked into the hallway.

"Have you seen Nick today?" she asked Richard.

"No, ma'am. His office door has been closed all day."

"Has he eaten? It's dinner time."

"He hasn't requested me, and he's asked to be left alone so I have. The chef isn't coming today, due to the snow, so I would guess he'd have made himself some food, but I haven't seen him."

"I was going to make dinner for myself and Max. I wonder if Nick would like something to eat." She thought about the kindness he'd shown her this morning, and she wanted to repay it. "Would you mind keeping an eye on Max for a few minutes? He's really fine on his own, but if you could just check on him. I won't be long. I just want to offer Nick some dinner."

"I'm sorry, Ms. Fuller. He's asked not to be disturbed. By anyone."

"That's fine. I'll tell him you tried to stop me."

"I wouldn't advise that you interrupt him."

"I won't keep him long."

Richard was still shaking his head, trying to convince Abbey to stay put, but she wanted to check on him.

When she got to his office, she knocked and he called for her to come in. Nick was at his desk, his hand on his forehead for support. He looked up. He had dark scruff on his face, circles under his eyes.

"Have you been sitting here since you left us?" she asked.

Nick nodded and looked back down at some sort of spreadsheet. He rubbed his temple with his fingers.

"Have you eaten at all today?" She searched his desk for empty plates or some indication that he'd been out of that chair. There was nothing.

Nick shook his head, grabbed his calculator, and typed in a few numbers, his attention on his work as if she weren't there. He inhaled, his eyes moving from the calculator screen to the spreadsheet, back and forth. "I've had some bad news about one of my investments, and I really need to be left alone with it. I'm sorry. I'm not trying to be rude, but this requires all my concentration at the moment."

She leaned down into his line of sight.

He looked at her.

"You need to eat something."

"I have to finish this or I'll lose my train of thought. This is more important than eating. I'm about to lose a sale, and if I don't get it…" He shook his head. "There are millions riding on it."

"You're tired. Some good food might help clear your head, and you can look at it with fresh eyes."

"I like being with you and Max—but I have to work."

The doorknob clicked.

"Hi, Nick!" Max was standing in the doorway. He waved and then looked at his mother, his face oblivious to what had just transpired before he'd opened the door. "Mama, I'm hungry. And bored."

"Oh!" she said, wondering where Richard had been, but then realizing that it wasn't his job to watch Max. "Well, I was just going to cook Nick some dinner. He needs to eat, even if it's at his desk," she said as she looked over at him. She could tell he'd heard her, but he didn't look up. "Want to help me?"

"Okay." Max walked over to Nick and put his face right between Nick and his papers. "Are you going to eat with us, Nick? Please?"

Nick looked up at Abbey and then at Max, his face tired but kind. "I have a little more work to do, but I promise I'll eat with you," he said.

"Yay!" Max said, jumping up and down, his little fists in the air. "You're gonna love my mama's cooking. She makes *great* food!"

"And I still owe you a dinner from our bet," she said with a smile.

Nick smiled but it didn't reach his eyes. Then, as they left, he looked back down at the papers on his desk.

It had taken Abbey fifteen minutes to locate all the ingredients she'd need in that big kitchen. Nick had everything she'd ever want to create a meal, and she'd settled on homemade macaroni and cheese, fried chicken, corn on the cob, and the sausage casserole she had because of Adrienne's party. Max had helped Abbey choose what to prepare, and he'd also helped her cook. She took the dishes through the swinging double doors and into the dining room where Max was already waiting. He'd asked Abbey to sit at the end, an empty chair between them, "for Nick," he'd said.

"When's he coming?" Max asked.

"I texted him that dinner was ready about five minutes ago. Let's give him a few more minutes," she said, hoping the food wouldn't get cold.

Max nodded, looking around at the dining room. "Nick's house is fancy," he said.

She smiled at him and nodded. "It is fancy."

"I wonder why he likes things so fancy."

"Probably because he grew up that way and he's used to it."

"The table's a really long way from the kitchen," he noted.

"Yes."

"If I had this house, I'd just put a table in the kitchen."

Abbey smiled again. "That's because that's what *you're* used to. But when you're a man, you certainly can if you want to. When you grow up, are you going to have a house this big?"

Max pursed his lips in thought. "Maybe. Or maybe something middle sized."

"That sounds like a plan."

They sat, talking—just the two of them like they were used to doing—for quite a while, and eventually, Abbey dished up a plate for Max. The food was only lukewarm at this point, and she figured he'd better eat at least. She could always warm hers and Nick's up later.

Max looked disappointed, his eyes fluttering over to the empty chair every so often. He'd been so excited to tell Nick that he'd helped to choose what was for dinner.

"Nick's food is going to be cold," Max said. "He promised he'd eat with us."

Max had never experienced anyone who didn't keep a promise. Nick's absence—whether intentional or not—was upsetting her. This wasn't just about letting her down; it was about letting Max down as well. And while dinner had been her idea, he'd agreed to it. He should've kept his word.

Max finished his dinner, and Abbey tried to keep conversation upbeat, but she was still flustered over Nick's absence. "Do you mind if I go find out why Nick didn't come to dinner?" she asked Max. He nodded. "Let's go upstairs and you can build with your Legos in our room." They cleaned up their dishes and went upstairs.

She smiled as she left the room where Max was. Once Max was out of sight, she walked down to Nick's office and opened the door without knocking.

"Did you not see my text?" she asked sadly without even a hello.

Nick wasn't looking at her. His desk was scattered with more papers. He was hunched over them all, a pencil in his hand, scribbling madly between bouts of punching buttons on his computer. She walked to the edge of the desk to face him, and he finally looked up at her.

"Did you see my text?" she asked again.

"I'm sorry," he said, his voice ragged. "No, I didn't."

She leaned down in front of his face. "Look at me, please," she said.

He looked up.

"I get it. You feel you need to make this sale. This job is important to you." She leaned closer to ensure that she had his attention. "But it isn't all of you. You are so much more than this job, and you're denying all the other parts of who you are. You aren't aware of what you're doing. You've been alone for so long, you've forgotten how to be with people. We were waiting. For you."

His face softened slightly, but he looked defensive.

"You promised Max you would eat with him. Can you even fathom what I felt for my son when you didn't show up after you said you would?"

His gaze dropped back down to his desk. He took in a deep breath and let it out.

"You promised," she said. "You promised Max you'd come to dinner. He saved you a chair between us. And you didn't show. You can't do that." She walked back to the other side of the desk. She could feel the lump in her throat—protectiveness of Max making her feel vulnerable—and she worried she was going to cry.

Nick rubbed his eyes, his remorse clear. He stood up and walked around the desk to face her. He reached out and hesitantly touched her arms. He moved his hands up until they were almost near her shoulders and he held on to her tenderly. She looked into his blue eyes. She had to look up to see him, and she thought about how gentle he was, despite his imposing physique.

"I should've been there," he said. "I'll find a way to make it better. Maybe I can get him a present—a teddy bear or something."

"You don't need to *buy* him things. He doesn't want a teddy bear. He wanted to eat dinner with you. The best thing you can do for him is to simply apologize."

"I know I don't need to buy him things. It would be a token of my regret for not being there for him."

"You can't fix the problem with money. *You* have to fix the problem." She kept her voice calm. She had to make him see. "What does that teach him? That he can do whatever he wants to people as long as he buys them something to say he's sorry? That's not how I'm raising my child. You should've come to dinner, and you didn't. Now, it's up to you to make that better."

Max was already asleep when Abbey went to check on him. He'd been waiting for her to come tuck him in, and she'd been busy cleaning up the kitchen even though Nick had assured her that the staff would take care of it. That was probably true, but it was her mess, so she cleaned up herself. She expected him to still be awake, but the day's events must have been exhausting for him.

When she'd finished checking on Max, Abbey hurried to the bedroom to work on taping the rest of it off. She could feel how tired she was, but it didn't matter. She had to get it finished. Without another thought, she pulled a long piece of tape from the roll and got started.

Abbey looked at her watch. Eleven o'clock. She rubbed her eyes, her fingers sticky from the adhesive of the tape. The whole room was supposed to be painted by now and drying so she could put it back together and decorate it tomorrow. She tried not to think about it as she lined the cans of paint on a drop cloth that Richard had found for her. She opened the paint and inserted a wooden paint stirrer. As she swirled the paint around, it looked slightly different than the original color she'd chosen, but wet paint sometimes did look different, so she continued to stir.

When it was mixed pretty well, she dumped it into the paint tray and dragged her roller back and forth in the gray mixture. Even on a long pole, given her height, the roller couldn't reach the ceiling, so she had to teeter on the ladder to get up to the top. She left a few inches between the crown molding and the wall so she wouldn't bump the woodwork with her roller. She'd have to go back and paint that with a brush, but even at the top of the ladder, she had no idea how she'd ever reach it. She rubbed an itch on her forehead with her wrist but still managed to get paint on herself. With a sigh, she kept rolling.

After she'd painted about two-thirds of the wall, she got down off the ladder to look at it. Part of it had dried somewhat already. In the dark of night, with the glow of the chandelier, it was difficult to tell if the paint was the right color. It didn't look right, but she had to go with it. It was the best she had, and with the snow, she'd never be able to get out and buy more.

It had taken ages and she wasn't even finished with one wall. She'd have to paint around all the woodwork and fireplace by hand, and she was getting tired. The room smelled of paint, and it was a wreck. She'd never get it finished and decorated by tomorrow. What had she been thinking? She should have added extra time into her schedule. She could've had her mother watch Max more often, and gotten ahead in anticipation of something like this happening. This room was huge. It could easily take her three days to paint.

Abbey had two more rooms she planned to paint. She had lighting to rewire, new chandeliers in a few of the rooms. She wanted to replace some nicked pieces of woodwork around an ornamental accent on the ceiling that encircled the chandelier. The snow would put this entire process behind because she couldn't possibly do it all herself. And now, as she watched the paint drying, she finally admitted to herself that it was completely the wrong color. Her watch read nearly midnight. She'd spent a hour and hadn't even finished a wall. Tears pricked her eyes.

She took in a deep breath to try to keep herself together but it caught, and she sucked in ragged breaths instead. This project meant a lot to her. It was the first time in her life she was doing something that made her happy. She was living out her dream. It was the shot of a lifetime. If she could pull this off, people would trust her and hire her for more projects. She might even be able to open her own business one day.

She was tired. She could feel her tears surfacing. With a sniffle, she put the roller back into the paint and started again.

"How's it going?" Nick's voice echoed through the room.

Abbey's frustration and exhaustion had been building with every paint stroke, and if she spoke, she'd start to cry, so she just looked at him, her lip trembling against her will.

His face flooded with concern and he walked closer to her. "What's wrong?"

She shook her head, holding her breath to keep the sobs at bay.

"Tell me," he said gently.

"The paint's the wrong color," she said with a sniffle. Tears were filling her eyes, blurring her vision. She felt so unprofessional, but then again, she was covered in paint and still there, doing it all alone at midnight. None of it was going according to plan at the moment. "And the painters canceled." She took in another jagged breath and a tear escaped down her cheek. She quickly wiped it away and tried to breathe to release the tension in her chest. She had to get herself together.

Nick reached over and ran his finger across her cheek. Was she still crying? She was so embarrassed.

He held up his gray finger. "You have paint all over your face," he said with a small smile. He turned around and looked at the room. "Are you painting all the walls in here?"

"Yes."

"And when do you need to be finished with this one?"

"Yesterday," she said.

He looked at her, more concern on his face. Was he worried that she wouldn't get it done? Was he second-guessing his decision to hire her?

"I know," she said, answering her own questions. "I should have a team doing this, but the snow caused my painters to cancel on me. There's no one but me to do it."

"Hmm," he said. "I understand. I'll see what I can do."

Without another word, he left the room. Who was he going to get to help her at midnight? Was he going to personally have the roads plowed all the way to the paint company? There was nothing his money could do to help her now. She'd have to just do it herself. She rolled her head on her shoulders and tried not to think about how tired she'd be taking care of Max tomorrow after painting all night.

Abbey opened up another can of paint and poured it into the tray. Then, she started painting again. With every stroke, she worried more and more about finishing this tonight. It was proving to be a much bigger job than it had looked, but she kept painting.

"Tell me what to do," Nick said from the doorway. He had on a T-shirt, jeans, and bare feet. He walked over and pulled one of the rollers off the floor, ripping the plastic packaging off and putting it into the paint.

"You don't have to do this," she said, putting her roller down and walking over to him. "You've hired me to do it. I'd feel terrible making you work."

"You asked once, how would I show someone I cared if I didn't have my money to fall back on; remember that? Well, my money won't help us tonight. So, I'm painting *with* you. Because I care." He pushed the roller back and forth, filling it with paint and put it on the wall. "Just go up and down?"

With her tears still present and a smile on her face, she nodded. "Like this," she said, moving her roller up and down at a slight angle. "Thank you," she said as they both started to paint.

They both painted quietly, their rollers making wet, spongy noises against the wall. Abbey noticed how much more quickly it was going with two people, not to mention that Nick's height allowed him to cover more of the wall with his strokes. He was also able to get up near the ceiling around the crown molding that she couldn't reach. She'd shown him how to avoid brush strokes by going around the doorframe. After a few practices there, he'd done the area by the ceiling with ease.

As they finished the last wall, Nick said, "The color isn't that bad." He stopped and took a step back to look at it. Abbey turned toward him and laughed.

"What?"

She laughed again at the sight of him. "You have paint on your nose."

Nick tried to wipe it off, only smudging more across his cheek.

"Now it's on your cheek."

"Well, we match then. Except you have some on your forehead as well."

She walked over to him and looked up into his eyes sweetly. Then she dragged her hand across his forehead, making a large, gray streak. "*Now* we match," she said.

He took a step back, a suspicious look on his face as she bent down, pretended to cover her roller, and wiggled her fingers around in the paint. He lifted his T-shirt to wipe his face. When he did, he revealed his bare chest and waist, the sight of it causing her to drop her roller. Paint splashed up on her, dousing her shirt with gray. He laughed, clearly realizing what had happened.

"Why did you drop your roller?" he asked.

"I was finished with it," she said, having trouble making eye contact.

"Well," he chuckled again, obviously seeing through her answer. "Now you have paint on your neck *and* your face. Would you like me to wipe it off with my T-shirt?" he asked, barely able to get the words out without laughing.

She faked a serious expression and turned away from him, glad the paint was covering her blushing cheeks.

"So, is this room finished now?" he asked, changing the subject.

She turned around. "I still want to fix the woodwork in that ornament on the ceiling."

"Where?" He tilted his head back to look up at it.

"There," she pointed at the spot.

"I don't see it."

"How can you not? It's right there?"

"That little break?"

"Yes."

"No one will see that. Don't worry yourself with it."

"They will if they're lying in bed."

"They'll be sleeping."

"What if they aren't? They'll see it."

"Where's the bed going to go?" he asked.

"Here." She walked over to the spot where she'd planned to place the king-sized four-poster bed. "Look." She lay down on the drop cloth and patted the area of floor beside her. "Come lie down and look at it. It's an eyesore."

Nick lay down beside her, their shoulders touching, and stared at the ceiling. "Are two people really going to be sleeping like this? Like statues?"

Abbey laughed.

They stared at it for a while, and Abbey could feel the drop of her eyelids and the silence that was settling upon them. It was nearly four in the morning now, and neither of them had stopped for even a breath. She let her eyes close.

Abbey was aware of the birds outside her window and the chemical smell of paint. She tried to open her eyes but they wouldn't budge. She was too tired. Had she slept in the bed with paint still on her? Was she ruining the sheets? She forced her eyes to open and gasped. Nick stirred under her. They were still on the floor of the bedroom. As she tried to move, she had an ache in her hip and her lower back from sleeping on the wooden floor. Nick had his arm under her neck, his hand on her shoulder, and she was lying half on top of him and half on the floor. When she attempted to sit up, her shirt pulled away from her, causing her to stop and look down.

"Morning," he said with sleepy eyes. She wanted to take in the adorable way he was looking at her, but she was in a slight panic as her shirt pulled further down her body. His eyes slid down her neck and she wriggled down to keep him from seeing anything else.

"Our shirts are stuck together," she said. "The paint on my shirt must have dried last night while we were sleeping."

"One of us will have to take our shirt off then," he said with a crooked grin.

She cut her eyes at him.

"Okay," he chuckled. "I'll take mine off. You aren't holding any rollers, are you?"

"Oh, hush," she said, trying not to smile.

He pulled his arms out of his shirt and, as she held on to hers, trying desperately to keep herself covered, he slipped his off his head. Abbey wadded it up along the front of her and crossed her arms, trying her best not to look at him sitting there in only a pair of jeans.

"Thank you again for helping me last night. I hope I didn't pull you from your work."

"Nope," he said with a smile. His dark hair was messy, and he had stubble on his face.

She swallowed, trying to keep her thoughts from showing.

"I got the company." He grinned at her. "It cost me a million more than I'd wanted it to, and a dinner with Max, but I got it. I promise to make it up to him."

"I believe you," she said, and she meant it.

Chapter Seventeen

Abbey was tired today, so she switched a few things on her timeline and focused on the living room. It wasn't as big as the ballroom, but it was still quite a large space. The ceilings were high, the walls a deep brown color with oversized moldings in stark white, making the room quite bright, and she already liked the color choices, which meant no painting was required. After last night, she was glad about that. The room had a lovely brown leather sofa and two matching chairs with a big-screen television on the wall.

She added mahogany side tables with oversized lamps, magazine racks for each side of the sofa, filled with the latest copies of travel and food magazines. The sofa was full of down-filled throw pillows in reds and deep blues, providing the pop of color that it needed. She hung a painting she'd found at an art gallery online on the large, blank wall opposite the sofa. It had all the colors tied together in streaks of bright paint on a stark white background. In the corner was an empty Christmas tree. Abbey was waiting to decorate that one. She had some plans to do it in a more traditional fashion, and she'd need Max to help her with it.

She looked around at how warm and cozy this room appeared after she'd had her hands on it. The recessed lighting in the ceiling, which was on a dimmer switch, was on, so she could make the room feel like it had more lamplight instead of harsh overhead lights. She'd adjusted the lighting and put the throw on the sofa when Nick came in.

"Hi," he said as he looked around. "Wow, you don't stop, do you? I could hardly get a cup of coffee in this morning."

"I'm trying to keep my schedule," she said with a smile. "But I have a quick moment for a break. Have you come in to relax?"

He smiled. "Relax?"

"Yes. I just figured you'd come to the living room to relax for a minute. Kick your feet up. Do you usually relax in here?"

"No," he said, running his fingers along the new side table. "I hardly ever come in here. If I'm up, I'm working."

"What if you were stuck in this house with no computer or phone—nothing to connect you to your job—what would you do to entertain yourself?" she asked as she sat down on the sofa.

He sat down beside her. "I don't know."

"Yes you do." She nudged him playfully with her shoulder and he looked down at his arm, that curiosity evident again. "What do you love?"

"I'd compose music. For piano," he said quietly.

Abbey remembered the sound of the notes he'd played and how they'd affected her. "Really?"

"Yes." He allowed a small smile to emerge.

"Do you have anything you've composed?"

"I have whole folders full from when I was younger. Before my father died."

"Where are these folders?" This conversation had taken such an unexpected turn. Abbey knew all too well what this was like for him. She had files of decorating pictures, ideas jotted down, torn-out pages of magazines. She still had them all. Just like he still had his music.

"In my office."

"Would you play me something that you've written?"

"I've never played for anyone before."

"Do you like my decorating?"

Nick blinked, obviously trying to tie the question to the conversation. "Yes."

"Do you really like it?"

"Yes." He smiled at her.

"The way you feel about playing me your music is the way I felt when I started decorating your house. I was worried too. Play me something." She stood up.

"We'll wake up Max."

"Play softly then. And he sleeps like a log. You won't wake him." She grabbed his hand, and she could see the immediate response in his body. He was nervous. He stood up and looked down at their hands. She twisted her fingers in his grip and intertwined hers with his. For just a moment, he rubbed her hand with his thumb and the feeling was so intimate that she worried she'd start to tremble herself.

They walked together to his office. Nick was very quiet the whole way, and she knew why. This was a big deal. He'd said he'd never played his music for anyone before. She assumed that meant his family as well. He'd never played for Caroline or his sister. He'd never played for his parents. But he was going to play for her.

As they entered the office, Nick clicked on the light and walked over to the dark wood bookshelf that spanned one entire wall. He pulled out two brown folders and set them down on top of all the papers on his desk. He opened one, revealing sheets upon sheets of papers with music notes scratched in pencil on printed lines, all stuffed inside the pockets. She could see the remnants of marks that had been erased and rewritten several times, and she imagined him at the piano, tinkering with the notes as he changed them on the page. It made her impatient to hear him play now. There was something so calming, so attractive about watching him.

He was studying the pages, turning them then turning back, obviously deliberating on which one to play. "May I choose?" she asked.

He stopped for a moment and looked at her. He was unsure, she could tell. She looked down at the pages. The notes meant nothing to her, so she read the titles. Carefully, she thumbed through, page after page, reading them until she got to the last one: "Dreams." The title struck her. It was perfect.

"Play this one," she said.

He slid it out of the folder's pocket. As he turned to leave, Nick took her hand again, but this time it was like he was holding on to her for strength. This confident, wealthy businessman needed her?

The ballroom was bright with the morning light when they entered. Abbey let go of his hand and turned on the white lights of the two Christmas trees, and the lights looked like yellow stars against the gray sky outside. They cast a glow along the floor. Nick sat down. He propped the paper up on the music stand in front of them. Abbey sat down beside him. He turned to her, a subtle smile on his lips. Then, his foot settled on one of the pedals, and he placed his fingers on the keys.

He began to play. It was quiet, gentle, like the music boxes Max had had when he was a baby. The music was so beautiful that she closed her eyes to hear it better. It sounded tinkling and smooth at the same time, the notes bouncing around together softly. She'd never heard anything like it. It reminded her of a lullaby. Just hearing it took her back to those sleepless nights she'd had, a terrified new mother, all by herself with Max when he was a baby. It reminded her of rocking him, listening to his little sucking sounds once he'd fallen asleep, the smell of his hair. Like a slideshow, she thought of the smile Max had in his crib every morning, his first steps, the smear of birthday cake on his one-year-old lips, his first hit at his baseball game—so many memories.

Without warning, she could feel the swelling of tears in her closed eyes and she sniffled. Nick hadn't even finished playing yet, and she already wanted to hear it again. She opened her eyes and a tear escaped down her cheek. She wiped it away. Never before had she had this kind of experience, and it made her feel differently in that moment. She felt like anything was possible.

The song ended and Nick turned toward her, immediately showing concern when he realized she was crying. "What's wrong?" he asked.

"Nothing at all." She smiled and sniffled again. "It was beautiful."

He stared at her for a moment as if deciding something. Then, he leaned in slowly, her heart speeding up with the realization of what was happening. He stopped just before meeting her lips. She could feel his breath, every inch of her body wanting to press herself against him. She couldn't get close enough to him and the space between them was killing her. "I'm glad you liked it," he whispered. Then, he closed his eyes and, under the mistletoe that hung over the piano, his lips met hers. The warmth of his hands as they moved around her, the tenderness in his kiss, the perfect way they fit together—she didn't want it to end.

But, before she was ready, he gently pulled away. Thoughts were clear on his face. He swallowed. "This… was completely unexpected," he said. She knew just what he meant. His money, his upbringing, his ridiculous choices for spending his earnings—none of it seemed as big as the way she felt at this moment.

To Abbey's surprise, the painters had made it out to do the other two bedrooms this afternoon. Abbey was so excited, she'd gone to find Nick. Last night, he'd offered to help her with the others. While she'd enjoyed herself, painting with him, she didn't want to impose on his time, and she was happy to tell him he wouldn't have to help her.

Abbey found him in the ballroom, and he was on the phone. He motioned for her to come and sit on the sofa as he finished his call. She looked around the room so as not to make eye contact and appear to eavesdrop, but as she let her eyes fall on the piano, she heard something about him traveling somewhere.

"Are you taking a trip?" she asked, standing up to face him as he hung up the phone. She worried about him flying in all this snow.

He cleared his throat. "I'm going to New York the day after tomorrow. I'll be gone all week," Nick said.

"Oh."

"I'm going because I'm house hunting. I'm planning on moving just after Christmas. I haven't told anyone except Robin yet." He looked over her head for a moment as if he had to collect his thoughts. "It's just easier to do what I do from a larger city. I could make more money in New York, and I feel that if I could be more hands-on with the business, be able to meet with people face to face, be available on a moment's notice—if I could do that, things could grow on a grander scale than they are here. My living in Richmond is the last remnant of my marriage, and I'm ready to make a change."

She stared at him, taking in this news. It was like someone had kicked her in the stomach, and all the possibilities rushed right down the drain. Her mind went to Max. She walked over to the piano bench and sat down. "You promised to go to Max's school," she said quietly.

"I will keep that promise," he said.

Reality set in, the weight of it slamming against her temples and making them pound. He'd only just met her. They didn't have any kind of relationship that would warrant keeping him here.

She understood that it should be easy to walk away, for the very reason that they hadn't known each other very long, but the thought of not seeing him again and Max's loss of a real man in his life made her feel like she had a cinder block on her chest.

"I can tell you're upset."

She tried to straighten out her face but was unsuccessful.

"I'm sorry I kissed you," he said sitting down next to her.

His face came into a sharp focus. "You're *sorry*?"

"I was simply acting on my feelings, and I should've thought it through. I didn't mean to cross the personal–professional line."

"What about eating tacos, dancing with me, the snowball fights, painting… Those weren't crossing the personal–professional line? You even said you cared about me."

"I do. And I don't think we should allow things to move any further given my plans to leave. It was my fault for allowing it to progress as much as it has. After Christmas, I'll be gone."

Abbey realized something at that moment. "Is Caroline moving with you?" she asked. If he planned on taking Caroline with him,

Abbey would be out of a job. She felt sick. She'd have to start looking as soon as she could get her car out. What was shaping up to be the best Christmas was now looking like one of her worst.

"Yes. She'll be leaving as well. I was going to give you a month's pay with your notice."

"I think I need to have a moment to myself to process all of this," she said. "I'm just going to go upstairs." She stood up, blinked her eyes clear, and took in a breath. But then she turned around. He was still, his eyes on her. "I'm not sorry I kissed *you*," she said. "I'm not sorry at all." She walked back over to him, still not ready to leave this conversation.

"I'm glad I kissed you too. I meant it. I just think it made things harder, and that's why I'm sorry."

"Then why didn't you say that?" she said, sitting back down next to him. She was so glad to hear him opening up a little and telling her how he really felt.

"I'm not as practiced at telling my feelings as you are."

"What do you mean I'm practiced at telling my feelings?" she asked.

"You're really good at it," he said, his face shifting into a happier expression. "I can honestly say that I am fully aware of all your emotions as you are having them." He was smiling at her now.

"Is that so?" She looked up and put her arms around him. The skin between his eyes wrinkled as he waited for an explanation for her behavior. Without another word, she leaned down and gave him a kiss.

"What was that for?" he said, their faces still close.

"I had to," she teased. "We're under the mistletoe."

"Mmm hmm," he said, leaning in for another. Then, he looked up at the mistletoe and shook his head.

The next morning, the plows had finally come and Abbey could go home to pack properly for her and Max's stay at Nick's. Given his recent news, however, the wind had been taken out of her sails, and she was apprehensive about staying there with him. It would only make things more difficult.

Richard helped her put the few bags she was taking back to the apartment into her car as Max climbed into the backseat. Richard had returned her house key and assured her that someone would bring all her food by once the power had come back on at her apartment.

Once Max was in his seatbelt, she made her way down the long drive. Max was quiet, clearly sleepy from all the excitement yesterday, and she was relieved because it gave her time to clear her head. It was probably good that Nick would be gone next week. Then, she could just finish decorating what she could get done and have maybe only one more week after he returned. She wished things could be different... Abbey stopped herself. She wasn't going to do any wishing. There were no Christmas miracles. She needed to get a grip and get over him.

She drove straight to her mother's. She was leaving Max there for an hour or two to go Christmas shopping for him before she went home to pack. The good news was that she would get her check from Nick soon, so she could afford to spend a good amount on her son for once. She even planned to get Nick a present.

Abbey was already worrying about missing Nick. Her mother would help her through this. As she drove, Abbey wondered exactly what *this* was. She wanted to see Nick. She didn't want him to go to New York. Those were the facts.

They pulled into the drive, and sitting on the front porch was Señor Freckles. He darted across the yard to the car, which was surprising. Abbey got out and walked around to make sure Max could get out all right on the ice. When she did, she couldn't believe what she was seeing. Señor Freckles was at Max's door, purring. Max reached down to pet him, and the cat ran away. Didn't that ridiculous cat know that if he would just hold still, and allow it, they'd cuddle him and pet him?

Abbey's mom opened the front door, that motherly expression on her face. "Have you been snowed in this whole weekend?" she asked, tiptoeing her way across the icy porch to greet them.

"We stayed at Nick's house!" Max answered for Abbey, and she felt her face go white.

It was silly to make a big fuss of it. Her mom had always said Abbey picked the wrong guys, and what Abbey didn't ever tell her was that she knew that. Nick wasn't like the others at all. He was far from it. And she knew what her mom would be thinking. She knew that her mom would be thrilled beyond belief if something were to happen between them. And if her mom got excited, it would only get Abbey thinking about how much she liked him. She looked over at her mother who was eyeing her, her eyebrows raised in anticipation.

"It was so fun, Nana," Max said. "We built a snowman and watched TV on a giant screen, and I played 'Hide and Seek'!"

Her mother flashed an excited grin.

"It was very fun," Abbey said for Max's benefit but her face told her mother something else. "I'll fill you in when we get settled." Abbey opened the door, Señor Freckles darting between them into the house. Max rushed in after him, trying to catch him, but Gramps intercepted Max in the hallway.

"Hiya, buddy," Gramps said, tousling his hair.

"Hi, Gramps!" Max said as he wrapped his arms around Gramps's waist.

"Come on in and get warm," Abbey's mom said as she put her hands out to take their coats.

"Where did Señor Freckles go?" Max asked as he plopped down on the sofa and crossed his legs. "He ran too fast for me to catch him."

"He doesn't want to be caught," Gramps explained, gingerly lowering himself down beside Max, his knees wobbling with the movement. "He's a wild cat. He's used to being strong all on his own. When you see him again, just talk to him. He likes that."

Max nodded.

As Gramps began a conversation about how he'd originally found Señor Freckles, Abbey's mother ushered her out of the room.

"Tell me!" she said. "What were you doing at Nick's all weekend?"

"My power was out. He offered for us to stay with him."

"How did he know your power was out?"

"He was shopping with us."

Her mother's face lifted, the interest building. So much had happened that Abbey didn't really even know where to begin.

"Why was he shopping with you?" she asked, her words elongated to denote her delight in the idea of Nick spending time with her daughter.

"I asked him, and he came."

"Will you see him again?"

Abbey chewed on her lip, trying to figure out the answer to the question herself. In what capacity would she see him? She wanted to be near him again, feel his lips on hers, his arms holding her, but she didn't know if that would be a possibility.

"He's going out of town tomorrow for the week. We'll see what happens after that. Actually, I need to text him something before he goes out of town. Do you mind if I step out for just a sec?"

"No, not at all. I'll keep an eye on Max." Her mom leaned in to take a peek at him and then she made eye contact with Abbey. She looked hopeful, and Abbey wanted to tell her mom everything, but she wanted to call Nick too.

"I won't be long."

"I'll make us some coffee," her mom said.

Abbey took her phone into her childhood bedroom and lay on the new comforter. Nervousness ran through her fingers as she typed his number, and opened the text screen. She got straight to the point.

She texted: *I forgot to tell you the painters came. They did the other rooms. You won't need to help me paint, but thank you so much for your help and for the offer.*

He responded: *That's great news. May I call you?*

Yes, she texted back. The phone rang and she answered it.

"I wanted to make sure you're okay. I was hoping to break the news about me planning to move in a better way. I didn't have a chance to get my thoughts together first. Will you be able to find a job in a month's time? Does that sound reasonable?"

"It's fine," she said. "I'm going to really miss Caroline, though. I really enjoy spending time with her."

The line was quiet for a while. "I'm in too deep with the business to consider staying," he finally said.

"I'd never ask you to."

Abbey didn't want to be some kind of anchor, a weight, keeping him in a place he didn't want to be. He wasn't going to change his plans for her, and that was understandable, given that they'd just met, but it made her so sad. She'd just found him and now she was losing him.

"Who will care for Caroline?" Abbey asked quietly. She'd grown attached to Nick's grandmother. Even not seeing her some weekends was really hard. Caroline was fond of her too, and she might be all alone in New York.

"Robin is there with her family. She's going to find a suitable nurse to take care of her."

"Will you sell the house?" She was grasping for anything. Maybe they'd come back. Maybe he wouldn't like New York.

"Maybe."

Abbey's mom poked her head into the room. "Coffee," she mouthed. The coffee being ready was a legitimate reason for peeking in, but Abbey knew her mother was just checking on her.

Abbey held up one finger and smiled her best smile as she whispered, "One sec." Her mom closed the door but left it open a crack and walked back toward the kitchen.

"Do you need to go?" Nick asked.

Abbey rubbed her forehead. "I have to go shopping for Max. I haven't bought any Christmas presents yet and Mom's going to watch him for me. Why don't you come with me?" The truth of the matter was that, after Christmas, he'd be leaving Richmond and too far away from her, so there was no use in seeing him again. But she couldn't help herself.

"I'd love to."

"What time?" she heard herself ask. Despite her best efforts, she couldn't stay away because, when it came down to it, all she wanted was to see him.

"What time were you planning on going?"

"In a few minutes."

"I'll pick you up. You're at your mother's—at Maple and Ivy?"

He remembered. She smiled. Of course he remembered. "Yes."

"I'll be there in ten minutes."

Abbey ended the call and made her way to the kitchen where her mom had two steaming mugs of coffee made. One of the mugs was painted with finger-paints—it had been an art project of Max's that he'd made for her. She could hear Max playing a card game with Gramps in the other room.

They sat there quietly for a while before her mother spoke. Her mom had been wiping counters, her back to Abbey, but Abbey could feel the questions hanging in the air.

"Want to tell me what all this is about?" her mom finally said, sitting down next to her. She picked up her mug and blew the steam off the top.

"It's so… hard to explain," she said, feeling her worry settling in her shoulders.

"You like him," her mom noted.

"Very much. I think there's so much more to him than he allows anyone to see. I can feel it. I used to think that I was the one with few experiences, but I wonder sometimes if he's got fewer than I have. …Or maybe just not very rich experiences. No pun intended," she smiled. "Did you know that he's never been to a baseball game?"

"Really?"

"Really! And I took him to The Crazy Corner," she smiled wider at the memory of him dancing.

"Alma's restaurant?"

"Yeah. He loved it! He even danced with me."

"He seems to like you."

"I think so."

"Then what more is there?"

"A lot. He said he isn't having any kids, and I've got Max." Her mom was about to respond, but Abbey stopped her. "And he's moving to New York after Christmas." She took a sip of her coffee and held on to the mug, warming her hands.

Her mom was still, her head tilted, her eyes wide. "Oh, no."

"Oh, yes."

"What are you going to do?"

"Well, to start, I'm going to go shopping with him today," she said, huffing out a little laugh of disbelief. She put her head in her hands and covered her eyes. With her voice muffled by her fingers, she said, "He'll be here in ten minutes. After that, I don't know."

"Ten minutes?" her mom nearly shrieked.

"Who's coming in ten minutes?" Max asked, entering the room and nearly tripping over Señor Freckles. The cat, who'd come out of nowhere, darted away before Max had regained his balance, and he dropped the deck of cards on the floor. "I have to *keep* picking up cards," Max said, a slight frustration to his voice.

"Nick's coming in ten minutes," Abbey answered his question, taking her mug with her to sip her coffee as she helped Max with his cards. "Where's Gramps? Did you two finish playing your game?"

"Yes. He's tired and wants to go to sleep. He kept dropping his cards."

"I'm sorry," she said. She worried for Gramps. Was he really tired or just annoyed at having a tough time holding the cards?

"Were you patient with Gramps?" she asked. "You know things like holding cards are difficult for him, and it aggravates him."

"Yes. I was. …Nick's coming?" Max said with a smile, and Abbey could feel the tension in her body as she saw his excitement. She didn't want him getting close to Nick only to have him leave. It hurt her enough to think about him leaving; she didn't want to have Max's disappointment to deal with.

"I don't think he's coming in. He's just picking me up to go shopping."

"May I go?"

"No, but you can see him when he comes to the door. Okay? Why don't you look out for him?"

"Okay!" Max ran to the living room to watch through the window.

"Max sure does have a fondness for Nick," her mom said, a cautiousness to her voice.

"I know. Nick has been wonderful with him. Max seems to have connected with him so quickly. I've never seen him like this."

"Nick's a great guy. Maybe Max just senses that. He hasn't had a lot of great guys in his life."

The doorbell rang, and she heard Max opening the door. "Hi, Nick!" she heard him say.

"Hello, Max… Oh," she heard Nick say. She got up to see what was going on.

Abbey entered the room to find that Max had wrapped his arms around Nick and given him a hug, but what surprised her most was the complete adoration on Nick's face as he looked down at her son.

He liked Max—it was clear—and she had to cough to keep the lump out of her throat.

Nick looked up, and as soon as he saw her, he smiled.

"We'll be back in a few hours," Abbey said to her mom, trying to keep the butterflies at bay. She grabbed her coat and handbag as Max stepped back and allowed her to exit.

The Mercedes was purring in the drive. It looked out of place against the small homes surrounding it. Nick put his hand on her back to guide her down the icy steps and into the car. She slid inside and waved goodbye to her mother and Max through the window.

Chapter Eighteen

"Let's start at the sports memorabilia shop," Abbey said as they walked the open-air mall. A group of carolers was singing "Deck the Halls" at the entrance, their voices like angels as Abbey and Nick walked by. Along the bricked walkways, they passed life-sized nutcrackers, towering Christmas trees, and more white lights than there was snow outside. Abbey took in the large swags of greenery, the lights, the bows on every shop door—it was like a Christmas wonderland. The weather was freezing outside, and she could feel the numbness in her nose and cheeks. There was a slight breeze that felt like an icy stab every time it hit her face.

"You don't have a scarf," Nick said. "Aren't you freezing?"

She was freezing. "I'm fine," she said. They were there to shop for Max and, since it was the first year she had a sizeable amount of money coming to her, she was eager to get started. She didn't care in the slightest if she had on a scarf, even if she was shivering.

"I'll feel better if you're wearing a scarf. Do you want gloves?"

"No, I'm fine."

They kept walking. Everywhere she looked the surfaces of the giant Christmas trees and wreaths were still covered in snow and ice. The walks had all been shoveled, but the white snow on the edges of the paths, the grounds, and the branches of the trees gave it all such a festive feel. As she looked at Nick in his tailored coat and scarf, she wished she could remember like he did. She wanted to keep this moment forever.

"I know. Come with me," he said, warmth in his eyes. She didn't want to notice it, but she had. Nick placed his hand on her back again and led her to the coffee shop where he opened the door and motioned for her to enter. He found a table, nestled along a dark wood windowsill that was big enough to double as a bench, and pulled out her chair. "Tell me what kind of coffee you like."

"Just a regular coffee is fine," she said with a smile. True, it was cold out, and a coffee sounded wonderful, but there was a buzzing energy to him that made her think he wasn't just there to get coffee. He was grinning at her, his eyes full of some sort of insider knowledge. What was he doing?

"Cream and sugar?"

"Just cream, please."

"Be right back," he said with another grin.

As she watched him standing in line, making his order, she wondered why he'd asked to come today. He knew as well as she did that any connection they had wasn't going anywhere. So why was he doing this? At that moment, as she caught him stealing glances at her, she didn't care. She didn't want to think about anything other than him and her right then.

"Here you are," he said, returning and setting her coffee in front of her. "Sit tight for just one more second. I'll be right back."

To her surprise, he left the shop. Where was he going? As she sat by herself, with her thoughts, she wondered if she was being too careful, worrying about how everything would play out. As a young girl, she'd thrown caution to the wind and she'd done whatever she felt in that moment. Should she jump in with both feet and do that now? Max had changed her; *he'd* made her more careful about things, and now she had her family—Gramps—to think about. She just wasn't that young, naïve girl that she'd been. But that girl was still there. She could feel the impulsiveness lingering under the surface, telling her to just go for it. The only problem was the grown woman that she'd become was reminding her of how badly all those impulsive acts had turned out. All but one: Max.

Max was that one light in her life, that one good thing that had come in the midst of all her troubles. And when she looked at him, she didn't mind the money struggles, the job juggling, or the fact that things hadn't worked out with his father. None of it mattered because she had Max. And she felt so lucky and blessed to have him in her life.

Nick walked past the windows carrying a paper shopping bag. She didn't recognize the store name. She hadn't been to this mall very often—most of the stores were out of her price range—but given Max's Christmas list, it had been the most logical place to come. Nick came inside and sat down, a look of satisfaction on his face. He reached into the bag and pulled out the most gorgeous pearly white scarf Abbey had ever seen. It looked so soft. He stood up again and wrapped it around her, then sat back down.

Abbey ran her hand along the luxurious surface of it. It *was* soft, softer than anything she could remember feeling. Her fingers slid down to the very end where the price tag still hung. She caught sight of the numbers just as Nick reached across and grabbed it, obscuring it in his fist and pulling it off into his hand.

"Did that say one hundred fifty dollars?" she asked in horror. There was no way she was letting him spend that kind of money on a scarf that, given her lifestyle, would get stuffed in a handbag, dragged on the floor, or lost in a closet.

"No," he said, but his eyes gave him away. "It said a dollar fifty."

"It did not." She reached for his fist.

He squeezed it tighter and then threw the balled paper behind him over his shoulder. She watched it land across the room. He was looking at her playfully, clearly enjoying the fact that he'd just spent a ton of money on her and she couldn't do anything about it. Then he leaned close to her—too close. His face was right in front of hers. "Let me buy you something, and just enjoy it," he said softly. "I know you'll be just fine without it, but I *wanted* to buy it."

When he showed her his playful side, he was irresistible, and she knew that if they just had enough time together, she could bring that side out more than his working side. It made her long to try. "Why are you doing this?" she asked suddenly. She couldn't play these games. She needed to know.

"Doing what? Buying you things?"

"No. Why are you here with me today?"

He leaned away from her, righting himself. "I don't know, honestly," he said, looking at the floor as if the answer were there. "I just wanted to see you."

"I won't see you once I'm done working on your house. This…" she wagged a finger between them, "will amount to nothing." She could see disappointment on his face. "I'm just being brutally honest."

"Let's not think about the future," he said. "You and I are both here until Christmas. Why don't we just enjoy the holiday?"

"I agree," she said. "Let's get Max's presents and have fun." She smiled. "Thank you for my scarf. It's beautiful." She ran her hand down it one more time.

"You're welcome. So. What is on little Max's list?"

"He wants a Willie Mays baseball card," she said. "I'm not so sure I can get him one, but we could look and see."

"Shall we take our coffees and have a look?" Nick suggested.

Abbey nodded, standing up, and he followed. As they neared the door, Nick reached around and pulled it open for her. Then, with her new scarf and her coffee to keep her warm, she headed out to the shop to find Max's present. Nick stepped up beside her and, as she walked along the cobbled pathway to the shop, she noticed that he was walking slowly to keep her pace. She peered up at him, and he was already looking at her, a small smile on his lips.

She worried about shopping for this baseball card. It could cost a lot of money and she might have to leave the shop without buying it. While she wanted to get a good card for Max, she wasn't going to spend upwards of a thousand dollars on something that small for her six-year-old to lose. Nick would certainly offer to pay for it because, to him, it was probably nothing. But the trouble was, Abbey didn't want him to buy it. Every time she saw Max look at that baseball card, she wanted to remember how she'd used her own hard-earned money to buy it for him. It would have sentimental value then. She didn't know if Nick would understand that.

When they reached the shop, Nick opened the door for her, and they walked in. Abbey approached the counter, a glass structure that had every baseball card she could imagine displayed inside it. There were so many.

"May I help you?" a stout man with thinning white hair and round glasses asked from behind the counter.

"We're looking for a Willie Mays baseball card," Nick explained.

The clerk pulled out two cards and set them on the counter. Abbey studied them, unsure of what qualities to look for in a collectible baseball card. She wished she had Gramps there with her. He'd know.

"How much is this one?" Abbey asked the clerk as she pointed to one that looked as though it had a portrait on the front.

"That's a 1952 mint condition Topps card. It's five hundred."

She felt her cheeks heating up with the answer. *Don't try to buy it*, she thought, hoping that Nick had mindreading skills to match his memory. Surprisingly, he didn't say a thing.

"What about this one?" She pointed to a green card with three photos side by side of Willie Mays catching a ball.

"That's also Topps, mint condition. It's not nearly as rare. It'll run you fifty dollars."

"I'll take it," she said, digging in her purse for her credit card. Fifty dollars was still a lot of money for a baseball card, but it was a lot less than the other one.

Nick had remained very quiet the whole sale. Whenever she looked at him, he smiled sweetly at her, but he hadn't said anything more than his original comment to the clerk. She signed the receipt and the clerk put the card into a small handled shopping bag.

As they exited the shop, Abbey turned to Nick. "I was worried you'd offer to pay for it," she admitted.

"Yes." He placed his hand on her back to steer her around a couple that had stopped to look in a store window. She was getting used to the feeling of his guiding hand. "I figured that, so I didn't offer. Although," he smiled again, sending her heart soaring, "I would have."

"Why would you have bought it?" she asked.

"Because I make a nice amount of money and I don't have anyone to spend it on. I like spending money on people I care about."

For so many years, she'd cared about people, she'd tried to show them what love was, but she never really got that love in return. This time, she felt something for someone, and he cared about her too. Why did he have to go to New York?

She knew what it was like to need a job, and she didn't want to judge him. Just because he had a lot of money didn't mean that he didn't need to keep making that money to make ends meet. But at the same time, couldn't he downsize a bit and make his life what he wanted?

"Why are you so insistent on making your father's company profitable?" she asked, feeling like he was making the wrong decision by moving.

"Because he trusted me to do so."

"Yes, but I doubt he wanted you to do it at the expense of the rest of your life."

"You don't understand," he said as he walked.

She shuffled up in front of him and stopped him. "Then make me understand."

"I don't think I can." He politely moved around her and she walked up beside him. "Let's work on getting Max's Christmas presents. I still have to tie up a few loose ends before I get on a plane in the morning."

Chapter Nineteen

The ride home from shopping was quiet. She hadn't meant to put a damper on things. She just felt in her heart that the business wasn't right for Nick. It was holding him back from so much happiness.

She was tired of things being serious. Instead of taking the exit toward home, she asked him to go straight. She wanted to meander through the city instead, taking the long way. Then, she had an idea.

"Where are we going?" he asked.

"I know you have a few things to tie up," she said. "But I want you to buy me something." He looked over at her. She knew that would get him.

For the first time since they'd left the mall, a real smile spread across his face all the way up to his eyes. He knew she was up to something. "You're asking me to spend money on you?"

"Yes," she said, chewing on a smile.

"I'm intrigued. And a little surprised at your forward behavior. I've never had someone ask me to spend money. They usually just allow me to."

"I make it clear what I want," she teased. "Pull off there."

Nestled in the skyscrapers of the city was an ice skating rink. She could hear the Christmas music through the windows of the car.

"You want me to buy you an ice skating rink?"

She let out a little giggle. "No. I want you to buy us each a ticket and two skate rentals. I have this new scarf and no reason to wear it. I'd like you to take me ice skating."

He looked over at the rink and Abbey followed his line of sight. There was hardly anyone there. She noticed the clerk. He seemed so cold—he was hunched over a Styrofoam cup of steaming liquid, looking miserable. Nick had noticed him too.

"He doesn't have my scarf," she said with a grin.

"I've never been ice skating," Nick admitted.

"I haven't either."

"What if we slip and slide all over the place?"

"Might be fun," she said with a devious look. She had no problem at all with the thought of falling in a heap on top of him.

He absorbed that comment and immediately opened his door. "Absolutely. You're right. Let's skate."

Nick purchased their tickets and skates from the frozen clerk and they sat on the bench, lacing up.

"What if we break an ankle?" he asked.

She pursed her lips and looked over at him. "You are awfully cautious," she said. "You won't break an ankle. I'll hold you up if you fall."

"As small as you are, you would never hold me up."

"Then don't fall." She stood up on her skates, wobbling slightly before getting used to standing on the small blades. He stood up beside her, grabbing the bench for balance.

Abbey slid out onto the open rink, and turned around to view Nick. Strings of lights stretched above them, their bulbs yellow against the gray cloud cover. A Christmas tree sat at one end of the rink. She'd only noticed it because Nick had looked at it as he bobbled and wiggled his way onto the ice.

"That's just waiting for someone to plow into it," he said as he looked at the tree.

"Please don't let it be one of us," she laughed, reaching out to grab his hands.

They skated slowly, holding hands, her going backwards and him in front, leading precariously.

"Why is it that you wanted to do this?" he asked, only half serious. He jerked, catching himself before he pulled them both down onto the floor.

"It's romantic!" She let go of his hands and turned around, gliding slowly but balanced across the ice. She turned back around and pushed against the skates until she was skating toward him again.

He stood in front of her, one toe in the ice to steady himself. "What could possibly be romantic about this?" He was asking the question but his eyes were saying something else.

She skated to him, bumping into him slightly and wrapping her arms around his waist for support. She looked up into his eyes as he steadied them both. "This," she said, and she pushed herself up with one skate to reach his lips. He bent down, putting his arms around her, and kissed her right there in the middle of the rink.

He pulled back to focus on her face. "You didn't have to put me in these skates for that," he said with a crooked grin. "I'd have done that in the car."

"Don't give me any ideas," she said as she pulled away from him and skated away.

When they both felt they should be getting back, Nick drove Abbey to her mother's. He turned off the engine as they sat in the driveway.

"Thank you for taking me," Abbey said.

He nodded, a smile on his lips.

"I should have the house nearly finished when you get home on Friday—just a few rooms will be left by then."

He nodded again. She turned for the car door handle but he stopped her and she faced him. He put his hands on her face and kissed her.

"Thank you for today," he said. "I had a lot of fun."

"You're welcome." She stepped out, and pulled the presents from the car, setting them down by her feet. "Okay," she said, wishing there would be some way she could make him stay, but she knew there wasn't. "I'll see you next week," she said.

"I'll look forward to it," he said, and his real smile came through again, making her lightheaded with emotion.

She shut the door of the Mercedes, picked up her bags, and gingerly stepped over a pile of shoveled snow to allow Nick room to back out. Feeling very cold, she tightened her new scarf as she watched him drive down the road. She didn't move until the car was completely out of sight.

When there was nothing left but her, her bags, and the silence of the icy air around her, she put the presents in the trunk of her car. She'd gotten Max everything he'd asked for. She'd spent way more money than she'd ever in her life, but, just this once, she was going to make magic.

"Max sure had a lot to say about that new friend of yours," Gramps said as she entered the house. He was sitting on the sofa, his hand bouncing furiously against his leg. Abbey remembered those hands as they'd pushed her on the swings at the park. He'd grab the chain at the base and pull her up almost over his head before letting go. As a child it had seemed like he was pulling her as high as the treetops. Gramps's shaking hand came back into focus.

"Yes," she said, acknowledging his comment. "Max really likes Nick."

"And what do you plan to do about that?"

"Is there anything to do? He's only a friend."

"Is that how you say goodbye to a friend?" He shot a glance over to the window where she noticed a perfect view of the driveway. He'd seen their kiss.

"Max has his heart set on seeing him again. Did you know he told me about their sock races? He told me how Nick had talked to him when Max was in his office. When I asked what they'd talked about, Max said, 'Big man work stuff' and he seemed quite pleased to have had the chance to talk to him. His hopes are sky high, Abbey. I've never seen him like this."

"Well, he's done that himself," she said feeling frustrated. "I've done nothing to get his hopes up like that."

"No," Gramps said, eyeing her in a way that told her otherwise.

"What?" She felt defensive.

"Nick Sinclair has been taking you to a lot of places recently. You stayed at his house during the snowstorm. You could've stayed here…"

"That's not fair. He happened to be with me when the power went out and then the storm hit. That wasn't my fault."

"Have you considered his motivations in all of this? Why is he always around? What does *he* want?"

What does *he want?* she wondered herself. *Does he even know?*

She and Gramps could always talk. As a teenager, he was that neutral party who would listen when her mother would've been more judgmental. Her mom would worry about her choices, tell her what to do, but that wasn't what Abbey needed to hear. She knew that her choices were sometimes not the best ones, but she went with her heart, and nothing her mother could say—even lovingly like she had—would change that. Gramps had a way of listening and guiding without pointing fingers. Looking back on all their conversations now, she realized that he wasn't so neutral, and he had plenty of his own thoughts on the matters of her life; he just knew how and when to give his opinions, and she found that when she didn't listen to him, later, she'd understand that he was right. Every time.

"I haven't figured it out yet," she said honestly. "He seems to care about me, Gramps. Things have moved very quickly between us, but we have a lot going against us."

His body was unstill, and she could tell the medicine wasn't working like it should, but his eyes were the same eyes that had guided her for so many years. She couldn't imagine what it would be like one day when he wasn't there to help her.

"Like what? His money?"

"Well, there's that, but that isn't really the issue. He's moving to New York, and no one can convince him otherwise. His business is demanding it."

"And you wouldn't consider going to New York to see him?"

"I wouldn't want to pursue anything long distance, Gramps. The travel would be really hard on Max. Plus, all that running around would give me less time to see you." She smiled, but didn't receive a smile in return.

"Don't you dare make a decision about your future based on me."

How could he say such a thing? Of course she would. She was going to use some of Nick's money to buy his new medicine. She'd want to be around to monitor him if they tried it. And if it didn't work, she'd want to be there to find something that did. Over the years, Gramps had given her and her mother a whole lot; she couldn't possibly give him all that he'd given her, but she could darn well try.

"Gramps, I'm not going to leave you."

"If it will affect your life, you'd better."

She knew that he wasn't going to budge, so she had to come at it from the logical standpoint. "I'm going to help you with the Parkinson's as it progresses," she said. "I'm the one in the family who knows your options and how to handle the disease. Do you really want me to leave all the decisions on Mom's shoulders while I run back and forth to New York?"

She'd made her point, but he didn't like it, she could tell.

"And what decisions do we have? Meds or no meds? Options to keep me from being a grump? What are you going to do for me, Abbey?"

"I think I can buy those trial meds you need."

For an instant, he was stiller than he'd been, hope washing over him, but then, it dissipated and he connected the dots. He knew the only way she'd have that kind of money was if she used Nick's payment for the interior decorating. She didn't even have to say anything.

"Max needs that money more than I do."

"Max will be just fine. You need it, Gramps. If those meds will help you, I'll get them. It's worth a try."

"For what—to prolong the inevitable?" His fingers were jumping all over his lap now. "I've had my life, Abbey. You and Max and your mother have not finished yours. Don't waste it on me."

"How's it wasting it if I'm spending it on making someone I love better?"

"When your grandmother got sick, you were only little, so we kept you from a lot of it, but there came a time where the cancer was everywhere and she asked that we not do anything too invasive. She just wanted to live out the rest of her days. That was it. We all have a certain amount of time here. Live out *your* days. Invest that money in an interior decorating business! Do something other than sink it into an old man. Enjoy life! Stop trying to prolong mine. I've had a great run."

She didn't want to be having this conversation. It was almost Christmas for goodness' sake. She wanted everything to be great this year. She wanted a dream holiday—the kind like the movies. But life wasn't like that, and, while she'd do her very best, it would never be exactly the way she wanted it.

"Hi, Mama!" Max said as he entered the room, Abbey's mom behind him. "Look what I made with Nana." He held out a coloring page that had every detail colored.

"It's pretty," Abbey said.

"How'd the shopping trip go?" her mom asked, more questions than just that one hanging in the air between them.

"It went fine," Abbey said. "Nick got me this." She stroked the scarf that was still around her neck. She hadn't taken it off with her coat when she'd come in. Señor Freckles was sitting in the corner of the room by the kitchen door, presumably ready to make a run for her new scarf. The only thing deterring him was the fact that there were people present. Was he zooming in on it right now? It sure looked like it.

"Wow," her mom said as Max ran his fingers along it. "That is a very nice gesture."

"I couldn't believe he bought it for me." She wiggled it while looking at the cat, knowing he'd never dare get close enough to play with it.

"Nick seems very nice," her mother said.

"He is."

To her surprise, the cat began walking low to the ground, like a precursor to a pounce, its eyes on the fringe at the bottom of the scarf.

"Don't you dare," she said to the cat, tossing the ends of her scarf over her shoulders.

Señor Freckles jumped onto the arm of the chair, and when it did, she could hear him purring. The cat stepped up on the back of the sofa directly behind Abbey. They were all watching to see what he would do. The cat had never been so bold before. To her disbelief, he started pawing gently at her neck, his purrs loud in her ear. Max reached up and touched his back, and the cat let him.

"Ever since I got that cat," Gramps said, "I've hoped that he would come around. He will. It just takes time. All he has known his whole life is how to be alone. He has to learn how to be with people. That's all. Then he will know that being alone isn't as good as being with those who love him."

Chapter Twenty

"Is that a new Christmas tree?" Abbey asked.

"Yes," Caroline said with a smile. She turned her head toward the small, three-foot spruce with crystal ornaments and red balls. "I had it delivered and I decorated it yesterday. Isn't it pretty?"

"Yes. It's so nice."

Caroline nodded in agreement then turned and faced Abbey. "Robin called," she said as Abbey took her blood pressure and scribbled the numbers onto her chart. "She and the family are coming early in an attempt to avoid the impending snow in New York."

Abbey was relieved the house was nearly finished. She still had a few projects left, but nothing that would get in the way of visitors. "Have you ever been to New York?" Abbey asked, trying to seem nonchalant in her approach.

"Yes, dear. It's nice there."

"You like it? I've never been." She checked Caroline's heartbeat, and then pulled her stethoscope out of her ears and let it dangle around her neck. She wrote down more notes in the chart. "I'm guessing the city is busier than here. Which do you like better?"

"I can live anywhere at this stage in my life, but I particularly like it here. I get to see you, and Nick is just down the road... I'll even move into Nick's giant house if it suits everyone. At least I can trust you've made it habitable. In New York, the only family there is Robin, and she's so busy with work and her son. I'd never see her." Then she stopped talking and looked at Abbey. "Why are you asking?"

"No reason," she said. "I was just curious since I'd never been there."

"Mmm," Caroline said, her mind clearly moving to something else.

Abbey shouldn't have mentioned it. She should have just kept quiet. But she was worried for her friend. She didn't want just anyone taking care of her. There were things about Caroline that she knew only because she'd worked so closely with her. Would someone else know that she liked her pillows from flattest to puffiest going down the middle of the bed because it helped her arthritis? Would they know not to give her anything with grapefruit because it upset her stomach? Would they know that her blood pressure went up just slightly throughout the day and only went down after around six o'clock and that was okay?

"Nick's father, Aaron, lived in New York," she said, her eyes like lasers. "His business was there and it was very profitable. Nick took a risk coming to Richmond, a small, southern city. People warned him not to, but he did anyway because Sarah wanted him to. That's why he's going back."

"You know?"

"Yes. He told me everything over the phone last night."

"I wish he'd have told you in person," Abbey said, shaking her head.

"It's okay. He's a busy man."

"You cater to him sometimes," Abbey said boldly. "You should've made him come tell you."

"You would've if you were me, wouldn't you?" Caroline smiled a devious smile. "That's why I like you so much. You're good for him. I'm glad he met you."

Abbey smiled.

"It's a shame things couldn't be different. I will miss you," Caroline said.

"I'll miss you too. But, it looks like I'll be moving into the main house very soon, so we'll have a bit more time together."

"I'm excited about that."

"So," Caroline said, sitting up and clearing her throat to change direction. "Did we get my test results?"

"Let me look through your mail and see. They were supposed to overnight it on Friday, which should definitely put it here today." Abbey thumbed through the envelopes that she'd brought in from the mail on her way to see Caroline. Sure enough, she saw it. "Want me to open it, or would you like to?"

"Open it, dear. You can decipher the results better than I can. But wait. Before you do, let's have some pie. I've made fresh peach cobbler."

Caroline got two plates from the cupboard. Abbey noticed the delicate pink floral design around the edge. Caroline cut a generous slice from the pie and slipped it onto one of them.

"Your plates are beautiful," she said. "Are they antique?"

Caroline offered a wide smile. "Yes. They're my mother's. I used them as a girl."

"What was your childhood like?" Abbey asked, watching the way Caroline managed to get the slices of pie onto the plates without breaking the crust at all. She was a skilled hostess, but Abbey knew that about her. Caroline was the epitome of grace. She was polite, gentle in her movements, reserved in her comments, and she could entertain amazingly well. Even her home was bright and clean, no evidence whatsoever of aging—no extra dust, none of the smells or sights she'd encountered when she'd cared for people in the past. Caroline added a fork to each plate. Abbey picked up the two plates and set them on the table that was still covered in the cream tablecloth Abbey had bought when she'd decorated.

Caroline smiled, acknowledging her question, but in true form, she wasn't planning to answer until they were comfortably sitting at the table. "How about some coffee first?" she asked. "I just brewed some for myself. I made an entire pot. There's plenty." Abbey nodded and Caroline pulled a shiny silver creamer from the fridge and set it on a silver tray. Then, from the cupboard, she got a matching sugar bowl. She placed them on the table with two spoons, their handles intricately designed in silver roses.

Once the coffee was served and they were seated, Caroline very courteously placed her hands in her lap, leaving her food and drink untouched. "You asked about my childhood," she said with a smile. "That is why I love you so much, Abbey. You're the first person to ask."

"Really?"

"The others are so busy, I can't blame them. You are too—don't misunderstand me—but your job allows you time to focus on people. I really admire your attention to detail and your caring nature."

"Thank you," Abbey said, the compliment warming her. She hadn't received a lot of praise in her line of work, and it just went to show the bond that she and Caroline had. She gently dragged her fork against the corner of the pie, scooping up a bite.

Caroline took a slow sip of her coffee, resting the dainty cup in the palm of her hand. "My childhood was quite different than the generations after me. What's considered acceptable in our family now is quite dissimilar to my day. I had a good childhood." She took another quiet sip and then set it down to take a bite of pie. They sat in silence as she finished her bite. Then, she continued. "I was expected to do the things my mother taught me to do: I was taught manners; I learned how to receive guests; I did what I was told. But I played too. I had dollhouses, a wooden rocking horse, blocks. I was like most children when I was allowed to play." Her voice was quiet and a little sad.

Abbey paid attention to what Caroline was saying. She was telling her something more than what was on the surface. She was *too* careful with her words, *too* mannerly, to say what she wanted to say, but Abbey could see it on her face. In her description, she hadn't used the word "love" once. She hadn't said how great her parents were or how good they'd been with her. She hadn't spoken about trips she'd taken with her family, only what she'd been asked to do.

"My son and his wife, Susan, raised Nick and his sister in a different manner," she said. "Aaron was busy—he worked all the time— but when he was there, he made those kids feel like they were all that mattered. They had a bond with him that no one can ever take from them, and they miss him dearly. I had to find that kind of devotion later in life with my husband rather than my family, but it was fine. I am who I am because of my life's path. It just took me a little longer to find my way."

"Do you ever worry about your grandkids finding their way?"

"I don't worry about Robin. She's happily married with a son. She left as soon as she possibly could. She's just like her mother, and she found it much easier to be happy on her own. Then there's Nick." She took another sip of her coffee and stared into the brown liquid for a while before she started talking again. "Nick is a little lost, at the moment. He needs someone to show him the way."

"And you think that person is me," she said, no longer worried about what Caroline might say. It was pretty clear what she was getting at.

She smiled, and gingerly set her cup down onto its saucer. "I can only hope that person is you, my dear."

"Please don't get your hopes up," Abbey said. "Our lives are taking very different turns."

"I *knew* he was going to New York," Caroline said. "Before he'd even said anything, I knew eventually he would." She set her hands back into her lap in a very restrained manner. It was obvious that she was using everything she had to keep herself controlled. She probably worried terribly for him. "I know you are the right person to show him how to live, how to really *live.*"

"How do you figure?" Abbey asked.

Caroline was watching her closely, an unreadable look on her face. "You only know the Nick who you've seen. But he's not the Nick that his family knows. The Nick we know does not stop working. He's made it his personal goal to keep Aaron's business successful and he works around the clock to make it happen. He misses meals, he doesn't visit, he barely even takes a phone call. He *doesn't* stop, Abbey. But, after meeting you, I've had a few more phone calls, a visit or two, and I've heard about the things he's done with you. All of that is wonderful, but what really hit me was how many times you have been able to make him want to stop working. You're the only person who can do it. Even Sarah didn't get as much attention as you're getting from him."

"If what you say is true, then why is he still planning to move to New York? Why isn't it enough to make him see that work isn't everything?"

"All he's known his adult life is an inability to make things work. His marriage was a disaster—he closed up right after all that—and now all he has is the business. He doesn't want to let his father down."

What if he was afraid at failing with Abbey? Was he worried he'd give it all up, like he had with Sarah, only to have it not work out between them? Was it up to her to show him that they were worth a shot? "And you expect me to convince him to stay?"

"I think you're doing a pretty good job already," she said with a smile. "Now, let's take a look at those test results."

Chapter Twenty-one

Abbey sat amidst the pile of papers she'd used to scratch out ideas for Nick's Christmas party. She'd sketched table designs for the dining room, listed food pairings she thought would fit the season, and she'd created a wine and beer list. There were still a million little things she had to do to organize it all and get it ready. It was a far cry from her usual decorating. This was more of a favor than design, but she didn't mind doing it for Nick. She'd never had a chance to plan a party like this before, and she figured she could always add it to her portfolio. However, she had questions that he wasn't there to answer, and she knew, at some point, she'd better talk to him about Caroline's test results.

She got out her phone and texted: *I got your grandmother's test results back. Want to know what's going on with her or shall I wait to fill you in when you return?* She hit send and put her phone down on top of the wine and beer list.

The response came immediately: *Let's talk tonight. When is a good time to call?*

She was supposed to buy gift basket items for Max's school this evening, shop for Nick because she wanted to get him a Christmas present, she also had to finish planning for the party, *and* she had to get Max to do his homework, cook dinner, and get him to bed. She was already tired and needed to get to bed early but the idea of hearing Nick's voice was too enticing to pass up. She texted back, *How about nine o'clock tonight?*

Whatever works for you, he texted back. *Chat soon.* ☺

She peered down at her phone. Was that a smiley face? Had he inserted an emoticon in his message? "Haha!" she laughed out loud. It had surprised her.

Abbey was so excited at the thought of talking to him. She knew she had to stop this, and get over it, but she just couldn't. Caroline had mentioned that he needed her to show him how to live, but what Caroline hadn't said was that Abbey needed him too.

Nick brought something out in Abbey that made her feel more alive than she had in years. She hadn't told him, but she'd never danced with a man before at Alma's restaurant—only with Max or in her living room when Alma came over. She'd never have stopped to ice skate. But with him, she wanted to. The way his face changed when he was around her made her want to be with him. She craved his attention, and loved the thrill of seeing his playful side. When she'd first arrived at that big house of his, and the rooms seemed massive and unlivable, she wondered how he could live there, but now, his house was shaping up to be a wonderful home, and his money was just a part of who he was—she hardly noticed it. She loved sitting in that enormous ballroom on those fluffy sofas in front of the fire. All the glamour and luxury of that big house didn't overwhelm her anymore.

Max's affection for Nick only made things more difficult. As young as he was, could Max tell a difference in his mother when she was around Nick? Could that be part of the pull Max had toward

Nick—Max's yearning for that perfect little family that his classmates seemed to have?

Abbey got up and pulled her hair back, straightened her clothes that had been wrinkled from sitting on the floor while party planning, and got herself ready to go out. She needed something to keep her mind off Nick for a while, and she had to buy items for Max's gift basket at school. She thought about the theme: "Stay Warm and Comfy." She knew very well what made her feel warm and comfortable, but she couldn't think about that now.

Abbey had been shopping for an hour. Every year the school classes created Christmas gift baskets to be auctioned off. They were huge, over the top, foil- and plastic-wrapped prizes that were so well planned and presented that they fetched anywhere from fifty to a hundred dollars per basket. The money was then given to the students in need for supplies, winter clothing, and food. The list of items for the gift basket was crinkled in Abbey's hand as she held on to the shopping cart handle. She smoothed it back out and read the list of suggestions: quilt, slippers, bathrobe, decorative pillow…

Last year, the theme had been "A Day of Fun," and the basket had been filled with movie passes, bowling gift certificates, children's painting kits—all sorts of things. Abbey had purchased what she could afford that Christmas. She'd donated a box of microwave popcorn. She wanted to donate something wonderful, something so decadent and irresistible that the basket would bring in a ton of money for those kids in need. With her artistic eye, she could make those baskets amazing. She just didn't have the free cash to do it. As she looked at her list, she had no fear this year.

Abbey had decided to visit a small shop that was full of unique, upscale gifts. It was there that she found a quilt in gorgeous blues and creams and turned over the tag. Fifty-five dollars. She put it in her shopping basket and tried to keep the smile from spreading across her face.

After Vince left, Abbey had changed everything about the way she lived. Her free spirit had been crushed just a little when things hadn't worked out. And then having Max had made her feel like any blunder could be disastrous for him. As a single young woman, she could live without a dinner one night or camp out on a friend's couch if she couldn't afford an apartment, but she would never dream of causing an upheaval like that for Max. She saw her free spirit in him, and she didn't want anyone or anything ruining that. Childhood had been the one time when she'd felt invincible. She wanted that for her son. Now, when all his classmates brought in their items, even though he may never notice the difference in his contribution, she had the satisfaction of knowing that she and Max could provide something wonderful for the school.

Wouldn't it be nice to make a living all the time like she did with her decorating job? Maybe it was the Christmas music piping through the store, or the decorations hanging from the ceiling, all the happy faces plastered along the walls… She thought it could be possible to start her own business. As she walked through the shop, her mind traveled to the what-if's that didn't seem so far fetched anymore. An interior designer needs an office. She couldn't meet with clients in her apartment. She didn't even have an empty room. That would take money. …Money that she had from doing Nick's house. She could snap photos of her mother's, of Caroline's, and of Nick's and take out a few ads.

If she didn't try, she'd never know. Caroline would move away, and she'd find herself nursing again, her hours sporadic, her mother having to get up in the middle of the night and watch Max for her again. Could she have a better life if she just let go of her worry and tried this? Maybe she could start something part time… As scared as she was, all the ideas were flooding her, and the thrill of it was filling her with every step.

As she walked along the aisles, the quilt in her basket, she let her eyes slide along every shelf. There were so many wonderful things that she wanted to buy them all. She was heading toward the register when she stopped right there in the store and gasped quietly. Slowly, she reached out and grabbed the book off the shelf. It was deep brown rich leather, and it was made for holding music. Abbey ran her fingers along the front where it advertised possible engravings on a gold plate on the front—monograms, names… She knew what she wanted to put on the front. Beside it was a new book of sheet music for Christmas carols. She grabbed it and took it all up to the register.

"Did you brush your teeth?" Abbey asked Max as he put his things back into his backpack for tomorrow. He was wearing his pajamas with the trains on them, and his socks were bunched up at his ankles.

"Yep," he said, stuffing his reading book inside and zipping his backpack.

"Wait." Abbey grabbed the plastic bag off the counter and pulled out the quilt. "Give this to your teacher," she said, feeling a little joy from her purchase. But she kept her face light for Max's benefit. "It's for the class gift basket."

Max took the quilt and stuffed it in his bag.

"Can we read my bedtime story out here?" Max asked, his eyes roaming the small living area. "I want to be able to see the Christmas tree."

"Sure," she said, glad to have the power back on again so they could enjoy it.

In the corner of the room, Abbey had a small live tree with a few ornaments and a couple of strands of colored lights. Max had picked them out. It wasn't anything spectacular, but in the dark of night, the lights shimmered off the glass of the ornaments and it looked magical. It made her think about the living room at Nick's. She had planned a traditional small tree in that room, one that Max would enjoy. She was moving into Nick's tomorrow; maybe they could decorate that tree then. She'd packed them each a fresh bag, figuring she could always come home and switch out their clothes if they needed more. Max should have a tree that was familiar. She couldn't wait to make some ornaments or a homemade garland for it.

Max ran down the short hallway and returned with a book and one of the blankets from his bed as well. They sat together beneath the lamplight and snuggled up under the blanket.

"Do you think Santa will bring me lots of presents this year? " he asked and Abbey thought of all the gifts she'd bought with Nick, which were safely hidden away and waiting to be left by Santa.

"Yes." She smiled down at him, so happy that she'd gotten him what he wanted.

"What are *you* going to unwrap? You never have presents to unwrap on Christmas morning. It's just me. That's not fair."

"Aw, it's okay. Grownups don't get presents like kids do." She knew that in some families they did, but she didn't want Max feeling guilty at all. This was supposed to be his special Christmas.

"Grownups need surprises though," he said.

"You are my surprise and every year that I spend with you watching you open your gifts is a gift for me. Now, what book do you have tonight?"

He handed her his story for the night and they read together until Max could hardly keep his eyes open. Once she put him to bed, she went to the bathroom to check on the sheet music. She'd ripped out the pages from the Christmas carol book and soaked them in tea to give them an aged look, and now they were drying on a plastic sheet in her tub. The sheets were nearly dry.

The apartment was quiet. Max was asleep in his bed and Abbey had her phone in her hand. It was exactly nine o'clock. Her fingertips were cold and numb from nerves. She couldn't wait to talk to Nick. All day she'd waited and now, it was finally time. Before she could dial his number, her phone rang.

"Hello?" she said.

"Hi."

Hearing his voice was the best sound. He hadn't even been gone a day and she already missed him. She missed the way he looked at her when she surprised him with things she said, the way it felt to wake up with his arm around her after painting, the feel of his hand in hers.

"I only have a few minutes," he said, and she felt her heart drop into her stomach. "I had to know about my grandmother, but after today, if there's anything else, just let Richard know. You're moving in tomorrow, right?"

"Yes."

"He has my emergency number if it's required for any reason. Otherwise, I won't be available."

"You don't sound like yourself," she said. He sounded distant. It was so different than his regular cadence—it was short, choppy.

Nick cleared his throat. "I'm just busy," he said a little more gently this time. "I'm in the middle of a large acquisition at the same time that I'm house hunting."

"Oh," she said.

"So, shall we just get right to it then?" he asked.

"Okay," she said reluctantly. "But first, why didn't you go and *see* Caroline to tell her she was moving in? She said you called."

"I was in New York."

"Couldn't you have told her before you left?"

"Abbey," he said, his voice sounding tired. "I'm sure you would've done things differently, but you aren't me. I called her. She knows. She took it well."

"She did?" Abbey asked, his last comment of more interest to her than arguing with his approach. She had noticed how Caroline hadn't seemed very upset, although she had mentioned in conversation before how she'd never want to live there. "She never wanted to live at your house before, but now she's okay with it?"

"She didn't want to live there when the house was empty and I was always at work, but now the house is amazing. She will have you and Max, and Robin should be coming. She's fine with it."

"The house is amazing?" Abbey asked with a smile.

"Yes." She could feel his smile in that word. "Now, tell me what's going on with her."

"Caroline has an arrhythmia," she answered. "I suspected it, but was waiting for a diagnosis before I said anything."

"What does that mean?"

"It's an irregular heartbeat. It can escalate with age. By itself, it's just something to monitor, but I worry about it with her arthritis and the hip problems she's been having. If she needs surgery, the arrhythmia might make it impossible."

"She can't fall. She can't walk around too much," he worried aloud. "I'm glad she'll have your care."

"I enjoy taking care of her. I'll miss her when she's gone," she said.

"I'm sure you will."

She hated the idea of Caroline leaving.

"I have to go," he said. "Thank you for keeping me informed."

"I have some questions about the house," she said quickly, before he ended the call.

"Ask Richard. I've told him he can make decisions this week while I'm gone. And, as always, I trust you to do what you think is right." There was a small pause, and she could feel that he was going to say something else. "You're great at what you do, Abbey," he said, his voice soft. "You're a wonderful nurse, but you're an even better decorator." That was the best compliment she could've received. And she could tell by his honest voice that he was serious.

"Thank you," she said.

"I'm not kidding at all. You are great."

Where was this coming from? He'd never cared one way or the other about what she did. It was clear, after seeing his bedroom, that he had an eye for that sort of thing, but he'd never bothered to offer his opinions before.

"Well," he said, his voice sounding unsure all of a sudden. "I should go."

"Don't." She worried that he was holding back. She was desperate to keep him on the line. If she could just talk to him, maybe she could make him see that he needed to stay; maybe they could find some sort of middle ground. His change in tone had been enough to give her the strength to try to stop him.

"Abbey, I have to go," he said gently.

"Why?"

"I just do. Richard is there if you need him. Have a good week."

The phone line went dead. She thought about calling him back, but decided against it. She'd surprised herself tonight. She'd never needed anyone before, she'd been fine on her own, but tonight, she felt, for the first time in her life, what it was like to yearn for someone, to wish with everything she had that he'd stay on the line. With a heavy heart, she went to bed.

Chapter Twenty-two

Abbey let Max run through Nick's house as she placed their clothes in drawers and set the suitcases in the closet. Nick wasn't there anyway, so it was just the two of them and the staff. She'd texted him this morning to remind him that Max's "Bring Your Daddy to School Day" was next Wednesday, and she hadn't heard back. She was so worried that he wouldn't show up, especially with him being as busy as he was at the moment. Max needed a positive male role model in his life and that was one thing that she couldn't give him. But Nick could give him that.

Her phone lit up with a text just as she was thinking of him, and Abbey almost fell over the bed to get it. She could see Nick's number; her heart slammed around in her chest. She opened it and read, *Just a quick note to say Robin is actually flying in tonight. Feel free to decorate around her. Just wanted to give you the heads up.*

Abbey felt a mixture of exhilaration at seeing his text and complete despair that he hadn't even bothered to say hello first. She didn't know what to think. She just stared at the words until her phone's screen went dark. What about Max's day at school? He'd gotten the text, surely. He hadn't even responded.

Abbey had spent a whole lot of time at Caroline's today, helping her get what she needed moved into the mansion, and now she was scrambling to get as much of the house done as she could before Robin arrived. She got Caroline all settled into one of the chairs in the living room with a book, her cell phone, and a cup of coffee, and told her that she was a text away. She'd be outside.

Before she went outside, however, she put Max in the bath to play and sneaked into Nick's office. She pulled his music folders from the shelf. They were old and worn on the edges. She thumbed through the music and pulled out a few titles she liked, making sure to find "Dreams." She slid the folders back onto his shelf and carried the small pile of music she'd taken to the room with her things. She pulled the new book she'd bought for Nick from the front pocket of her suitcase and blew a tiny speck of dust off the engraving. Then she opened it and put the music inside it.

Once she had it all the way she wanted it, she pulled the tea-stained sheets of music from her bag. She'd been meticulous about getting the edges of each sheet perfectly lined up, creating a large, shiny piece of Christmas carol sheet music wrapping paper. She set the book in the center of it and cut the paper to size. Then, she folded it around the book, taping the edges closed, and secured it with a wide, wine-colored ribbon, tying an oversized bow on the front. Snipping an obscure piece of holly from one of the bedroom's arrangements she'd made, she tucked it under the bow. When it was all finished, she hid the present in the closet.

After Nick's gift was well hidden, and Max was out of the bath, Abbey stacked the rest of the exterior wreaths that had been delivered. She'd ordered more because, in a last-minute decision, she'd decided to put one on every single window on the house, all the way around. Why not? Nick needed a little Christmas cheer. The groundsmen were putting them up using ladders that were so large they looked like scaffolding. One of them had explained that it was the way they cleaned all the windows four times a year. Max had come outside and was digging in the snow with a plastic shovel he'd brought with the rest of his outside toys.

A wheelbarrow the size of a dump truck held boxes of exterior white lighting. She'd drawn a diagram of which trees to string with them and how closely to place the lights on the branches. One of the groundsmen was already setting up a ladder next to a small maple tree, its base sinking in the pile of snow underneath it. She had two of the boxes of lights in her hands. The spruce trees flanking the front door were in need of some sprucing up themselves. She started with those—shaking the snow off their branches—and then she'd move to the greenery along the railings leading to the front door.

The exterior and the living room were the only two large areas left to complete. After that, she had to put the finishing touches on the ballroom, and then add a few decorative items in the bathrooms and hallways. Then, the house would be finished.

She pulled her new scarf up around her mouth to keep her face from freezing as she got the greenery out and laid it straight along the steps to see its length before beginning on the large iron railings lining the steps. Her breath was puffing out in front of her and she could barely feel her nose, but when she saw that black Lincoln town car, she couldn't deny the heat in her face. Abbey tried not to stare as it rolled along the snowy drive in front of her and came to a stop.

Richard got out and opened the back door. A thin arm reached out and dropped a designer bag onto the snow. Then, a pair of boots revealed themselves, their heels so tall that it was a wonder the person in the car could walk at all in these conditions. The woman wearing those boots was finally visible, her face a feminine version of Nick's, her skin so milky and soft that it looked like the porcelain dolls Abbey had had as a child. The woman's dark brown hair was silky and shiny despite the weather, falling in waves along the shoulders of her perfectly tailored black trench coat with a patterned buckle that cinched the belt at the waist. Richard picked up her bags and they started walking toward Abbey.

She watched the woman out of the corner of her eye as she wound the wire around the greenery to hold it on. The task was difficult with her mittens on but it was too frigid outside to take them off. The woman wobbled on her boots, her face neutral like Nick's had been when he'd first met Abbey, but with every little slip, the woman pursed her lips in what seemed like concentration as she tried not to fall.

Abbey's gaze moved past the woman, back to the car, as a little boy got out. He, too, was perfectly dressed—Max had never worn anything that nice, even on picture day. She looked over at him now, his jeans soaked at the knees from playing in the snow. Max stood up, eyeing the boy with anticipation on his face. The little boy's coat and snow boots matched, both a deep hunter green. The collar of his coat and the rims around the tops of his boots were navy. The boy's complexion was like his mother's, the navy of his coat bringing out the blue of his eyes. He ran up beside her and Abbey heard her warn him gently not to run on the ice.

A man, presumably the husband of the woman, was getting out of the car just as the woman stopped and made eye contact with Abbey. "Oh!" she said, her gaze moving from Abbey to the house. "This is completely amazing!" She walked up the steps carefully, those tall boots working hard to keep her steady. "I'm Robin, Nick's sister. Are you Abbey?"

She knows my name? Abbey thought. She nodded, wishing she'd spent a little more time on herself. Robin's expression was kind, not judging, and it set her at ease a little.

"Nick has told me so much about you!"

"He has?"

"Yes! He tells me you should be my decorator."

"He did?" She was so surprised that he'd recommended her to his own sister.

"Yes! I have a loft in New York. If I like your work, I'll have to fly you up."

Jet-setting around the coast to decorate people's homes sounded preposterous for her, but no more preposterous than getting the opportunity to decorate a multi-million-dollar home. She thought to herself how different her version of "normal" had become. She could actually do this.

The little boy, who had stopped to drag his fingers in the untouched snow, and the man both joined them on the steps.

"This is my son Thomas…" She patted his head. "And my husband James. This is Abbey, the decorator."

James held out his hand to Abbey. He was strikingly handsome—he had a square jaw, a warm smile, and his hair was curly but perfectly cut. She shook his hand. Max stepped up beside them as they finished their introductions.

"It's nice to meet you," she said. "This is my son, Max." Abbey looked down at the two boys standing side by side. "This is Thomas," she said to Max. "Maybe he'd like to play with you." The moment she said it, she worried that perhaps his mother didn't want to get his clothes messed up, but when she looked at Robin, she was smiling.

Richard opened the door and ushered them inside. Abbey followed behind, needing a break from the cold. Max and Thomas were already chatting as Max kicked his snow-covered boots off at the door and unzipped his coat.

Robin gasped, her eyes going immediately to the giant Christmas trees in the entranceway. "Oh," she said slowly, turning to Abbey and handing her coat to Richard at the same time. "These trees are positively *gorgeous*."

Richard motioned for Abbey's coat, so she shrugged it off and handed it to him along with her scarf and mittens. He scooped up the kids' things and disappeared.

"Is this where Santa will leave our presents, Mommy?" Thomas asked as he stood next to one of the twenty-five-foot trees and tipped his head up to see all the way to the top.

"Probably not," Robin said as she headed toward the ballroom, her heels clicking on the gleaming floors. She walked through the arching doorway and stopped in the center of the room then turned around. "Abbey, this is amazing work. These trees are fantastic. And that fireplace! Oh my goodness!" She threw her hand to her chest in dramatic excitement.

Thomas ran into the ballroom to see what his mother was raving about as Max followed.

"Wow," James said as he entered, looking around.

Abbey was thrilled by their reaction. Having decorated around Nick and received so small a response to what she'd done, this was a welcome surprise. Hearing their praise, all the worry that she'd had about her lack of experience, picking high-end furnishings, and making the right decisions for such a wealthy client were totally gone. She caught herself smiling from ear to ear. She'd created the feel of this home all by herself, and now she realized that she could do this. Interior design was a possibility for her.

Thomas grabbed his father's hand and began swinging it back and forth. "Is *this* where Santa will come?" he asked.

"I've put a smaller tree in the living room too," Abbey offered. "Although I'm still decorating the house and I haven't finished that tree. I thought maybe we could make some ornaments for it or something."

"Lovely! That would be a more suitable place for Santa, wouldn't it?" Robin said to Thomas. "It's cozier in the living room, I'm sure."

Abbey smiled. While it did have more casual furniture, the mere size of the room had removed it from any definition of "cozy" that Abbey had ever had, but she'd been able to pull it together with furniture, lighting, candles, and artwork, and now it was as comfortable as anywhere else.

Richard poked his head in. "Your bags are upstairs," he said to Robin. "I wasn't sure which room you'd choose, so I set them in the hallway. Please let me know if you need any further assistance."

"Thank you, Richard," Robin said, and Richard left the room.

"Show me what else you've done!" Robin said, walking over to Abbey. "This house has been transformed! I haven't been here since Sarah had it decorated with all her things. The whole house has a different feel now. It's so…" She looked around the room as if trying to find the right words. "So, comfortable. You've really given it a personality. It's just lovely." She grabbed Abbey's arm. "Show me the rest! And where's my grandmother? I'm dying to see her! What does she think of all this?"

"I'm just going to take Thomas to get a snack," James said to Robin. "Max, would you like to come too?" Max looked over at Abbey for approval and she nodded. She was so glad to have someone here now to give Max a little attention.

Abbey watched as little Thomas ran and slid in his sock feet just like Max had done. Max, delighted by the sight, joined him. It made her think of Nick. She pushed the thought away, the worry about Max's disappointment if he didn't show at school still lurking in her mind.

Abbey led Robin upstairs. "Caroline is probably in the living room," Abbey said. "That's where I left her just before you came. I'm sure she'll be happy to see you." They walked into the first bedroom. The enormous four-poster bed warmed the room, the oversized linens and navy and white throw pillows anchored the space, and drew in the deep blues of the bedside lamps that were casting a glow around the room. Abbey looked down at Robin's boots, wishing she'd kick them off and feel the softness of the rug underneath them.

Robin took in a breath of excitement as she pushed her shiny hair behind her shoulders, her bright red nails revealing themselves between the strands. "I want this room! I'm staying in here," she called. "I love it! Where's my grandmother staying? Certainly, she can't get up all these stairs on a regular basis."

"There's a small room at the back of the house downstairs. I believe Richard had it made up as her room with the things from her house. I'm going to check it out and make sure it's suitable for her. I helped her bring most of it over and we left it with the staff. I'll put the room together for her if they haven't."

"Good, good," Robin said. "Show me the other rooms."

Abbey walked her down to the room with the picture she'd taken from the closet and then through the rest of the rooms.

In the last one, Robin sat down on the bed. She patted the spot beside her, asking Abbey to sit. "I hope you have some free time in your decorating schedule," she said, "because I would love to fly you out to New York. I have several friends who were just asking for interior designer recommendations. You'd be perfect."

"I'm not a full-time decorator." Could she be? Robin was lining potential clients up for her. She decided tonight she was going to begin to research small businesses and find out what she needed to do to make this happen. Her dream was right at her fingertips. Perhaps she could decorate a few more homes for Robin and her friends, add them to her portfolio, and then begin doing it full time.

"Well, we could work around your schedule. Are you booked up?"

Abbey chuckled. "No. Not at all at the moment, although I'd love to do it full time. I'm a nurse. I care for your grandmother."

"Wait. You're the same Abbey who is the in-home nurse for my grandmother? She loves you! She talks about you all the time!"

"Yes."

"Well that would make sense."

"It would?"

"Nick has nothing but wonderful things to say about you too. And not just your decorating." She winked. "I've heard about your Mexican dancing," she said laughing. "I wish you would've recorded that. I've never seen Nick dance in my life."

Abbey's face was suddenly on fire.

Robin laughed again. It was a light, giggling laugh. "Nick has a crush on you. He told me! He tells me everything."

He'd told her that? she thought. Abbey caught herself smiling and no matter how hard she tried, she couldn't stop.

Robin stood up and started to leave the room so Abbey got up too, trying to iron out her expression so she wouldn't look like a crazy person. "Any word on when Mother's planning on coming?" Robin asked.

"I haven't heard," Abbey said.

"Who knows with her," she said, shaking her head. "It's funny: she and Nick were always so close when we were kids. They got along famously. But after Dad died, it was as if she couldn't be near him because he was so much like his father that it kept her in some sort of depression. She moved to Colorado not long after my father passed. I wish she would've stayed, though, to see how well Nick has managed everything. He's so hard working. Persistence is one of his talents."

"Did you know that Nick plays piano?" Abbey asked. He wrote beautiful music. People needed to hear it.

"Yes. He's very gifted."

"And he writes his own music."

Robin stopped and looked directly at Abbey. "You know that?"

"He played me some."

Her eyes got big, causing Abbey to notice her long, thick lashes. She was very beautiful. Outside of this situation, Abbey would feel intimidated near someone like her, but Robin was so kind and talkative that she almost didn't notice how gorgeous she was. "He played for you?"

"Yes."

"He hasn't even played his music for *me*. As far as I know, he hasn't played it for anyone. Except you, apparently. He guards it like some big secret, not letting any of us in on it."

"Why would he do that?"

"You tell me."

They made their way downstairs and headed into the living room where Caroline was dozing in a side chair. Abbey took in with pride the two dark wood side tables with coordinating lamps, the throw pillows for the sofas, and the whole host of indoor plants from the nursery. Thomas and Max were on the floor next to the spot where the bare Christmas tree was, playing with a small train set.

James was drinking a beer, the bottle resting in his lap. He had football on the big-screen, the volume low. He stood up when they reached him as a polite gesture. "I spoke with Caroline for a few minutes, but she fell asleep," he whispered.

"Did you know that Nick played his music for Abbey?" Robin said to James.

He turned to look at Abbey, his eyes as wide as his wife's had been. "Really?"

"Yes. I must get to the bottom of this."

"Wait," Abbey said, nearly breathless. "I don't know if he wanted me to tell you."

"Well, it doesn't matter. I'm his sister and he tells me everything." She bent down, her long hair nearly touching the floor, and smiled at Thomas and Max. "That looks fun," she said. The boys both smiled at her, holding train cars in both hands.

"It is," Thomas said, smiling. He handed her a train car. "This will be yours."

"Thank you," she said, standing up and putting it in her pocket.

"James, do you need another beer? I'm going to get a glass of wine."

"No thank you, dear. I'm fine."

"Abbey?"

She shook her head. "I don't want to impose."

"You aren't imposing at all! We can talk decorating."

"Well, just the one glass then."

"Excellent!" Robin clapped her hands together quietly, her diamond rings swinging around her thin fingers. "Come with me. You can choose your wine."

Abbey followed her through the house as they made small talk about her choice in décor.

In the kitchen, Robin opened one of the cabinet-like doors, revealing a huge wine cooler—stacks of wine went from floor to ceiling inside the cabinet. The whole thing was at least eight feet tall! "Reds are on the left, whites on the right," she said.

Abbey didn't know about wine. She didn't know what was good and what wasn't. Did Robin expect her to say the name of a wine? She had no idea...

Her confusion must have been evident because Robin stepped in and said, "I really love this white wine." She pulled the bottle from its holder. "It's my favorite. It's a little sweet, more on the dessert wine side, but very nice and crisp. Have you ever had it?" She turned the bottle around so that Abbey could read the label. She'd never even heard of it.

Abbey shook her head.

"Want to try some?"

"Yes. It sounds great, thank you."

As Robin poured the wine, Thomas came into the kitchen. "Mommy, may I have something to drink too? Daddy said to come ask you." He climbed up on one of the swiveling high-seat chairs that lined the bar in the center of the kitchen. His tiny feet dangled as he swung them back and forth.

"Sure. What would you like? Uncle Nick probably has everything."

"Hot chocolate, please."

"Mmm, hot chocolate sounds nice and Christmassy! Would Max like some?"

"He said he wanted to keep playing with my trains."

Robin nodded and pulled a mug from the cabinet.

"How old are you, Thomas?" Abbey asked, taking her wine and sitting down beside him at the bar.

"Six."

"I thought you looked like you could be six. Max is six too."

"Did you know that Max will be staying here with us until Christmas? You two will be able to play every day," Robin said. She looked over at Abbey. "Nick told me that you'd be living here to be on call for my grandmother. What a wonderful surprise to find out that your son will be here as well. Thomas was very worried about leaving his friends until after Christmas."

Robin spooned some hot chocolate mixture into the mug and poured hot water over it. Then she mixed it and handed it to Thomas. She grabbed her wine and took a sip. "Now, tell me," she said to Abbey, "how is my brother? He's out again on one of his business trips, I'm assuming."

"He's fine, I think."

"Well, between conversations about what to do for my grandmother's care, he sure had a ton to say about you, and he sounded more than fine."

"What did he say about me?"

"He was almost giddy—well, as giddy as Nick can get. But I've never seen him like that. He said he can't keep his mind on his work, and that worried him. You were distracting him," she said with a smile.

"Yes, he's told me that too."

Robin smiled wider. "I can understand your pull on him. You have an honest face, and you're a good listener. Your demeanor puts people at ease. I'll bet you're a great nurse."

"Thank you. That's very nice of you to say." Abbey set her wine down on the counter and Robin refilled it without asking.

"I've only known you a few minutes and I feel like I could tell you anything." Robin rolled her eyes. "Maybe that's just me, though. Maybe I'm too chatty."

"No, you're fine. I'm enjoying myself."

"I'm going to see Daddy and Max," Thomas said.

Robin held up the train car that she'd kept in her pocket. "Want me to join you and we can play?"

"No, thank you. I can play with Max."

"You sure?"

Thomas nodded, took the train car, and left the room. Robin tidied his spot, rinsing his mug and putting it in the dishwasher. Then she sat down on the tall bar chair, crossed her long, thin legs, and swiveled herself toward Abbey.

"Listening to Nick talk about you," she said, the glass of wine dangling from her fingertips, the liquid tilting in the glass. "I took an instant liking to you—before I'd ever met you—because you were able to do something that none of us have ever been able to do: make Nick stop working. Anyone who can do that is someone special."

"That's what Caroline said too—no one can pull him from work. Can you tell me, Robin, why does he feel the need to keep his father's company going? He's tried to explain it and I just don't understand."

The question made Robin straighten up a little more, her eyes focused. "My father worked all the time on that business. He built it from nothing, and he made a ton of money. He risked everything for that company—even his family. We barely saw him. My mother was very upset about all his working—I heard their quiet arguments at night. She wanted him to spend more time with us. When Nick was very young, he would walk around in my father's work shoes; he could knot a tie at four years old. Nick wanted to be with him every moment. So when my father passed, Nick took it the hardest of all. Nick feels that if he lets the business fail, then he'll fail his father."

"But he moved to Richmond for family. And Richmond wasn't the best location for his business. That looks like a step in the right direction."

"Ah, but he was trying to do both at full steam, and what he learned the hard way was that, while my mother put up with it from my father, other women will not. Sarah wasn't having it at all. And I believe—just my opinion—that it was the reason she left."

"Do you think he's scared?" Abbey asked.

"What do you mean?"

"Do you think he's scared to do something other than what his father had done? There could be lots of reasons he'd be scared," Abbey said, the words coming out at the same time as she was processing them. "…Scared that he might not be as successful doing something else, scared that he'd let his family down, scared that he wouldn't have a plan or know what to do." She realized as she was listing those things that they were all the same reasons she had for not following her dreams. It silenced her as soon as she'd realized it.

"I've never thought of him as anything other than strong, but you know what? You could be right. So, how do we show him it's okay to do something even if he's scared?"

Robin was using the term "we" as if there were some reason Abbey would be involved in changing him. "I don't think *we* are going to do anything, but you can if you'd like."

"Why?" Robin asked and then trailed off, immediately clasping her perfectly manicured hand over her mouth. "Are his feelings one-sided?" she said through her fingers.

Abbey thought about Nick's eyes—how curious he'd been when he looked at her, that smile lurking, just waiting to come out and knock her off her feet. She thought about how sweet and tender he could be, how it felt to kiss his lips. Did she just have stars in her eyes? She wanted to text him right then and find out how he felt about her exactly, but she didn't. He'd been pretty clear, telling her to direct all questions to Richard.

"You're quiet. It *is* one-sided," Robin said.

"It's not that," Abbey tried to explain. "He made it pretty clear that he didn't want to talk to me. He told me if I have any questions to direct them to Richard. I have to plan a party for a hundred people here. I've never done that before. I want to do a good job, make him happy with what I've chosen, and have it all completed in a timely manner."

"I'll help you plan the party. I do it all the time. You just weigh in on what you like design-wise and I'll help with the rest."

"I don't feel right asking you to do that. This is your Christmas holiday. You need to spend it with your family, not do a job that I'm being paid to do."

Robin laughed. "Nick hired you as a decorator. He only threw the party on you because he didn't want to do it himself, and he knew that when it came down to it, you'd be great at it. I know him too well. You and I can plan the party together. Nick won't care one way or the other who gets it done as long as he can tick it off his list."

"What about your time that I'm taking? You need to enjoy your family."

"I will! It doesn't take long to plan it—a few things here and there. You'll do all the ordering of supplies. We'll be able to do it while our boys play tomorrow. Easy."

"Are you sure?"

"I'm sure."

Chapter Twenty-three

Abbey had gone herself to pick up Max after school. She took a moment to admire the exterior of Nick's home as she drove up to it. All the exterior trees were lit in their white lights, the trees by the door lit as well, the dark green spruce wreaths on every window, their dark cranberry bows popping against the brick exterior. It was such a beautiful, Christmassy contrast to the muted daylight through the gray sky.

She parked the car and got out, tugging the scarf Nick had bought her a little tighter to keep out the frigid temperatures. Max had his coat on, but she had to zip it up as he got out. They weren't even to the steps before the huge front door opened and Thomas stood there in his socks.

"Hi," he called out in a very matter-of-fact way.

When they got to the top of the steps, meeting him at the door, Max smiled at his new friend, and they ran inside. Abbey went back to the car to get some extra toys she hadn't yet unpacked, although, from the looks of it, the boys were already keeping themselves busy.

Richard met her in the drive and insisted on carrying everything in for her. She didn't feel comfortable when he did that because she wasn't employing him, but he assured her that he'd do it anyway. She liked Richard. He kept his personal thoughts separate from his professional life, but she could tell that a lot of what he did for the family and for her was simply because he cared. He was very quiet but thoughtful—it came through in his actions. He said he'd put it all in the living room. Then, just before he walked away, he told her that Nick was home.

Abbey immediately went to his office and knocked but no one answered. She'd had enough experience by now to know that he was probably busy. She hated when he didn't answer the door, so without another knock, she opened it. She couldn't wait to see him. To her surprise, the room was empty. Taken aback, she slowly closed the door, wondering where he was.

She found Robin and Caroline in the kitchen. "Nick's home," she said. "But he isn't in his office. Have you seen him?"

"He was on a phone call, but I assumed that he went to the office after. I was helping Caroline with her sewing," Robin said.

"Is he with James?"

"James isn't here. He went to do a little Christmas shopping."

"Okay," she said. "Well, I'll check on the boys."

She made her way to the living room, but when she got there, she had to close her gaping mouth. Nick was not only in the living room—where he never went—but he was on the floor on his back while the boys were building a train track over the top of him!

"Hi," he waved carefully from under the track.

"Hi," she said, kneeling down beside him. "What in the world…" The sight of him like that made her want to kiss him right there on the spot.

"I had a very stressful time in New York. When I got home, I came to see you but you were gone, so I thought I'd come in here and *relax*." He smiled and eyed his half empty beer on the side table.

"Thank you for using a coaster," she said with a grin. "You came to see me?"

"You're welcome and yes. I was in New York all alone, working in between trying to find a house, and I kept feeling uneasy. I couldn't place it, but it was driving me crazy. I went through the motions, but something was different this time. All I wanted was a distraction. My work wasn't holding my attention." He winked at her. "When I couldn't find you, I figured I'd get a beer and kick back."

"That's not like you."

"No, it isn't. And it feels very weird. Even weirder when being under a train track."

"Pity you can't reach your beer," she said with a grin.

Thomas sat on his knee and added another piece.

"Yes it is. Thomas had other ideas."

"That perfectly good beer going to waste…" She walked over and sat down on the sofa next to it, picking it up between her two fingers and pretending to inspect the label. It was some kind of fancy microbrew. "I didn't know you drank beer." She tipped it up to her lips and took a swig. It was good.

"Get your own beer," he said, but his eyes were affectionate.

"I just wanted a taste."

Carefully, he pulled himself from under the track and the boys moaned in disapproval. "Sorry, boys," he said. "I'll play again soon."

"You don't have time to play," she said. She handed him his beer and tried to keep her hands at her sides when all she wanted to do was put them around his neck.

"I got the company I was after in New York. After that, I decided to take a little time off for Christmas."

"Is that so?"

"Yes."

"I didn't expect you back so soon," she said, leading him out into the hallway.

"I found a house very quickly. Well, I just stopped looking after the first showing. I don't really care where I live as long as it's in a central location and decent."

"You found a house?"

"It's an apartment."

"Are you drinking beer?" Robin interrupted their conversation, the tapping of her heels reaching a crescendo against the floors as she neared them.

"Yes. I drink beer on occasion," Nick said to his sister.

"What occasion?" she teased. "Never mind. I'm not going to talk you out of it. That's a good thing. It's better than having a phone in your hand."

"I'm taking some time off for Christmas," he explained.

"I can't believe it," Robin said dramatically. "James should be home soon. We should have a big dinner."

"Whatever you like. Just let Richard know. I need to do a little work today to tie up a few loose ends. It shouldn't be too long. Then we can all eat dinner."

"May I cook?" Abbey asked, and they both looked at her.

"Certainly. If you want to. It's a big crowd," he said with a smile.

"I'm up for it. I'd like to cook you some of my favorite foods. Would that be okay?"

"I'd love it," Robin said. "Surprise us!"

Nick agreed.

"Are you sure?"

"Yes," Nick said. "I can't wait to see what you cook."

"Great! I'll go get started."

The bag of odds and ends Abbey had requested from Richard was still on the counter when she finished up each of the dishes. She had it all on the bar of the kitchen buffet-style as everyone came in. She pulled a bag of white hamburger rolls from the grocery bag and opened the twist tie, leaving them at the start of the buffet. There were paper plates, napkins, hot dogs, hamburgers—with or without cheese— baked beans, potato salad, and her famous green bean casserole.

Max ran in ahead of Thomas. "Yummy, Mama!" he said, reaching up for a plate at the end of the counter. The others followed.

"Grab a napkin and fork with your plate!" Abbey said with a giggle as she looked at them. They were all scanning the bar with inquisitive faces. "Ketchup and mustard are at the end of the line."

"It's like being at a picnic!" Caroline said with excitement. But then nobody moved. It was as if they didn't know where to begin.

"I'll start," Abbey said, pulling a plastic fork from the cup she'd stuffed them all in, and grabbing a plate and napkin. She pulled a bun from the bag, left it open on the plate, and added a burger with cheese. "Get your burger and then you have all this to choose from." Max stood next to Nick, trying to reach the plates. "Nick, if you'll help Max, I'll make yours. Do you want everything on your burger?"

"Make it however you like and I'll try it," he said.

"Excellent." She added onions, tomato, lettuce, mayonnaise, ketchup, and mustard. When she closed the hamburger, it was so high that she had to secure it with a toothpick. "Baked beans?" she asked.

"Yes. Thank you. What is that bowl of yellow…?" he asked as he opened a bun and set it on a plate for Max.

"Potato salad. It's my mother's recipe. Want to try it?" Abbey had her plate and Nick's teetering on the edge of the counter beside each other as she piled on the food.

"Potato... Salad. Is there salad in it?" he asked, peering over the bowl.

"No. There's mustard, mayonnaise, and relish, among other spices. You might like it." She scooped up a glop of it and lumped it on his plate. "You've been living in Richmond all this time and you've never encountered potato salad?" He just looked at her. She tried not to giggle. "I'll put a little of everything and you can try it all." His face was priceless.

The others were slowly filling their plates, watching Abbey and smiling. Robin had set her food down and was leaning into the wine cooler. "What goes well with this meal? Red, maybe? It's beef..."

"Anything is fine," Abbey said.

Robin pulled out a bottle of Zinfandel and uncorked it. "Who's having wine?" she asked as the bottle breathed in her hand. The adults accepted her offer, and Abbey poured milk for the kids.

They all took their plates and drinks with them into the dining room.

Nick let out a punch of laughter. "What's on the table?" he asked.

"A paper tablecloth," Abbey said as she set her paper plate down on the Christmas tree printed paper. "It's festive. And at the end, you can ball it up with everything on it—easy cleanup."

With another chuckle, he sat down beside her. Abbey looked around at the faces that were there tonight. Caroline was cutting her burger with her plastic knife and fork, clearly being a good sport, her paper napkin in her lap; Robin and James were both helping Thomas get situated; and Max was holding a burger as big as his head!

Abbey recalled those first nights with Nick, sitting in silence at that huge table. She leaned over to Nick. "Now this is what the dinner table should be like," she said quietly to him.

Nick smiled and discreetly pointed at Max as he tried to take a bite of his burger, half the toppings falling out the other side.

Abbey laughed. "Well, you helped him make it."

"I just followed your lead." He pointed to his own and grinned at her.

Abbey turned to address the group. "Has anyone tried something new?"

"It's my first taste of potato salad," Nick said. "The jury's still out…"

"I like it," Robin added. "And I like this green bean casserole as well."

"When I first started working for Nick," Abbey said, "he made me dinner and I didn't know what it was. It was zucchini, wasn't it, Nick?" She looked at him for agreement. "Anyway, it was delicious. I wanted to share something new with you all. I hope you're enjoying it. I've made apple pie for dessert."

"That sounds delicious, Abbey," Caroline said. "Thank you for all of this." She dabbed the corners of her mouth with her paper napkin. "When was the last time we all ate as a family?" Caroline asked.

Everyone looked around at each other and shook their heads.

"We don't do this enough," Caroline said. "Promise me that when your mother gets here, we'll all get together again. We lead such busy lives. We need to stop and remember our family."

Nick stood up, holding his glass. "To family," he said, and they all raised their drinks. Abbey joined too and asked Max to lift his cup. While this wasn't her family, it was a great one, and she was toasting to that. Nick added, "And good friends," as he winked in Max's direction.

"Cheers!" Max said, and clinked his cup with Nick's glass. They all laughed.

It was getting late, and Max hadn't had a bath or gotten his homework finished, but tonight, Abbey didn't mind at all. He was having the time of his life. And so was she. She didn't let herself worry about missing this family once they were gone, or the fact that Nick was still moving to New York. She didn't have a care in the world tonight because she was too busy enjoying the people around her.

"Who's next?" James said, bending down to pick up one of the kids. Max jumped into his arms as if he'd known him for ages. James held her son out like an airplane, spinning him around and up and down, Max's giggles bubbling up with every dip and spin.

Caroline sat under an afghan that Abbey had brought down for her, smiling as big as day as she watched the kids play. They played together so well, and it was wonderful to see how Max interacted with another child. He was courteous, he listened, and they tried to help each other through the tasks they'd created. They'd started by building a bridge on the train set, and both boys worked marvelously well together to build it. They'd asked Nick to be the base again, but he gently declined, telling them he hadn't had enough time to spend with Max's mommy and the rest of the family, and they needed some attention too. The boys had played with a few toys together while Abbey chatted with Nick, the women, and James. It was nice to have some adults to talk to.

Both boys started climbing on James, causing him to topple over, and Abbey worried about his nice clothes. James didn't seem bothered, laughing as he sat back up on the floor.

"This is so much fun!" Max said, and everyone laughed.

"I'm having so much fun too," Nick said in her ear and then kissed her cheek, surprising her. "I can't remember being this relaxed."

"It's got to be the living room," she teased.

"Yes, of course," he played along. "More seriously, it could be all your decorating. You've given me a place to relax." A smile still lingered on his lips. "You've given us a wonderful space where we can all get together. Thank you for that. I'd said that this would be the last room you need to decorate because no one would come in here, but you pulled it together anyway. What I hadn't planned on was you pulling us all together too. And now, this is the first room we needed—the *family* room. So thank you."

She went to kiss him on the cheek but he turned to catch her lips, planting a kiss right on her mouth.

Chapter Twenty-four

That morning, after assisting the electricians with changing out the last bit of lighting in the house, Abbey had planned on microwaving a bag of plain popcorn to string for the living room Christmas tree—their family tradition. But Richard had given her a popcorn popping contraption instead, with a jar of unpopped kernels. She sipped her coffee as she opened the pamphlet with directions and spread it out on the counter to read it.

"Good morning," Nick said from the doorway. Max was holding his hand.

"Max, did you bother Nick in his office?" she asked.

"No," Max said with a big grin. "I caught him before he went in!" He said it as if he'd done something right, and it made Abbey laugh.

"Sorry," she said to Nick.

"I was just going to check email quickly. It's fine. What are you doing?" he asked.

"I'm trying to figure out how this popcorn popper works. Do you know?" She lifted a plastic tube and peered into the end of it, trying to figure out where to snap it together.

Nick shook his head. "I've never popped popcorn."

"Ever?" Max asked.

"Nope," Nick said with a smile. "Why are you popping popcorn at eight in the morning?"

"To decorate the tree!" Max said with excitement.

"You put popcorn on trees?"

Max giggled. "Yes! Where else would we put it?"

"In your mouth, I suppose."

Max doubled over laughing and Abbey caught Nick trying to smooth out his amusement at the sight of him.

"What tree are you going to shower with popcorn?" he asked Abbey.

"The living room tree." She pushed the tube into a slot and heard it click. "I cannot figure out where this piece goes." She held up a yellow handle-like crank. "I think that's the last piece and then it'll be ready to go."

"I'm going to get Thomas!" Max said, running out of the room.

Nick walked over beside her and picked up the pamphlet. His brows pulled together as he scanned the directions, and Abbey tried not to smile at him and distract him. "Maybe here," he said, pointing to a spot on the machine. When he did, he noticed her looking at him. "What?"

"Nothing," she said, smiling despite her attempts not to.

"Why are you looking at me like that?"

At this point, she might as well just be honest with him. "You just looked cute reading the directions, that's all."

"Cute?" He said the word as if it was new to his vocabulary.

"Yeah."

He grinned and took the crank from her hand. "Let's see," he said, snapping it into place. It fit. Then, he unscrewed the cap of the corn kernels and poured some in. "Would you just plug it in, please?"

Max and Thomas entered the kitchen running full speed just as the machine started to make a sound. A kernel popped loudly, making everyone jump, even Nick. He quickly centered himself, his eyes on the machine. The pops became faster, and the kernels were becoming white fluffy popcorn, but they started to pop so rapidly that Abbey couldn't get her sentence out before they were shooting all over the room like snowy missiles. The children both shrieked with laughter as popcorn spewed all over the kitchen. Abbey went to unplug it, but Nick stopped her.

As the kids danced around, trying to catch the popcorn in their mouths, Nick held up one last piece of the machine—the lid. He waved it in the air, taking a step toward Abbey. "Don't worry," he said. "I'll have the staff clean it up after. Look at how much fun they're having."

"Catch one in your mouth, Nick!" Max called, stopping Nick before he had reached Abbey. He set the lid on the counter.

Abbey could've easily placed the lid on the machine or unplugged it at this point, but she didn't because she was so surprised to see that Nick seemed to be enjoying himself. She watched as he moved closer to the children, the popcorn floating down around them like warm, buttery snowflakes. He got down on his knees to be at their level and opened his mouth. Abbey let out a laugh and quickly quieted it with her hands as he caught a piece in his mouth and chewed it. He swallowed and tried again, this piece hitting him in the cheek and falling to the floor. He caught a few more after that. Max caught one and cheered.

Nick turned toward Abbey, still on his knees, and gestured for her to come over with them. "Your mom hasn't caught any yet, Max," he said, looking over at Abbey in a challenging way. "I've caught three. How many have you caught, Thomas?"

"Two!" Thomas said enthusiastically.

"And you, Max?" The popcorn popper was still shooting popcorn wildly around them.

"One."

"And your mom has zero. It's going to be a tough comeback, Abbey, but I think you can win it."

A piece of popcorn flew through the air at her and she caught it in her mouth. While chewing it, she grinned at Nick.

"Oh!" he yelled as if he were watching a football game. "That's one for Max's mom!"

"I have two now!" Max called.

Nick lunged on his knees to catch a piece and nearly fell over, sending the boys into fits of laughter.

When the last piece had popped, Nick stood up and reached out to help Abbey who'd been on her knees as well. She took his hand and stood up.

"Now," he said. "What do we do with all this?" The entire kitchen floor was covered in popcorn.

"Do you have plastic kitchen bags?"

Nick rummaged around in a few cabinets before pulling out a box of them.

"I need four bags, please."

He drew them out and returned the box to the cabinet.

Abbey handed each person, including Nick, a gallon-sized bag. "Everyone fill your bags with popcorn. No eating it! It's been on the floor *and* it's for the tree. When you're done, we'll take it to the living room and make a Christmas garland."

Nick stood holding his bag, watching her.

"Go ahead," she said, nodding toward the popcorn scattered across the floor. "Fill your bag. You started this mess; now you have to help us decorate the tree." With a wink, she bent down and started filling her own bag as the two boys dove across the floor to get their popcorn.

"Nick and I will thread the needles," she said to Thomas and Max as the rest of the family looked on. Caroline had gotten up from a nap, and she'd said she was glad she had because she had to see Nick thread a needle. Robin and James were on the sofa watching as Abbey demonstrated how to string the popcorn by poking the needle into the soft part and sliding it along the thread.

Nick was having trouble getting his needle threaded, and Caroline couldn't have been more amused. Abbey took the thin, white thread from his fingers and put it in her mouth to wet the end of it. "That always works," she said, but his eyes were still on her lips. Gingerly, she placed the thread through the eye of the needle and pulled it from the other side. "There," she said, handing it back to him.

The kids began giving Abbey and Nick popcorn from their bags to be strung—one after another until both of them had a sizeable strand. Robin jumped in and threaded another needle, giving them three long pieces of garland.

"What do we do with it now?" Nick asked Max.

"We start at the top of the tree and then wrap it around."

Nick handed his popcorn garland to Max.

"I'm too short!" Max said, but before the words had completely come out, Nick had scooped him up into his arms, lifting him to the top of the tree. It was a small tree, only a little over five feet tall, and it was dwarfed by the large space. With a giggle, Max draped the garland on the top branches as Nick walked around the tree to allow him to cover every bit of the top with the popcorn. Abbey watched how Nick handled Max now with ease, how gentle he was with him, and how relaxed he seemed around him. He'd changed so much since that day they'd had their sock races. Max draped the last bit of his garland around the tree, and before Nick put him down, Max wrapped his arms around Nick's neck and gave him a hug. She couldn't imagine anything better.

The builders she'd hired were buzzing through the wall in the hallway while the kids played outside in the snow. Abbey came in to check their progress. She was putting in a built-in shelving unit like the old telephone coves, but she was planning to fill it with antique books she'd found at the second-hand store. She had two more built-ins she wanted to do, and she was hoping that, given his relaxed demeanor lately, Nick would actually take a look at her plans this time.

"He's not here," Richard said from behind as Abbey peeked her head into Nick's office. She hadn't seen him since this morning when they'd decorated the tree. "He's gone to look at a possible acquisition in Chicago."

"He just up and left? In the middle of the day? He's supposed to be taking time off for Christmas! His sister and her family are in from out of town and Christmas is only a couple of weeks away."

Richard said nothing. She knew he wouldn't. It wasn't his place, and she felt bad for even voicing her concerns. It put him in an odd spot.

"Sorry," she said, and he smiled a knowing smile.

"He did tell me that you'll have one more bedroom to complete. It's the fourth bedroom upstairs."

Abbey stared at Richard paralyzed, trying to figure out what he meant by "decorate." That room was finished. She started toward the hallway leading to the staircase and Richard followed as she went up-stairs. The buzzing of the saws had ended, leaving her in complete si-lence as she got to the bedroom. Abbey opened the door and gasped, every emotion she had draining right out of her.

"He had us clear the furniture early this morning and donate it to a halfway house."

The nursery was empty.

Was this some sort of grand gesture to put a point on the end of his sentence that he wasn't the guy for her? Was he telling her that in no way did he want children? Was he telling her that he'd never want Max, let alone a child of his own? She felt sick, staring at the empty walls, the bare wooden floor, the naked windows. But then, she got herself together. Nick was probably going to put the house up for sale. Perhaps he needed the room to be more neutral to help the home sell faster.

"Did you see what Nick did with the nursery?" she heard Caro-line's voice float up over the balcony from the entranceway. "What a shame."

"I was coming over to your room in a little while," Abbey said, looking down at her. She looked so small standing at the bottom of the first floor.

"I was taking a walk. It's a nice place to be when it isn't just Nick clicking away on his computer at one end of the house."

"Why did he dismantle the nursery?"

She met Caroline at the bottom of the steps. "He claimed it would be nice to give away the furniture at this time of year because the donation would spread some Christmas cheer." Caroline pursed her lips in disapproval. "It was such a lovely room."

"I'm going to text him. Do you mind if I excuse myself?"

"Go right ahead," Caroline said with a wink.

Abbey went into the ballroom, sat down on the floor in front of the fireplace, and leaned against the bottom of the couch, her legs crisscrossed. She pulled her phone from her pocket, brought up Nick's number, and typed: *Why are you in Chicago when you said you were taking time off for Christmas? When are you coming home?*

He must have checked it immediately and began typing. She waited for the little bubble on her phone to show his words. Finally they appeared: *I'm sorry, Abbey. I got an email about an interest in one of the properties I'm selling. It's a huge offer. I'll be home probably Wednesday of next week.*

She thought things were better. She thought she could make him see… She texted back: *Why so long?*

Nick: *I'm in negotiations for the sale of the corporation here in Chicago and it takes some time to get them to meet me somewhere in the middle. They're playing hardball but I know they'll offer more. Why? What's wrong?*

What's wrong? Was he serious? He'd left without telling her at all, and now he was wondering why she was asking? She typed: *I want to know what happened to the nursery.*

Her screen lit up with a text: *Someone else needs that furniture more than I do. I felt guilty leaving it unused.*

She really wanted to talk to him. She wanted to hear the tone in his voice, to feel his emotions as he spoke. Her phone rang.

"Hi," she said. "How did you know to call me?"

"You always end up asking me to, so I did."

"I thought you were planning to take some time off for Christmas?" she asked.

"I will. I promise. When I get a lull."

"When you get a lull? What if that doesn't happen again until after Christmas? Why did you feel the need to sell this company in Chicago right now?"

"It's a big offer. I wanted to pursue it before the buyer lost interest. It could really help my own company's standing."

"Would it help enough to keep you from spending all your time working?" She waited for his answer with shaky hands. She was letting him in on her feelings.

"I'm still going to chase things when they come up. And things will always come up. It's the nature of what I do."

Abbey let the words linger in the air, feeling the icy chill of them. The thing was, though, it was Christmas, a time when miracles happened, when people showed each other how they felt. "I watched you with Max this morning. Is moving to New York what you want? What *you* really want?"

The buzz of the line echoed in her ear as she waited for his answer. It wasn't immediate, and she knew that it probably frustrated him because the pause itself was an answer. "Yes," he finally said. "It's what I want."

She wasn't trying to argue with him; she just wanted to make the point that there was so much here for him if he'd just give it a chance. "You never told me why your dad left the business to you in particular. You'd only guessed that Robin couldn't or wouldn't run it. Perhaps your father didn't ever intend for you to run it. Maybe he just wanted you to figure out what to do with it. You could sell it, get it off your shoulders, and be done with it…"

"Then what in the world would I do? I'd just come up with some other business and I'd have to start from the ground up. I'd rather not."

"You could write music."

He laughed. It wasn't a funny laugh, though. "You're dreaming, Abbey. That isn't a career. It's a few pages of rambling notes I put on paper."

"No it isn't," she said emphatically. "Look, decorating your house has been a huge challenge for me. I was terrified, but I did it! It took me deciding to take a risk and believing that I could do it. Nobody knows what tomorrow will bring. You're good at putting down bets, at taking risks."

"Calculated risks. You're asking me to be ruthless with my choices, to risk my income on a dream."

"It's not all about money, Nick. You don't strike me as a person who cares to impress those around you. Who are you making all this money for? You never enjoy it, you always want to spend it on someone, but you won't let anyone get close enough to let you."

"I really need to go."

"No! You're not going to get off that easy. Talk to me."

"What do you want me to say, Abbey? That I'm going to give up a two-generation company that makes me millions of dollars so I can live in Richmond and scribble notes on paper all day, doing nothing with my life?"

"That's not what I want you to say at all. I want you to say…" She didn't want to admit it. She didn't want to have to voice it. Just the thought of saying what she was about to say was filling her with anxiety and she was trembling all over.

"What? What do you want me to say?" His voice was quieter now, anticipating what she was about to tell him. Did he know? Did he want to hear it from her lips? Or would she make a complete fool of herself?

"I wanted you to say that you liked being relaxed. That you wanted to spend more time with me and with Max and your family. That you'd rather give up your millions than lose the chance for a wonderful life with lots of memories of time spent with people you love. There are people here who love *you*. There are people who want you here."

"I would let my mother down. I would dishonor my father. I would lose my ability to maintain my lifestyle. It isn't as easy as running off into the sunset, Abbey."

"I know that. Believe me. I know."

"I wish it were."

He did? He wished it were that easy? Then why didn't he work at it? "Come home," she heard herself say.

The line was silent. She could hear his breathing on the other end, a swallow. What was he thinking? Why wasn't he talking? "Aaarrgggh," he said very quietly under his breath. She smiled, not meaning to frustrate him but glad that he didn't have a cut and dry answer. It meant that he was thinking about it.

"Can I ask you something?" The fire in the ballroom was low, spitting sparks upward, but the warmth still filled the air around her.

"Yes."

"Why did you play me your music? I mean… Why me?"

There was a huff on the end of the line and she could feel his smile coming through. "I knew you would get it."

"Why though? I don't play piano."

"Yes, you do," he was chuckling. "You told me so."

"Yeah, I remember… Haha."

He let out a small laugh and the sound of it sent a thrill through her. "It was a grand rendition of 'Chopsticks'."

"Why did you think I would get it?"

"Because you are an emotional person. You wear your feelings on your sleeve at all times. You are artistic and thoughtful and passionate about everything you do. I wish I were more like you."

"You are a lot like me. You just don't allow yourself to be. You're artistic—you write music! And it is beautiful music. It was so moving that it brought me to tears, Nick. You need to share it with everyone. You're thoughtful and kind and generous. You bought me pies, and you took Max to see Santa, you were a human train track for the boys. And you're passionate about what you believe in. So passionate that you're willing to give up opportunities for happiness just to honor your father."

"I'm sorry, Abbey," was all he said, his honesty coming through in his words.

Her shoulders slumped at his response. "Me too." The fire popped, bringing her thoughts back into the reality of the day. She looked at her watch. "I have to check on Caroline. Text me if you want anything special for the nursery. Otherwise, I'll make another bedroom for you."

"Okay," he said quietly, and it was apparent his mind was elsewhere.

"Why did you, all of a sudden, think someone else might need the nursery furniture?" she asked.

"I saw family at my home for the first time, and it inspired me. Someone out there is building a family, and if they don't have what they need, I wanted to be the one to give it to them because families should be happy."

"Nick…"

"Yes?"

"I still want you to come home."

There was silence.

She cradled the phone to her ear. She didn't want to leave the call but she knew it was coming to an end.

"I know you do. We'll see."

"Bye," she said against her will.

"Bye, Abbey."

Chapter Twenty-five

It was amazing how much time Caroline was spending walking around at Nick's since Robin and her family had come. Once they'd gotten settled, Thomas was busy most of the day with private tutors, arranged to keep him on track with the school work he was missing until Max got home from school. James was in and out, and Caroline, Robin, and Abbey spent time talking. For the past few days, they'd settled into a friendly routine. It was so nice to have them to talk to.

"Mom's coming in today," Robin said with a loaded look to Caroline as Abbey rearranged a few knickknacks.

"Is she?"

"Yes. She says she has something to tell us."

Caroline eyed Robin, her interest palpable. "Oh?" she said, her word drawn out in an interested manner.

"I wonder what it is."

"Whatever it is," Caroline said, her lips pursed in disapproval, "I'm glad it prompted her to bless us with her presence. She's been in hiding since Aaron died, and she needs to be with her family." Caroline looked over at Abbey as she straightened a picture on the wall in the living room. "This room looks amazing, Abbey," she said. "The whole house does."

"Thank you."

"Would you like to do my loft?" Robin said. "If Caroline is moving closer to me, perhaps you could come for a working visit." Robin smiled at her in a playful way.

"Do you think I should? I've been considering the idea of doing more decorating. I'm just a little nervous about taking the leap to having my own business."

Abbey thought about it. She'd get to do what she loved, see Caroline again. See Nick. "What would I do with Max?" she asked. "I couldn't leave him with my mother—I'd miss him too much—and he has school."

"Easy," Robin said. "I'd throw tutoring into the contract."

Caroline smiled at this. "You're making it difficult to pass up, Robin."

"The loft is much smaller than this," she waved her arms around the giant living room. "This house is huge. And! Nick's going to need someone to decorate his new apartment, I'm sure. We could do a two-for-one deal."

Abbey laughed, the excitement getting to her.

"I'm serious," Robin said. "It would probably only take three or four weeks. I don't have a crew like you had here. I only have cleaning. We'd have to move all the furniture in ourselves unless you'd like to negotiate a staff…"

"Are you still serious?" Abbey asked.

"Yes. But I have to warn you, my friends are going to die of envy when they see your work, and you might get busy."

There was no long-term security with the decorating job, even though her prospects were promising. What would happen when she'd exhausted Robin's friends? Then what?

"Say yes."

Abbey surfaced from her thoughts to see Robin awaiting an answer.

"I'm dying for your expertise."

She knew that if she didn't take the chance now, she might not get it again. Here were possibly two more opportunities to decorate and add to her portfolio. If she didn't make the leap now, she never would.

"Just think about it," Robin said as she stood up. "I'm going to check to see if lunch is ready."

When Robin had left the room, Caroline leaned toward Abbey. "Are you going to take Robin's offer?" she asked.

Abbey had told Caroline about Gramps. "I worry about leaving Gramps," she said, voicing her fears. "But I know it's a good thing. I'm seriously considering it."

"I understand." She looked thoughtful. "You are very thoughtful to consider your grandfather, but I'm sure, if he's anything like me, he'd tell you to go for it."

"Look who I found when checking for lunch!" Robin's voice broke into the conversation between them. Abbey turned around to see a striking woman, maybe in her sixties, her dark brown hair positioned into perfectly sprayed waves, an enormous pair of sunglasses pushed up on top of her head, causing the waves of hair to cascade symmetrically on either side of her face. She had red lips and long eyelashes, her fur coat nearly reaching the floor, allowing a view of her fashionable high heels. She carried a designer bag in the crook of her arm.

Caroline stood up and Abbey followed suit. "Susan," Caroline said with a welcoming smile. "I'm so glad you decided to come visit your family." It was clear that she was teasing and Abbey noticed no hostility whatsoever. "We have missed you." As Caroline got closer, she ran her hand along the coat. "Dear Lord, child, is that fur?"

"Faux, of course." Susan kissed Caroline on each cheek. "I've made a lot of changes in my life, but my personal values haven't changed a bit."

"Still eating only salads then?" Caroline allowed a chuckle.

"How else can I fit into this dress?"

The two women had an easy way of talking to each other, although their conversation was so different to any that Abbey had had with her own friends. Watching their interaction was mesmerizing—like watching a movie on TV. Right in front of her were three generations of wealth. Caroline was refined in her actions, Susan, more open but clearly affected by it, and then Robin who, while wealthy, was so down to earth that Abbey barely noticed the money that surrounded her. It was so interesting to watch them.

"The house is stunning!" Susan said, her eyes roaming the room. "Has Nicholas found himself another little trophy who decorates?"

Abbey felt her eyes widen at that statement and she had to consciously hide her astonishment.

No one answered, and Susan added, "If so, this one knocks Sarah right out of the park in decorating. Sarah was lovely, though, wasn't she?"

There was an uncomfortably giddy silence still lingering.

"What?" Susan said impatiently.

Caroline put her hand on Abbey's arm. "Susan, this is Abbey... My nurse."

Susan seemed a bit taken off guard, having been pulled from the line of conversation, but she recovered and reached a delicate hand out to Abbey. "Oh, forgive my rudeness. It's so nice to meet you," she said, smiling warmly at her. "I'm Susan, Nicholas's mother." She let go of Abbey's hand and looked around the room as if she'd lost her keys. "Where is Nicholas anyway?"

"In Chicago," Robin said.

Susan rolled her eyes. "What for?" she said in mock annoyance.

"Work."

"Ugh," Susan said. "In and out, in and out. Never still. He's just like his father."

Abbey tensed at that comment—Susan's comments seemed to straddle that edge of inappropriateness, but no one seemed overly bothered. She had to admit, his absence was maddening to her as well. She tried not to think about the fact that tomorrow was Max's "Bring Your Daddy to School Day."

"Well, if he's not here to show me this gorgeous house of his, then please, Robin, take me around! The entrance blew me away. I want to see what else he's had done." She shrugged off her faux fur and draped it on the sofa, then turned to Caroline and Abbey. "Ladies, would you like to join us? I'm dying to hear what company he hired to decorate. I'm feeling all Christmassy!" She fluttered her hands in the air before turning and swishing down the hallway toward the front of the house.

Chewing on a smile, Abbey followed slowly with Caroline, her confidence in her talent growing miles with every step.

Chapter Twenty-six

Abbey hit the gas, trying to balance going fast enough to exceed the speed limit and yet not fast enough to get a ticket. Nick hadn't come home last night. Her last day decorating had ended with little fanfare other than Susan's complete surprise when they'd finally told her who'd done the decorating. All she had left were a few more finishing touches on the living room tree.

When she'd dropped by her apartment to get the mail last night, she'd seen a legal envelope with Nick's name and address as the sender. She opened it and had to steady herself as she read the numbers on the check. He'd overnighted her seventy-five thousand dollars. The envelope was absent of any correspondence. It was just the check.

Now Abbey was trying to get to Max's school as fast as she could. Since Nick had not come home from Chicago, she'd had to prepare Max for the disappointment; the regret she had over it was almost too much to bear as she saw his face. It had been her fault. Max had fallen hard, just like she had, and now, he had to deal with the fact that Nick wasn't around. Nick had warned her enough, but she'd thought she could change his mind.

She'd tried to shield Max as much as possible this morning, telling him how Nick had gotten caught at work in Chicago, and that he had to fly in an airplane to get back home. He wouldn't be able to make it. Then, in the silence of the morning, with all the doors in the house still shut but theirs, she promised that she'd come instead so he'd have someone there for him.

"But you're not a daddy," he'd said, his distress clear. She'd assured him that it would be fine if she came instead, but she could tell that he was uneasy about it.

The light turned green and she hit the gas again.

In minutes, Abbey pulled the car into the lot at Max's school and got out. Her heart was pounding as she looked at her watch. She was late. She ran up to the door, trying her best not to slide on the ice, and hit the bell to enter. Her head pounded with every tick of the clock as she filled out her name and got her visitor's badge in the office. The woman behind the counter was smiling, slowly completing her information for her. She wanted to snatch the badge out of her hand and run down the hallway. Max was waiting for her with no parents, probably watching the other dads with sadness in his eyes. She looked at her watch again.

The woman finally handed her the badge and she peeled the backing off as she ran down the hallway, rushing past two students who turned around to look at her. She stuck the yellow visitor sticker on her coat and came to a stop outside Max's classroom door. She took one more second to get herself together and catch her breath before going in. When she opened the door, the teacher greeted her. All the children were at their tables, their daddies beside them, sitting in little chairs, their knees all resting higher than the tables themselves. They were smiling, talking quietly to their children as they made a craft with craft sticks and paint.

Abbey scanned the crowd for Max. The teacher had moved seats, and he wasn't in the same place as he'd been when she'd visited last. She looked for his brown hair, his blue shirt, and then, she stopped, her entire body freezing in surprise, tears filling her eyes. She blinked to clear them so that she could be sure that what she was seeing was real. Max had his back to her, and beside him, holding a craft stick and talking sweetly to her son, was Nick. She walked over and squatted down beside them.

"Hi, Mama!" Max said, a proud look on his face. "Nick came!"

Kneeling down, she was eye level with Nick and she could tell that he'd noticed her emotion. "I wouldn't have missed it," he said quietly to her in almost a whisper, and she felt like her chest would explode. "I caught the red eye last night and got in very early—it was the best I could do."

She tipped her head back to try to keep the tears from falling.

"It's okay," he said into her ear, causing goose bumps down her arm. "I know by your actions that you're not used to being able to trust people, and I haven't given you much opportunity to trust me. But you can. You taught me how important it is to just be there."

She nodded, trying to calm down and enjoy her complete relief.

Abbey sat next to Nick as they finished their craft—a small bird-house. Nick had helped Max paint it, his fingers red even after wiping them off. It made her smile. Max had stood with the other students in his class and they all sang a song. Finally, there were refreshments. When it was time to say goodbye, Max hugged Nick a little longer than the other boys and asked Nick when he'd get to see him again. Nick had said that he wasn't leaving anymore this week. It was Nick, not Abbey, who'd gotten him settled back at his seat. Then, they both said their goodbyes and walked into the hallway.

"What are you doing now?" Nick asked her.

"I was going to go shopping for teacher gifts for Friday, but that can wait. What's up?"

"Feel like chatting with my mother?"

"Why?" She smiled suspiciously.

"She has… news. She wants us all together to tell us. I'm a little worried about it. We never know with her what she might be up to. I can't do it alone," he teased. "And, she said she likes you." He smiled down at her. "We're meeting for lunch at Lemaire." Abbey had never heard of it before. He clarified, "It's in The Jefferson Hotel."

She had heard of The Jefferson Hotel. It was a grand hotel, built in the late 1800s and only a mile from the James River. It was breathtakingly beautiful inside with its marble floors and columns and stained-glass domes. There was nothing else like it in the city.

"I might need to change," she said, worrying already that she didn't have anything nice enough to wear. "I'm not sure I have anything… clean," she said as they walked to the door.

"It's right near Carytown. There are tons of dress shops," he said, opening the door, the frigid cold hitting her and nearly taking her breath away. They walked until they were at his car. "Let me buy you something. Then you don't have to worry about anything. It'll be my treat for your company at a lunch where my mother is going to dominate all conversation." He smiled.

She looked at him, deciding.

"Please?" he said, opening the passenger side and gesturing for her to sit. "We'll come back and get your car after lunch."

She got in.

The Mercedes started with a purr. "I really enjoyed that today," he said as he backed the car out of its spot. "Max is really a great kid, Abbey. He's so kind," he said, pulling out onto the road and merging onto the highway. He smiled at her, the happiness lingering subtly on his lips as he drove.

Abbey hadn't even known this shop was here—she'd never been down to Carytown for anything more than an ice cream or a ninety-nine-cent movie. Most of the shops here, while amazing, were completely out of her price range. She stood in the pristine dressing room, staring at the wooden hangers with the brass hooks that held a perfectly tailored pair of navy wool trousers and a matching blazer with a silky white top that Nick had picked out for her.

She slowly slipped off her jeans and sweater and tried them on, still unsure, immediately noticing how they felt against her. They fit like they'd been sewn together to match just her body. She slid on the coordinating high heels and looked in the mirror at the person staring back at her. Her reflection didn't look a thing like her, and it startled her. Was this the kind of girl Nick dated? Was this what he'd want her to look like if they ever got together? He'd picked it out after all. She tried to imagine a time when she'd feel normal in clothes like these. Would they grow on her like the ballroom had? The trouble was, the ballroom was just a space, whereas how she dressed was a representation of who she was, and this wasn't who she was at all. She ran her fingers through her hair and then dug around in her handbag for her powder and lipgloss. She freshened up her makeup and fluffed out her hair.

"Or there's this," she heard from the other side, and Nick's hand appeared above the dressing room door, a green dress in his hand. A shoebox slid toward her on the floor through the open space under the stall.

She took the dress from his hand and hung it up, then opened the door to show him the first outfit. There was a visible reaction and his eyes slid from her face down to her feet. "That's…" he looked back up at her, "really nice." He swallowed and handed her a pair of navy teardrop earrings. "These would go with that if you decide to get it."

"Do you want me to try the dress on, or do you like this?" While beautiful, none of it was her style anyway, so it was up to him.

"It's what *you* like. Get what makes you comfortable." He cleared his throat, clearly still affected by how she looked. "But, yes," he smiled. "I'd like to see you in the green dress." His eyes moved around her body one more time, and she couldn't help but feel a little self-conscious.

She went back into the dressing room. As she took off the suit and hung it up, she noticed the price tag on the blazer and nearly fell over. One thousand eight hundred ninety dollars? She grabbed the tag on the trousers. One thousand seven hundred ninety-five. She didn't bother to look at the shirt. There was no way she was going to let him buy something like this for her. She slipped on her Chuck Taylors and opened the door.

"The dress didn't fit?" he asked, but she didn't answer. She was still in a daze, trying to figure out if people really paid that kind of money for clothes when she waited for the thirty percent coupons to come in the mail so she could apply them to a twenty-dollar top at her local mall shops.

"I didn't try it on…" she said, still thinking.

"You're going with the blue then? Good choice."

She attempted to push away her growing worry, willing herself to focus on the conversation. "Um… No. I'm not getting either… They're so expensive…" she nearly whispered.

"Well, it's Gucci. Of course it costs more than an average brand. It's well worth it."

She remembered how the fabrics felt against her skin, how perfectly they'd fit, and she knew he was right, but she couldn't bring herself to make him spend that on her.

"It's fine," he assured her.

She shook her head. "No. It's not fine at all."

He looked at his watch. "I'd suggest going somewhere else, but we're running out of time. We only have about twenty-five minutes. You looked amazing in the blue, but if you want to wear what you have on, I'd be just as happy sitting beside you."

"Would you? Or are you just saying that?" She looked back at the outfit still hanging in the dressing room. It really was beautiful, but she was paralyzed by the price. She just couldn't let him pay that much for something that she'd never wear again.

"Sarah loved this shop, so I thought since you needed to dress up that perhaps this would be a shop you might like as well. I didn't want you to feel out of place wearing your regular clothes, that's all."

"I'm not Sarah," she said. "At all, in any way."

"I know, but—"

She cut him off. "And you thought I'd feel out of place?" *Or was it that he felt I was out of place in what I have on?* she worried.

"I just want you to be comfortable," he said. "It's a dressy occasion."

"Well, I'm not. I'm not comfortable in a fancy restaurant in jeans but I'm also not comfortable in what you've picked out."

"Well, which makes you the least uncomfortable then?" he asked. She didn't have an answer.

"I'll tell you what," he said. "I'll buy it and when we're done today, we'll sell it online and donate the profits to your favorite charity. Would that make you feel better?"

"Okay," she said, still feeling uneasy about wearing it in the first place.

"Good." He took the shoes, earrings, suit, and top up to the register. "We'll have these, please," he said to the salesperson. "And then if you could assist Miss Fuller with the tags so that she can change immediately, that would be fantastic."

"Yes, sir," the salesperson said, her black hair straight as an arrow, a scarf tied around her neck in a small knot at the side. She looked over at Abbey and smiled, clearly working overtime to keep her eyes from appraising Abbey's current attire.

"And please offer Miss Fuller any of the cosmetics that she may need," he said as he pointed at the makeup options displayed along the back wall. "You can put them on my bill."

Was there something wrong with her makeup?

Nick turned to Abbey. "I'll wait up front." He grabbed a navy handbag off the shelf nearby and set it on the counter before leaving. "That too."

Chapter Twenty-seven

"What do you think this big news is?" Abbey asked as Nick stood by her side of the car, holding the door open for her. He reached out and offered his hand to help her step over a small pile of snow in her heels.

"There's no telling with her," he said. "She has a very unique personality. She's extremely outspoken, which is funny, because my dad was always more reserved… You know, she really likes you. She told me about a hundred times."

"Why would she?" She didn't mean the question to come out like that. "What I meant was, what in particular does she like so much about me? She and I are so different."

They walked together between a pair of giant evergreen shrubs in pots, their limbs cut in a spiral shape and covered in white lights. They stepped under the long awning that had "The Jefferson" in curly gold writing on the front, each side of their path lined with red poinsettias. The doorman opened the door for them.

Nick nodded his thanks to the doorman and then answered, "I think it's because you both are sort of no-nonsense in your own ways. She liked your honesty and transparency. You are always yourself no matter what is put in front of you. I like that about you too."

They entered the lobby of the hotel, and Abbey stopped walking. Nick looked over to her to see what was wrong and then, out of the corner of her eye, she saw him smile and wait for her to take in the amazing view surrounding her.

The entire room, as big as a sports field, was surrounded by balconies, their edges draped in fresh greenery, their railings anchored by large, marble columns. There were so many poinsettias that it would take all night to count them. The marble floors were covered in an enormous rug, small seating areas arranged along the edges. And in the center a twenty-eight-foot Christmas tree that stretched all the way up to the stained-glass dome above it. Every inch of the tree was covered in traditional ornaments and white lights.

"It's so beautiful," she said, having difficulty keeping her emotions in check. They moved from the red carpet runner leading up the stairs to the piles of Christmas greenery on the railings going up. She let her gaze wander the two floors and marble columns, the detail and ornamentation on every surface.

"Yes. Very beautiful," he said, but he was looking down at her.

He ushered her forward and they walked toward the restaurant. The marble floors gave way to hardwoods, the round columns turning square and in front of her, in the ornate style of a cathedral, was a bar, the lighting illuminating the edges in a gold glow. The stools with burgundy padded seats were perfectly lined along the front of it, and it almost looked like a piece of art. They walked past it into the dining room where Susan was standing and waving ceaselessly.

Every table was covered in white linens, the chairs a burnt orange to match the drapes and rug covering the hardwoods. Chandeliers dripped down from the ceiling in various places. Abbey's eyes followed the ornate moldings around the windows and the ceiling. A huge fireplace sat at one end of the room, the mantle covered in candles and more greenery, the wall-sized mirror above it reflecting its light.

Nick guided Abbey to the table where she met Robin, James, Thomas, Caroline, and a man she'd never met before. Thomas was sitting quietly, his hands in his lap, his hair perfectly combed to the side while James was playing "I Spy" with him. Susan walked around the table to greet them, kissing them both on each cheek. She held Abbey's hands and pulled her arms out by her sides.

"You look fantastic!" she said to Abbey.

"Thank you." Abbey smiled, feeling a little like an imposter in those clothes. She was glad they'd already met the real her because she surely didn't feel herself dressed like this.

"She looks like a runway model, Nick," Susan said, her eyebrows jumping up and down in excitement. "Come! Sit! I am bursting at the seams!"

They sat down and Nick eyed the man across from him, a slight crease forming between his eyes. He smiled politely at him and held out his hand across the table. "I'm Nick Sinclair, Susan's son."

"Hello," he nodded, shaking Nick's hand. "I'm Carl Simmons."

"And you know… my mother?"

"Yes!" Susan butted in. "Everyone, I have an announcement to make." She held up a finger to one of the wait staff and he brought over a bottle of champagne, uncorked it with an echoing pop, filled champagne glasses, and then set the bottle inside a silver bucket at the end of the table.

Abbey politely took the glass she was offered.

When the waiter had disappeared, Susan continued. "Carl and I have known each other for quite some time. Last month, he proposed." She held up her hand and turned it around so everyone could view the boulder of a diamond she had hanging off her ring finger. "So, I wanted you all to meet him."

Everyone burst into an excited chatter at once, congratulating them and smiling, toasting, and drinking champagne. Nick followed along with everyone, but Abbey could tell there were thoughts in his eyes. He seemed genuinely happy for her, but he was thinking about something else too.

When the food was served and they'd broken into smaller conversations, Abbey whispered to Nick, "What are you thinking about?" He'd been quietly listening, nodding at the right moments, and smiling, but there was something on his mind.

"It's nothing." He pushed around his grilled chicken gouda cavatappi—she'd heard him say it and she'd asked for the same since she'd had no idea what to order.

"It's something, I can tell."

"I miss my father," he said in her ear.

It was a very honest piece of information, and it made her feel closer to him. She reached under the table and put her hand on his.

"Things keep moving farther away from him. I feel like I'm the last person to keep his memory alive. Everyone else seems to be going along just fine without him."

Caroline seemed to notice their conversation, and Abbey wondered by the look on her face if she'd heard it. She, too, looked like she was contemplating something, but she only smiled when their eyes met.

After dinner, they had drinks at the bar in the hotel, so they moved to a more casual location, allowing Susan to float around the bar and chat with everyone. She came up behind Nick and put her arm around his waist, her cheeks rosy from the champagne at dinner.

"Are you okay with this?" Susan asked. She sipped the red wine that she'd gotten at the bar. "I know how you feel about your father."

"I just miss him."

"Well, you know you're a grown man. Carl wouldn't dare try to take the place of your father. He's simply a friend to you. And he'd do anything for you."

"He seems very kind," he said. "I'm happy to see you get so much attention. You deserve it. I know my father wasn't always the most attentive husband."

"No," she agreed. "But he loved his children." She smiled and took a large drink of her wine.

Robin poked her head into the conversation. "Pardon," she said with an unknowing smile, cutting through the seriousness of the last minute. "I wanted to catch Abbey. Can we finalize the party details on Monday? The chef is going to have us all taste-test his dishes."

"Yes," Abbey said with a smile. "And we also still need to finalize the favors and music. I know we were down to only a few choices."

"Abbey *is* coming to the party, right?" Nick's mother asked. "She'd better. Nick, have you asked her? If not, get with it, son!" she teased.

Nick looked down at Abbey, rearranging his lips to keep his smile from emerging. "Would you like to come to the party rather than sitting upstairs in your room?"

"Okay," she said with an unsure smile. She wasn't sure if he'd only asked her because he was prompted, or if he'd already planned to ask her. But she knew that she wanted to be with Nick despite their obstacles, and this would give her yet another chance to spend time with him before he left for New York.

"Max can come down too. I'm letting Thomas stay up for it. You won't have to arrange childcare or anything."

"Thank you. That's very thoughtful."

"Speaking of Max," Nick looked at his watch. "We should probably get you back to your car." He walked over and shook hands with Carl and James, then he kissed each of the ladies on the cheek. "We must be going, but we'll see you back at home shortly."

They said their goodbyes and walked out into the bright sunlight, the sky an electric blue against the snow on the ground. It looked like the storms were finally departing. Then they got in and Nick started the car, the seat warmers giving Abbey shivers with their heat as they pushed the chill out of her.

"Thank you for taking me today," Abbey said. "It was very nice, although I don't think you needed me." She grinned playfully at him.

"Actually, I did. It made me feel more comfortable hearing the news that my mother was moving on with her life. I handled it better knowing you were beside me." He looked over at her and then back at the road.

Abbey felt her heart lurch.

"I enjoyed it," she said.

"I'm glad."

They drove quietly until they pulled in to Max's school. She thanked Nick for the wonderful lunch and told him she'd see him back at the house. He got out and opened her door. As she exited the car and stood beside the open door, he grabbed her hands and looked down at her.

"I was thinking about New York while we were driving," he admitted.

She waited for what he had to say.

"You can stay with me if you decide to decorate Robin's home. Are you considering it?"

She nodded, her mind going back to the feeling of waking up beside him.

"I'm glad to hear that," he said with a smile. "I'll see you back at the house." Without warning, he leaned down and kissed her lips. "Bye, Abbey." He jogged around to his side of the car and got in.

With a ridiculous grin, she went in to get Max in her five-thousand-dollar outfit.

Max was holding his craft stick birdhouse and an envelope with holly he'd colored all over the outside. "What's that?" Abbey pointed to the sealed envelope. She loved hearing about the things he'd made at school.

"It's a secret," he said, his face animated.

"So you can't tell me?"

He shook his head. "It has my secret Christmas wish in it."

"Oh!" Abbey was itching to know what Max's secret Christmas wish was. This was supposed to be his big Christmas, the one to top all others. It would be wonderful if she could make that secret wish come true. What else did Max want? "Will you ever tell it to me?" she asked.

"I have to wait and see if I get it for Christmas first. Then, after Christmas, I'll tell it to you."

"Deal," she said, thinking of ways to steam open the envelope.

Max hugged it to his chest as he walked to the car. The snow was starting to melt, making the curbside drain sound like a waterfall from all the melting ice. Max climbed into his booster seat and fastened his seatbelt.

"I'm so glad Nick came to my school today," he said as they drove home.

"I'm glad too. You know he flew back from Chicago just for you! He took a very late flight so he could get to school like he'd said he would."

"I like him so much."

She smiled. "Me too." She looked at Max in her rearview mirror and she thought how lucky she was to have had Nick there today. He'd made Max a happy boy.

Chapter Twenty-eight

It was early. Max was still sound asleep in the bed and Abbey's stomach was growling. Slowly, she climbed out from under the covers and padded over to get her robe and slippers, then left the room to get something to eat. The house was eerily quiet as she made her way down the stairs. They were solid, not a creak at all.

The sun wasn't even up yet, the stars shining through the great ballroom windows as she passed by them. The sconces on the wall were lit like nightlights. They led the way down the enormous hallway to the kitchen.

She entered the room and nearly jumped with fright. Nick was sitting on one of the barstools, the morning paper in his hands. He set it down and looked over at her. His eyes went from her hair down to her slippered feet, interest showing on his face.

"Good morning," he said, a small smile playing at his lips. His eyes were unstill, and she wondered what he must think of her. Had she known anyone would be up, she'd have at least dragged a comb through her hair.

"Good morning," she returned. Nick was already dressed, shaved, and perfectly handsome as always. "Do you just wake up like that?" she teased, trying to make light of her own appearance.

Nick looked down at his clothes. He allowed a smile. "Do you just wake up like *that*?" he teased back.

She laughed quietly so as not to wake anyone else. "I was just coming down to find something to eat. I'm starving."

"The chef won't be here until seven. Let me cook you something."

"No. You don't have to do that. I'll find something. Have you eaten? Let me cook for you! I make a mean omelet."

He smiled again, his eyes shifting down to his newspaper, affection oozing from his face.

"You're in a good mood today," Abbey noted, rooting through the cabinets for a frying pan. She retrieved the eggs and cracked some into a bowl she'd found. "Whisk?" she asked.

"Top drawer to your left."

"Thank you. So, what are your plans today?"

"I'm putting a bid on a paper corporation. You?"

"Making handprint ornaments for the living room Christmas tree."

He laughed. "Busy day for both of us, then."

"Yes," she grinned, pulling a green pepper and an onion from the fridge and dicing it. "Good thing I'm cooking. We'll need a good breakfast. I thought you were taking time off for Christmas."

"I am. It's only one bid."

Abbey pursed her lips in playful disapproval, although she was half serious.

She slid the egg mixture into the pan she'd heated up and began dropping the diced peppers and onions in. The eggs sizzled as she turned down the heat on the stove and then walked over to Nick.

He'd picked his paper back up, and she leaned over his shoulder. "What are you reading?" she asked, their cheeks nearly touching.

He turned to look at her. "The business section."

She reached over and took the paper out of his hands. He watched her, his forehead creasing in interest. She turned one page after another and then stopped. "Here," she said, sliding the paper back over to him. "This is the only part I read."

He looked down at it. "The comics."

"Yep."

"I've never read this section."

"What?" She pushed the paper a little further down so it lined up with his line of vision. "Look at this one," she said, pointing to one of the comic strips. "Read that." While he was reading, she walked over to serve up the omelets. Her back was to him when she heard a laugh escape his lips and she turned around.

"That's funny," he said, scanning down the rest of the page. He stopped on another one on the opposite side and chuckled again.

"See? You don't have to always be all business." She winked at him as she slid his plate toward him. When she'd prepared her own plate, he folded his newspaper and set it aside, allowing her to sit on the barstool next to him.

He took a bite and swallowed. "This is delicious," he said.

"I'm glad you like it." After a moment's silence, she asked, "Will you have time today to make ornaments with us?"

"What time?" he asked.

"I can work around you," she said, trying not to let her excitement get the better of her. "What time would you be free?"

"How about around noon?"

"Done."

* * *

Abbey had spent the day finalizing the music and favors for the party. The house looked amazing, and Robin had already sent photos to two of her friends who were going to call Abbey for price quotes on her decorating services. She'd had a busy day, and she hadn't seen Nick, but she'd promised to make ornaments at noon, and she was there and ready. She looked at her watch. He had one minute. Thomas and Max were sitting at the bar in the kitchen, the bowl of ornament dough waiting to be rolled out.

"He'll be here," Abbey said despite her reservations as Robin stood up to go get him. "Let's give him a chance." He'd proven himself at Max's Daddy Day at school, and she wanted to believe that he would be there today.

"Hello, everyone," Nick said, coming into the kitchen and Abbey let out a breath of relief.

"I thought you were going to be late," Robin said to him.

"Nope. Not for this. I am intrigued with how to make a hand-ornament." He walked over to the boys. "Thomas, have you done this before?"

Thomas shook his head.

"Max? Have you?"

"Yes. Mama and I do it every year. She has one for every age I've been."

"Then you're the pro at this. Will you show us how it's done?"

"Yes," Max said with authority. "You have to roll up your sleeves."

Nick complied, unbuttoning the cuffs of his shirtsleeves and folding them up to his elbows. "Now what?" he asked, reaching over to help Thomas roll his sleeve up. Robin was on the opposite side helping with the other sleeve.

"Mama, would you put the flour down, please?" Max said.

Abbey dusted the surfaces with flour.

"Now, grab a big glop of dough." Max reached in and grabbed a fistful of the white mixture. He dropped it onto the floured surface.

Nick followed his lead and put a wad of it in front of himself.

Abbey handed each of them a cup. "For rolling the dough," she said.

"Would you like a rolling pin?" Robin suggested. "Nick, you have one, right?"

"That's okay," Abbey said. "We always use a cup and it works just fine."

Nick rolled his cup, his ball becoming flat but lopsided due to the shape of the cup. He rolled again, looking over at Max. Max had done it so many times that he had a perfectly round, flat shape, ready for his handprint.

Abbey reached her arms into Nick's space to help him smooth his out. As she did, he whispered, "Thank you," in her ear, and a prickle of excitement slid down her spine.

"Well, you looked like you needed help," she said with a grin, their faces dangerously close.

After Robin had helped Thomas with his, the boys and Nick each sat in front of a round piece of dough. "Use the end of the cup to cut the dough into a circle. Then press your hand in. I like to do my right hand," Max said. "You press it like this." He placed his hand in the center of the dough and pushed down. When he withdrew his hand, there was a perfect print in the center. Abbey scooped it up with a spatula and set it on a cookie sheet. Nick and Thomas followed.

"I'll bake them," Abbey explained, "And then we can paint them for the tree." She turned on the water at the sink. "You two can wash your hands and I'll let you know when they're ready to paint."

The boys washed and dried their hands and Robin went with them into the living room. Nick walked over with dough still in his fingers. "Thank you for including me in this," he said. "I've never done anything like it before." He tried to brush his hands off by clapping them together but only succeeded in getting gooey dough on both hands.

"You're welcome," she said, and she meant it, unable to hide her amusement.

"I like doing things like this with you."

"Really?"

"Yes. It…" he searched her face as if she had the rest of his sentence, but she stayed quiet. "It makes me wonder about things."

"What things?"

"How different things with you are."

"Good different or bad different?"

He smiled and it went all the way up to his eyes. "Good different. I want to kiss you right now."

"But that wouldn't be a good idea," she said.

His face became somber. "Why is that?"

"Well, your hands are full of dough."

He grinned a crooked grin. "So, you wouldn't want these on your face," he said, holding up his hands. The dough was sticky and crumbly at the same time, a small piece falling to the floor.

"No," she said, shaking her head.

He took a step toward her. "You wouldn't want me to run them through your hair."

She watched him, not believing for a second that he would actually touch her with those fingers. "No," she said, but honestly, she couldn't care less what was on his hands if he were kissing her. She got closer until she was looking up at him, telling him with her eyes that she wanted him to kiss her. He'd shown up today, he'd been involved, he'd talked to the kids. There was something so attractive about that, that she couldn't deny what she was feeling.

He put his hands on her cheeks, the wetness of the dough cold against her face. She didn't notice it for long because, in less than a second, his lips were on hers. The soft warmth of them was making her lightheaded. She put her arms around his neck, kissing him back. Playfully, she bit his lip, and his eyes flew open for just a moment before he resumed kissing her. He pushed his hands up the back of her neck and into her hair, the dough trailing behind, his mouth moving on hers urgently.

"I should make ornaments more often," she said.

"Yes," he said, leaning down for one more kiss.

"The chef is here. He's got a lot of food already," Robin said.

"Robin has asked him to make literally everything she's ever had at a party before," James said. "We have to narrow it to six hors d'oeuvres, two main dishes, and five desserts." James and Robin were seated at the bar area with a line of white plates in front of them. Susan was standing at one end, a white cloth napkin dangling from her fingers.

Nick walked in the room and stood next to Abbey. "Looks good," he said.

Susan clicked over to them on her high heels and gave him a kiss on the cheek. "Hello, darling," she said and then she looked at Abbey.

"I'm so glad you two are both here! I'm trying to keep busy while Carl is out golfing. He doesn't know a soul, yet he'll be the first to chat with strangers if there's a tee in the vicinity."

"Want to help us decide between the garlic-roasted shrimp cocktail and the ham, Gruyère, and honey-mustard palmiers?" James said to Nick.

"Absolutely." Nick went over to the sink to wash his hands and Abbey followed suit. Then, he walked around to the bar and picked up a little croissant-looking pastry.

It must be the ham-whatsits James had mentioned, Abbey thought. To her surprise he'd come back to her and was offering her a bite as she finished drying her hands. She leaned forward and he popped it into her mouth. It was the most savory, delicious thing she'd ever tasted.

"Those are my favorites," he said with a little grin. "I used to ask for them whenever my parents had a party."

"Mmm hmm," she said, nodding, still chewing. She swallowed and set the towel down just as he handed her a stemmed glass with sparkling wine—another item set out for them to try. "It is very good."

"The wine goes well with it," he said.

She took a sip, and he was right. "If you already know what's good and what you like, then why are you tasting things? You could've just told me what to order."

"We have to have a consensus," Robin said, her gaze darting back and forth between Nick and Abbey. "I can't help it if you two have the same taste." She winked in their direction. "I'd like to try them all."

"Well, why don't you call us when you're ready to do the deserts?" Nick said. "Since Abbey seems to be on the same page as I am, I'd like to take a few minutes to talk with her, if that's all right."

They all agreed a little too energetically.

"Shall we go to the ballroom?" he asked. "I've had Richard start a fire in there."

"Sure," she said.

"We'll be back," he told them as the chef set another plate in front of the others. They smiled and waved them off down the hallway.

"I was hoping to discuss your plans for Christmas Eve," he said gently as they walked. "You're staying to take care of Caroline. No staff works on Christmas, but I'd like you to stay."

She hadn't really thought it through yet. The party was on Christmas Eve. She could attend that with him, but Max would certainly be too tired to drive all the way home with her. It would be very easy to put him to bed upstairs. The only problem was that this was supposed to be the perfect Christmas for Max, and Santa would have to arrive at an empty apartment. He wouldn't get his gifts until they'd gotten back home. She considered this as they entered the ballroom.

Nick offered her a seat on the sofa.

"I'm just thinking about Santa Claus," she said.

Nick nodded, looking thoughtful. "Well, he can either leave the gifts at your house and you can get them the next day, or he can leave them at mine. You could set out a note with his cookies and milk," he said.

She didn't want to have Santa leave the gifts in an empty house, but she also didn't want Max to compare his gifts from Santa with whatever in the world Thomas was going to receive. She wouldn't be able to compete.

"Something's bothering you," he noticed.

She chewed on her lip, trying to figure out what to say, and stood up. He followed suit.

"What is it?" he said.

"I want Max to have the perfect Christmas," she said. "So I don't want his Santa loot to be left at an empty apartment."

"Fine. He can leave it here."

"But…" It was so touchy. How would she explain it without making him feel guilty or, worse yet, make him want to buy more things for Max?

"But what?"

"I'm worried he'll compare what he's gotten with what Thomas gets, and I can't equal what Robin will be able to buy." He opened his mouth to speak but she kept going. "And I don't want you to buy him things to bridge the gap either." He shut his mouth. "I know Christmas isn't about how much we get, but for a little kid, he already feels the pressure of pinching pennies. He hears what his friends have gotten and he wonders, since Santa can get anything, why Santa isn't bringing it to him. It's a tough situation. I don't spoil him; I never have. But I want him to feel like he's just as good as his friends, and if that means buying things, then so be it. I can explain it all to him later. But I want those things to be from me."

"How many things do you have for him from Santa?" he asked.

"Three. I wrapped the others up from me."

"Then we'll put out three for Thomas."

"Isn't he used to getting more?"

"Not necessarily. Robin doesn't like to spoil him either. Mothers are all the same," he smiled.

"Are you sure Robin will be okay with that?"

"I'm sure."

"Thank you," she said, feeling relieved.

"So," he said with a smile. "That means you and Max are staying the night on Christmas Eve."

"I suppose," she said with a grin.

"Perfect! I didn't want you driving after the party. Now, I have another money question for you: I want to get you a Christmas gift."

She was very interested to see what he had to say.

"It would make me feel good about going to New York, knowing that you're taken care of."

What kind of gift was he considering?

"My grandmother told me about your grandfather. About how he can't get good medicine on his insurance plan."

She swallowed. He was going to offer her something that she would have a very difficult time refusing; she could feel it, and she was gearing up for how in good conscience she could tell him no thank you.

"Let me pay for the medicine."

She shook her head, anxiety surfacing at the thought of pushing away what could help Gramps. But she couldn't ask for it.

"Why?" he pleaded. "It will make him better. Let our family physician recommend specialists for him, and we'll get him what he needs to be comfortable and to have a better quality of life."

What would happen when Nick was gone? Who would pay for that kind of care once time had inched between them and she was left on her own again?

He cupped her face in his hands, her body tingling with his touch. "Let me do this for you," he said in a whisper. "Your happiness and security is all I want for Christmas."

The man who had everything had found something to ask for this Christmas.

"Please," he said, and his eyes told her that he meant everything he said.

Reluctantly, she nodded, and with a huge grin, he leaned down and kissed her lips.

He pulled back to look at her. "Thank you," he said.

She smiled at the sight of his happiness. For whatever reason, he wanted to do this for her, and it wasn't out of pity. It was because he was looking out for her. He was taking care of her, and she didn't mind it because it was out of affection for her, not obligation.

"I'll take care of all his medical care," he said. "If you need anything, let me know. He has an appointment on January fifth with a specialist recommended by our family physician." He grinned a crooked grin. "You know, just in case you said yes."

Her limbs felt weak, her head dizzy. She sat down on the sofa to keep herself steady. This was too much. In one conversation, all her problems with Gramps had been solved. Certainly, he'd still have to deal with the Parkinson's, and her mother would have to help him while also watching Max so she could work, but Gramps might be close to his old self, and that was more than she could've hoped for.

"Are you okay?" he asked, sitting down beside her, grinning from ear to ear.

She nodded, tears falling faster than she could hold them back, relief so overwhelming that she felt a sob rise in her chest. Nick wrapped his arms around her and held her. "Merry Christmas," he said, and kissed the top of her head.

Chapter Twenty-nine

The morning had gone by in a flash, and it was already noon. Abbey and Max were back at her apartment. They had spent the morning with Gramps. Gramps could hardly control his jitters when she'd told him about Nick's gesture. Then, they'd all cried—her mom, Gramps, and Abbey. It was the most emotional Abbey could remember being in a very long time.

"Look, Mama!" Max had called out, and their tears had turned to laughter. Señor Freckles had allowed Max to pet him. It only lasted a second, and he darted away, but it was more than they'd ever seen him allow in all these years. Perhaps that was his Christmas gift to the family.

"He better not get too cozy," her mother had teased. "I'll put a Christmas sweater on him." They all laughed out loud at that.

They were at the apartment to get clean clothes and do laundry before they went to Nick's tomorrow. Now, they were doing what they always did the day before Christmas Eve: they were making cookies for Santa. Max was wrist-deep in the dry ingredients, most of them now on the counter or on his shirt.

"Be sure to mix them up really well," she said with a giggle.

He turned to look at her, and in doing so, moved the wooden spoon a little farther to the edge of the bowl, dumping a lump of flour, sugar, and baking soda onto the counter.

"It's time to add the wet ingredients," she said, plugging in the mixer and putting it into the bowl.

They'd made cookies for Santa many times before, but this time would be different. They were taking them over to Nick's tomorrow. Max had written a note to Santa Claus, explaining the situation, and Abbey had assured him that this kind of thing happened all the time. They'd taped the note to the fireplace mantle. The only other thing they had to do was finish the cookies.

"Will Nick have enough milk?" Max worried aloud.

"I'm sure he will."

"And a plate for the cookies?"

"Mmm hmm."

"Okay."

Right about the time they'd put the cookies in the oven, the doorbell buzzed. Abbey wasn't expecting anyone. She'd cleaned her hands and dried them before opening the door. When she stepped out to look, she nearly tripped over a box.

"Hello, ma'am," a man said as he came into view. He was writing on a clipboard. "Are you Abbey Fuller?"

"Yes," she said, wondering what this was all about.

"I just need you to sign here," he said, and she signed.

"Thank you, and Merry Christmas."

She smiled in return and picked up the box to carry it inside.

"What is that, Mama?" Max asked, coming into the living room and bouncing on the sofa.

"I don't know." She picked at the tape on the edge of the brown freight box until she had enough to grab on to. Then, she pulled it off the seam and opened the flaps. Sitting on top of a mass of tissue paper was an envelope. She pulled out the card and read the inside. It read, *For tomorrow night. Love, Nick*

She pulled back the tissue paper as Max leaned over the edge of the box. "Is that for me?" he asked with an excited bounce. It was a perfectly sized tuxedo. She laughed out loud at how small it was.

"You get to dress like Nick tomorrow," she said, pulling out the black shiny shoes to match and checking the size. He'd gotten it right. He must have somehow noticed Max's size. Perhaps it was when he'd taken his shoes off at the door.

Max ran around the room whooping and laughing. "I get to match Nick! I get to wear a big man's outfit!"

She laughed again at his enthusiasm. There were more sheets of tissue paper in the box. She pulled them back and stopped. Then a smile spread across her face. Underneath a lining of wrinkle-care plastic was the green dress and matching high heels. There was another note in Nick's handwriting that said, *Don't overlook the tiny box at the bottom.*

She pulled the dress out and hung the hanger over the top of the kitchen door. Then she set the shoes underneath it. A small green clutch with beaded accents was in the box too. She set it on the side table. At the very bottom of the box was a smaller gift box. She pulled it out carefully, noticing an unfamiliar jeweler's insignia on the top. She opened it and gasped out loud.

"What is it, Mama?" Max came over to her to see. "Oh, that's so pretty."

It was a necklace with emeralds and diamonds that went all the way around it. There was another note peeking out below it, and she smiled through her astonishment over the jewels and picked it out of the box. It said, *Don't lose it. It's on loan. See you tomorrow. Nick*

Abbey had known she had to sleep last night. Nick had given her the night off to get everything together for Christmas Eve, and Max had mentioned that he missed his bedroom, so they'd stayed in her apartment. Being in her own comfortable bed, she'd thought for sure she'd have slept better.

She and Max had made the cookies and packed them in a Christmas tin. They'd worked to clean the kitchen. They'd watched a Christmas special on TV, and they'd read all of Max's Christmas stories before bed—the books were still in a pile on his floor. The whole afternoon and evening had been relaxing, uneventful, but that dress hanging on the door kept sending thoughts of complete excitement through her mind.

All night, she'd thought about Nick and her life. She no longer had to help financially with Gramps. She'd been offered a decorating job in New York. She'd make a lot of money. She might even stay with Nick. The problem was, she knew that she couldn't live that far away from her mom and Gramps indefinitely. They only had each other. They certainly couldn't afford to live in Manhattan on her mom's retirement, and for that matter, Abbey probably couldn't afford it either, even with the decorating job. Rent would eat up all her profits. Not to mention that she didn't want to live in New York. It wasn't her at all.

And Nick had tried to run his business from Richmond—it didn't work. He had nothing tying him here except her and a few friends and family members to whom he didn't seem terribly close. Their lives just didn't fit.

But she was falling in love with him. The woman who had always been so independent found herself wishing he was there sitting beside her, to talk to her. She wanted to hear more of the music he'd written. She wanted to show him what a baseball game was like. She wanted to do everything and anything with him—it didn't matter what it was. And the excitement of seeing him on Christmas Eve was almost more than she could bear. It had kept her up most of the night and occupied her thoughts all day.

They'd spent the day at her mom's and Max and Gramps played card games while she and her mother baked a pie for Christmas Day. She was glad for the distraction, although Nick still made his way into her thoughts most of the day. Her mom had come back to her apartment that evening to help them get ready.

While her mom was in the other room getting Max all put together for her, Abbey slipped the green dress over her head and let it shimmy down her body. It was amazing—low cut in the back, scoop in the front with a fitted waist that gave way to a free-flowing skirt. It ended above her knees, showing more leg than she was used to, but drawing the eye to the matching high heels. With nervous hands, she clasped the necklace around her neck and then let down her hair. Her blonde curls fell softly over her shoulders.

She heard a gasp at the door and turned around. "Wow," her mother said, clearly at a loss for words.

"I feel like I'm in a movie," she said.

"I've never seen you more beautiful." She stepped aside to let Max enter and Abbey had to hold her tongue so as not to embarrass him. His hair was combed down to the side like a little Robert Redford, his tux fitting him like a glove. He tugged at his bow tie.

"You look so cool," she said, still holding back.

"Thank you." He squared his shoulders in pride.

Abbey's phone lit up on the bathroom counter and she checked the text. It was Nick. It read, *Richard should be there any minute. If you're not ready yet, take your time. He'll wait.*

She slipped her phone into her new clutch and walked with Max into the living room to watch out for Richard, but when they got there, he was already waiting out front. Her mother handed her the tin of cookies.

"Thank you," she said to her mom, kissing her on the cheek, and nodding toward the window at her car with Max's presents.

"You're welcome. Have fun! I'll lock up! See you tomorrow evening."

They walked out to the car. Abbey waved to Richard who got out and opened the back passenger door for her. She felt her chest tingle with a thrill when she saw that Nick already had a brand new booster seat in the back waiting for Max. She swallowed to keep the lump out of her throat. They got in and Richard popped the trunk, inconspicuously taking the bag of Santa loot from Abbey's mother as she hobbled around the car as quickly as possible with her bad ankle to meet him out of sight of the backseat. He placed it into the trunk of the car along with their suitcases. Abbey shivered in the warmth, not having wanted to wear a coat and wrinkle her nice dress. With another wave once her mother was back at the steps, Richard headed toward the party.

The streets were finally clear, the temperatures inching up just above freezing to melt the snow off the roads and walkways. Abbey was glad for that when they parked out front because both she and Max were wearing slippery shoes. Richard hurried in front of them and opened the front door.

Abbey could hear music in the ballroom, and through the large doorway, she could see all the people who had gathered. A shot of anxiety pelted her as she wondered if she could find anyone she knew in the crowd, but before she could even process the thought, she was processing another. Standing right at the front of the crowd waiting for her was Nick with little Thomas by his side.

"Hey," Max said to Thomas. "We're twins!" They inspected their tuxedos as Nick reached out for Abbey's hand.

"Now *that*," he said, "is a dress." He spun her around, the skirt flaring out around her. "You look stunning."

"Thank you. You look quite handsome yourself," she said as she took in the look of him in a tuxedo, the neutrals of the crisp white shirt and black jacket drawing attention to those icy blue eyes.

Still holding her hand, he led her to an area of the ballroom where a quartet was playing instrumental music. The music was soft yet a little jazzy, the perfect dancing music. Caroline waved from a nearby chair and Abbey waved back just as Nick spun her inward and put his arm around her waist, leading her as he danced in clearly rehearsed and well-learned steps. He was so good at guiding her that it didn't matter that she wasn't familiar with the dance. He pulled her in and they were pressed against each other swaying to the music, her hand in his.

"You were holding out on me at The Crazy Corner," she teased.

He twirled her around.

"This is amazing," she said. "The dress, the necklace, the car to pick me up, and now dancing. It's a little overwhelming."

"Like Cinderella," he smiled.

He'd remembered from when they first met how she'd said this ballroom was like Cinderella. Of course he'd remembered.

"The good news is that it all won't turn into a pumpkin at midnight."

She smiled up at him as he spun her around again. *No*, she thought, *it won't turn back into a pumpkin until after Christmas when all of this will no longer be here.*

"Oh!" a voice cut through the music and Susan was there beside them, breaking them apart for a kiss on the cheek. "Hello, my dear! You look gorgeous!" she said a little too loudly. Carl came up beside them, offering his hellos. "You have outdone yourself with this house, young lady. I am so thrilled at the results. You have a very bright future ahead of you in interior design."

Abbey could hardly contain her excitement. She'd done it. It had been tough at times, but she was a natural at it. She decided then and there that she was going to give her dream a chance. After Christmas, she'd set up times to meet Robin and her friends. She still had the suit Nick had bought her to use for her meeting, and she promised herself that she'd buy another one with her first earnings from her next job and finally donate the blue Gucci one to charity like she and Nick had planned.

"Now!" Susan clapped her hands together, her wrists dripping in diamond bracelets. "Let's see what that food we ordered tastes like. You and Nick were too busy enjoying each other to offer the final opinion but we went with Nick's favorite. Champagne, you two?"

"I'll get it, Mother."

"He likes to have your attention all to himself," she said with a wink, making Abbey smile. She liked his attention too, and she liked it when it was just the two of them.

"Mama!" Max said, running over with Thomas.

"Walk, please," she said gently.

"I want to show you what they have!" He grabbed her hand, pulling her away from Nick and Susan and nearly dragging her to the edge of the room by the two big Christmas trees. Along the large window, there was a small table covered in white linens. It was filled with licorice, giant swirled lollipops, gumdrops, hard candies of every kind and a giant chocolate fountain with marshmallows, pretzel sticks, and fruit arranged on skewers. In the center was the tin of cookies Abbey and Max had made yesterday.

Robin came up behind them. "I figured they need a party too," she said. "I put this together at the last minute. I hope that was okay. We can get them all sugared up and then let them crash tonight while they wait for Santa. And I saved Santa two of your cookies." She offered a conspiratorial smile.

Nick met them at the table. "What was that about Santa?" he asked.

"Mama and I made these for Santa and we saved him two of them," Max said, pointing to the tin in the middle.

"Those look delicious," Nick said. Then he made eye contact with Abbey as he continued talking to Max. "Santa would love to have anything you and your mother made, I'm nearly sure of it." He squatted down between the two boys. "You two enjoy the treats. I'm going to take Abbey to the dance floor and spin her around some more." When he smiled at Abbey, it was a big, genuine smile, and she could hardly help the flutters in her stomach. "Look," he said pointing above them. "Mistletoe." He leaned in and gave her a kiss. Then he grabbed her hand and pulled her onto the dance floor.

It was late. Abbey had taken her shoes off because the heels were starting to pinch her feet, and most of the guests had left already. The party had been amazing. There were so many people, but Nick had given almost all his attention to Abbey. Max and Thomas had gotten tired around eight, and Robin and Abbey had left the party long enough to tuck them into bed. Richard had helped Caroline get to her room when she'd decided to turn in for the night. Now, the quartet was packing up, but Abbey and Nick were still dancing, neither one of them letting go.

"I'm dying for more music!" Susan said, her arm slung around Carl, a glass of wine swinging from her fingers. "Nicholas, play us something on the piano."

Abbey stood up on her toes to reach Nick's ear. He'd straightened up to address his mother over Abbey's head, so she really had to stretch to reach him. "Play your music," she whispered.

He shook his head subtly.

"It's the perfect time to show them. Everyone's here."

He looked down at her, that very rare vulnerability on his face.

"Do it," she whispered with an encouraging nod.

"Play us something, Nick," Robin said.

He cleared his throat and took in a slightly nervous sounding breath. "I have to get the music from my office," he said.

"Come with me." Abbey took his hand. "We'll be right back," she told everyone. Then, she led him to the stairs. "Wait right here." She ran up to her room and tiptoed inside past Max who was sleeping. In the dark, she opened the closet door and slid her hand along the top shelf until her fingers hit the gift. On her toes, she stretched up to get it. Then, she ran across the room and let herself out. Nick was standing at the bottom of the steps. He looked so gorgeous in his tuxedo.

"What is that?" he said quietly as she came down the stairs.

"It's your Christmas gift." When she reached the bottom, she handed it to him.

He turned the box around in his hands to view the handmade paper. Then, he slipped the holly out from under the bow and untied the ribbon. Together, they sat down on the steps as he slid his finger under the paper to loosen it. The thick paper popped open and he set it aside, his eyes on the music book.

"I had it engraved," she pointed out.

"*Make your dreams and then follow them*," Nick read aloud and then opened the book and realized that she'd taken some of his music and filled it, the song "Dreams" on top.

"Thank you," he said, and he kissed her softly.

"You're welcome. You've made your 'Dreams'," she said, pointing to the song. "Now you just have to follow them."

"I've been thinking a lot about it lately. It seems ridiculous until I'm with you and then, for some reason, it all seems like it could work."

"I know the feeling," she said with a tiny laugh. "Let's start small, shall we? Baby steps. Play for your family."

She took his hand and they walked down to the ballroom. This was a big step for him. With his music, he was showing his emotional side, the soft underbelly of that hard businessman, and he'd probably never shown that to his family before.

Nick walked in and sat down at the piano. His family joined Abbey around it, Susan clapping in excitement. He opened the book and set it on the stand. She could see the nervousness in his fingers. It was very slight, but she knew him well enough to know it was there.

"This is…" he looked up at his family, his eyes moving from one to another as he hesitated. And then, as if he'd made a decision, he said. "This is an original piece I wrote. It's a lullaby."

Abbey looked around at the faces of his family. Susan and Robin were perfectly still, their eyes on his fingers, eagerly awaiting this mysterious song that they'd known existed but had never heard.

He began to play, those familiar notes swirling their way up into the air, and, this time, Abbey didn't think about Max. She thought about what it was like to hold a brand new infant child, to feel the softness of its skin against her, the pink of its lips, the curl of its fingers around hers, the way it would look nestled in little Max's lap, and suddenly, the absence of those experiences nearly overwhelmed her. Each note brought her to the reality that her dreams of a big family, years of bedtime stories, a loving husband who helped her tuck her children in at night—it was still a dream. A tear rolled down her cheek and she wiped it away quickly, but as soon as she did, that glorious music hit her again and again, its sound so soothing and yet heart-wrenching that she could hardly breathe. She looked up to see if anyone had noticed, and to her surprise, Susan and Robin were both crying too. Even James's and Carl's eyes were glassy.

Nick had been looking at the music the entire time, and when he finished, he looked up. Susan had her hand on her chest, her eyes full of tears. "Nicholas," she said, her voice breaking, "you have been holding on to this amazing talent and no one has been allowed to en-joy it. I am in awe of your ability, and as your mother, I am filled with pride. This is one of the best pieces I've heard. It moved me to tears—it moved us all to tears. Why aren't you doing something with it?"

Abbey protectively sat down next to him. She, too, wanted him to pursue something with his music, but this alone was a big step for him.

"I just get busy," he said.

"Doing what? Aaron's damn business? That company took him away from his family far too many times. I put up with it because I knew he loved it and it made him happy, but I resented those nights when you asked for him and he wasn't there. Do you really love what you do, son? Do you love it as much as your father did?"

Nick sat up, and Abbey could see the defensiveness in his demean-or. "I love it *for* my father," he said, his voice controlled and even, as it had been on previous occasions when his emotions were challenged. "Because he isn't here to love it anymore. And no one seems to get that except for me."

Susan's shoulders dropped in compassion for her son. "I loved your father," she said, smiling at Carl to acknowledge him. "I didn't like how much he worked, but I'd promised to be with him until death do us part, and I honored that promise. You have always been the most like your father, but you are very different as well. He didn't have the kind of passion you have for things. He had drive, yes, but not pas-sion. When I see you work all the time on that company, I don't see your passion, and it bothered me so much that I moved away so that I didn't have to watch it. Because I know how stubborn you are and how I wouldn't be able to change your mind. That company won't love you in return. It won't give you the time that you've given to it. Look at your father. He'll never get that time back."

"He left it to *me*," he said quietly, still refusing to expose any emotion he had on the topic.

"Do you know why, Nicholas?" Susan asked, her eyes pleading for his consideration.

He looked directly at her, waiting.

"Because he loved you. He loved you so much. That business was the very best he had to give. It was what he'd spent most of his life working toward. So when it came time to figure out who got what, guess who got what he loved most? But not because he wanted you to run it, because it was the grandest gesture he could make to show his love for you. When parents say they'd give you the world—well, he gave you his. In the best way he knew how."

Nick sat silently, digesting this information. Abbey reached over and grabbed his hand, hoping he was okay. She wanted to cry for him, to sob for the loss of his father because it was clear how much Nick loved him. What she'd only now realized was that Nick showed his love by how much he worked. Her mind raced to all those things he'd done for her—the pies on Thanksgiving, the trips around town, the scarf, the clothes, the arranged drivers, the nights at his home, Gramps's money—it was all his way of showing he cared. And with his father's company—he'd make himself sick with sleepless nights and barely eating just to show his father how much he loved him.

"I'm sorry to have brought the conversation around to this," Susan said. "Please don't let it put a damper on this wonderful night. Your music was incredible. I hope you will play it for Caroline tomorrow. I'm sure she'd love to hear it."

Robin walked around and kissed her brother on the cheek. "I loved it," she said with a smile. "It's been a big night in many ways. I think I'll set out Santa's gifts and head off to bed." She grabbed James's arm and blew a kiss to everyone with her other hand as they made their way to the doorway leading to the stairs.

Susan put her hand on his shoulder. "Thank you for playing it for me," she said. Then she gave Abbey a little smile and left with Carl.

It was just Abbey and Nick. There they were in the same place they'd first met; it seemed like a million years ago. She got up. He swiveled around still sitting on the piano stool, facing her as she stood in front of him, and wrapped his arms around her waist. As he looked up at her with those gorgeous blue eyes of his, his stubble showing on his face at the end of the night, she thought how different he looked to her now. She felt like she knew him—she knew the way he smiled, the lines at the corners of his eyes, the way his hands felt in hers. She put her arms around his neck and pulled him to her. When she did, she could feel his body relax.

The staff was moving around them, cleaning, the clinking of dishes and the rustling of bags filling the air. "We should probably get Max's Christmas set out and call it a night," she said, still holding him.

He squeezed her tighter.

"Can I tempt you with cookies?"

He looked up at her and smiled, his eyes so tired. She wanted to go upstairs with him, to get into comfortable clothes, to curl up beside him and fall asleep, or… something else, but she pushed those thoughts out of her mind. Yes, Nick was a talented composer, but she doubted he would make his millions publishing music. She didn't live in his world, and she didn't know how to give him options. He had to decide. So going upstairs with him tonight would only make it more heartbreaking when he left. And she had to face the fact that all of this would be over tomorrow.

She pulled him up and together they left the room.

"Mama!" Abbey heard through her sleep. "Mama!"

Abbey opened her eyes and took a minute to register where she was. Last night, she'd left Nick with a kiss in the hallway and climbed into bed with Max. With the previous night of not sleeping mixed with the events of Christmas Eve and the bedding she'd bought for the bedroom at Nick's, she hadn't had much of a chance to contemplate things, and sleep had consumed her almost immediately. She sat up and rubbed her face.

"Good morning, baby," she said, rubbing Max's arm.

"It's Christmas!" Max said, as if she'd forgotten.

"Yes," she said with as much excitement as she could muster for him. Sleeping in that bed had made her feel like she hadn't slept in years, and she could stay right there for days. "Let me quickly get ready so that I'm somewhat presentable and we'll go downstairs. Put your clothes on and I'll get your teeth and face in a minute."

After they'd gotten ready, Abbey and Max headed downstairs— the glorious smells of breakfast wafting toward her—and her tummy rumbled. She'd arranged Max's two-wheel scooter, his iPad, and his Willie Mays baseball card beside Thomas's specially made craftsman building kit, his child-sized drivable jeep with working headlights and CD player that took up most of the room, and his collectible train set.

"Good morning." Nick met them at the bottom of the stairs with a big smile on his face. "Merry Christmas." He leaned in and kissed her cheek, brushing his lips against hers as he pulled back. He bent down and grinned warmly at Max. "Merry Christmas to you too! Did you leave Santa a note at your house?"

Max nodded.

"I thought maybe you had because he's left quite a bit of loot for you in the living room. Would you like to see it?"

Max's eyes lit up and he started to run down the hallway.

"Wait, Max! I want to get a picture!" Abbey said, scrambling behind him as quickly as she could. Nick picked up his pace as Abbey pulled her phone from her back pocket. They arrived just in time to catch his expression, and Abbey snapped a photo. "Phew," she said to Nick. "I almost missed it."

"Mama! Look what I got!" Max grabbed his iPad and turned it on. "This is so cool!" He set it down and got on his scooter. "Look at this! The wheels light up!" He rolled over to her to show her and the orange wheels glowed as he rode across the floor. Carefully, he set it down a few feet away and ran back to where they had been. "Mama! I got Willie Mays! I can't wait to show Gramps!" Thomas climbed off of his jeep to see what Max had received.

Robin and James were sitting next to Susan and Carl, with Caroline in the chair across the room. All of them had their eyes on Abbey with very odd expressions on their faces. She smiled, looking at them all.

"Merry Christmas," Caroline said to her.

"Merry Christmas." She looked around and couldn't believe where she was. She'd only noticed just then that Nick had his arm around her, a loving look on his face. Thomas and Max were playing together, showing one another their new toys. With the Christmas lights, the tree, the presents, and the delicious aroma of breakfast, she couldn't imagine a better holiday. She'd wanted the perfect Christmas—well, she got it.

"I got you a present," Nick said, and Abbey immediately felt anxious. He'd already given her so much with Gramps's care. "It's in my office. Would you come with me to see it?"

Everyone was looking at her expectantly, their faces full of excitement.

Nick grabbed both her hands and looked down at her. "Come with me," he said as if she were the only one in the room.

She looked over at Caroline, who nodded in encouragement.

Nick took her hand and they walked to the office. There was an excitement to his walk, and a contentment to the way he held her hand. He pulled it up to his lips and kissed her fingers.

When they entered the office, there was a small gift wrapped in green and red paper with gold scrolling. The ribbon tails cascaded over the edge of it.

"I do have one more Christmas wish, but first, here's your gift. It's just something small." He took the gift off his desk and placed it in her hand. Abbey sat down in the chair and unwrapped it as Nick leaned against the desk watching her, a smile on his face. She couldn't help noticing how much he'd been smiling lately.

Abbey pulled the paper off. It was a picture frame. She turned it around and felt a flutter. The frame was unfussy, just a simple black one—she wondered if he'd thought of her apartment when he'd gotten it—and inside was the picture of Max on Santa's lap.

Abbey stood up and gave him a kiss. She lingered there on his lips, wanting more, but he pulled back and set her down gently in the chair.

"It's for your new office, if you plan to actually follow your dream and become a full-time interior designer," he said. "It's very small, but I know you'll decorate it well."

"What?" she asked in disbelief.

"It has two offices and a conference room. It's downtown. Centrally located. I own the building so it's rent free." He smiled.

She threw her arms around him and gave him a kiss. "Thank you," she said. "I'll be happy to pay you rent…"

"We'll work all that out," he said. "Now, you surprised me with that amazing music book but it's time for your second gift to me." He pulled an envelope off his desk, and Abbey noticed how similar it looked to the one Max had with his Christmas wish in it. It was sealed just like Max's. "In Max's class, the sons and fathers were supposed to write wishes to each other and share them next year. I modified our assignment since I wasn't Max's father. I told Max, instead, to write what he wants most in this world, and then I'd do the same, and maybe they'd come true."

Nick kneeled down in front of Abbey so that they were eye to eye. She waited, her heart pounding for what he had to say. He took the framed photo from her hands and set it behind him on the desk and then turned back to her.

"Would it make you happy if I kept this house in Richmond and stayed here some of the time?" he asked.

"Yes," she said, nearly breathless.

"Would it make you happy if I were here more than I was in New York?"

What was he doing? "Yes," she said again.

"Would it make you happy to be… with me?"

She nodded.

"My last Christmas wish is in here." He held up the envelope. "I want this for Christmas." He handed her the envelope. "Open it."

She tore it open.

The paper had black writing at the top that had been copied for every student and father. It said, "Dear _____," and Max's name was written in the blank. "My Christmas wish is…" and there were lines for writing wishes. In Nick's handwriting, it said, *I wish I could make your mom happy.*

The words blurred on the page as she read them. She'd never had anyone try to make her happy before, and it was a wonderful feeling. She looked up at him, blinking to clear her vision.

"I tried very hard to carry on with my life after I met you," he said. "And I just can't. For the first time ever, I want something more than my work—you. When I'm with you, I feel like my career doesn't matter, I want to see my family more… I kept holding on to my father's business to save me from the grief of being completely without him, but when I'm with my family, I realized that I can actually honor his memory more because I can see all the people he loved right there with me. You've shown me what life can be like when I'm not alone. And it's fantastic. I love being with you, doing things with Max, visiting my grandmother, seeing her smile. You've made me realize that I can have so many things that my father never had.

"Even buying the apartment in New York, I was having doubts, but I didn't say anything because I'd never had to deal with feelings like this. I'm still going to work, but I'm going to try to balance the two. Before, with Sarah, it didn't work because my heart wasn't in it, but now it is. I find myself wanting that balance. I'll keep the apartment in New York for when I have to run up there. You're welcome to use the apartment for your interior design business as well. But we'll go together."

He took her hands and he guided her up. Then, he put his hands around her waist, leaned in, and kissed her like he'd never kissed her before. But, before she was ready, he stopped and looked at her, pushing a curl away from her face. "We have breakfast cooking and the whole family knows I'm staying. They're very excited about it," he smiled. "Let's have breakfast and then I want to call your mom and your grandfather, and invite them over. I want to celebrate. You have made this the best Christmas ever."

Abbey smiled. Just like the decorating, she'd done her job a little better than she'd expected.

Epilogue

"Nick!" Abbey ran in with a delivery box.

Nick looked at her curiously, a loving grin on his face as he grabbed playfully at Max in an attempt to tousle his hair. Max, now almost ten, and getting lanky, wriggled out of his grasp, grinning deviously at him. He gave Nick a squeeze around the waist.

"I think it's the audio of your music!"

With Abbey's insistence, Nick had finally published his music. She ripped open the freight box and pulled out one of the audio boxes along with a stack of flyers with the same cover for promotional purposes. "The cover looks beautiful," she said. It was a soft purple with music notes sketched in white across the front—she'd designed it. She handed it to Nick and plucked one of the promotional flyers from the package. "I'm stealing this for our memory book," she said.

Nick turned the cover over in his hand, his face content and happy. "I like it," he said. "What do you think?" He held it out for Max to inspect.

"Let's play the piano!" Max said with excitement. Nick had been teaching him how to play piano in their free time. The two of them were nearly inseparable. Nick had cut back on the business to give himself more family time. He found that it was still lucrative enough to afford him the finer things in life, but he didn't have to sink every waking moment into it. And now, he'd told Abbey, he didn't want to spend every moment doing that. He had a family to care for.

"We'll wake the baby," Nick worried.

"No, we won't," Abbey said. "She sleeps through anything."

Corinne Sinclair was born two years after she and Nick were married. The wedding had been a quiet ceremony on the grounds of their home, next to the James River. Susan had wanted to invite all of Richmond, but Nick and Abbey insisted they wanted family only. So, on a hot summer's day, with a gauzy white sundress and a flower in her hair, Abbey had held a bouquet of red tulips wrapped in satin and said, "I do" to the man of her dreams. Max was the ring bearer-slash-best man. It was perfect.

"I'll just go check to see if she's still sleeping," Abbey said and headed upstairs. They'd changed the room with the photograph to the nursery, and Abbey had painted it a glorious mint green with white trim. The crib was built as if it had been inspired by an enormous sleigh, all white with curly edges, and framed above it was the original version of Nick's lullaby. She peeked in on Corinne. She was still covered in her blanket, her blonde curls, like her mother's, haphazardly spread across her little pillow.

Corinne had just started to try to walk, but when Nick played his lullaby on the piano, Abbey would swear she was attempting to dance, her little patent leather shoes with soft soles tapping on the floor a few times before she'd fall on her lacy bottom, her dress flaring out around her.

Abbey stopped in to her home office to slip the flyer into her memory book. Her decorating business had become rather popular in Richmond, and, after her experience decorating Robin's loft in New

York, she was building quite a clientele. She still took care of Caroline, but it was much easier to do now that she was living with them full time. Abbey loved her as if she were her own grandmother.

There was one more person who had taken residence at the Sinclair home: Gramps. On his new medicine, his tremors were significantly decreased, and he required minimal support. He was so good, in fact, that Abbey and Nick were planning to redo Caroline's cottage for him. He'd wanted his independence back for so long, and he was finally going to get it. Abbey's mother was delighted to have her house to herself, although she'd said it was very quiet. With her ankle finally healed, she'd started a few small projects that she'd wanted to complete.

Caroline had actually suggested Gramps moving into her cottage. She'd said that she loved living with Nick, Abbey, and the children so much that she didn't ever want to be alone again. Señor Freckles had been hanging out around the cottage a lot, probably to explore the grounds of the enormous house he now found himself living in.

As Abbey flipped the pages in her memory book, she smiled when she got to a certain one. It was the page where she'd saved Nick's and Max's Christmas wishes. Nick had wished that he could make her happy. And, a year later, Max had finally let them open his. It read simply, *I want a daddy.* And now he had one.

Abbey finally had her big family, her dream business, and more happiness than she could believe. Gramps still asked her, "How's life treating you?" and now, she could tell him. Because life couldn't get much better than this.

Letter from Jenny

Thank you so much for reading *Christmas Wishes and Mistletoe Kisses*. I really hope that you found it to be a feel-good festive treat!

If you'd like me to drop you an email when my next book is out, you can **sign up here**:

www.itsjennyhale.com/email/jenny-hale-sign-up

I won't share your e-mail with anyone else, and I'll only e-mail you when a new book is released.

If you did enjoy *Christmas Wishes and Mistletoe Kisses*, I'd *love* it if you'd write a review. Getting feedback from readers is amazing, and it also helps to persuade other readers to pick up one of my books for the first time.

Until next time, and Merry Christmas!

Jenny

PS. If you enjoyed this story, and would like a little more Christmas magic, do check out my other Christmas novels – *Coming Home for Christmas* and *A Christmas to Remember.*

ALSO BY JENNY HALE

Coming Home for Christmas
Love Me for Me
A Christmas to Remember
Summer by the Sea

Lightning Source UK Ltd.
Milton Keynes UK
UKOW06f2343141115

262712UK00016B/194/P

9 781910 751558